THE
STRANGE
INHERITANCE
OF LEAH
FERN

THE
STRANGE
INHERITANCE
OF LEAH
FERN

A NOVEL

**RITA
ZOEY
CHIN**

MELVILLE HOUSE
BROOKLYN, NY/LONDON

The Strange Inheritance of Leah Fern

First published in 2022 by Melville House
Copyright © Rita Zoey Chin, 2022
All rights reserved
First Melville House Printing: October 2022

Melville House Publishing
46 John Street
Brooklyn, NY 11201
and
Melville House UK
Suite 2000
16/18 Woodford Road
London E7 0HA

mhpbooks.com
@melvillehouse

ISBN: 978-1-61219986-3
ISBN: 978-1-61219987-0 (eBook)

Library of Congress Control Number: 2022938608

Design by Patrice Sheridan

Printed in the United States of America

1 3 5 7 9 10 8 6 4 2

A catalog record for this book is available from the Library of Congress

FOR C.E.

The moon laid a blazing finger on our bodies,
And drew us into the dark waters.

The black waves reached for us—
She lifted us gently.
The waves broke into points of fire against our bodies
And fell back—
She sang to us, rocking,
"Sleep, sleep!"
But all the fire of the moon-path was in our bodies—
We could not sleep.

—MARGUERITE ZORACH, "THE MOON ROSE"

In this life, you've got to use all of your forces.
In this life, you've got to use all of your senses.

—EKOVA, "TEMOINE"
(FARMAKIT EXTENDED REMIX)

ONE

LEAH HAD IMAGINED it for years, the way some girls imagine the ordered rituals of their weddings—the dress, the march, the ordained officiant, the declarations, the dance, the toss, the waves goodbye before crossing that threshold—but here, in her dark iris velvet dress, in her small candlelit apartment in the tiny town of Hilda, South Carolina, where Mozart's Requiem in D Minor was moving toward its crescendo and the beat-up ebony grandfather clock she'd lugged home from a roadside sale was gonging through the hours, she was the sole officiator and attendee of this, the grand ceremony of her last breath.

Why not Mozart? This was a celebration, after all, one deserving of a timeless and lofty orchestration. Though this day, April 4, 1999, marked Leah's twenty-first birthday, it was not her birth she was celebrating. Having lived more than half her life feeling penned in by the impenetrable wires of solitude, weighted by the kind of shapeless helplessness only the abandoned know, she felt powerful now to claim her own death, to schedule it on her own watch, her own grandfather clock as it were. What she didn't know yet was that her plans were about to be undone by a more powerful force.

There was no one to say goodbye to. She had never made friends in the small town of Hilda, though at first she tried. Shortly after her mother left her there, in the care of the saintly-patient Edward Murphy, who would become, through a peculiar marriage of force and kindness, a father to Leah, she was invited to the house of fellow second-grader Cynthia Lewis, in whose flouncy bedroom Leah unveiled her most prized possession by lifting it from its wrapping in one theatric sweep of the arm: a fox skull she'd found in a field. Her eyes gleamed as light touched the bone, but before she could tell Cynthia and her friends about how beautiful she thought it was, how amazing that its jaw still hinged open and shut, one of the girls said "Ew," and that was followed by a series of yucks and additional ews, along with tears from Cynthia Lewis, who begged her to "put that dead thing away," and finally Cynthia's mother, who suggested Leah go back home and find something else to share with her new friends, something not dead. But death hadn't scared Leah then, and it didn't scare her now.

She held nothing back on this day, moving through her death rituals with a rapt intensity, not unlike the way Mozart's quill must have moved through each of his compositions, all the notes now mounting in their urgency alongside the whole of her collected days, which had coalesced here to form a swiftly moving current that would carry her out to an unknown sea. She had initiated the ceremony by lighting the two red candles Edward Murphy had once given her for Christmas. "Smell 'em," he'd urged excitedly as she pulled them from their wrapping. "Just like cinnamon!" That year she'd given him a new Mozart album to add to his record collection, the same album she was now blasting through her apartment. He had been attempting to branch out from the reliable rock classics to something "more cultured," as he put it, but now it was completely her own.

When Edward Murphy died and she had to move out, she took the candles from their small dining table, wrapped them in tissue paper, and stowed them on the top shelf of the nearly bare pantry in her new apartment. They had never been lit. But now they flickered dangerously, leaping toward her each time she came wildly gesticulating past, then threatening to go out. She had never moved this way before—all body, flinging herself back and forth through the small space of her living room, her arms darting up erratically, painting invisible pictures in the air, as if to finally answer every question about her sanity that had ever been lodged in her direction by the various small-towners who wondered why, even in the thickest heat of South Carolina summer, she always wore black. Why those heavy combat boots? Perhaps more than anything, people wanted to know "what on God's green earth" she was doing wearing that "ridiculous" nail-studded belt and collar. "You'll poke someone's eye out with your neck!" said Dr. Hammershire, the local dentist who found his comment so amusing that he repeated it every time he saw her.

As she came thrashing again past the candles, a loosened flame herself, even her hair, ink black, shaved close on the right side, spiked longer on the left, seemed to be participating, each barb moving like its own baton, conducting along with Mozart on the fringe of abandon. She couldn't remember dancing before. She couldn't remember being so sure of anything.

The rituals, long-planned in a thoughtful order, had begun at 4:44 that morning with the lighting of the two red candles and would continue for one full rotation of the earth, one sunrise and one sunset, twenty-four hours that she would peel each minute from with Herculean intent. She'd chosen this time not only because her birthday fell on the fourth day of the fourth month but also because the number four struck her as whole—four chambers of the heart, four ventricles of the brain, four elements, four seasons, four winds, four principal phases of the moon—and she wanted to close her life feeling like she, too, was whole.

After lighting the ceremonial candles, Leah recited aloud Mary Oliver's "Sleeping in the Forest," which Edward Murphy had first read to her when she was a child. "Your mama was nuts about Mary Oliver," he'd told her. "She was carrying this beat-up old book of hers in her purse when we met." It had been almost fifteen years since Leah had heard her mother's voice, though she could still conjure it from fifteen birthdays before, her sixth birthday, the last one she would spend with her mother.

))) ● (((

IT WAS APRIL 4, 1984, in the Alabama fields of the Blazing Calyx Carnival, and Leah had just blown out the six candles adorning a chocolate-covered mound of fried dough. Her wish was the same wish she wished each time she saw the first star appear in the sky: to meet a real live elephant. "Did you wish for elephants again?" her mother asked, tapping her cigarette against the rim of the ashtray. Leah plunged her fingers into the melted chocolate. She didn't answer because Perilous Paul had told her that you should never tell a wish if you want it to come true. Her mother reached across their little fold-up table and stroked Leah's cheek. Her eyes went shiny as they sometimes did when she felt what she called "a little love spell" coming on. "When you were born," she said, "right here, in this very trailer, I had no idea what to call you. You were such a sensitive baby. I could tell right away you were different." Leah watched the tip of her mother's cigarette glow orange as she pressed it between her lips and was mesmerized by how the cigarette changed before her eyes, just like one of her mother's magic tricks. "You were always looking around with those big eyes of yours as if you already knew everything there was to know, secret things. And you never wanted to sleep. That summer, when you were only a few months old, you'd stay up all night just looking, not making a sound. And I thought of a legend I once read about, how if you find the seed of a fern in bloom on a midsummer night, you get special powers."

"Powers?" Leah asked, pushing a handful of dough into her mouth.

"You become invisible, and then only will-o'-the-wisps can see you."

"Will-o'-the-wisps?"

Jeannie nodded slowly for emphasis. "Yep, that's right. Will-o'-the-wisps. Spirits made of light. And when you find them, they lead you to hidden treasures that no one else can see."

"What kind of treasures?"

"I don't know," said Jeannie, pulling hard enough on her cigarette to make it crackle. Her voice crackled, too, when she exhaled. "You'll have to tell me when you find the seed."

Leah smiled. "I'll take you with me," she said, "to the treasure."

"Nah, I'll always be just a person," she said pensively, tapping her ash and looking out at a distance Leah couldn't see. "But you,

Miss Fern, are different. That's why you're not named after a person. You're named after magic."

"Did your mama name you Jeannie Starr because she knew you'd be a magic star?"

Leah's mother stubbed her cigarette out in a small orange ashtray. "My mama never knew anything about me."

"Why not?"

She reached for Leah's face again but stopped midway, as suddenly as if something had bitten her hand. "You just eat your sweets, okay? That was a long, long time ago."

Leah thought for a moment. "Do I have a dad?" she finally asked.

Leah's mother laughed the kind of laugh that isn't really a laugh. "Ah, your daddy," she said, "could have been any one of a few handsome cowboys."

LATER THAT DAY, Leah's two favorite friends—Her-Sweet, the Bearded Lady, and the Rubberband Man, the carnival's contortionist—arrived bearing gifts. Her-Sweet presented Leah with a book called *The Almost Anything You Might Ask Almanac*, and the Rubberband Man unveiled a crystal ball with a wooden stand, thereby tapping Leah on the top of her head with one spindly finger and declaring her The Youngest and Very Best Fortuneteller in the World. Leah didn't know if he was serious or joking, but she liked the way the sphere turned everything upside down when she peered into it.

Jeannie bent down to get her own look inside the crystal. "I keep telling you, I think she's too young," she said, exhaling a fresh stream of cigarette smoke that swirled over the crystal.

But the next day, the Rubberband Man sat Leah down in a tent at a small round table adorned with her new crystal ball and a white egg timer. Four black pillar candles burned on slim wooden tables, one in each corner of the tent. From a small cassette deck Romani music played in the background, while on a poster on the wall opposite Leah, an elephant charged toward her. Jeannie had sent her off that morning wrapped in one of her magic capes—a diaphanous crimson silk edged with purple velvet and silver sequins—that hung to the floor on Leah. "You're gonna tell people their fortunes," the Rubberband Man explained as they walked toward the tent, while Leah tripped every few steps on the velvet edge of the fabric. "With those eyes of yours, and those smarts, people will listen to anything you say."

Leah fidgeted in her dazzling cape. "But I don't know what to say."

"Tell 'em something about themselves. Whatever you feel."

"What if I don't feel anything?"

"Then tell 'em one of your stories. Or tell 'em something that might happen to 'em—best to make it nice, though. Or just tell 'em something you know." And as he stepped out of the tent, he turned back. "Just do what comes natural. And remember, hit the timer when they sit down!" Within seconds she could hear the Rubberband Man's voice rollercoastering outside the tent. "Step up, step up! Get your fortune told by the World's Youngest and Very Best Fortuneteller! This six-year-old marvel will blow your mind!"

She went along with the Rubberband Man's idea not because she understood what she was supposed to be doing, or even what a "fortune" really was, but because she loved him. What she loved most, besides his gentle nature and his smooth bald head, which always smelled faintly of cloves, was that being with him was like opening a treasure chest filled with mysterious things. Sometimes the mysteries came when he pointed up at the night sky and described event horizons or when he talked about the phenomenon of frog rain or when he showed her a phantom inside a piece of quartz: "If you look into the crystal," he showed her, holding it up to the light, "you can see how it's grown. You can see the ghost of what it used to be." But other times the mysteries glowed inside him, still unrevealed, and Leah liked simply knowing they were there.

"It's love, I tell ya. It's all love!" he sang. "This child will *enlighten* you! She will *enliven* you! She will *resurrect* you!" And with that, Leah's first client, a soft-bellied woman in a shirt patterned with peacock feathers, entered the tent. Leah pressed the button on the timer the way the Rubberband Man showed her, but she had no idea what to do next. So she sat calmly, radiant in her mother's crimson, and watched the woman. The woman, who appeared to be in her sixties, stood at a distance, holding up one skeptical eyebrow.

"Would you like to sit down?" Leah asked.

The lady smoothed the fronts of her slacks in flat, measured strokes. "I don't really believe in this," she started. "And look at you. Such a wee thing. You should be off playing hopscotch, not sitting here pretending you know things you don't know."

Leah touched the top of the crystal ball nonchalantly with her fingertips. "I'm not pretending," she said. "I know a lot of things."

"Like what?" asked the woman. She took a few steps toward the table. "What do you know?"

Leah clasped her hands on the table. "I know about elephants."

"What do you know about elephants?"

"Pretty much everything. I know their herds are led by females." Leah scratched her forehead. "They're called cows."

"Cows, huh? I didn't know that. The woman took another step toward Leah. "What else do you know?"

"I know you didn't tell the truth."

"I beg your pardon?" The woman stepped back and folded her arms across a row of peacock feathers.

"When you said you don't believe. That wasn't true."

The woman half exhaled, half laughed. "How do you know that?"

"I don't know."

"So you *don't* know?"

"No, I know. I just don't know *how* I know," Leah corrected.

"You have pretty eyes. Do you know that?"

"Do you want to sit down?" Leah asked again, reaching her hand out in a sweeping gesture, the way she'd seen her mother do when she invited someone onto the stage before sawing them in half.

"All right."

The lady approached the empty chair and lowered herself onto the flimsy seat without taking her eyes off Leah. "So, what do you know about my future?"

Leah knew a lot about elephants, about their diet and behavior, about how their bodies worked. She knew a little about magic tricks, mainly that the trick is to make people look where you want them to look, not where they want to look. She knew how to read books meant for older children, including science books. She knew that sprites are patterns of red lightning over thunderheads and that snowflakes form from specks of dust. She knew that birds evolved from dinosaurs, that we're made from the explosions of stars, and that one can make a smoke bomb for a magic show by combining sugar, baking soda, and potassium nitrate. She knew how to count to one hundred in Spanish, and she knew her mother was the most beautiful woman in the carnival. But what any of that had to do with her own future, let alone the future of this now eager-eyed stranger sitting across from her, she didn't know. So Leah simply asked the woman to put her hands on the crystal ball.

"Like this?" the woman asked, tentatively cupping both palms around the sides of the crystal.

Leah nodded as if she'd done this a thousand times before. Then she placed her small hands over the woman's hands. But before she could even close her eyes, she felt a weight on her chest that took her breath. Leah drew her hands back and, in doing so, startled the woman.

While Leah was used to knowing how people around her were feeling at any given moment—she knew from across the room, for instance, when Her-Sweet was sad, even if she was smiling; she knew by the pitch of Hank's voice when he'd be paying a visit to their trailer to see her mother; and she knew from the moment her mother opened her eyes in the morning whether she'd dreamed good dreams or bad—an ability that had always been intensified by physical contact—she had never felt an awareness of another person in her own body as powerfully as she did now. Did the crystal ball actually work? Was it her mother's magic cape?

The woman looked at Leah anxiously. "What is it? What did you see?"

The Rubberband Man had told her to say something nice, but he also told her to do what came naturally, so Leah sat frozen, not knowing which to do.

"Is it bad?" the woman asked. "It's something bad, isn't it?"

"Your heart isn't smooth," Leah confessed.

"What do you mean it isn't smooth?" demanded the woman in a shaky voice.

"It's a little bit bumpy. Kind of like the Peppermint Punch roller coaster." Leah reached out and touched the lady's hand once more, this time for comfort. "But it's a good heart. It'll be okay."

"Are you sure," the woman asked, tears filling her eyes, "that it's a good heart?"

Leah sensed that something had shifted, that now they were having a different conversation. "Yes." Leah nodded purposefully. "It's a very good heart."

"Thank you," said the woman, pulling a tissue from her purse and dabbing at her eyes. "I wasn't sure. I was never sure."

Leah gave the crystal ball a quick peek, to see if maybe something would be revealed to her in it, but nothing appeared.

"What else do you know?"

Leah thought for a moment, running the cape's edge through her fingertips. "One way to tell the difference between an Asian elephant and an African elephant is that an African elephant's ears are shaped like Africa."

"That's wonderful, dear. But what about my future? What else about my future?"

Leah looked up at the elephant poster behind the woman. "That is your future," she said.

"Yes," said the woman, nodding gravely, as if she had just been handed the answer to her life. "Yes, of course."

And at that moment, as if by design, the timer buzzed.

"Please exit to the left," Leah instructed.

And so began Leah's first job. She was an instant success, sitting calmly, sage-like, unlike most children her age, as she placed her hands on people's hands and told them what she felt, told them elephant facts, told them stories: "And Ozzy, the peanut-shaped elephant—elephants don't actually *like* peanuts, so he would have rather been shaped like a banana—had a special gift none of the other elephants had: he could speak. He knew three sentences: 'I am Ozzy,' 'Some winds lift me,' and 'I love you.'"

And that, she quickly learned, was what people cared about the most—that they were loved. Sure, people asked about jobs, health, childbearing, lifespans, but the questions, no matter how uncomfortable it made people to ask them, almost always led back to love. The question of love came in all tenses—*was I loved, am I loved, will I be loved*—and varied measures—who loves me, whom do I love, how much I am loved, does person X love me more than person Y, what makes love love, am I truly lovable, and so on. *Yes*, Leah told them again and again. *You are loved.*

Two weeks after the peacock lady left with her unsmooth heart, she returned to tell Leah two things. The first was that she'd gone to her doctor, who did in fact find a small problem with her heart, which she was able to correct with medication. And the second was that she'd been thinking of what Leah had told her about Africa being shaped like an elephant's ear, and she realized that she'd never been a very good listener. To remedy this, she called her sister, whom she hadn't spoken to in years, and, for the first time, she listened.

"We got on grandly," she told Leah, "and now we're making up for lost time. So I stood on that long line out there just so I could give you this," she said, beaming as she placed a small bronze elephant in Leah's hand, its trunk reaching toward the sky.

That summer the carnival stayed put right there in that field in Eclectic, Alabama, where people flocked from all over to see the glacier-eyed wonder child peer into the mysteries of their futures.

IN LIFE THE carnival had been a noisy place, filled with bells and shrieks and bulbous music, but in Leah's dreams it was always quiet, reduced only to motion and light. And on a night shortly after Leah's sixth birthday, when she couldn't sleep, she snuck out of the trailer she and her mother lived in. "Don't you go wandering off anywhere!" her mother had warned, as she always did before leaving for her nightly magic act. Then she whisked up a small ceramic elephant from the bedside table, made it disappear in midair and reappear on Leah's pillow while Leah looked up with awe at her mother's large green eyes and pixyish smile.

Every time Jeannie left the trailer, Leah had to adjust. It wasn't being alone that troubled her; it was the transition—those moments right after her mother closed the door, leaving their shared space suddenly silent. In the vacuum her mother left behind, a bereft feeling would come over Leah, for which she would turn to her nightly comfort, her bridge into sleep: the contemplation of infinity. Earlier that year, when Her-Sweet had introduced Leah to the word, she folded her arms in disbelief. "How can something have no beginning and no end?" Leah asked. Her-Sweet pulled a silver band off her middle finger and handed it to Leah. "Show me the beginning and the end," she said, and Leah turned the ring around and around, transfixed.

No beginning, no end. Infinity, infinity, infinity . . . Leah lay in bed, her eyes squeezed shut, her mind on the never-ending loop, but on that night, her eyes popped open. She was awake. In the orange glow of the night-light, the trailer still flooded with the woodsy spice of her mother's perfume, Leah got out of bed and picked up a glinting sequin that had loosened from her mother's bustier and fallen on the floor. Holding it in her hand, she crept down the trailer steps and set out barefoot into the field. A fog had settled, so thick that as she walked through the weeds she felt no sense of distance between her and the trailer she was moving away from— only the feeling of being enveloped. She wondered if maybe this was infinity—this silver mist she kept walking into.

As she stepped through a kind of dreamtime, she found herself wanting to know new things, like what made the fog and what other sort of life might be out there, on the other side of the fog. Another carnival, perhaps. Or maybe a farm with pigs and goats and weeping willows. Or a seashore lined with swings. Or a castle spiraling up into the clouds. Or a tunnel . . . She wondered and wandered, farther and farther, until the fog began to break and she found her answer: the edge of a forest draped in silvery moonlight. She turned around and faced the carnival, her true and only life, so far away—a small world shimmering in the dark distance. A terror lit through her then as she felt herself, for the first time, separate. Separate from her mother, from her friends, from the only home she'd ever known. It was almost as if she knew, or as if in her brief pilgrimage had possibly even *conjured*, what was to come. Still, she ran as fast as she had ever run, through the shifting moonlit mist, back home.

TWO

FIFTEEN YEARS AFTER her birthday wish for elephants, five hours before she would begin her dance to Mozart, Leah made seven more wishes upon seven resounding gongs from her grandfather clock. She'd been rehearsing and revising these wishes for years, one for each of the Pleiades's seven sisters, and now as she spoke them out loud, a funereal formality settled over her. "Electra," she began, "I wish peace for all animals." Her voice was as crystalline as the blue of her eyes. "Maia, I wish for music on the other side. Asterope, I wish to know all the answers to my questions. Merope, I wish to be able to fly. Taygete, I wish to go back in time and see the dinosaurs. Alcyone, I wish my mother a happy life." This wish surprised Leah, for in all of her rehearsals, those words had never come.

Leah had one last star. "Celaeno, if I am reincarnated, please don't let me come back as a tick, leech, or mosquito. Thank you." She opened her eyes and blew out the candles, unsure if the last wish was one or three. One, she decided, carrying her candles into the living room, where she placed them on the coffee table and relit them.

Since Her-Sweet had given her *The Almost Anything You Might Ask Almanac*, Leah had remained fascinated by the night sky. The colorfully illustrated book—which covered topics ranging from lightning storms to worms to garlic, from the seasons to the zodiac to witches to facts and curious musings about the moon—told how there was a time when "scientists thought the moon was covered with oceans full of serpents" and that it was bad luck to point at it. So she was always careful not to point as she flung her imagination up at its glowing surface, where she sometimes saw a jack-o-lantern's face, hills made of diamonds, the smile of the Greek moon goddess, Achelois. "You must be related to her," Her-Sweet had once said, "because you wash away people's pain." Leah inquired up at the stars, too, hunting for con- stellations—Pegasus, Ursa Major, Cassiopeia the queen, Corvus the crow, Hydra the serpent, Draco the dragon, the Seven Sisters—some of which she'd first discovered in the back of her almanac. And while the heavens changed with the seasons and the phases of the moon, what never changed was the light she felt turn on in the secret dark of her belly each time she looked up at that vast and glittering distance.

In addition to the two red candles, her coffee table was populated by a collection of sea stones and shells she'd gathered with Edward Murphy on their only vacation together. There was also a sketch- book she'd filled with pencil drawings and watercolors, mostly of animals and plants. And there was her fox skull, now in two pieces. Not long after she'd brought the skull home from Cynthia Lewis's house, its lower jaw fell off. She considered wiring it back on but then decided to let it be and wrapped the bones back up in her mother's scarf. The scarf was indigo, spattered with flecks of silver and white, and it reminded Leah of the night sky. A stunning contrast against her mother's fair features and red hair, the soft silk was the last thing her mother had given to her. For years it held traces of her perfume, Mitsouko, which Leah had treated parsimoniously, allowing herself only an occasional sniff, lest she sniff all the molecules away. But over time, the scent faded, like Leah's memories, into something more resembling a wish. The scarf was not on the table.

With the eighth strike of the clock, Leah lay on the floor and tried, as she'd done as a child, to imagine infinity—an endless hall of mirrors, a ceaseless sea of stars, a roller coaster forever looping through space.

With the ninth gong, she sat beside a stack of books and visited some of her favorite artworks. Among them was a girl riding her bike into an unknown future in Giorgio de Chirico's *Mystery and Melancholy of a Street*, a woman lying beneath a lion's gaze in Henri Rousseau's *The Sleeping Gypsy*, and Antoine de Saint-Exupéry's Little Prince walking the cliffside well. She had always been drawn in by how the artworks exist on a precipice, and how all possibilities—wonder, danger, magic—exist within them. But she had never understood them the way she did now, as she bid them farewell from a precipice of her own.

On the tenth hour, Leah removed from her bedroom closet a small canvas, a palette of watercolors, and a single brush. These, too, were gifts from Edward Murphy, though she'd let them sit untouched for years. But now, on the morning of April 4, 1999, Leah filled a small glass with water, dipped in one of the brushes he'd given her, and beside the burning red candles she brought an elephant to life—a chubby calf, its trunk pointed up to a lavender sky. She hung it on the wall just in time for the clock to strike eleven, which is when she put on Mozart's first symphony and followed it with his Requiem in D Minor.

The record player, along with three boxes of records ranging from classical to classic rock, had belonged to Edward Murphy.

She'd frequented that turntable as a child, losing herself in the dark chords of Jethro Tull, The Moody Blues, and Led Zeppelin. After a day filled with varying degrees of alienation and humiliation, as most school days were, she found the intensity of these musicians comforting. They sang about "broken luck," "gathering gloom," "dogs of doom," and she felt as if they were singing for her, as if they *knew* her. They slipped in through the darkest corridors and stroked that secret place of unrest inside her.

Now, having leapt and spun with Mozart through the noon gongs, hurling herself closer and closer to her death, she was ready to switch from Edward's old record player to her CD player for *Rage Against the Machine*. She went straight to the second track, "Killing in the Name," and grabbed a chocolate chip cookie, which she pumped into the air between bites. Tossing her head forward as the song climbed into its fury, she screamed along, "Fuck you, I won't do what you tell me! Fuck you, I won't do what you tell me . . . !"

In the distance, there was a tapping. Whether in the distance of the music or the distance of her apartment, Leah wasn't sure. She barely registered the sound. Or maybe she registered it just enough, because her tempo began to slow as she peered out from her singular rhythm, as if out of a dream, and looked suspiciously at her CD player. No, the tapping was not in the music; this she became certain of in the same moment she became certain of the tapping itself.

A rivalry ensued: Rage's urgency against the increasing urgency of the tapping, which had graduated to banging. She turned the volume even louder, but the banging would not be outdone. So she lowered the volume and listened. As if in response, the banging also receded, and she realized then that it was someone knocking on her door. She turned the music off.

The knocking persisted. Her heart pounded.

She wondered who it could be. People almost never knocked on her door. Yet now someone was doing it with surprising fervor. For several minutes she didn't move, though she could tell from the increasing dullness of the knocking that the knocker was tiring. And eventually, when the knocking stopped, Leah waited several more minutes before she tiptoed over and peeked through the peephole to be sure that whoever it was had gone. But at the same time, a face came toward her on the other side. She gasped and jumped back.

"Hello?" the man called. "Leah Fern?"

Leah held her breath.

"Please, I know you're in there. I could hear you, uh, *singing*. My name is Peter Minkin. I'm an attorney."

Leah opened the door part way and got a better look at the perspiring, balding, beleaguered-looking man. "Hi," he said, smiling with relief. He was holding a plain brown box in both arms, shifting its weight back and forth as if it housed a bowling ball he was attempting to balance. They were both somewhat winded. She let the door fall open a little more.

"Are you okay?" Peter Minkin asked.

Leah folded her arms across her chest. "Are you?"

The two of them stood there, blinking at each other. Sweat had blossomed out from the man's armpits, darkening his white shirt.

"Are you Leah Fern?" he asked.

"What's in the box?" she asked. For a moment it was unclear whether either of them would ever answer a question that the other asked.

Peter Minkin cleared his throat. "Well, if you're Leah Fern, this box is your inheritance."

Leah's stomach dropped. Her inheritance? She could scarcely find the breath to ask, "My mother?"

"Was Essie East your mother?"

"Essie East?" Leah asked incredulously. She took a step toward the door and began to close it on the man. "You've made a mistake. I don't know who you are or who you're looking for, but you've got the wrong person."

"Please," he nearly squealed. He pushed the box forward, inserting it in the way of the door. "I've been calling you for days. I just called you an hour ago, before I drove here from North Augusta. You never answer, and it seems you don't have an answering machine."

She looked over at the phone, which was unplugged on the kitchen counter next to the remaining chocolate chip cookies.

Peter Minkin shifted the box in his arms again. "Why do you think I drove all the way out here, on Easter Sunday no less? I figured I was bound to catch you today, and since I'm Jewish, well . . . you know. No Easter eggs for me."

"It's Easter," said Leah. "I almost forgot."

"As you can see," he said, motioning toward her with the box, "I'm eager to settle this matter and move on. I don't want Essie East haunting me, that's for sure."

She regarded the now profusely perspiring man and considered that he might be a psychopath, but in that same instant she sensed the surprising truth: he was the one who was afraid.

OVER THE YEARS, being an empath had taken its toll on Leah, particularly the physical discomfort she felt when she perceived pain in someone else. When Edward Murphy once sliced his finger on a tuna can lid, for instance, she winced at the twinge that seared through her ribs. When Miss Emily hobbled into the feed shop after knee surgery, Leah felt as if her own knees were swelling. When a stranger wept onto the steering wheel of a car in the Minnie's Minimart parking lot, Leah's left hand inexplicably began to throb. In crowds, she quickly became inundated by the onslaught of so many feelings, as if other people's inner volumes were turned on high in a frequency only she could hear. And the closer she was to a person, emotionally or physically, the more acutely their feelings became hers.

There were no rules for how others' suffering manifested in her body, except that it was different every time. The art, of course, had always dwelled in her ability to interpret what she felt, as if her intuition had its own separate language for the seemingly endless permutations of pain. She attempted to protect herself by dodging physical contact with others, but that gave her little more than a modest respite from the most extreme transmissions. It was exhausting, this whole feeling business, a curse she was ready to be rid of.

It hadn't always been that way. In the early days, when she still lived at the carnival with her mother, she simply felt people's feelings without discriminating: she hadn't minded feeling their hurts any more than she'd minded feeling their joys. Whatever she felt simply *was*. There was a wholeness to her exchanges with others, a natural ebb and flow, like breathing. But on the day her mother drove away and left her with a stranger, something catastrophic happened quietly inside her: she lost access to the frequency of joy. From that moment forward, all she could perceive in others was their pain, amplified through the lens of her own.

For a short time, though, her talents had shone, and her job as The Youngest and Very Best Fortuneteller in the World had given her a unique power: she'd been able to ease, and even transform, the innumerable fears and heartaches people lugged into her tent. Her desire to make people feel better was an impulse she would later suppress but never lose, and it was present now, as she opened the door to a stranger.

"THANK YOU. AND thank God," said Peter Minkin as he walked in. "Is here okay?" He motioned with his chin toward the kitchen counter. Leah nodded, and he released the box, perhaps a little faster than he intended to, so that it landed on the counter with a thud. "Sorry about that, Essie," he said. Then he pulled out a handkerchief and dabbed at the sweat on his forehead.

Leah had known Essie for the last year, albeit cursorily, as her downstairs neighbor—an elderly woman who wore men's clothes and whose gray shoulder-skimming hair was perpetually disheveled. She possessed a rugged handsomeness and a clipped manner that no doubt rankled in their Southern locale, and she walked with a flamboyant limp, for which she sometimes carried a cane. She and Leah had exchanged only the briefest occasional nods whenever they happened upon each other entering or exiting the building, until four months earlier, New Year's Eve 1998, which was the only time Essie had ever knocked on Leah's door. When Leah opened it, Essie pushed a plate of pink and green confections toward Leah's chest. "Here," she said. Reluctantly, Leah accepted the plate, and Essie turned and began to hobble back down the stairs. "They're called peppermint meltaways," she added, without looking back.

For hours, Leah eyed the cookies suspiciously. She wondered if maybe they were poisoned, for that seemed as good a reason as any for this random delivery. But each time she lifted the plastic wrap, the sweet minty scent lured her closer, until she could no longer resist.

Leah sat down on the arm of the couch and trained a questioning eye on Peter Minkin.

"Yes, well," he said, "I'm sorry to tell you this, but Essie passed away last Tuesday."

"I'm sorry," said Leah. "But what does that have to do with me?"

"You don't know?"

"If I knew, would I be asking you?"

He knocked on the box three times, as if it were a door. "She left this to you."

Leah stood up. "That's a mistake. I barely knew her."

"That may be," he said, "but clearly she knew you."

"What's in it?"

Peter Minkin cleared his throat, then cleared it again more forcefully. "A check."

"Must be a big check."

"And other things."

"Such as?"

"Essie's remains."

"No, thank you," said Leah, picking up the box and thrusting it toward Peter Minkin.

He took a step back and put his hands up in surrender. "This is yours now, I'm afraid. Feel free to throw it away if you wish. But if I were you, I'd take a look inside. At least read the letter she left you."

Leah put the box back down on the counter. "A letter? To me?"

"Yes," he said, "to you."

They shared a moment of silence—each of them looking at the other and at the box—before Peter Minkin dabbed at his forehead again. "I just can't get used to this Southern heat. Yankee boy all the way." He pushed the handkerchief back down into his pocket and motioned toward the burning candles. "Anyhow, it looks like you're in the middle of something here, so I'll let you get back to it." He placed a business card beside the box. "In case you have any questions."

She grabbed a glass and filled it at the kitchen sink. "Have some water before you go."

Peter Minkin took the glass and emptied it in five loud gulps. "Thank you," he said, putting it down beside Leah's chocolate chip cookies. His eyes widened. "Those look delicious."

Leah picked up the plate and offered it to him. "Don't mind if I do," he said with a sheepish grin as he grabbed one. "Actually, better make it two," he said, reaching for another. "Last thing I need, but the first thing I want!" With that, he and the two cookies were out the door.

Leah stood motionless in the center of her kitchen. The box did not stir. The clock struck one.

THREE

IT'S HARD TO measure what, exactly, Leah's momentum had been on that April afternoon as she whirled through her apartment in a state hovering between ecstasy and fury, except to say that she'd been moving with the greatest force of her life. And now that she'd been brought to a swift and unceremonious halt by an opposing mass—this mysterious, if unimpressive, cardboard box, which she now stood facing—she had no thoughts, no feelings, no inclination toward motion; nothing but dumb shock, which left her unable to do anything but stare blankly at the box's blankness.

After a time, the natural questions began to surface in her mind—chief of which was: why were the remains of her neighbor sitting on her kitchen counter? She recalled the last time she'd spoken to Essie beyond hello. She'd gone to return her plate. Though Leah didn't scare easily, it had taken her days to gather the nerve to knock on Essie's door, and when she did, she knocked so quietly that Essie didn't answer and she had to knock more assertively a second time. This time Essie swung her door open accusingly. She was wearing pinstriped wool pants and a white V-neck T-shirt, partially tucked in on one side. Her feet were bare, her jaw clenched, setting off the weathered hollows beneath her cheekbones. "Your plate,"

Leah said offering the flowery dish. "They were good. Thank you." But Essie neither took the plate nor responded for many seconds. Instead, she peered at Leah, taking her time to run her eyes over her face, her hair, her clothing. Of the two women, it was clear that Essie was not only the more brazen one but also the more honest. While Leah used a word like "good" when she meant "one of the most delicious things I've ever tasted in my life," Essie had no such reservations. Instead, she was a seemingly egoless creature, something of a pained old dog who might pee on your foot, or take a bite out of it.

"You look like her," she said, squinting.

"Pardon?" asked Leah, who began to wonder if perhaps Essie was suffering from dementia. "Your *plate*," she tried again. "I'm *returning* it to you. *Thank* you."

Essie cocked her head to one side as she studied Leah's face. "You have to look to see it, but it's there." She furrowed her brows. "Your hair certainly isn't doing you any favors, though—that's for sure."

Leah thought she should feel insulted, but Essie's words were mediated by her English accent, which graced everything she said with an air of decorum.

Essie touched the tip of her nose before adding, "I didn't see it at first. Or maybe I didn't want to. Anyway, we'll all look like dirt eventually."

Leah took a step back and slowly knelt down. "I'll just put your plate right here, then." With that she left the plate at Essie's feet and scurried back up to her apartment, from which she peeked out a few hours later to find Essie's door closed and the plate gone. And then they were even, each having knocked on the other's door once.

But now Essie had reached through death to knock again.

Leah stood up and took stock of her surroundings. The candles were still burning, down several inches from the morning; the elephant was still poised under a lavender sky; the clock would soon strike two. The fox skull was pointed in her direction, sleek and ready, it seemed, to exhale a great wind. And as the sun began to edge down the slope of the afternoon, warm light gathered behind her closed blinds. Suddenly the hours seemed to be burning off like steam, her date with Death drawing closer.

Eyeing the box suspiciously, Leah restarted the Rage Against the Machine song and resumed her death dance, this time even more extravagantly than before. "Fuck you, I won't do what you tell me!" she shouted at the box. "Fuck you, I won't do what you *tell* me!" But there was a problem, she soon realized, with this box. She could feel it staring back at her, possibly even mocking her, in its silent boxy way.

Leah stopped the music, grabbed a kitchen knife, and sliced the box open in one sleek motion. Inside stood a large bubble-wrapped object, which she took out and began to unravel. With her first glimpse, she gasped. The urn, which was not urn-shaped at all, but rather an obelisk sculpted out of a quilted maple that had an almost holographic appearance, was inlaid with gemstones that gleamed in every color of the rainbow. Ranging from the size of a lentil to the size of a birch leaf, the gems were set into blossoms that wound around the wood on an etched vine. Sunstone, moonstone, garnet, tourmaline, opal, turquoise, lapis—each stone possessed its own distinct beauty; collectively they formed a riot of color and bedazzlement. Some stones sparkled wildly. Some appeared to blink when you tilted them. Some were boldly saturated and opaque. Some were translucent and emitted an ethereal glow.

Leah, who held in her hands more gems than she'd seen in her life, owned three pieces of jewelry: a large black watch with a wide band, a gold dolphin necklace, which Edward Murphy had given her on thirteenth birthday (and which she never wore), and a silver ring she'd found in a pile of leaves. She'd been walking home from school when she noticed a quick flash like the scale of a fish, and though she happened to be, in that same moment, in the process of getting teased by a gaggle of seventh-graders who trailed behind her, she stopped to reach down and unearth her find: a crescent moon and three stars, which fit her right middle finger perfectly. *A magic ring*, she thought, turning to present that same middle finger to the kids behind her.

From then on, she would hold her right hand up to things and point her moon and stars at them, casting imaginary spells mostly in the form of directives: *you will all stumble and fall*, she wished the children behind her; *you will land on my arm*, she commanded a dragonfly; *you will not dream of the carnival*, she told herself before sleep, eyeing the ring in the dark—but the kids strode upright; the dragonfly dipped near but didn't land; and the dreams came. Occasionally, Leah would wish for something she knew would happen—*you will roll off the table*, she instructed a pencil she'd lightly pushed—just to restore her faith enough to keep wishing.

She never took the ring off, and now it clicked against the smooth wood as she turned and tilted the obelisk in her hands. "Why?" she heard herself say.

She put the urn down and reached back into the box for the two envelopes wedged along one side. The first was a plain business envelope on which her name and address were typed on the front. Inside was a check handwritten in small shaky writing to Leah Fern for $9,999.99, which was a fortune to her, one that seemed more like a riddle than an actual representation of cash. Even her own name looked foreign, like a thing she knew she was supposed to recognize but couldn't.

The second was a padded nine-by-twelve envelope sealed with red wax. On the front was a single word written in gold ink: BEGIN. Through the padding Leah could feel something hard and lumpy, but before she could rip the envelope open, a memory stopped her. She could hear herself many years earlier, chiding Edward Murphy for being so hasty in opening the Christmas presents she'd given him. She had always taken her time with the wrapping—drawing wintery scenes on the paper, using an X-Acto knife to cut out the stars and Christmas trees she carefully pasted on in layers—and Edward Murphy always tore right in, spending only a second or two admiring her artistry. "Why do you always have to open your presents so fast?" she finally snapped. "Why can't you just appreciate them for a minute before you rip them up?" A shadow of shame passed over his face, and she instantly regretted her behavior. "I'm sorry, sweetie," he said, "but I *did* appreciate it. I loved the little dogs sledding down the hill." His kindness only made her feel worse, and when he took his time opening her next present, she wanted to cry and she wanted to pummel herself with her own fists. "Open it fast," she urged, trying to repair what she'd damaged. "Open it like you normally do!" And when he looked at her, he smiled a knowing smile before ripping into his gift with gusto, because that's how they were together, always wanting to make things right.

Now, as she held Essie's envelope in her hands, she didn't wait another second. With a quick slip of the finger, she ripped the seal. The scent hit her first—herbal, resinous, mildly astringent, and a momentary wooziness washed over her, as if she'd suddenly changed altitude. Leah peeked inside to find a folded letter, some sort of photograph printed on transparency paper, and something dark at the bottom. She took out the letter first, and as she unfolded it, a sprinkle of confetti spilled out onto her lap and the floor. She gathered the pieces into a pile beside her and began to read.

July 7, 1998

Dear Leah,

You should know straightaway that it wasn't a coincidence I moved into the apartment below you. In fact, I paid the former tenants to vacate so that I might move my life's worth of belongings into this incurably musty and remote hovel, from which I've had the distinct privilege of listening to your hippopotamus- like footsteps over my head for the last year.

Why, you might ask, have I gone to such lengths to spend the last of my days here below you? Why are you now in possession of my remains—and in such an unfitting vessel, no less?

I'm 71 years old as I write this. I predict I will die in nine months. If I'm right, don't be impressed. People have been predicting their deaths through the ages. Mark Twain did it. So did Nostradamus and Schoenberg. Children do it all the time. A lot of people we never hear about do it. I think mine will be quick as an explosion.

As for you, you're already dead.

LEAH DROPPED THE letter as if it had scorched her fingers. How could Essie have known? Or was this some kind of joke? No, she reasoned, Essie was not the joking type. Yet she couldn't be certain. This was, after all, a woman who had inexplicably given her a plate of pink and green confections. Leah launched to her feet, flung her door open, and rushed down the stairs. This time she would not be shy. With a heavy fist, she knocked on Essie's door. When no one answered, she paused for a moment and listened, looking defiantly at the peephole, below which hung a large brass knocker and nameplate that read EAST. She knocked again, this time delivering a series of demanding blows. "Open the door!" she insisted in a volume she wasn't accustomed to using. But her calls met only silence. "I'm serious!" she shouted, knocking even harder, faster. "Open the door!" And at some point the steadiness in her knocking broke into an arrhythmic two-fisted fury that didn't stop until her knuckles were raw.

When she finally let her hands drop, she put her ear up to the door and listened again, and this time she thought she heard something. A breath? A whisper? A slipper against carpet? She held her own breath and waited, but all was silent, except for the rage now rising into her throat. "Come take your box back! I don't want it!" She pressed her eye to the peephole but saw only darkness. She wanted to kick the door down. She wanted to rip the knocker off with her teeth. She wanted, more than anything, for someone to open the door. "Please?" she eventually begged, her voice tiny as a hummingbird. But the door remained closed.

Defeated, she climbed back up the stairs. Her apartment door was still open, as was the box. The candles, now nubs, were still burning. The urn stood sparkling, as if it were the most alive thing in the room. The new elephant still hung on the wall, its trunk pointing skyward. The fox skull was still poised on the table amid a sea of ocean stones and shells. And yet none of it felt like hers anymore. It was almost as if *she* were the ghost, standing in the middle of someone else's apartment.

Essie's words rang through her mind—*as for you, you're already dead*. Had Essie been right? Had she already gone through with it? Was she, in fact, dead? And was this strange world of beleaguered lawyers and bejeweled urns some sort of purgatory? Leah pushed her finger onto one of the nails in her belt.

She was alive.

As the gong struck three o'clock, she turned to the candles and blew them out. The clock was next. She opened the glass door, reached in before another minute passed, and stopped the pendulum. And so the death of death had been marked, and time, which Leah had not prepared for, mattered no more.

FOUR

HILDA, SOUTH CAROLINA, 1999

LEAH HAD NEVER received a letter in her life. Birthday cards from Edward Murphy, yes. Valentines that her second-grade teacher instructed all the classmates give to each other, yes. But an actual letter meant specifically for her? This letter from a dead woman was the first. And there was nothing else for her to do now but to finish reading it, as she faced not her own death, but Essie's.

From where I sit at my window, I watch you come and go. It doesn't take a genius to see that you're barely in this world—a shriveled flower still stuck to its stem. The difference is that a dead flower can't rise again. The question is, will you?

This might help: I knew your mother, Jeannie Starr. Our lives, for a time, coincided in ways you might be interested in knowing about. If you want to know more, there are nine letters waiting for you in nine post offices—General Delivery under your name. Each letter will give you more of your mother's story as I know it. The letters will also have instructions

about where to release my ashes along the way.
I suggest you drive.

I'm making a simple offer here—one journey
in exchange for another. I've rarely asked
anyone for anything in this life. I'm not
proud of that, but there's not much that can be
done with wisdom that comes too late.

It's July as I write this. Last night
the thunder was so forceful it rattled the
windows. I heard what sounded like a tornado
barrel past, and for some reason, it made me
laugh—the force and fury of it all. *Hecate!* I
called, laughing. *Bring down the house!*

Hecate, goddess of sorcery, of doorways. In
1977, five of us opened the door to an unusual
journey, one that would span nine places and
nine months. We traveled largely on instinct
into the world of the unseen, and those nine
months were the happiest and also the worst
time of my life.

Regret is a useless thing, yet since 1977,
it's the feeling I've known best. But now I've
figured out a way to go back, and you're the
only one who can take me, just as I am the
only one who can take you.

Your mother stayed with me in my New York
apartment for six months in 1989. She'd left
the carnival by then, but I can assure you she
was no less a magician.

Overlooking Gramercy Park, the apartment
had wide-planked wood floors and a large

marble fireplace, where the urn you now
have stood front and center on the mantle.
"Fancy." That was what your mother said when
she came. To her, everything was fancy—the
apartment, the New Yorkers in their long
wool coats, the chocolate croissants from
Marguerite's Bakery, the doorman downstairs,
the bright lights of Broadway. She liked
to draw it out—*faaaaancy*—almost as a joke,
leveled at both her own naivete and her
Southern accent, both of which I admit I
found charming.

Your mother was born on September 7, 1951,
in Philadelphia, of all places. You might
not have known that, because she didn't much
care to talk about the past, and you were
young when she left. I guess you could say
that while I wasn't one to ask for things, she
wasn't one to look back. That isn't to say she
hadn't meant to come back for you. It's just
that she couldn't find her way.

This, however, is your way: Post Office, La
Pointe, Wisconsin, 54850.

Yours,

Essie East

That isn't to say she hadn't meant to come back for you. Leah kept
reading that one sentence, which felt at once like an ache and a salve.
And yet, what did those words even mean? And why the past tense?
Would Essie's letters, if Leah chose to follow them, lead her at last to
her mother? Was her mother even alive?

And what of Leah's own long-planned date with Death, so swiftly undone? Does one reschedule such a thing? Would she even want to now? So many questions tumbled through her mind.

Leah put the letter down beside the urn and the confetti and reached back into the envelope, this time for the photograph. Holding the transparent sheet up to the light, she found the white rise of a tombstone, around which there were other graves built like small houses. The photographer had taken the shot through a split rail fence, so that the wooden rails framed the cemetery. Beyond the cemetery, an icy lake reached to the horizon. The graves bore no names that Leah could see, the snow no footprints. "Where is this?" she asked, looking at the urn. But the stones flashed back at her in silence.

Leah placed the photograph next to rest of the box's contents and then reached into the envelope for the last thing—the dark object at the bottom. "Ouch!" she yelped, quickly withdrawing her hand and rushing her finger to her mouth. Whatever it was had drawn blood, on the same finger she'd stabbed earlier with her belt.

She was more careful when she reached in again, this time with her left hand, and slowly extracted what had pecked her—a black stone crow no bigger than a half dollar. Finely carved, its beak was sharp enough to pierce through skin, and its wings were spread in flight. Leah balanced the bird in her palm and noted how heavy it seemed for how small it was.

As she held it, its weight seemed to transfer to her, as a fatigue descended upon her and made her limbs feel like lead. She let go of the crow and stood up, but her arms and legs only grew heavier, until she imagined she might fall straight through the earth. She swayed on her feet, fighting to keep her eyes open, then woozily shuffled to her bedroom. She barely managed to kick off her boots and remove her spikes before falling onto the bed and succumbing to a deep and dreamless sleep.

As she slept, the setting sun leaked through her blinds and took its slow strokes over her skin, painting her face golden. She was on her back, her face turned slightly toward the window, and her tar-black hair had fallen away from her cheek and forehead, fully exposing her angular but delicate features, features that could have, in this particular light, conjured paintings by the old masters, such as da Vinci's radiant but unfinished *La Scapigliata*. And like *La Scapigliata*, Leah, too, was a half-formed creature, though she couldn't have known this yet. In fact, as she slept, she was the absence of knowing. She was, in these hours, a tabula rasa: she was art being made and remade by light. And as the sun dipped below the horizon and the light dimmed and blued, Leah's face transformed in the gloaming from glowing amber to a silver sculpture. It happened the way coronas happen during total eclipses—at once quickly and slowly, wondrously and terrifyingly—though there wasn't even a spider in her web to see it.

FIVE

BLAZING CALYX CARNIVAL, 1984

"WHY IS HER-SWEET in the tank today?" Leah asked the Rubberband Man as they walked past it on a sweltering afternoon. At six feet tall, Her-Sweet was an imposing woman with deep brown eyes and a mothering sensibility. It wasn't unusual to find, in the back tent where all the performers gathered during their off hours, a person curled up in her lap—sometimes two people at once. "There, there," she'd say while stroking someone's forehead or cheek. "There, there." But her maternal nature was not without its formidable side. She was often the one summoned when a carnival patron had downed one too many beers and needed to be escorted off the property.

"Probably cause it's so gosh-darned hot. So hot you could probably fry an egg on the street."

"It's not *that* hot," said Leah, cutting her eyes as him. She pushed a fluffy piece of cotton candy into her mouth and hummed a small happy sound as it melted. It was a Monday, their shared day off, when he didn't have to perform at night or guard Leah's tent during the day and Leah could spend hours tagging along with him.

"Goddamned freak!"

Leah and the Rubberband Man shot their attention back toward the dunking tank, where the voice had come from. Inside the tank, Her-Sweet sat on a narrow ledge in a red bathing suit, laughing and pointing her finger at the enraged man who was shelling out another three dollars for three more chances to dump her into the water.

"You couldn't pitch a strike on a Little League field!" she taunted.

"You're gonna fall hard, fucking freak!" he warned, gripping the first of his three balls.

"Hey there, watch the language," warned Magson the Giant in his deep rumble of a voice. "This here's a good all-American estab-lishment for children."

But the man could no more hear Magson than he could throw that ball anywhere close to the big red release button outside the tank. "You throw like a drunken grandma!" chided Her-Sweet. "I'm more man than you are!"

"Why is she making him so angry?" Leah asked the Rubberband Man.

"She's not making him anything other than what he already is," he said, brushing the top of her head with his long fingers. "Besides, some people like to get angry. Let off a little steam. It's a kind of release."

"A release?"

The man missed again.

Her-Sweet tossed back her beautiful dark hair and laughed some more.

The Rubberband Man headed toward the dunking tank, and Leah followed. When Her-Sweet caught sight of her, she called out to the man who had finally given up and begun to walk away. "I bet this six-year-old girl can throw better than you!"

The man stopped walking and looked over his shoulder, as if he were deciding whether or not to get angrier.

"Go on, now," the Rubberband Man urged, giving Leah a gentle push, "give it a try."

Magson held a ball out to Leah, and Her-Sweet called, "C'mon, sweetie, give me a bath!"

But Leah shook her head, clutching what was left of her cotton candy. "I don't want to."

"I'll hold your cotton candy for you," said the Rubberband Man with his big stretchy smile. "Give Her-Sweet a release. She wants you to."

Leah handed the Rubberband Man her cotton candy and took the ball, and the Rubberband Man started to chant, "Le-ah Fern, Le-ah Fern," and then the crowd joined in, people slapping their thighs and stomping their feet with each syllable of her name, until Leah stepped up to the line. The chanting stopped, and Her-Sweet sang Pat Benatar from her wooden perch, "Hit me with your best shot!" Leah fixed her eye on the red button and threw the ball, but as soon as it left her grasp, she closed her eyes. It was the sound that told her—first the clang of the ball against the metal button and then the splash—that she had spilled Her-Sweet into the water. Leah opened her eyes. The crowd applauded, and the Rubberband Man cheered, "That a girl, that's our girl!" Leah watched Her-Sweet hoist herself back up out of the water, her once bouncy hair now drooping and plastered to her face, her mascara inking black streaks down her cheeks, as if everything about her was still falling. Somehow Leah couldn't register that Her-Sweet was smiling, that the atmosphere had turned jovial, that the angry man had decided not to get angrier and had instead disappeared into the crowd. What she registered was that Her-Sweet had been diminished, that she had lost actual physical volume—her hair gone flat and her eyelashes dripping down into her beard—that she had been distorted. Regret surged through Leah, a pain that radiated through her throwing arm and made her wish she could rewind the throw. Instead, she turned and ran.

She ran through mazes of people and chatter, around the Bump-n-Grind's grating noises as it jostled its passengers in sudden forceful bursts, past Rattle the Snake Charmer, who was guessing people's ages while hanging upside down like a bat ("Guess it young," she'd once heard him say, "always guess it young"), past Perilous Paul, who was juggling fire on a unicycle. But it didn't matter how fast she ran or how far or in which direction; she couldn't escape the ache of dunking Her-Sweet, which now throbbed in her arm like the red strobe light on top of the Ferris wheel. Still, she kept running.

Breathless, Leah flung the door open to her favorite place in all the carnival, the House of Tricks Treats and Creatures, a hodge-podge of a structure built like an odd insect with four legs of varying lengths sprawling out from its center. Part haunted house, part medical museum, part magic shop, part perpetual Halloween night, it was one of the carnival's biggest attractions. Within its secret corridors, guests could meander down the Hall of Mirrors and watch their reflections change and distort, or they could venture into the Hall of Windows, where unexpected faces sometimes appeared amidst the dioramas. They could enter the Hall of Figures, populated by animated wax statues, including a roach-covered bride and, inexplicably, a statue of Donny Osmond, which some guests said scared them the most. Or, if they were feeling strong in the knees, they could crawl through the Puppet Portal—a twenty-two-foot tunnel lined with red lights that had a habit of flickering off—which was the only way to get to the infamous shows of the Puppet Beasts, a collection of hand-animated creatures that included a giant slug, a cauldron of bats, a mercurial wizard, a red-eyed mongoose, a three-eared rabbit, a daydreaming hyena, a very small frog, and a stand of talking trees. But some would say that the center of the House was its most brash territory, exhibiting a mechanized seven-foot bronto-saurus wearing pearls and a chandelier cap; a collection of specimens in jars, including a two-headed fetal pig, a transparent salamander, and a large horn said to have come from the head of an Egyptian prince; an antique record player crackling out 1920s music; an array of games, candy, and magic tricks for sale; an enormous poster of a dragon lady being pleasured by a satyr; and a rotating cast of live performers.

Leah typically took her time poring over everything in the House whenever she had the opportunity, but on that relatively quiet Monday, she ran past it all and shimmied into the Puppet Portal. When she was halfway through the tunnel, the lights went off, and she curled up like a small nut, burying her face in her knees. In the darkness, she could pretend that nothing had happened. She could pretend she had never been born.

"Excuse me, excuse me, Leah Elephant Fern?"

Leah instantly recognized the slightly raspy voice of the Rubberband Man, only now it was coming through a megaphone. She tightened up into an even smaller nut.

The lights came back on.

"Please report to the chocolate insect bin."

Leah picked up her head.

"We're going to need you to report to the chocolate insect bin immediately. We have several infractions against you, including abandoning a half-eaten cotton candy, closing your eyes while in possession of a throwy ball, and leaving the scene of a crime. Over."

Leah didn't mean to, but she laughed. And when she crawled back out of the tunnel, she came face-to-knee with the Rubberband Man and Her-Sweet, who towered beside him, dressed now in a long white skirt and a pale pink blouse embroidered with delicate red flowers. Her hair was still wet but had sprung back to its curly glory. "Time to pay your penalty," she said, smiling down on her.

Leah stood up and wrapped her arms around Her-Sweet's hips. "I'm sorry I made you fall."

Her-Sweet pulled her in close. "Are you *serious*? Child, I *wanted* to get wet. I was tired of sitting in that hot cage. I love to be in the water. I'm like a fish!"

"Like a bearded catfish," added the Rubberband Man, and the two of them broke into laughter, while two small children wedged their way past them to crawl into the tube bound for the Puppet Beasts.

Leah disengaged from the hug and looked up at her bearded friend. "Her-Sweet?"

"Yes m'love."

"Why were you mean to that man? Were you giving him a release?"

"A release? Hmm, I suppose you could call it that." Her-Sweet knelt down to face Leah. "Truth is, people out there hate freaks like us. We scare them because we're different. So I was just giving him the chance to, I guess you could say, *express* his emotions. Besides, Hank told me I need to start bringing in more money. Gotta earn my keep, after all."

"That there is just ridiculous," said the Rubberband Man. "You do plenty around here, and Hank's just a greedy son-of-a-bitch."

"Shhh," warned Her-Sweet, and they both cast a glance around to make sure they were in the clear.

But Leah wasn't satisfied. "How can someone hate you if they don't know you?"

Her-Sweet fluffed her skirt. "Oh, honey, a lot of times people just hate themselves and need someone to blame it on."

"Enough of this talk!" said the Rubberband Man, leaning back until he was in a full backbend. "It's time to pay your penalty. Please exit under the bridge."

Leah stepped under the arch of the Rubberband Man, and they exited the House of Tricks Treats and Creatures. "What's my penalty?" Leah asked, smiling under the blazing summer sky.

"Wouldn't you like to know?" taunted the Rubberband Man. "Just follow us."

The three of them wound their way through the carnival and scurried across a field to a narrow road. The sun beat down with such vigor that Leah could feel the heat boomeranging off the asphalt and into her face. "Tell me! What's my penalty?"

"What do you think?" the Rubberband Man half-whispered into Her-Sweet's neck. "Is it time?"

Her-Sweet gave Leah a considered look. "It's time."

The Rubberband Man gave a decisive nod and reached into his pocket. He held his closed fist out to Leah.

"What is it?" Leah giggled. "Show me!"

The Rubberband Man opened his hand.

"An egg?"

"You, little miss, are going to cook us breakfast by cracking this here egg on the street and watching it fry, just like I told you it would."

"It's not breakfast time!"

"Okay, lunch. You're going to cook the lovely Her-Sweet and me lunch. Now go ahead—we don't have all day!"

Leah took the egg from the Rubberband Man and knelt down on the empty street. For a moment, the world seemed suspended, as if there were nothing else in it but three people and an egg. Leah cracked the egg, and the insides oozed out, the bright yellow yolk like a second sun. The three of them presided there together, between the two suns, for what seemed like a very long time, until it began to sizzle.

SIX

LEAH SAT UP, rubbed her eyes, and scratched the top of her tufted head. Her first feeling was one of confusion. Was she supposed to be somewhere? Had she dreamt that a man knocked on her door and handed her the remains of her neighbor? She glanced at her alarm clock and saw that it was 6:19 a.m., more than an hour past the time she'd planned to take the pills. Beside the clock, the bottle of narcotics she'd been saving since the extraction of her impacted wisdom teeth still stood unopened. Another morning's twilight seeped in through a slat in her blinds. A woman had died. That woman was not her. These were facts.

Her mother had meant to come back for her. She could not say this was a fact. Yet this was the thought that rushed to the fore of her mind.

Leah rose from her bed and trundled down the hall, stopping just short of her living room. Slowly she peeked around the corner. There on the table was her fox skull as she'd left it, next to what remained of the two red candles. Mozart's Requiem in D Minor leaned against the record player. Her elephant painting was now one day old. She took another step and peered over the table, half expecting the floor to be empty. But there it stood—Essie's bejeweled death tower—beside a black stone crow in a sea of confetti. Leah stood unmoving, the way so many children had stood just inside the carnival entrance, bewildered by all they saw, unsure which way they should go first. And just as they'd crossed through the turnstiles into another world, Leah had crossed through, too, from one life into another, and years of unanswered questions and ungranted wishes crossed with her, reanimated. She closed her eyes tightly and watched a pinpoint of light push deeper into darkness. She could feel it, that speck, as if it were her very own soul. If only she could follow it. If only she knew where it wanted her to go.

With her eyes still closed, she became aware of the slim road she lived on, which bisected the three square miles of Hilda. She could feel its quietness, its reliable *thereness*. And she could sense the web of roads that sprawled out from it, away from Hilda, away from South Carolina. She had spent most of her life scanning those Hilda streets for her mother, always waiting—until now.

"La Pointe, Wisconsin?" said Leah, taking the urn into her arms. "Wherever that is." The stones seemed to be waking up as Leah turned the urn in her hands—the opals flashing bits of fiery red and orange, the luminous moonstones glowing blue, the pyrite flecks in the lapis glinting like gold. Though she had never held a baby, she imagined the urn was as heavy as one.

As Leah cradled her new future, there was no denying that a deal had been struck. Without ceremony, without words, without even fully comprehending what had happened there in her small apartment in Hilda after she'd turned off the music and stopped the clock and fallen into a galactic sleep, she had traded one date for the possibility of another. She had traded death for her mother.

From her earliest days, the carnival had instilled in her a fascination with death. In some ways it was a shrine to the dark side, with its haunted rides and skeletons and its mysterious House of Tricks Treats and Creatures, which displayed death in jars. Whether it was the dove she found pulsing with maggots in the woods, the sleek fox skull that had scared away her prospective friends, or her own last breath—death had always drawn Leah's interest and awe. And now, as she held the remains of Essie East in her hands, she felt that same curiosity. She gave the urn a little shake and felt the contents clump around inside. She unscrewed the tapered wooden top and peered into the narrow opening, but it was too dark to see much more than a shadowy gray. She put her ear up to the opening the way people do with seashells and heard a whisper as inscrutable as the sea.

Leah closed Essie's urn and began to scoop up the confetti that had fallen from the envelope the day before. As she collected the thick bits of paper, she realized that they had once been a photograph—a patch of grass, part of someone's leg, a bit of sky—pieces of a puzzle she now began to arrange on the floor. Matching sky to sky, foot to leg, an eerie feeling crept over her, and when she came upon part of a face, she understood why. Quickly she located the other half—the dark spiky hair, the smooth sweep of the cheekbone, the sleek angle of the jaw—and pushed the two pieces together to find, there at her knees, her own face come into being. Essie must have snapped the picture from inside her apartment. *As for you, you're already dead.* Though she had barely heard Essie speak, she could hear her words as if she were in the room speaking them. "What the fuck?" Leah said, standing up and stepping back.

Suddenly she couldn't breathe. She couldn't focus. A kettle screeched inside her ears. A prickly heat flushed her face. Without another thought she turned and ran out of her apartment, down the stairs, and out onto the sidewalk, the same sidewalk she'd been on when Essie had taken the photo of her. Everything felt blurred, as if she were racing through space, even though she was standing still. "I just need to focus," she said to no one, peering intently across the street at the row of straight-trunked loblolly pines that lined the road. She gulped down a breath, and then another, and as the ringing in her ears began to abate and her breathing began to calm, the hairs on the back of her neck started to tingle. Was someone standing behind her? She quickly peered over her right shoulder at Essie's window, certain she would catch her standing behind the glass. But the window was empty, the morning slow as molasses.

Leah walked into it, the morning, and away from the house, though she couldn't resist looking back at Essie's window several more times. It was hard to know what was real anymore. Everything seemed tenuous, shapeshifting, ghostly.

The heat was already rising. There were no cars on the road. There were no birds darting about. Everything had a languorous feel to it, as if it would take all day for a single sparrow to spread its wings. But Leah was picking up speed. If she kept heading south on Old Salem Road, she'd be out of Hilda in a blink and would eventually hit Thunder Road, which always made her think of the Bruce Springsteen song of the same name, and if she continued going south from there, she'd find herself on Crazy Road, which seemed fitting.

But who was she kidding? This wasn't about Hilda's sixteen streets. This was about whether or not she would really ever leave Hilda at all.

Since her mother had left her with Edward Murphy, she'd never again crossed the South Carolina state line. Even the one vacation she and Edward Murphy had taken was to a South Carolina beach. And though Leah had stood a reasonable chance of getting into an out-of-state school, she applied to only one college: the University of South Carolina, where she made the hour-and-fifteen-minute commute from Hilda three days a week.

It had been there that her lifelong love for animals, elephants in particular, had blossomed in the field of biology, and when her professor received a grant to study the progression of elephant endotheliotropic herpesvirus on afflicted elephants in Cambodia, he'd selected her to be a researcher on the project. After he gave her the news, she smiled the whole way home from campus, then smiled herself to sleep. She was even smiling when she had her passport photo taken the next day, which was the only post-carnival photograph in existence in which she was smiling. But when the day came to board the plane, Leah couldn't move. *What if she comes back while you're in Cambodia?* Her mind besieged her. *What if you miss her? What if you miss your only chance?*

She lay in bed for hours after her flight departed and stared up at the ceiling as if it were a window to the sky. Though she had never boarded a plane, or even been to an airport, she imagined hurtling through the clouds the way she sometimes did in dreams, when her body sailed weightlessly, as if there were no body at all. That's what death must be like, she'd often thought: a birth into flight. So she lay there wishing she had no body, while her stomach growled and her bladder filled and her skin itched here and there, and she didn't move to scratch a single spot. Instead, she flew in the sky of her mind, while the daylight, along with her life's dream, vanished.

On that day, she set her big date: April 4, 1999.

But now it was April 5, 1999, and Leah's walk through Hilda had led her, without her thinking about it, to the house she'd grown up in, the house that Edward Murphy had willed to her mother. More than a year after Edward's death, it sat empty and overgrown, while the town lawyer, Paul Montgomery, was still attempting to locate its rightful owner, the elusive Jeannie Starr, who, by all accounts, had pulled the greatest disappearing act of her life. Edward had also bequeathed to Jeannie his Feed & Seed shop, where Leah had worked since she was a child. Upon Edward's death, the lawyer had explained to Leah that she would be able to work at the shop for three months at her hourly rate before they closed the doors, at which time she would be left jobless and homeless. And even if, after ten years, they failed to locate Jeannie Starr, Edward Murphy's modest estate would pass not to Leah but to his legal next of kin: his estranged son, wherever he was.

Leah had no legal link to her mother, either. Because Leah had been born inside a carnival trailer and had arrived at Edward Murphy's house with nary a document to confirm her existence, it was this same lawyer who'd had to obtain a delayed birth certificate and a social security number for her.

"The day you were born, I did my best magic ever," her mother had told her one night as she tucked her into bed. "I didn't feel a single labor pain for the whole performance—and let me tell you, people went crazy seeing a pregnant lady swallow a sword! But I swear, I've never been that keen again." Jeannie tapped the tips of her fingers together. "It was almost like you were amplifying my magic, like you were helping guide the sword." Leah beamed at that part of the story. "Just that one day, as you were fixin' to be born, I felt like maybe I could do anything. And then at the very end, while people were clapping and throwing their dollar bills up on the stage, my water broke. Right there in front of everyone. And you know what? They thought that was a trick, too! But things happened real fast after that, and before you knew it, Her-Sweet was pulling you out of me, right here on this bed," she patted the mattress, "in this very trailer."

Leah recalled this story as she stood facing the humble ranch house she'd once called *home*. If she blurred her eyes, she could almost see Edward Murphy appear before her. Yes, there he was, pushing the lawnmower in straight strips across the yard. There he was, filling the birdfeeders with the best seed from his shop. There he was in his straw hat, tending the garden, pulling beetles off the cucumbers, slugs off the cabbage, yellow leaves off the tomatoes. "You have to talk to the plants," he'd told her, "thank them for growing." Leah reached her hand toward him, toward the ordinary occurrences she'd once taken for granted, and the ghost of Edward vanished.

Even the house was a ghost—a shell of peeling white paint and faded black shutters standing among the garden's limp remains, the downed birdfeeders buried in the weeds, the battered fence warped and toppling. She had never realized how quickly entropy can set in to an unloved thing.

BACK IN HER apartment, Leah knelt before the photograph Essie had torn to pieces and taped the grass and sky and herself together again. She was businesslike about the whole matter, carefully aligning edge to edge, then flipping the growing photograph over each time to tape it from behind. When she was finished, she paused only for a second or two to admire the finished product, which had an eerily beautiful mosaic quality, before she returned it and everything Essie had given her to the two envelopes they'd arrived in. Then she tucked the envelopes, along with Essie, into her black backpack. She moved with purpose, stepping out of the velvet dress she'd been wearing for two days, wasting no time in the shower, swiftly packing the suitcase that had once been meant for Cambodia. She wrote a check to her landlord for another month's rent and added a book of poems, a sketchpad, her fox skull, and her mother's scarf to her suitcase. She started out the door but then turned back and pulled her watercolor elephant off the wall and the remaining chocolate chip cookies off the counter. She left the pills on her bedside table.

Then she hauled everything into her black 1985 Ford pickup, which she revved straight out of Hilda, heading north.

SEVEN

"I LIKE YOUR SPIKES."

"I'll just take this, please," said Leah, pushing a 1999 Rand McNally road atlas for the United States, Canada, and Mexico toward the gas station attendant.

"What are they?" he asked, ignoring the atlas. "Nails?" His lower jaw hung open in an eager smile as he extended an ET-like finger toward Leah's neck.

"Not," said Leah, stepping back, "a good idea. Just the atlas, please."

The boy closed his mouth and quietly rang up the atlas, his face red as sunburn. This was a shortcoming of the spikes, these moments when people saw them not as a shield but as an invitation, or even a challenge. And now Leah could feel her own cheeks flush at the boy's embarrassment, as if it were her own.

She'd made the belt and collar by cutting up one of Edward Murphy's old belts when she was twelve, then driving one-inch roofing nails through the leather from behind and securing them with glue. She put the nails only in front of the belt and collar, lest she poke holes in any furniture she dared lean back on. "What do you want to go around looking like a porcupine for?" Edward Murphy had often asked gently, with one side of his mouth tipped up toward a smile. But Leah never answered.

"They're roofing nails," she told him, placing her credit card on top of the atlas.

The boy narrowed his eyes at her. "You don't look like a roofer."

"Well, I am," Leah lied. "At this very moment, I'm heading to Wisconsin to put a roof on a symphony hall that was damaged by a tornado."

"Oh!" said the boy. "That's why you need the atlas, huh?" He picked up her credit card but then paused midway between the atlas and the credit card machine. "They get tornadoes in Wisconsin?"

"Not usually. But this one took off the roof and swept up ten harps. People said that when it happened, they heard the most incredible music in the wind."

The boy smiled with delight but then cocked his head with suspicion. "Are you putting me on?"

Though they might have been the same age, Leah felt ancient next to him. "Nah," she said.

He smiled and swiped her card. "That's pretty awesome, then." And as Leah headed out, he called after her, "Have a good trip, see you next fall!"

Leah threw a look over her shoulder as she opened the door.

"Because, you know, you're going on a trip, not because you actually tripped, though that would have been funny."

"Thanks," she said, stepping out into the light.

DRIVING THROUGH COLUMBIA, Leah recognized the manicured expanse and motion of the city, and when she saw the

Cupcake House, the place where she'd often studied before tests, she pulled in. It was there that she'd once run into her favorite professor, the one who'd invited her to join his Cambodia team. "You can't beat the Cupcake House," he'd said, startling her. He hadn't even asked if she minded if he joined her; he simply sat down across from her, letting his backpack flump to the floor. "This triple-chocolate treasure will most likely accelerate my middle-agedness," he said, "but at least I can say I enjoyed getting old."

"Unless you're an immortal jellyfish," Leah said, remembering what he'd taught their class about transdifferentiation and the jellyfish species *Turritopsis dohrnii.*

"Can you imagine," he'd asked, "true immortality?"

Leah had learned so much from him, and yet she couldn't recall any of it now without feeling an immediate and gripping sadness. When he'd returned from the elephant sanctuary in Cambodia, after she'd abandoned the project at the last minute, he'd been kind enough to allow her to earn her internship credit by sorting through all the data they'd gathered and writing the paper that would detail the study's findings: the drug had worked quickly to heal some elephants but seemed to hasten the demise of others. The next phase of the study would involve looking for gene variations between the two groups, research that Leah would have applied for had she been able to face him, the professor who'd believed in her the most. Instead, she completed the paper, received her credit, and, a year shy of graduating, left the university.

And now, there would be no going back into the Cupcake House either, despite the temptation of chocolate. Instead, she would open her atlas to Wisconsin and peer, dumbstruck, at the two-page sprawl of roads and the tiny shapes of countless towns. "La Pointe," she said out loud, scanning the map. "La Pointe La Pointe La Pointe." And then, as if she'd always known where it was, her eyes fell upon a little town at the very top of Wisconsin, on a small island in Lake Superior—Madeline Island. Leah unzipped her backpack just enough to catch a glimpse of the gems inside. "So you want to go Madeline Island?" she said to the urn. "Then we have one more stop to make."

At the bank, Leah took a green lollipop from the lollipop bowl and handed Essie's $9,999.99 check to the teller. Two weeks prior, she had sent most of the money she'd saved from working at Edward's Feed & Seed shop to the elephant sanctuary in Cambodia. After she'd dropped it in the mailbox, she'd felt a passing impulse to call her professor and tell him, so that he would know how deeply she cared about the elephants. She'd wanted to thank him, too, for what he had done for her. She imagined writing a whole book of all the things she'd never said and calling it *The Book of Unsaid Things*.

THOUGH LEAH HADN'T been out of South Carolina since her mother left her there, she had been to an island—John's Island, home to Angel Oak, one of the oldest southern live oak trees. She was thirteen when Edward proposed they take the trip. "What we need is some ocean air," he'd decided. "That always clears things right up." The next day, he tacked a CLOSED FOR VACATION sign on his Feed & Seed shop, and they took off for the shores of South Carolina. He'd pulled the sign from the shop's storeroom, where it had been leaning against the back wall, covered in years' worth of dust. The last time he'd used it, he'd just fallen hard for Leah's mother—though Leah had not yet been born—and he would have let all the birds in South Carolina fly away with his seed if only she'd be his. According to him, Jeannie told him that she could never be his, but she giggled when she said it, which Edward took "not as a definitive no but as a no with possibility." They met—or, one could say, he found her—when he'd made the hour drive to Augusta, Georgia, for the best peanuts anywhere.

"You have to understand," he'd explained, "Jimmy Carter had just been elected, and suddenly everyone had a hankering for peanuts. Miss Emily told me about the peanut farm, and I thought maybe I could buy a bunch and sell some at the shop. I figured even if I ate the profits, I could at least break even. Anyway, I'd loaded up with peanuts and was heading home when I saw this orange flash in the woods. I thought it was some type of bird at first, but something told me I'd better stop. I didn't even bother to close my car door. I just left it swung open on the side of the road and walked over to what I realized was an actual woman. She was all balled up, sitting in the ferns, hugging her knees and crying. 'Hey there, miss,' I said. 'Can I help you?' And when she looked up at me and I saw how beautiful she was, I couldn't move or speak. Could barely think for what seemed like a century, though it was probably only a second or two. She said she was fine, and I said that I didn't mean any disrespect but that I had to beg to differ, as a girl crying in the woods isn't fine. She said she'd had a fight with her boyfriend and that she'd gotten out of the car and run away. I asked if she had anywhere to go, and she said she was already where she needed to go, and I said maybe she should come with me and at least have some peanuts.

"When she got into my car, I remember thinking that I'd found my own little genie, as if she'd just come—poof!—right out of a bottle. And when she told me her name was Jeannie, I thought it must be fate that I'd found her. I knew then that my life had changed.

"A day later, I took a black marker and an old piece of scrap wood and made this closed for vacation sign—then wooed Jeannie Starr all the way to Hilton Head, where I spent two weeks lavishing her with lobster and wine, stuffed bears and porcelain angels, and a diamond ring that damn near cleared out my savings account. I kept thinking she would change her mind and stay with me, but she just swung that silky hair of hers like she was dancin' and told me I was a silly old fool. And that may be true. But mark my words, she'll be back. One day she'll show up right at our front door, and it'll be like she never left."

From that faulty promise grew the thickest bond that would ever exist between Edward and Leah: their shared wish that Jeannie Starr would return to them.

"What if she comes while we're away?" Leah had asked him when he told her to pack her suitcase. As soon as she had learned to speak, people sometimes had to look away when she asked them a question; her Caribbean-blue eyes were just too large, too unnaturally blue, too penetrating, too honest, too knowing, which made people—even good people—feel shifty and uncomfortable under her gaze.

But Edward appeared to be immune. "Oh, that's simple," he told her, meeting her eyes. "I'll leave her a note on the door and tell her where we've gone."

"What if somebody takes the note?"

"Nobody'll take the note. Even if someone does, I'm leaving a second note for her on the kitchen counter." He reached out toward her shoulder but then dropped his arm back to his side, having learned that was as close as she would let him get to fatherly affection. "Don't you worry, kid. She knows where I keep the spare key. She'd probably just wait here for us. Make herself some pancakes or something."

The first thing Edward and Leah did when they arrived at Folly Beach, South Carolina, was rush down to the beach and walk along the surf. While Edward matched the cloudy seascape with his silver hair, pale blue shirt, and khaki pants rolled up over his ankles, Leah, dressed in black, stood out like a crow among a shoreline of seagulls. They didn't speak as they moved along the shore to the sound of the waves crashing in. Leah stopped every few steps to examine a stone or a shell, and soon her pockets sagged with a variety of smooth treasures. Edward, whom people often mistook for her grandfather, walked through the water at a slow but steady pace, his face turned toward the horizon, as the distances waxed and waned between them.

HOW LONG AGO it seemed since they had taken that vacation and returned home to find the note they'd left for Jeannie Starr still taped to their front door. Edward had tried to shrug off his disappointment. "That just means we'll be here when she does come, and that'll be even better." Leah watched him throw the note in the trash.

Now, as she drove up Route 26, she wondered about the letter waiting for her on an island in Wisconsin. She started to speed up, but the sight of the North Carolina state line ahead stopped her cold. She pulled over on the shoulder and clicked on her hazard lights. Her heart was racing, her breath jagged. Cars rushed up behind her and whooshed past, while she felt as stuck as the highway sign. In a break in traffic, she stepped out and leaned against the front of her truck to face the sign that, for years, had been her imagined barricade.

There was nothing barricade-like about it. The sign was not riddled with ravenous crocodiles. It was not a gaping, fire-rimmed hole in the earth. It was a friendly green rectangle of aluminum, welcoming her to North Carolina with an image of a waving flag. Beyond it, hazy bluish mountains sloped softly into greater distances. Over the years, Leah had heard the phrase, "you can't go back," so many times that it had become cliché, but now the words came to her as if she were hearing them for the first time. Now she had something calling her forward. She climbed back into her truck.

"Bye," she said to the road and sky in her rearview mirror. Without fanfare, she pulled the last cookie from her backpack and crossed the line into North Carolina.

EIGHT

AS THE HIGHWAY stretched ahead, Leah retraced the year she and Essie had coexisted in their duplex. Had there been some look, some intonation in one of their few brief greetings that harkened to the secrets Essie had been carrying? What about the day Essie had brought her the peppermint meltaways? Had there been something in her eyes, some small but knowing spark? "You look like her. You have to look to see it, but it's there," Essie had said to her when she'd come to return her plate. How quickly Leah had dismissed her; how quickly she had cowered and looked away. "I didn't see it at first," Essie had added. "Or maybe I didn't want to." Now, of course, it made sense, and Leah felt seized by a deep regret for not asking more at the time, for not returning Essie's gaze. In fact, she couldn't even conjure the color of her eyes.

Like a compass invariably orienting north no matter how you shake it, Leah's thoughts turned back to her mother. She had never considered that her mother would have left the carnival, or that she, too, had grown older. In her mind, she was still performing in her sequined bustier on that same wooden stage, silks and birds and flames flying from her hands. She was still flopping onto their shared bed each night, where Leah had loved to wedge herself into the fragrant haven of her armpit. She was still gathering wildflowers from the field, still winking at her horrible boyfriend, still weeping in her sleep some nights, after the carnival had gone, for a brief spell, silent.

))) ● (((

LEAH TRAIPSED BEHIND her mother in the buzzing summer field, stretching her six-year-old legs with each stride so that her feet could land in her mother's footsteps. Jeannie was wearing a long diaphanous skirt, white and billowy. Every few feet, Jeannie stopped to pick a wildflower, until they entered a thicket of hickory and pecan trees.

"Ooh, look! Snakeroot!" Jeannie kneeled to admire the clusters of tiny white flowers, but she refrained from adding any to her bouquet of sunflowers, blazing star, and goldenrod. "This right here is the stuff that killed Abe Lincoln's mother."

"A flower killed someone?" asked Leah, astonished.

"Well, not directly. She drank milk that came from a cow who ate the flowers. They're poisonous if you eat them, but if you mash up the root and put it on a snakebite, the bite just disappears."

"How do you know so much about flowers?" asked Leah, not having encountered much about them in any of her books. She knelt beside her mother to get a look at the small white blooms.

Jeannie stood and walked up to the edge of the stream to give the stems of her bouquet a drink. "I've lived a lot of lives," she said, exhaling a long audible breath.

Leah followed and squatted down beside her. "How do you live more than one life?"

Jeannie, who didn't look up from where the water swept around the flower stems, not even when Leah's knee bumped into hers, ignored the question. "The thing about flowers is that they can't hide who they are. A sunflower can't pretend to be a snakeroot, for instance. And this blazing star will just blaze right back up at the sun without a care in the world."

"Why would a sunflower want to be a snakeroot?" Leah asked, dipping her fingers into the cool water.

"You're taking it too literally."

Leah stood up and meandered slowly away from her mother, her cheeks stinging red. She hated when she missed something her mother was trying to convey, especially in those moments when her voice got all willowy and her words grew tails that stretched on and on—*without a caaaaaaaare in the wooooooorrrrld.* Leah picked up a gnarled stick and meandered in circles along the stream, pretending to be old. She let her weight fall onto the stick, jabbing it onto the ground with every other step—until she heard the sudden loud chatter of a cicada and her mother spoke a single word: "Stop."

Leah didn't understand at first and took another elderly step forward.

"Leah Fern, don't move." Jeannie spoke quickly, and the urgency in her voice halted Leah in her tracks. "Right there," Jeannie said, pointing the dripping bouquet, "beside you, under that tree with the rocks in front, is a rattlesnake."

Leah looked where her mother had pointed and saw it, coiled and aimed in her direction, its corncob tail erect and rattling. "What do I do?" Leah asked, more curious than afraid.

"Just be still a second. He doesn't mean you any harm. You probably just scared him is all."

"I'm sorry, little guy," Leah said to the three-foot viper. She remembered reading that most snakes are shy and bite only to defend their lives, so she stood still as a tree and watched the snake be still and rattle at the same time. And in that frozen moment Leah thought how in a way she and the snake were the same, both of them talking but not moving. She made a mental note to ask her mother if that's what she meant about a flower wanting to be like another flower.

"Now slowly start to move away from it and come on back to me," Jeannie instructed.

In slow, delicate steps, Leah made her way back to her mother, who pulled her into an embrace while the snake slid off in the opposite direction. As Leah pressed her face into her mother's warm chest and felt the cool wet flowers dripping against her back, she was thinking about how to ask her question about the flowers. But her mother spoke first. "That's what I meant about living lots of lives. It's kind of like how a snake sheds its skin. It's still the same snake after, but it's also new again."

Leah pressed more firmly into her mother, wanting nothing new, wanting only this.

"See how nature works?" Jeannie mused, as she disengaged from Leah. "Plants often grow where they're needed most. Like that snakeroot growing over there where the snake lives, or jewel weed, which soothes the itch of mosquito bites, growing in swampy places where mosquitoes live." Jeannie headed out of the woods, with Leah following in her footsteps, listening. "It's amazing, really. What you need is almost always someplace nearby. All you have to do is look."

NINE

LEAH'S FIRST STOP after crossing the South Carolina line was Asheville, North Carolina, where she purchased a sandwich, a package of cream-filled cookies, an assortment of marked-down Easter candy, and several bottles of water. As she walked through the little mountain-lined city, which felt as if it existed on the other side of the world from Hilda and not just on the other side of a state line, she was intrigued by the vividness and interconnectedness of the people—bright-eyed boys kicking hacky sacks back and forth as they strolled; a woman in a red dress busking on a street corner while passersby dropped tips into her jar; three dreadlocked drummers closing their eyes to the beat; an artist painting the scene in shades of lavender and green; a group of stern-faced doomsayers carrying Y2K signs proclaiming the end of the world. She slipped among them like a stray and wondered if the drummers' hands got tired and what the artist had painted yesterday. She wondered what kind of bed the singer slept on and what happened on those sidewalks very late at night. She wondered if her mother had ever been to Asheville, if maybe their footfalls had even touched the same bits of sidewalk. And she wondered what was beyond the city, beyond the mountains that enfolded it—and what was beyond that. Now that she'd crossed over into this new territory, the *beyonds* felt end-less, and they filled her with a sea of inchoate questions that glowed like the bioluminescent creatures of the deep.

"Cross the border when you get there." The growl of a woman's voice startled Leah from her thoughts. Dressed in tattered layers of varying lengths, an old woman was suddenly peering into Leah's face.

Leah stepped back. "Pardon?"

The woman stepped closer again, initiating a strange sort of dance. Her eyes bumped up in their sockets as she leaned in farther, kissing-distance now. "Here and there and everywhere. Vampires. They're all vampires." The woman veered off sharply then, mutter-ing to herself until her voice faded into the crowd.

BACK ON THE highway, Leah settled into the hum of the road and the steady click-clicks of her tires over the grooves in the pave-ment. Twilight crept over the land, and with it came a blue so sin-gular that it could have been the birth of blue. But in the span of a few miles, it, too, was gone. As night came fully and the Big Dipper rose straight ahead, Leah imagined it tipping, filling the back of the truck with miniature stars.

Eventually her mind began to quiet, to settle on the hum of motion as the road went on and the darkness went on and her head-lights pushed through it as if their light were her only future. As the hours passed and the darkness settled deeply into itself, she began to wonder if maybe infinity was simply a road like this one, a highway that you never get off.

Her sugar stash, however, was not infinite, and when it could no longer stave off her exhaustion, she pulled over at a truck stop outside of Lexington, Kentucky. She slid her elephant painting behind the bench seat of her truck, took off her collar and belt, balled up some clothes for a pillow, and lay down across the seat. She had never lain in her truck before, and as she curled up on her side and a quiet settled over her, she had the feeling of being cozy and vulnerable at the same time. She peeked into her backpack, which stood upright on the passenger side floor, and caught the sheen of a stone. "Where am I?" she whispered. And as she closed her eyes, the word *Kentucky* played in her mind. What did it mean? *Kentucky.* In the staggered dark of the truck stop's parking lot, through the sibilance of cars coming and going and the occasional jarring sounds of road-weary late-nighters remarking too loudly about french fries or fucking or things indiscernible, she repeated the word in her mind until she no longer recognized it. *Kentucky.*

BY THE TIME Leah arrived in Wisconsin the next night, crossing a state line felt no more significant to her than a cloud crossing the sky. She ventured down several small roads in search of an inconspicuous place to close her eyes as she'd done the night before, but what she found instead was a small shack festooned with retro Christmas lights. JOE'S BAR AND GRILL, the marquis read in removable plastic letters, as if tomorrow it could just as easily be something else. Realizing how hungry she was, Leah slung her urn-heavy backpack over her shoulder and went inside.

She had never been to a bar, but the few she'd seen in movies boasted charming white-teethed bartenders twirling glinting steel shakers and serving drinks decorated with fruits and umbrellas.

This bar had neither the gleam nor the umbrellas, and from the bartender's beard-shagged grimace, she could see that he lacked the enthusiasm of the big-screen ice shakers. What the bar did have was a pool table over which two men in leather jackets were hovering, a jukebox playing something twangy, and a row of old men nursing frothy beers. A pretty woman in an apron hustled past with plates of burgers and fries and delivered them with a casual expertise Leah couldn't help but admire, until a sudden eruption of laughter yanked her attention away from the server. It boomed out from a cadre of gray-haired men at the end of the bar, a foreboding kind of laughter. She could feel that, just as she could feel them aiming it in her direction. "Look who's here," one of the men said. "Edward Scissorhands!" A new wave of laughter crashed into Leah, and several of the men craned their necks around to get a good look at the girl with the coal-black hair and spikes. "She's even dressed like him!" said another.

Leah looked around the room, wondering if someone would come lead her to a table or if she should just seat herself. "Why don't you come show me how sharp your spikes are," the man taunted. "And I'll show you something, too."

Leah beelined over to him, a fireball, a meteor hurtling through space. She placed her hand on his right shoulder as if she knew him, and the men fell silent. Not a glass was lifted, not a head was turned, not a word was spoken. Everyone, it seemed, had come to a halt, waiting to see what she would do next. She swallowed. She could feel the man leaking into her, like sludge in the blood, but she wouldn't let herself retreat, not even when she began to feel as if a helmet were tightening around her head, not even when the pressure grew so intense that it made her list backward onto her heels. Instead, she steadied herself and let her voice flow forth, a wave that wrapped around the men like a ribbon. "In the movie you mentioned, Edward Scissorhands was a gentle creature, but the town mistook him for a monster." She turned away from the ringleader and consulted the others, keeping her grip firm on his shoulder. "When in fact, it was the people in the town who were the real monsters. Remember?" She felt the man's shoulder growing clammy under her palm. "Is that what you meant? That you're a monster?"

The man laughed nervously and looked to his friends, who shifted in their seats and looked away. "Hey there, miss," he finally said, "don't go getting your panties in a bundle. I was just playing around."

She took her hand off his shoulder and faced him squarely. "You're a lonely man, and you're a weak man. You probably have high blood pressure. You try to compensate for what you lack by harassing a woman one third your size. But do you see how you're only weaker now, and more alone?"

"She's crazy," the man said to no one in particular, clutching his beer as if it were the only thing keeping him from getting swept away.

"Would you like to have a seat?" a voice asked from behind Leah. It was the server, pushing a smile.

"Yes, please," said Leah. "Thank you." Then she turned back to the man one more time, and the last of the ribbon unfurled. It brushed against the scruff of unshaven cheeks, the sagginess of old necks. It swept across eyelashes and fingers, around rotund waists and swollen ankles. "It's not too late," she said, "to be something else." Then she followed the server to a table.

THAT NIGHT, LEAH didn't drive far. After she left Joe's Bar and Grill and the gray-haired men who resumed their vacant stares and small talk without another gesture in her direction, she followed a gravel road that eventually turned to dirt, and she pulled off to the side. A fat half-moon hung overhead, and she could feel its pull on her.

She thought about the men at the bar, how they'd left her no choice but to fight or flee. Why did it have to be this way, things always exerting power over other things? Rock-paper-scissors, something always beat something else. Stars absorb other stars; black holes swallow up mouthfuls of them; galaxies consume other galaxies; some twins even consume their siblings in the womb. For a moment, Leah felt ashamed of her own hunger. She unzipped her backpack and pulled out Essie's urn, cradling it in her left arm. The moonlight fell gently over the stones.

"Did you know the luna moth lives for twenty-four hours and has no mouth?" she asked the stones, which were sleepy but not sleeping in the blue light.

TEN

TWO DAYS, FIVE state lines, and over 1,300 miles after leaving Hilda, Leah arrived at the edge of Lake Superior. It was misty when she pulled into the Madeline Island Ferry parking lot, and even with her pickup's heater giving its all, she couldn't shake the northern chill she'd picked up somewhere in Indiana. There were only a handful of other cars in the sandy lot, and when she parked facing the choppy water, she didn't notice the man sitting in the green Oldsmobile a few spots away.

Leah unzipped her backpack and took out the urn. With each different light, every turn and tilt, the stones' moods changed, so that she never saw the same urn twice. Gazing out at the water, she could barely make out the island in the mist. She wondered why Essie and the others had chosen this place to start their journey, and whether the letter waiting for her in the post office would tell her. More than that, she wondered what the letter would tell her about her mother. Where was she? How did Jeannie come to know Essie? These questions had been pulsing in her nonstop, but now they embossed themselves onto the morning, becoming almost palpable. Unless, of course, there was no letter. Leah had to acknowledge this possibility. A letter could be lost, for one thing—or damaged, or maybe never even mailed at all.

She zipped the obelisk away again and buttoned up her black wool coat. She got out of her truck and started toward the gray building, where she presumed the ferry tickets were sold.

"Must have hit a nail." A voice came from behind her.

She stopped and turned around. An older man was looking at her from the open window of a green Oldsmobile, his tweed elbow resting on the car door.

"I beg your pardon?"

"Surely you must know."

"Know what?"

He motioned with his chin toward her truck. "I'd bet that by the time you purchase your ticket and come back, your tire will be completely out of air."

Leah walked to the front of her truck and saw the flat tire for herself. "Strange," she said. "I didn't feel it happen."

"Tires can go fast if you hit a nail in just the right way."

"Lucky me."

"Do you have a spare?"

"Um, no."

"Well, if you're not in any hurry, I can give you a lift to a tire place in town. Of course, you'd miss the last ferry of the day."

Leah looked at her watch. "But it's not even noon."

"Yes, and the last ferry runs at 12:30." The man looked at his own watch. "And I doubt we'll get you back here in the next thirty-seven minutes. I imagine whoever's expecting you will understand if you come a day late?"

"No one's expecting me."

"So you're just visiting the island for pleasure?"

"Sort of." Leah examined the man's face. He was a gentle soul, she could see that. "Not really."

"Sounds mysterious."

"I suppose."

The man smiled. "Mystery notwithstanding, would you like a lift into town?"

Leah looked out toward Madeline Island. The mist was lifting, the bumpy outline of the island emerging more crisply into view in wintery patches of brown and gray.

Back in Hilda, things had already begun to sprout and bud, but here snow lined the roads and the land was still asleep. She knew that the sensible thing to do would be to take the man up on his offer, but that muted patch of land across the water was calling to her. "That's a very kind offer," she said, "but I need to get to the island today. There's something at the post office I need to pick up."

The man gave a slow resigned nod and said, "A woman's gotta do what a woman's gotta do," as if it were a lesson he'd learned the hard way.

Leah went inside and purchased her ticket, and when she was walking back to her truck, the man picked up as if the conversation had never paused. "No Christmas trees this year," he said, a woeful weight in his voice. His neck was craned around so that he could see her.

Leah nodded politely and continued past his car toward her truck.

"First year in the history of the ferry."

Leah stopped and looked back at him. "I'm sorry, I don't—"

"This is the first year the lake didn't freeze. Usually it freezes up solid." He looked out at the water and then back at Leah. "You're not from around here, are you?"

"I'm from South Carolina."

"That's not what I would have guessed."

"What would you have guessed?"

"New York."

Fancy. She could almost hear her mother saying it, the way Essie had described. "Okay, well. Thanks again," she said, giving a little wave and continuing toward the driver's side of her truck.

Even out of sight, his voice came for her. "Every year until this year, there's been an ice road going across to the island."

Leah circled back to the Oldsmobile. "An ice road?"

The man lit up. "Oh yes. And every year after Christmas, when everyone in Bayfield tosses their Christmas trees, the town gathers them up and lines the ice road with them. But not this year, on account of the lake not freezing. They say the earth is heating up, that we're killing it, but if all that Y2K stuff is true, we'll all be gone soon anyway." The man chuckled at this final thought, and when the chuckle turned into a cough, he pulled a handkerchief from a pocket inside his tweed jacket and blew his nose. "Too bad you didn't come last year."

Leah studied the man's eyes, which were marked by deep lines and accentuated by tufted white eyebrows. They were the kind of eyes that tend to weep involuntarily, as they were doing now, and in their watery depths, Leah could see his currents of pain.

"The Christmas tree ice road sounds lovely," she said.

"Oh, it is! All those Christmas trees getting to have a second life—from our homes onto the ice!" He paused then, casting his watery gaze into the distance. "But I haven't had a Christmas tree in years. Enough about me, though! Where on the island are you staying, if I might ask?"

She cleared her throat. "I'm not sure."

"The mystery continues."

"The letter waiting for me at the post office will tell me where to go."

"Sounds like a treasure hunt."

"Sort of."

"Okay, listen. Since you're on a mysterious operation-slash-treasure-hunt, there's someone you should know, in case you need anything. She's a dear friend, and she loves helping people."

Leah detected a shimmer of pride in his voice. "That's very kind of you," she said.

"When you get off the dock, you can't miss the post office—it'll be staring right at you. From there, if you want to get to Brenda Wright's place, you'll turn left on Big Bay Road. Pretty soon you'll see Whitefish—the road, not the fish—and you'll make another left. Go just a little ways and turn right on Voyager, then start looking on the left for a red door set back in the trees. You'll know it when you see it. Go ahead and knock, and when you hear a woman call, 'Whoooo's thaaayeer?'—and she'll say it just like that—you just tell her Bob O'Malley sent you. She'll take care of you."

There was something about this man that made Leah want to hand him a warm bowl of soup. "So you're Bob O'Malley?"

Without getting out of his car, the man held out his hand. "In the flesh."

Leah eyed his hand anxiously. "Oh . . . I don't . . ." She pressed her hands against the front of her thighs. "I'm sorry . . . It's just . . . " But she couldn't bring herself to tell him that she didn't touch people, so she steeled herself and gave him her hand. "Leah Fern."

Through her hand, up her arm, into her chest, his sadness surged in.

"Yeah, that's right," he said, slowly withdrawing his hand back into the dim space of his car. "You just tell good old Brenda Wright that Bob O'Malley sent you."

"Aren't you coming to the island?" Leah asked, sensing this woman was someone important to him. "You could tell her yourself."

"Oh no. I just come here to think sometimes. Watch the people come and go."

Leah wondered what it was about the ferry lot that drew him there. She wondered about his life, his sadness. "May I ask you something?"

He smiled, visibly pleased to be on the other side of the questions. "Sure, shoot."

"If you like Christmas trees, why has it been years since you had one?"

Bob O'Malley thought for a moment. He tapped his fingers on the steering wheel, as if they were marking time. "Things change when you get old," he finally said. "Used to be Christmas trees marked the beginning of something—a new season, all kinds of anticipation. But now they're just a reminder of what's gone."

Before Leah could respond, the approaching ferry sounded its horn.

"Your chariot," he said.

Leah wanted more than anything to get on that ferry, but for a moment she didn't want to leave Bob O'Malley in the parking lot. "Wait!" she called, darting to her truck.

When she returned, she presented him with a page she'd torn out of her sketchbook. He held it out the window with both hands and examined it. "A tree?" he asked, his eyes bright with surprise. "For me?"

"It's a Christmas tree," said Leah of the shaggy conifer she'd sketched and filled in with watercolors long ago. "Already decorated with pine cones."

"You painted this?"

Leah nodded. "For you."

"I never . . ." he started, but then he trailed off as his eyes filled. "Thank you," he said, pulling the tree into the car with him.

Leah didn't know how to say goodbye. "Did you know that even from hundreds of miles apart, elephants can communicate with each other by pounding the ground? It causes a subsonic rumble."

"A subsonic rumble, eh? Maybe I'll stamp my feet and see if anyone over on the island can hear me. You let me know if you do, okay? You can look me up—I'm in the phone book."

She nodded and returned the smile before turning away from Bob O'Malley for the last time and moving toward the motor of her future: a boat that was about to take her even farther from Hilda, South Carolina.

ELEVEN

WHEN THE FERRY set off on the two-and-a-half-mile journey from Bayfield to Madeline Island's fourteen-mile stretch of land, Leah did not look back at Bob O'Malley's green Oldsmobile. She did not think about her flat tire or how she'd have no transportation once she got to the island. She did not think about the fact that she had no place to stay. Instead, she looked out at the water, its distances choppy with chunks of ice that any other winter would have solidified enough to drive on, and thought about the letter that awaited her. Though she tried to stop herself, she couldn't help imagining what she might say when she and her mother were finally reunited. *I still have your scarf. Edward died. I missed you.*

As Leah disembarked from the ferry, she spotted the post office straight ahead, just as Bob O'Malley had promised. With her backpack strapped over both shoulders, she broke into a run, and Essie came slamming into her back with each step. But she barely registered the hits or the cold wind whipping her face, and when she swung open the door to the post office, some small part of her was disappointed to find a stranger standing behind the counter and not her mother as she might have appeared long ago, emerging like a mermaid from the depths to shout, "Surprise!"

"I'm Leah Fern," she announced. She was winded from her sprint, and her words fell out in staccato bursts. "I'm here to pick up a letter, general delivery."

"Leah Fern," the woman behind the counter repeated. "Just one moment."

She disappeared, and in the "just one moment" she was gone, Leah watched a clock tick slowly on the wall. She eyed a display of stamps, including a collection in homage to the 1970s—disco dancers, smiley faces, Big Bird. She wondered what life had been like in 1977, when Essie and four other women set out on their mysterious journey.

The clerk returned carrying a padded envelope. "I just need to see some ID."

"Oh, yes, sure," said Leah, fumbling with the zipper on her backpack. As she rooted for her wallet, she felt as if her once-nimble hands had been replaced by concrete blocks, and when she finally retrieved her driver's license, she extended it forward triumphantly. "Thanks!" she called, darting out the door.

The sun had broken through the clouds, and the day grew suddenly brilliant. Leah sat on a step on the side of the post office and gazed out at Lake Superior, its turbulent mosaic of blues. The wind ruffled the post office flag, which made a pleasant flapping sound, while seagulls called to each other mid-swoop. The cold fell brightly on her skin. Everything around her felt so far from South Carolina, so different, especially the wind. Even her own hands, as she looked down at her slender fingers clutching the envelope on which her name appeared in a shaky script, felt almost as if they belonged to someone else.

She flipped the envelope over and saw it was sealed with red wax like the first one. Below the seal was a slash of white paint and the number one. Leah broke the seal, and as if in harmony, the wind, for a moment, ceased. She looked inside and saw another transparent photograph along with another uncertain object, but it was the letter she wanted. The wind kicked back up and rattled the paper as she read Essie's words.

July 8, 1998

Dear Leah,

So you've made it to Madeline Island, where the first of our nine full moon ceremonies began. What do I say to the girl in black who now follows in our footsteps? Have the courage to love. That's it, my one bit of advice.

The only thing I had any courage about was taking pictures. I didn't care what anyone thought; I just shot what turned me on. Sometimes I made transparencies of my prints, like the two you've received so far. This way you can see time as the illusion it is. I hold up a transparent photograph of Claire, and suddenly she's here with me in my apartment, smiling at me in front of my bookshelves or my window or this ostentatious urn that, by the time you read this, will belong to you. One world is a window into the next.

I've been living in two worlds—the one in which I sit at my typewriter and occasionally spy you lunking by either to or from your truck, and the world of the past, which lights up like foxfire in the forest of my mind. Lately there's been a third world: the one in which I imagine you in the future, holding this letter in your hands. How odd to think you'll also be holding what's left of these old bones.

You, the girl who walks pitched forward as if into a gale, as if all you hear is wind. You, a magician's daughter, one who once performed her own kind of magic. You, who now barely clings to the tattered hive of your own life, I give my death to you.

There were five of us who lived on the loop of a court in an artists' colony at the foothills of the Smoky Mountains in Tennessee. Athena was a sculptor who made imaginary beasts out of clay, much of which she dug out of the earth herself. She had wild black hair and one eye that occasionally wandered, often when she was talking about herbs. That was her other passion—making plant medicine. She wasn't shy about shoving all sorts of rooty and bitter decoctions at us and telling us, "Drink, drink," which we did, because they worked. They eased our dyspepsia, dissolved our headaches, helped us sleep. At times she was pushy and opinionated and loud. She tended to lean in too close when she talked. She wasn't always terribly meticulous about straining her brews. But she healed us. Because my mum had also been an herbalist, I had a soft spot for her.

Dee was a guitarist and singer who wrote songs that made the hairs on my arms stand up. She rode a motorcycle and once joked that if she could marry a piece of clothing, it would be her black leather jacket.

Linda was a watercolor painter perpetually enamored of the sea and its elements—lighthouses, piers, distant ships—and of her memories of sailing with her father as a child. The steadiest of the lot of us, she was a trove of arcane knowledge, including how to use a sextant—a talent that would serve us well.

I, at that time, was in a courtship with moss. That was all I wanted to photograph—these rootless plants that you have to get down low and close to see. Some mosses were fine and fernlike, some tall and willowy, some shaped like stars. It seemed each day I discovered a new miniature forest of moss as I tromped through hills and glades with my camera.

And then there was Claire. How can I describe her, except to say she was a master of everything she touched? She was a self-taught metalsmith (though I think of her as an alchemist) who made striking jewelry with gemstones that came from all over the world. She never told us how she amassed her collection, and I never thought to ask. It simply seemed natural that someone like Claire would have thousands of gems tucked up under her wing.

She was the only one of us who had already begun having some real success with her art. After one of her pieces was featured in a gallery show, collectors began seeking her out, paying top dollar for whatever she was willing to sell. But she was such a generous soul that she often gave away the things she made before anyone had the chance to buy them. I still have what she gave to me.

When the old poets describe women as fair, they must have envisioned our flaxen-haired Claire, always with a slight flush to her milky cheeks and rosiness to her lips. She had a sprinkling of freckles across her nose and a fetching smile that came easily and made it impossible to look away. I've spent my life studying light—its qualities of temperature, its angles, its sharpness, its softness—and she is the only person I've ever thought of as light personified. She was late afternoon light, warm, golden, gentle. And wherever she went, people wanted to be near that light. A man who bought a pair of her earrings for his wife came back that same night and serenaded her. The mayor of our town proposed marriage to her after one date. Children sought her out, repeating her name like a song.

It wasn't only people who sidled up to Claire. Deer ate from her hands. Dogs followed her home. Butterflies landed on her shoulders and in her hair. I don't mean once or twice. I mean all the time.

I didn't like many people—and still don't—but the five of us just seemed to work. Each day at 1:00 we took breaks from our studios and

met for lunch at the picnic table behind our
bungalows. We sat side by side so that we could
all face those green hills that rolled into a
specter of shadowy mountains. If anyone noticed
that I sat next to Claire whenever I could, I
didn't care.

We were having one such lunch when Athena
suggested we form a coven. She'd once intimated
that she'd been part of a coven before, but
she never elaborated. "You mean like *witches*?"
Dee asked, running her fingers through her
short blond shag, a habit Claire once called
sexy. "Call it what you want," Athena said.
Then she told us how the idea had come to her
in a dream. We were being summoned to perform
nine full moon rituals—a nine-month gestation
that would lead to the birth of our purest
creativity. Why else are we on earth, she
pointed out, than to create?

"To love?" Claire asked.

"Love is a kind of creation," Athena said,
"creation a kind of love."

We were all in agreement then, at least
about that.

Athena had been reading a book on sacred
geometry and the power of particular shapes—
and she suggested we travel the path of a
golden spiral, a pattern found everywhere in
nature, from flowers to hurricanes to our own
galaxy. I remember how she casually held her
sandwich out as she spoke, as if offering it to

those distant mountains, and how I felt as if I
might choke on my own sandwich. I couldn't help
thinking about what had happened to my mother
so many years before. "You'll just have to find
someone else to howl at the moon with you," I
told her. And at that precise moment, something
happened that I wouldn't have believed had I
not seen it myself.

We heard a scream. It sounded like the sky
was ripping open. Looking up, I saw a hawk
diving toward us, a black snake dangling from
its talons. It swooped down close and dropped
the snake right in the center of our table,
which made a terrible thud, but then the hawk
went quiet, except for the first flaps of its
massive wings as it flew away. None of us said
anything. None of us moved, including the
snake. It just lay there in a perfect spiral
from head to tail, as if it had been arranged
that way. We all thought it was dead.

And then the snake rose. It stood straight
up and faced us. I was sure it was going to
strike, but instead it slid off the table and
whipped down the hill faster than I'd ever seen
a snake move.

"So a spiral it is," Athena declared, her
sandwich still in midair. And then it was
decided: we would begin on the first full moon
of 1977, the wolf moon. This time I kept my
mouth shut.

We marked the first nine full moons of 1977

on our calendars, and Dee convinced a teacher
friend of hers to let us have one of those
oversized classroom maps of North America,
which we spread out on Athena's studio floor
and crawled around on like bugs, wondering
where the spiral would take us. Linda, our
seafarer, was charged with figuring that out
by using the Fibonacci sequence and a homemade
pair of compasses to plot our nine locations,
one at each turn of the spiral.

For the occasion, Athena had lit nine
candles, a white one to signify light,
initiation, and the purity of our intentions;
red, orange, yellow, green, blue, indigo, and
violet candles to represent each color of
the rainbow, a bridge to the supernatural,
an homage to the liminal; and a final black
candle—the counterbalance to white, symbolizing
the absorption of all colors, a bow to the
unknown.

The question was where would our spiral
would begin? We spent hours inching around on
the map, pointing here and there, until Claire
settled the matter by asking everyone to move
out of the way. Once the map was clear, she
tossed a tiny piece of quartz into the air. It
landed on Madeline Island.

"Do the honors," said Athena, handing Claire a
pencil. At the crystal's point, Claire marked a
small dot on the map. Linda used my transparency
paper to mark the degrees, minutes, and seconds,

then located the coordinates in an atlas. That led us to Bog Lake.

Just as your mother's story took time to unfold, it will take time to tell it. In the first weeks she lived with me in 1989, she started sneaking out of the apartment late at night, after we'd gone to sleep. I'm a light sleeper, so I felt her sliding out of bed and heard her tiptoeing out. And I heard her click the door closed when she came back in hours later. After a few nights, I followed her. She walked not with the briskness of most New Yorkers but unhurried, looking at everything as if she'd just been born. Eventually I realized where she was going—to a poky bar in the Village I'd taken her to on the night she arrived. By the time I eased in behind her, she was already sitting at the small piano in the corner. "Go Jeannie!" someone called. After only a few days, they knew her name. She sang one song, the Eagles' "Desperado," and got up from the piano. I left while everyone was still clapping, and for a moment I didn't know where I was or how to get home. I just stood there in the noise of the city, hearing her voice in my head.

Bog Lake is on the north end of the island. There's a small patch in the middle of the lake. Scatter me there.

Next stop: Post Office, Watersmeet, MI, 49969.

Yours,

Essie East

"Are you kidding me?" said Leah, staring down at Essie's words. "That's it? I came all this way for *this*?" She crumpled the letter and threw it toward the water. "Screw you, Essie East." The envelope was next. Though she winged it through the air like a Frisbee, it didn't go far. Meanwhile, the wind had caught the crumpled letter and was shuttling it toward the lake.

Upon the sight of the little ball of paper picking up speed, Leah panicked and began to run after it. "Please," she called. "Stop!" The ball, which took a sudden gusty turn left, would not be reasoned with. It skirted dangerously close to the water, even becoming airborne for a moment before she finally caught up and pounced, throwing herself over it as if it were life itself. When she hit the ground, Essie delivered one grand final thump to her spine. "I hate you," she said, clutching the balled-up paper in her hand.

By now the ferry had receded into the distance, a toy against the vast backdrop of water and sky. Leah stood back up and walked across the grass to where the envelope had landed. She sat down beside it and uncrumpled the letter. *You, a magician's daughter . . .* Once, she had been The Youngest and Very Best Fortuneteller in the World, but she was still and forever a magician's daughter—Essie had at least gotten that right.

Leah tucked the letter safely back inside the envelope, trading it for the transparency. Even more cryptic than the photo of the cemetery, this one centered on two tree lines converging downhill at an orb of light, like the moon but not quite. "Will-o'-the-wisp," she whispered.

The last item in the envelope was wrapped in red tissue paper. Remembering her mishap with the crow, Leah unwrapped it carefully: a small vial filled with water, its cork sealed with red wax. Tied around its neck like a scarf was a gold ribbon with small words penned in silver: *When the waters meet, they don't forget.*

"Witch," Leah heard herself say. Despite the eccentric cast of characters that had populated her early childhood, she had never met someone who claimed to be an actual witch, though the Puppet Beasts often told stories about them: *In the moonlight, the witches rubbed their bare backs against the rough hay of an October field, swishing this way and that until the sharp straw scratched through their skin and released the first unfurling of their black wings . . .*

BOB O'MALLEY WAS right: she recognized it instantly—the red door that gleamed through the trees like a present wrapped in metallic paper. Maybe it was the inflection in the way he'd said "good old Brenda Wright" that suggested to Leah that this little nest—set way back off the road with its fairy statues and copper wire dragonflies and ceramic birdbaths and multicolored ribbons streaming from branches and glass mushrooms in purple and blue set about in the thicket—could only belong to her. Leah made her way up to the red door and then stalled for several seconds before she finally summoned the gumption to knock.

"Whoooo's thaaayeer?"

"Um, I'm Leah Fern," she called, leaning forward hesitantly. "Bob O'Malley sent me."

The door swung open. "Did you say Bob O'Malley? Bob *O'Malley*! That old fool sent you here?" She laughed operatically.

"Hi. Yes." Leah inserted her hands into her coat pockets. "He said I should come if—"

"Come in, come in!" Brenda ushered Leah inside by extending her arm toward the interior of her little cottage, her many bracelets clinking. Framed by curly blond-silver hair that spilled out over her shoulders, Brenda's face had an ageless quality, and her eyes were warm and inquisitive—the kind of woman some might call fine in her bones, while others might call her unconventional, a loon. "Tell me everything!" she said, motioning toward the couch.

Leah couldn't think of a thing to say. She simply stood in the middle of Brenda's living room, mesmerized. Dangling from the ceiling, overflowing from shelves, rising like stalagmites from the ground, a museum of artifacts seemed to be proliferating before her eyes: an old canoe missing planks, a rusty trumpet, a collection of antique black telephones, a street sign that read WALKER WAY, numerous wind chimes made of wood and shells and metal, a haphazardly taxidermied elk, a crew of headless mannequins, vintage tennis racquets and bottles of perfume and board games, half-burned candles on nearly every surface, even wedged into the trumpet keys—

"Sit, sit!" exclaimed Brenda, patting the little bit of couch cushion that wasn't covered with stuff. "I want to hear it all."

"It's like the House of Tricks Treats and Creatures," Leah uttered, mesmerized.

"I beg your pardon? Did you say trick-or-treat? In April? You're my kind of gal!" Brenda clapped her hands together.

Leah set her backpack gently on the floor. "Oh. No. It's just— your house reminds me of someplace I've been before."

Brenda chuckled. "Must have been some crazy place!"

"Sort of," said Leah, sitting down between Brenda and a large metal object she couldn't identify. "But in a good way."

"That's a sculpture I'm working on," she said, pointing to the metal object, her bracelets jingling. "Sometimes I start things and then can't seem to finish."

Leah considered the sculpture, which looked to her like a cross between a five-legged animal and a film projector. "I like it how it is."

"Ah, you're too kind. Maybe I just like the excitement of a thing transforming. Once it's finished, it's kind of sad, an end of sorts." She patted the sculpture. "This way, it's always filled with possibility." She turned toward Leah. "Now tell me how you know Bob! And where are you from? And what brings you to the island? Oh, so many questions!"

Leah shrugged a little, worried she might let Brenda down. "I actually met Bob today, at the ferry lot. I'm traveling from South Carolina, and I was wondering if you might know how I can find transportation to get to the other end of the island this afternoon. A rental car maybe?"

"The ferry lot! What was he doing there? Oh, that man. You could put the whole world in his hands, and he'd look out past it, wanting the stars." A wistful expression came over her face, which passed like a rasp over Leah's heart. "Anyway, what brings you to the far end of the island?"

Leah thought about what to say. *I'm doing research on northern island vegetation in the spring. I'm recovering from amnesia and a place called Bog Lake is all I remember. I'm in search of a treasure.* "A witch," she finally said.

"Pardon?"

"I mean I'm doing a favor for a friend."

"Lovely! I'd be happy to give you a lift if you'd like."

"Thank you," said Leah, "that's very generous, but I kind of need to do this on my own."

"Ah, yes, I see. Can you ride a bike?"

Leah nodded, and Brenda Wright dashed off to root through some things in the next room. After some clattering and the sound of something falling, she returned with a buttercup-yellow bicycle. "Your wheels, mademoiselle!" she announced, rolling the small three-speed to Leah, who reluctantly took hold of the handlebars. The bike had a low banana seat, multicolored streamers dangling off the handlebars, and a wicker basket that held a bouquet of plastic flowers and a stuffed rabbit.

"This is great," said Leah. "But the tires look a little, um, flat."

"We can fix that!" she called over her shoulder as she darted out of the room again. And after a bit more digging, she returned with an air pump and knelt down to connect it to the front tire. She began pumping, but soon she was out of breath. "May I?" asked Leah, stepping in.

"Haven't been doing my sun salutations," said Brenda, handing the pump to Leah. "That's the problem."

As Leah inflated the tires, Brenda chatted about harmonographs and kaleidoscopes—"In some ways, they're very similar!"—and how she has not one, but two vintage Spirograph games—"also similar"—and how being one of the only people on the island in the winter is sometimes liberating and sometimes lonely, which prompted her to say, "That *Bob*," drawing out his name, as if the elliptical clause it pointed to would always be far away—like Bob's Christmas trees, like the people Leah had once loved, like the unknown places harboring her letters.

Leah thanked Brenda Wright, and after a protracted period of waving goodbye— Brenda from her front door, Leah from her banana seat—she pointed her newly inflated front tire toward a closer mystery: Bog Lake. She pedaled away from Brenda's wooded lot and then stopped to study the island map Brenda had given her.

When she first set off, the cold air was biting against her face, but soon her body warmed from the cycling. She passed a smattering of houses and then a small airport and then not much of anything but trees for miles. The sun edged out from behind the clouds, and occasionally, through the scrim, Leah caught Superior dazzling like a secret. The melting snow was seeping into the road, darkening it in Rorschach patterns. And she rode that old yellow bike through them, as if through a dream. She followed Big Bay Road to School House Road, where, in the absence of any signs of humanity, she pretended she was the only person on earth. She was not born from Jeannie Starr. There was no urn strapped to her back. There was no question of love.

She gazed up at the trees that lined her way, and she drank the cold into her warm body, and she looked down with sudden joy at the old pink-eared bunny in the basket, as if it had always been waiting for her to take it for a ride. Eventually she spotted a small lake in the distance, flat and dingy as an old piece of glass. This, the map told her, was Bog Lake.

She turned her bike onto the snow and began to pedal, but her pedaling soon devolved to swerving and failed attempts at braking as she careened down a slushy, bumpy, root-ridden slope. In what might have been the most protracted wipeout in history, she maneuvered between random trees and saplings, between bits of scrub and sinkholes, until finally the bike crashed down and deposited her—and Essie, the old pink-eared bunny, and the plastic bouquet—into a bush.

TWELVE

IT WAS EDWARD Murphy who had presented Leah with her first bike. And he had done so on the day they met.

On that roasting day in late August, Leah's mother pulled into Edward Murphy's driveway and announced, "Here we are!" as if they'd just arrived someplace grand. They had set off on an unexpected trip early that morning, and now Leah eyed the unremarkable white house and, feeling her mother's excitement—or was it nervousness?—she wondered what might be inside. Probably fossils, she thought, having just read about mammoth bones in one of her books, and maybe an octopus inside a water cave. Maybe there would be a hidden door, or a secret corridor like in the House of Tricks Treats and Creatures.

They got out of the car, and her mother took her hand. "I can't wait for you to meet good old Ed," she said.

"Is Ed an octopus?" Leah asked.

Leah's mother giggled—a high-pitched sound like glass breaking. "Well, I guess that's one way to think of the old goat."

"He's a *goat*?"

"C'mon," she said, giving Leah's arm a little tug. "You can see for yourself."

But when her mother gave a little knock and pushed the door open, all Leah saw was an old man napping in an old chair in a mostly empty room. "Anybody home?" Jeannie called. The man sprung up as suddenly as if something had bitten him and practically leapt to where Leah and her mother stood, smiling like a man half out of his wits. Leah held tight to her mother's hand. "Where's the goat?" she asked.

"Leah Fern, mind your manners! I haven't even introduced you yet."

"If it isn't Jeannie Starr, vision of visions!" said the old man, reaching for Leah's mother.

"Here I am!" she said, dropping Leah's hand and wrapping her arms around the man's neck. He was a tall man, with exceptionally long arms and a sharpness to his bones—prominent knuckles, elbows that could double as weapons, and cheekbones that looked as if they might slice right through his skin—and her mother had to stand on tiptoes to reach him.

They hugged for what Leah thought was too long a time, during which she took stock of her surroundings: the plaid chair the old man had been sitting in, an olive-green couch, a coffee table decorated with a dusty orange candle and several fly-fishing magazines, an old record player stationed atop a stack of three milk crates, and an unremarkable kitchen wallpapered in rows of staunch pineapples and furnished with a round table and four wooden chairs. There was a door on the other side of the kitchen, through which she could see part of a television glowing mutely. And that was it. No octopus, no goat, no hidden anythings. Just this sparse house and this gray-haired man whose eyes were filling, threatening to drop a tear onto Leah's mother's head.

"Can we go now?" asked Leah, tugging on her mother's white hip-hugging pants.

Jeannie extracted herself from the man's embrace and reached for Leah's hand. "Pumpkin, I want you to meet Edward Murphy. He's a dear old friend of mine." She turned toward Edward Murphy and rubbed her hand up and down his thin bicep. "This here is my Leah Fern."

Edward Murphy knelt down and peered into Leah's eyes. "Hi there," he said, extending his hand.

"Pleased to make your acquaintance," she said, shaking his hand.

"I hear you're six years old. That's a big girl!"

"You don't have to speak to me like I'm a baby. I'm almost six and a half."

Her mother and Edward Murphy broke into a fit of laughter, while Leah folded her arms across her chest in consternation. "Can we go now?"

Edward Murphy stood back up and pressed his long fingers into the curve of Leah's mother's waist. "Tell me you're going to stay," he said. "At least for a night."

"I'd love to," said Leah's mother, flashing her stellar smile, "next time." She took Edward Murphy's hand and pirouetted. "But there's always time to dance!"

Edward Murphy twirled her as if she were a lasso on the end of his rope, and she squealed as her red hair and blue and silver scarf swept around her. He ended with a dip, bringing her down so fast and low that Leah worried she'd whack her head on the floor. But for an elderly and somewhat rigid-looking man, Edward Murphy moved with unexpected precision and fluidity. "Supper, at least?" he implored, holding the pose, looking down into her eyes.

Jeannie Starr drew her hand up slowly from her belly to her face, her fingers as graceful as palm frond, in what Leah thought was a final dance move. But then she cupped her hand in front of her mouth and blew into it, causing a fine mist to spray onto Edward Murphy's face. The clown trick. Leah had seen her spray the faces of many men at the carnival, and they always looked at her as he was now, dumbfounded in a mixture of shock and enchantment. "I'm afraid I'll have to take a rain check on that, too," she said.

"Up to your old tricks, eh," he said, lifting her to her feet. And even after he'd let go of her entirely, he didn't bother to wipe the magic rain from his face. For a moment, Leah felt sorry for the sad old man whose smile had vanished.

"You know how it is," Jeannie Starr added. "The carnival calls!"

"The carnival calls!" Leah repeated as she moved toward the door, suddenly ebullient. "Nice to meet you!" It was the way her mother looked at her then—with a flash of sadness, or was it pity?—that made Leah's stomach go cold.

When Jeannie knelt down to face her just as Edward Murphy had done, Leah felt the inexplicable urge to turn and run; to bite her mother's fingers and their chipped red polish; to beg. But she did none of those things. Her mother untied the knot in her scarf and, in a single sweep, pulled the silver-specked silk from her slender neck and wrapped it around Leah's. She kissed Leah's cheek and whispered, "I'll visit soon." Then she stood up smiling, and as if she had done this a hundred times before, she casually opened the door, stepped out into summer, and pulled the door shut behind her.

Leah was stunned to stillness. Was this a joke? She watched the door. She heard the engine start. She heard the tires on the gravel driveway. She heard the transmission shift. She heard her mother begin to accelerate away.

Leah waited. Maybe it was a different car she'd heard. Maybe this was part of another magic trick, the one where Jeannie Starr disappears from one door and enters through another. Leah looked from window to window and toward the back of the house, where the television flickered in its empty room.

Then the spell broke. Leah flung the door open in time to see her mother's car gaining speed down the road. She took off running. Faster and faster, she chased that white car with all the muscle her small body could muster. Even her fastest wasn't fast enough to catch her, and when the car disappeared from sight, Leah gasped, "Mama!" as if her voice could still reach her. "Maaaaaaaa!" she called again, still running, her legs burning, the world a blur.

As she ran, her mind searched for answers to what she'd done wrong, what she'd done to cause this. Was it the time she left her fortunetelling tent in the middle of a fortune? Was it the night she wandered into the fog? Had she been too impolite to Edward Murphy? Whatever it was, she was sorry. As she ran, she started to yell those words as loudly as she could. "I'm sorry!" she called, finding a hidden gear and running even faster. "I'm sorry, I'm sorry, I'm sorry, I'm sorry!"

It was there on Barnwell Road, a narrow road in a tiny unfamiliar town far from everyone she knew and loved, that Leah came to a halt. A dry dusty heat settled around her. The road went quiet. A cicada rattled a rising note into the stillness. Leah stood in the street, confronted by an emptiness she had never known. It was as if the cicada lived in that emptiness, the sole occupant in the hollows of her chest.

When she saw a car in the distance, hope lit up in her again. In the span of the time it took for her to realize the car wasn't even white, her mind had already sped to the end of the story, the one in which the mother comes back.

Instead it was Edward Murphy who found her there in the middle of Barnwell Road. It was Edward Murphy who reached out his hand. He was holding her mother's scarf, cradling it guardedly in his large palm as if it might come to life. "You lost something," he said, and then he immediately shook his head as if to erase those words. "I mean, the scarf—it flew right off you."

She left it lying limp his hand.

"We should probably get you out of the road," he said, stepping over to the side. But she didn't move. He scratched his head and looked in each direction. Again the cicada pierced the air. "You know what would be faster?" he finally said. "Than running, I mean."

Leah looked down at the buckle on her sandal. Just the buckle, just this small silver thing.

"A bike, that's what."

She looked up hesitantly. "A bike?"

Feeding off her speck of hope, Edward Murphy, too, became hopeful. "Oh, yes. Absolutely!"

"I don't have a bike," she said, fixating again on her buckle. "I don't even know how to ride one."

Edward Murphy pushed Jeannie Starr's scarf into his front pocket and smiled. "What if I told you I have a brand-new bike just for you, and I could teach you to ride it?"

Suddenly Leah could feel a different end to her story, the one in which a girl pilots a bike and catches her mother. "Could you teach me to ride it fast?"

He nodded.

She put her hand on her hip. "Where is it?"

"It's at the house," he said, pointing. "C'mon, I'll show you."

That's how he got Leah to walk with him back up the road to his home, which would now be her home, too, and it was how he got her to throw her leg over that little blue bicycle and grab onto the handlebars with fiery determination.

"That there is a banana seat," he told her. "Best kind of seat if you ask me."

"I'm ready to go fast."

"Well, you see, it takes practice. I'll have to hold on to your seat until we can get you some training wheels. I could probably run into town tomorrow and pick some up."

"No," Leah said. "Not tomorrow. Now. I need to go fast now!"

Edward Murphy, who was not a stupid man but who also couldn't have known whom he'd just opened his door to, didn't know how to refuse Leah's command. "Okay, well, I guess you should just start pedaling. Just push the pedals down, one foot at a time. You want to make a circle with one foot and then the other."

Leah followed his instructions and began to pedal, and the bike began to move. Edward Murphy held onto the back, walking with her, slow at first, then faster, until she said, "Let go!" at which point he let go and she immediately crashed to the ground.

"Oh no! Are you all right?" He leapt over and helped her lift the bike, but before he could even get it fully upright again, she was already tossing her leg over and trying to pedal. "Hold your horses there, girl," he said, "you're bleeding."

Leah didn't care about the blood dripping from her knee. "Again!"

He pushed her again, and she pedaled again, and she told him to let go again, and again, she hit the ground. Somehow, the falling felt like the truest thing to her body—the violence of it, the rough thud and clang. When she demanded he push her a third time, he refused. "No more. Not until we get you training wheels," he said, turning the bike around and starting back toward his house.

"Tomorrow will be too late!" Leah urged. "I need to go now! I'll never catch her if I don't go now!"

Edward Murphy leaned the bike onto its kickstand and tried to put his arm around Leah, but she darted away.

"She's gone," he said, "and we're just gonna have to wait 'til she comes back."

"No!" said Leah. "I don't want to stay here with you! I hate you!" She lunged at him and punched him in the thigh, but the punch came back at her—not from a strike from Edward Murphy, who stood by with his hands hanging helplessly at his sides, but from what she felt when she made contact: even without the crystal ball, she could feel the depths of him magnified—his yearning, his old age, his pain. It was a pain that rebounded into her, almost as if she herself had caused it. It scorched through her like fire in her veins and sent her, once more, to the ground.

THIRTEEN

LEAH RIGHTED HERSELF and Brenda Wright's yellow bike, gathered up the scattered things, brushed the snow and twigs off her clothes and out of her hair, and wheeled the bike the rest of the way down the hill on foot. At the lip of the lake, Leah looked for the small island in the middle, where Essie had instructed her to scatter her ashes, but all she could make out on the frozen surface was a patch of reeds sprigging up from the ice. "I'm not walking on ice for you," Leah said, pulling Essie's urn from her backpack. Then, despite herself, she stepped onto the ice. She stood for a moment, bending and straightening her knees, then giving a few little jumps to see if it would break. When the ice held, she took a few more steps forward, grateful for the thick treads of her combat boots, and, one cautious step at a time, she made her way across Bog Lake. She wondered what she would have done had the lake not been frozen. Swim? Bring Brenda's living room canoe? How deep was this lake, anyway?

When she was only a few feet from the reedy island at the center of the lake, a sudden cracking sound below launched her from her thoughts as a bolt of adrenaline shot through her blood. She looked down. The ice was still solid as far as she could see. "I didn't come all this way to die," she said. And then she heard her words echo back to her, strange globe of a voice, as the clouds washed over the sun.

Leah took the last few steps to the "small patch" Essie had described and knelt down to unscrew the top of the obelisk. "I don't know what you did here twenty-two years ago," she said, looking around to be positive that no one was watching her, "but I hope it was more fun than this." She tilted the urn, and a small pebbly clump of gray ash fell into her palm.

She didn't know what to do next. Was there some prayer she was supposed to recite? Some special gesture of the hand? *Ashes to ashes, dust to dust,* she thought, but then she wondered what that actually meant, so she said nothing as she swung her arm, opened her palm, and released Essie. But the ash did not sail forth romantically on the breeze as Leah had envisioned; it dropped inelegantly onto the lake's hard, drab surface.

FOURTEEN

HILDA, SOUTH CAROLINA, 1984

AFTER EDWARD MURPHY locked Leah's new blue bike in the shed and convinced her to come inside the house, she stood at the window with her arms folded tightly across her chest and wouldn't move.

"Why don't we get some hydrogen peroxide on those scrapes?" he suggested. He stood behind her, his fingertips resting on the back of the couch that separated them. "The one on your left knee looks pretty bad."

Leah stared out the window without even the faintest acknowledgment that he was there.

"And a little Neosporin. That always makes it feel better."

—.

"You don't want it to go getting all infected, now."

—.

"Get gangrene or something."

—.

"Are you hungry?"

—.

"Thirsty? You want some orange juice? Or water? Or we could cut up a big old watermelon. Come summer, I could eat nothing but watermelon. God's perfect creation if you ask me."

—.

"I've got prune juice, too. Though I don't expect you'd want that, huh?"

—.

"How about whiskey?"

—.

"I'm just kidding about the whiskey."

—.

"I'm serious about the prune juice, though."

—.

Edward rounded the sofa and came toward her. "Listen, kid. I'm sad, too." He gently put his hand on her shoulder, but she flinched and ducked away. Startled, he sprang back and examined the hand that had touched her. "She'll be back," he said. "She always comes back."

Leah fixed her otherworldly blue eyes on him. "When?"

"Ah, you see, that's the thing about magicians. They live to surprise you, to appear when you least expect them." Edward Murphy cast a wistful glance out over Leah's head. "When you love a magician, you have to give her that. You have to trust that the next trick will be even better than the last."

"I don't want a trick," said Leah, turning back to the window.

"You think you don't now, but when she comes back, she'll do something that'll change your mind. That's part of the thrill of it." He walked over to the other window, and they both looked out onto the empty road. "Love isn't always what we think it should be. It doesn't always come in a neat box with a bow and whatnot. Sometimes it's wild-like. Sometimes it hits you like a tsunami in the middle of the desert, and all you can do is thank God for the water, that somehow it came." Edward Murphy patted the windowsill as if it were a live thing.

"If a tsunami hit you in the desert, you'd drown," said Leah, sneaking another look at Edward Murphy—his long fingers, his sad old face, the Adam's apple that bobbed up and down in his throat when he spoke.

"How do you know what a tsunami is?" he challenged.

"I read about them in one of my books," she said, uncrossing her arms and putting one hand on her hip. "How do *you*?"

"I saw a TV show about them."

They both fell silent then. Somehow an unspoken truce had been reached between them, two strangers linked by their knowledge of tsunamis and by the empty road outside their windows.

BY DUSK THAT evening Edward Murphy had convinced Leah to drink a glass of orange juice, but she still refused to eat. He cut up a watermelon into large squares, and the two of them sat at the table, Leah taking tiny sips of her juice, Edward Murphy slurping the melon. Leah, who had always been gentle—who had spent the last few months sitting at a table in a carnival tent making people feel loved—did not feel gentle or loving that night. She thought of hurling Edward Murphy's melon across the room. She thought of throwing her juice in his face. She thought of knocking the ceramic cookie jar off his counter, the fishing magazines off his coffee table, the gray wool hat off the coat rack. She thought of toppling his plaid chair. She thought of opening the door and running to the end of the earth. She thought of her friends and longed to touch the Rubberband Man's bald head or Her-Sweet's furry face. She longed for her mother, any small part of her.

"I'm sorry."

The sound of Leah's voice gave Edward Murphy a little start. "Look at me, all jumpy," he said, wiping a rivulet of pink juice from his chin. "What are you sorry for, anyway? I can't imagine a thing in the world you should be sorry for."

Leah looked down, shame reddening her cheeks. "I'm sorry for punching you in the leg."

Edward Murphy laughed. "You do have a good little right jab there, don't you?"

She stared into the depths of her juice, her cheeks getting hotter.

"You know how you could make it up to me?"

She looked up cautiously. "How?"

"You could let me help you with that knee."

Leah assessed the angry gash on her left knee. It was beginning to throb. "Okay," she said.

She followed Edward Murphy into the bathroom, and he put the seat down on the toilet and then the lid. "Gonna have to get used to having a lady in the house," he said.

Leah's stomach lurched. She wanted to say no, to scream no, to scream it so loudly that the sound blew all the watermelon and all the furniture and all the walls to smithereens. Instead, she took a seat on the toilet lid and watched Edward Murphy fumble with things in the medicine cabinet. He soaked a cotton ball in some hydrogen peroxide and tentatively reached it toward her knee. "Now, this isn't going to hurt," he said. "It's not like alcohol."

"Don't," she warned, holding her palm out like a wall. She didn't care if it hurt; it was Edward Murphy's pain she didn't want to feel. "Let me." Careful not to touch him, she took the cotton ball from his fingers and began to dab it onto her knee.

"Really get it in there," he instructed. "When you see it bubble up like that, you know it's working."

That's how Leah and Edward Murphy spent their first night together: peering into her open skin, watching a small eruption of white bubbles.

FIFTEEN

IT WAS NEARLY dark when Leah walked Brenda's bike past the now-shadowed fairies and dragonflies lining her walk. Beneath the porch light the red door still gleamed, but this time Leah couldn't bring herself to knock. Instead, she leaned the bike up against one of the sturdier-looking birdbaths and pulled from her backpack her last full package of marshmallow Peeps—yellow chicks, which she tucked into the basket with the plastic flowers and pink-eared rabbit.

With no ferry to catch until the next day, Leah made her way back to Voyager Lane and walked along the lake. She watched the rising moon, a waning gibbous, beam over the icy water, and she thought of Brenda and how the moon itself looked like a half-finished metal sculpture. She thought of Essie's ashes, a dark smudge on the surface of Bog Lake, being touched now by that same moonlight. She wondered if her mother, wherever she was, was being touched by it, too.

After sleeping in her truck for two nights, Leah was relieved to come upon an inn, grateful almost to the point of tears at the thought of having a bed and a bathroom. But once she was in her room, with its wiped surfaces, generic sheets, and muted prints on the walls, she missed the cozy familiarity of her truck. She flopped back onto the bed anyway and felt her limbs sink as if into wet cement. She hadn't realized how exhausted she was, or how good it would feel to let go of all she was carrying, even if only for that quick bridge into dreams, where now Brenda Wright's bracelets were jingling like bells and Bob O'Malley's disembodied hand was reaching toward her from inside his car and voices were sweeping through, old and new: *You could put the whole world in his hand, and he'd look out past it, wanting the stars . . . I just come here to think sometimes, watch the people come and go . . . Love isn't always what we think it should be . . .* And then Leah was falling, a bike crashing down. The sky was raining feathers. Edward Murphy was singing about the *Edmund Fitzgerald*. Essie's ashes were spilling down through the watery depths like glitter.

AT SOME POINT in the night, Leah had taken off her boots and gotten under the covers, though she didn't remember doing either. She also didn't remember opening her backpack and setting Essie's obelisk on the night table, but apparently she had done that, too. And when she woke at dawn, she felt as if she'd been on a long labyrinthine journey. She pulled from her backpack the only book she'd taken with her, a collection of poems that Edward had given her, and read these lines by Theodore Roethke: "I wake to sleep, and take my waking slow. / I feel my fate in what I cannot fear. / I learn by going where I have to go." As if in response, Essie's voice trailed through her mind: *You, the woman who walks pitched forward as if into a gale, as if all you hear is wind.* "I wasn't talking to you," said Leah, cutting her eyes at the obelisk.

Leah reached into her backpack for Essie's last letter, which was sending her to Watersmeet, Michigan. Though she wouldn't have wanted to admit it, she was eager for the next letter, hungry for any crumb about her mother that Essie was willing to drop. She picked up the phone and got the number for the Watersmeet post office, then called to get directions.

Next she took out Essie's first letter, in the envelope labeled BEGIN, and revisited the transparent photograph—the snow-covered cemetery with the house-like graves and the backdrop of water. Had Essie taken that shot here on Madeline Island? Might this cemetery hold some clue to her mother? Leah felt her throat constrict as she put the ghostly image away. "No," she said out loud. "She's alive. She has to be."

At the front desk of the inn Leah asked, "Are there many cemeteries on the island?"

"Cemeteries?" The same friendly woman who'd checked her in the night before smiled at her eagerly, as if she'd been waiting there all night for that question. "Do you mean the La Pointe Indian Cemetery?"

"Maybe. I'm not sure." Leah handed her the photo. "You have to hold it up to the light."

The woman held up the transparency and immediately began to nod. "Yes, yes! That's right up the street. It's a burial ground for the Chippewa Tribe, the first occupants of the island. It's become quite famous—maybe because there are rumors about hauntings there—though it's not open to the public anymore. But you can still view it from outside the fence."

"How would I get there?"

"Just go around the marina and turn right on Chief Buffalo Lane. It's on the water—you can't miss it."

"Thank you," said Leah, relieved to know that wherever her mother was, she wasn't at the cemetery.

"That's an interesting photo you have. Looks old."

"Yes, quite old," said Leah, scratching the shaved side of her head. "It belonged to an English priestess," she whispered, "who wound up in an insane asylum. I'm retracing her footsteps for a documentary called *The Secret Estuaries of Essie East*."

The woman nodded knowingly. "Sounds fascinating. Good luck—I hope you find what you're looking for."

Leah headed out into the bright chill of a new morning. When she reached the burial ground, she held the transparent photo out in front of her as she walked along the perimeter. A few of the graves had been wiped clean of snow and decorated with coins and beads, while most were topped with mounds of snow that made the tombstones appear to be growing. Still, no view seemed to line up with the image she was holding in her hands.

"What am I supposed to do with this?" she asked out loud, holding the photograph out over the snow, scrutinizing it again, the way a person keeps looking in the same drawer for something they've lost. But there was no response from the urn or from the graves, no message in the sky or snow.

Leah opened the front pocket of her backpack and grabbed a handful of Jordan almonds, her breakfast. She crunched into the quiet, while the Great Lake spoke in varied hues of blue. And it was then, as she relaxed her focus, gazing out past the cemetery at the water, that she spotted something. Candy in one hand, photograph in the other, Leah ran up ahead, holding the transparency in front of her like a viewfinder. When she came to a halt, what she held in her hand matched what existed beyond the fence: a crooked tombstone, which had lost some additional degrees of verticality over the years, and five spirit houses in its company.

A modest flock of starlings touched down in front of her. They spoke in tiny sounds, pecking and flitting about in a tight cluster. She marveled at their freedom, at how, though she wasn't permitted to enter the cemetery, they could go anywhere they wished. As she watched them, something strange began to happen. They were making a shape. Spreading out, they turned themselves into a star.

"You're not real," said Leah, shoving the photograph into her backpack and abruptly turning away from the birds.

O N   T H E   F E R R Y   ride back, Leah found herself hoping, even expecting, to see Bob O'Malley right where she'd left him, but when she arrived, there was no green Oldsmobile to be found in that waterfront parking lot, no old man in a tweed jacket. She felt a pang as she headed toward her truck, still without a plan to address her flat tire situation. But her tire was no longer flat. In disbelief, Leah circled her truck thinking maybe she'd misremembered which tire it was, but all her tires were intact. Tucked under one of her windshield wipers, a piece of paper fluttered in the breeze.

Dear Leah,
One gift deserves another. Your Christmas tree has been great company. Let me know if you hear any subsonic rumblings.
Your friend,
Bob O'Malley

Below his name he'd written his address. Leah hugged the note to her chest. "Thank you," she said, casting one last glance out toward Madeline Island. Then she stepped up into her mended truck and set off for a post office in Watersmeet, Michigan.

Compared to all the driving she had done since she'd first left Hilda only three days earlier, the two and a half hours to Watersmeet barely registered. In many ways, the two-lane pine-lined road she took from Wisconsin through the sparsely populated towns into Michigan reminded her not only of Hilda but also of her earliest, vaguest memories of driving through the south with her mother.

It was her last drive with her mother that always trumped all her other memories of driving, for it was the trip she'd recalled again and again in the days and weeks and months after her mother drove away from Edward Murphy's house. Each time, Leah tried to uncover some forgotten word or gesture, something that might suggest her mother was feeling even a modicum of remorse for what she was about to do. What Leah remembered each time was her mother's insouciance, how she smiled and sang along with the radio, how they'd stopped for lunch and then again for frozen custard, how that silver-specked scarf tied on the side of her neck caressed her bare shoulder as the wind poured in the open windows.

Parked outside the Watersmeet post office under a mottled sky, a breeze ruffling in through her window, Leah broke the wax seal on the envelope marked with red paint and the number two.

```
July 18, 1998

Dear Leah,
    In the days following our visit from the
hawk, I had tried to convince myself that the
snake it dropped on our table was nothing
```

more than a coincidence. What happened next
disabused me of any further inclinations. It
was mathematical, remember—Linda's plotting
of the golden spiral. We were bound to each
logarithmic turn, wherever it took us. When
Linda's pencil came down on the ninth point,
even I gasped. Our spiral had ended as it had
begun: on a lake on an island. What are the
odds? "I turned the grid to three hundred and
thirty-nine degrees," Linda told us. "It just
felt right. Maybe because three threes are
nine." Yes, we all agreed, it felt right. Maybe
Athena's dream had read the great cosmic tea
leaves after all.

When Athena was a child, her grandmother
left her a Book of Shadows—a kind of
instruction manual for incantations, healing
elixirs, magic dusts, animal summoning, astral
travel, manifestations, and more—and it was
from this thick black book that she first
learned about herbs. One day, she pulled it
from the rest of her esoteric collection—
old spiritual texts, bestiaries, books on
astrology, meditation, tarot—and shared it
with us, its worn pages stained with brews and
dusts and what appeared to be blood.

Instead of using Athena's grandmother's book,
we decided to create our own Book of Shadows.
"We all have our own unique keys to unlock
portals into the deeper realms. The magic,"
Athena said, her voice rhapsodic, her wild eye

straying, "is in learning how to use them." Dee pointed out that someone had to write the very first Book of Shadows just the same, so why couldn't we? Imitation is for those who lack intuition and imagination, the very things we wanted to enhance, so though we would use some traditional tools and tenets—no sense in recreating the wheel—we would generate our own rituals, along with the path that would lead us to them.

It's not so strange, really. We're a people of ritual, of symbolism: We make wishes upon birthday candles and stars; we wear masks on Halloween, wedding rings on our fingers, bindis on our third eyes, totems around our necks; we light menorahs and Christmas trees and funeral pyres. We tattoo blessings into our skin, offer feasts to the dead, throw fireballs off cliffs. We march in parades; we beat ceremonial drums; we spin, sometimes for hours; we climb holy mountains. All over the world, we conjure. We create. And that's what I was beginning to sense in 1977: the creative force that pulses through everything.

We spent many evenings together planning our expedition of moons. I couldn't deny I felt something mysterious happening as the first pages in our book took shape. Claire was the keeper of that book, carefully recording our visions and concoctions, illustrating the pages with vines and moons and pencil sketches of our faces. During that time, I also kept a notebook of my own because I wanted to remember as much as I could. I rarely need to refer to those pages, though. I remember it all too well as it is.

In the end, our Book of Shadows ended up with me, the one who, in the beginning, believed in it the least. Claire, I'd venture to say, believed in it the most—even more than Athena. For Claire, everything sparkled with possibility because she herself sparkled with it.

Sometimes she would sit for hours with hundreds of stones spread out on the floor, admiring them one at a time. That's what I caught her doing one night when I found myself knocking on her door. When she opened it, it was as if someone had slapped tape over my mouth. Did I even grunt? Who knows? I just remember staring at her, as if such a sight couldn't be real. Eventually I found my voice, and I can tell you now that sitting on the floor with her and her stones that night was better than anything I'd ever done with anyone else.

She had a fascinating collection of jaspers, I remember. Some of them looked like the landscapes from which they came—jagged rock formations against blue skies, undulating sand dunes, grassy plains—nature repeating the macro in micro, like my mosses. I thought, if everything repeats, let this, too, repeat. Let this woman keep placing stones in my hand.

Claire was the youngest in the group, while I was the oldest. At twenty-five, she halved my age. I hated thinking I was old enough to be her mother. Sometimes I would look at her and think *come up the years*, from a Jefferson Airplane song. Sometimes I sickened myself.

There was almost no one on Madeline Island when we arrived that winter. We drove from Tennessee—two long days—and Dee wedged her guitar in with us. Though it was cramped, we sang songs. There was a festive quality in the air. We were starting something, and beginnings always carry with them a certain frisson.

Any romantic notions about magic that I may have been harboring cut loose from me as we came sliding and tumbling down the snowy hill toward the frozen lake, laughing like kids up to no good. What were we thinking, going north in January?

The moon was so unabashed in its luster that night that we didn't even need our torches. I remember the texture of the snow, powdery and glinting like tiny specks of glass. "Would you look at that," said Athena, pointing to a small patch of vegetation in the center of the lake. "Another island! We must go to it." Linda tried to reason that maybe walking on the ice wasn't a good idea, but Athena ignored her and started out across the lake, poking her flame-carved wooden staff onto the ice with every other step. The rest of us followed.

"We go in to go out, out to go in," she said as she cast our first circle, a protective boundary around us. Athena arranged a small altar on the ice and then dipped a stone wand into a chalice of saltwater, to purify. With it, she traced the Orphic Egg—the mythological primordial egg coiled by a serpent—onto each of our throats and then onto her own, "To summon the spirit of Creation!" With the strike of a match, she lit her white candle and then lit Linda's, who lit Dee's, who lit Claire's, who lit mine. "Let our coven be formed," said Athena, as we pushed the flames of our candles into a single flame at the center of our circle. I felt a flash of something electric then, pure as lightning.

As part of our coven's initiation, each of us gave the others amulets we'd made. Then we swallowed a tincture of *Salvia divinorum*, so that, in Athena's words, we could "better see."

Athena's gift was a small unique beast she sculpted out of clay—"Magical Imaginaries," she called them. Mine looked like a combination of a leopard and a dragon. Claire carved five crows out of a black stone called magnetite—to guide us into the cosmos within, she said. Dee etched the first line of our first chant into five small stars of

sanded mahogany cut from a broken guitar:
Luna, illuminate our truths... Linda gave us
paintings on miniature canvases that fit in
the palms of our hands—full moons rippling
over dark waters. I gave them photographs
I'd taken of star mosses, each an original
transparency mounted on white silk.

In honor of the mosses, we had begun
referring to ourselves as the Moss Witches. It
started as a joke, but then somehow it stuck.
I'll admit, saying the word *witch* always
made me cringe—and despite myself, it still
does—not only because of what happened to my
mother, which I don't wish to discuss, but
because it made me think of caricatures of
hideous women riding broomsticks and wearing
pointy hats. "That's why we have to reclaim the
word," Dee had reasoned, and be "the wakeful
ones."

By the time we were finished giving our
gifts and reciting our chant, I wasn't feeling
wakeful at all. The *Salvia divinorum* had
started to tug at my mind. Nightmarish faces
appeared in the darkness, and I wanted to
ask if I was dreaming. I tried to call out
to Claire, but I couldn't form a single word.
The most I could do was moan in a way that
nobody heard. When I tried to swallow, I felt
a lump in my throat, and I considered that I
might die before my candle finished burning.
Then I looked up at the moon, and the lump in

my throat disappeared, and I thought maybe I
had swallowed a pearl. Maybe I had swallowed
the moon. I felt a moon-shaped sound rising
up from my stomach and into my throat, and
suddenly I began to howl, just like I said I
wouldn't.

On our way back to our hotel that night, we
stopped at an old burial ground, where I later
took the photograph you now have. We stood in
quiet respect until Claire whispered something
I'll never forget. "I think death must be like
going home."

Your mother ran away from home when she was
twelve and never went back. She told me it was
how she learned to be happy—by learning she
could fly. I thought she meant *flee*. But no,
she corrected me—*fly*.

Let me fly where the waters meet in
Michigan. From the intersection in the center
of Watersmeet, go north on Michigan Highway
45 for 3.3 miles and turn left on Sucker Lake
Road. Follow the creek to Sucker Lake.

Your next stop: Post Office, Friendship,
Wisconsin, 53934.

Yours,
Essie East

Leah sat in her truck for a long time without doing anything.
She watched people come into the post office, and she watched
them leave. She felt small breezes lap in through her open window

and land in cool splashes against her cheek. She watched a squirrel scamper into the parking lot and back out. She watched nothing at all.

What else could she do? Get out of her truck and throw the letter into the road, only to chase it again? The story would take time to tell, Essie had said, and Leah had to trust that; she had to trust someone. Besides, for now maybe these four sentences about her mother were enough.

My mama never knew anything about me. Leah could hear her mother's voice as it had sounded fifteen years earlier, on the day she told her the story of the fern seed on a midsummer night. *But you, Miss Fern, are different. That's why you're not named after a person. You're named after magic.*

"What were you running from?" Leah spoke into the cool air. "Where did you go?"

She wondered how a twelve-year-old runaway might get along in the world. Had her mother been hungry? Lonely? Scared? Or perhaps she'd slept in a hammock woven from honeysuckle vines and feasted on oranges from a secret grove? Yes, Leah decided, the latter. She was Jeannie Starr, after all.

The morning pressed on, and Leah reread the letter, pausing on the word *magnetite* each time. Where had she seen that word before?

She revisited Essie's begin envelope and took out the magnetite crow that had pierced her skin—the amulet she now knew Claire had given to Essie. How weighty it felt in her palm, this cold dagger of a thing. She ran her fingertips over its metallic sheen, over the fine etching of its spread wings, and then she slid it into the front pocket of her black jeans.

Only then did she finish unpacking envelope two, this time unraveling an object wrapped in red tissue paper: a spotted creature with a leopard body and a dragon face—Athena's Magical Imaginary. She placed it on her dashboard and peered at it, eye to eye. After a few minutes, when no other cars were in the lot, she roared at it like a cat.

The last thing in the envelope was another transparent photograph, only much smaller than the first two. Leah realized that Essie was giving her the gifts that the women had once given to one another—this one, mounted on white silk, was a photograph of moss, a miniature universe of stars.

LEAH PARKED HER truck on the slim shoulder of Sucker Lake Road and trudged through the snow, following an icy stream to the lake. The melting ice spoke in soft creaks and groans, like something waking up, while the pale sun hung like a paper cutout in the sky. She looked back at her trail of footsteps in the snow and could almost see the witches—a bloom of faces amid the sparse winterscape. They were coming toward her, floating almost, five women carrying roots in their hands, feathers in their hair. Their eyes shone with secrets that made Leah's heart quicken. But then she blinked, and they were gone.

Leah began running toward the empty space. She was all body, hurtling through the snow, away from the backpack, away from the urn, away from her questions—a sudden torrent determined to make herself fly: wind and legs and breath and then the opening of arms, the leap, the face tilted skyward, the second leap, the third, the slowing, the walking, the lungs wanting more, wanting weightlessness, the body staying earthbound a bit longer.

A girl who tries to fly and does not fly is not a girl who cannot fly.

BACK AT THE lake's edge, Leah thought about the water vial Essie had given her—*When the waters meet, they don't forget*—and suddenly she knew that the water in the vial had been collected here, from this water. She wondered if souls were like water—if, once they unite, they can never be fully separated.

She took the obelisk from her backpack and turned it in her hands, feeling that magnetic pull she always felt when she looked at it. There was one stone in particular that caught her eye—a round cabochon in the center of one of the flowers, which flashed red and green depending on how she tilted the urn.

Bob O'Malley appeared in her mind then. She thought about the reused Christmas trees that decorated the yearly ice road to Madeline Island and how it had been years since one of those trees had belonged to him. She thought about "good old Brenda Wright" on the other side of the lake and imagined that if one could have traced the direct line of his sight across the melting water, it would have landed precisely at her shining red door. Though Leah had grown up in a town so small it didn't even a have a gas station, the books she'd read and movies she'd seen had given her a sense that outside of Hilda, the world was bustling with hordes of people and their many important matters of business. But so far, her view of the world outside Hilda was mostly stark, and the people she met all seemed to carry with them their own private worlds of loss.

Essie had been no different. Though Leah had never touched her while she was alive, she had felt a force field of grief around her on the few occasions they had passed each other. What a strange and intimate thing, she thought, unscrewing the obelisk, to now hold these pieces of Essie in her hands. *Maybe we're all just carrying bits of each other,* she thought. She was about to pour some of the ash into her palm when it occurred to her that if she weren't careful, she could run out of ash before she reached Essie's final destination. She pressed her eye to the urn's opening in an attempt to gauge how full it was, and as she tilted it, a large clump of ashes shifted, causing a puff to rise up. "Ughhh!" she cried out, furiously rubbing her eye. She blinked and blinked, but the ash adhered to her iris like pollen to a bee. With one eye closed, Leah tipped a small amount of ash into her palm and dropped it dispassionately onto the snow. "Sorry about that," she said as she closed the obelisk. "I don't think I'm very good at this." And for a moment, she thought she heard Essie answer—until she realized that it was only the sound of hunger, growling in her stomach.

She drove back into town and found a diner, and when she went inside, the server who had come to seat her looked at her with concern. "Are you okay?" she asked.

"I don't know," Leah replied, half jokingly. "Am I?"

"It's just"—the server looked down shyly, then back at Leah— "you're crying."

In that same moment Leah had also become aware of the wetness sliding down her cheek. Quickly she wiped at her face with the back of her hand. "I don't cry," she explained reflexively. "I just have something in my eye." When she brought her hand back down, she saw what the server had seen: tears the color of ash.

SIXTEEN

IN THE FIRST weeks Leah lived with Edward Murphy, their lives jabbed together as sudden as a splinter, they stood each day, several times a day, at their respective windows, immobilized in a sheen of grief. They were tentative around each other—two castaways who were overly polite, strained, fumbling, and who were all the other had.

Leah had not cried once. In those first weeks, she looked as if someone had gouged out the core of her. She was pale, easy to startle. She walked hunched over, her head tipped forward as if she might fold into a somersault.

In time, she began to eat more than three bites of a given meal, which was the requisite number of bites upon which Edward Murphy insisted, and she began to stand a little taller. Having gone from a life of fanfare and uproar to the oppressive silence inside Edward Murphy's house, marked by the occasional creak in a floor or clink of a dish in the sink, she took comfort in the sounds of the television in the back room and in learning how to operate the old record player in the corner of the living room.

The sphere of people she missed only widened as she began to long not only for her carnival family but also for the strangers—the people who had traipsed through her daily sequin-caped existence. She'd become accustomed to a certain cachet with the adults who had come to take their turn at her table, where it wasn't uncommon for people to bow or even drop to their knees in reverence of her oracular tales, but she appeared to have no such pull on Edward. "Do you know why elephants curve their trunks into an S?" she asked him. "Do you know why they approach their watering holes at dusk?" And he joked, "because they know the alphabet" or "because they eat peanut butter sandwiches for dinner?" She responded by telling a story with practiced aplomb and a timely rise toward the denouement. ". . . Then the elephant wrapped its trunk around a fallen tree, which he was going to use to build a boat, when a whole army of termites marched up his snout. Right up his trunk, all one hundred thousand muscles of it! The elephant sneezed a humongous sneeze, which sent the termites zooming through the village with their mouths still full of wood. The end."

Edward Murphy had questions. "A boat for what?" he wanted to know. Leah restarted the timer in her mind.

"It was a boat to explore a hidden sea. The other elephants told secrets about it and always whispered because they didn't want the sea to hear them and creep up and steal them in their sleep. But Lumie the Elephant wasn't afraid. He was brave. He was ready to *explore*." Usually on a note like that, the patrons in Leah's tent would nod or smile or say, "yes, yes, *explore*, of course," as if they now knew the secret, too. Their readiness to be enlightened, coupled with the uncanny truths Leah told them about themselves when she put her hands over theirs, was almost always cause for them to stand from her table when the timer buzzed and thank her ecstatically, often in tears, and declare her *enchanting*, a *sage*, a *miracle*. Edward Murphy simply wanted to know if the elephant built the boat and found the sea. While he ultimately made Leah a far better storyteller, their early exchanges were not without their frustrations.

"You're supposed to tell me I'm *enchanting*," Leah instructed.

"You want to know what's enchanting? I'll tell you what's enchanting. The time your mother got an entire restaurant to dance."

Leah pressed her elbows onto the table and rested her chin in her hands. "How'd she do that?"

"She just started dancing." Edward Murphy squinted his eyes and smiled, as if he could see her in action. Leah squinted her eyes, too, wanting to see what he saw. "I had taken her to this really fancy restaurant all the way in Charleston—"

"Was that when you took her on the vacation? When you put the sign up on your shop?"

"Yes, yes it was," he said.

"Was she a magician then?"

Edward's hands came to rest on top of the table. "I reckon she was always a magician." He paused for a moment and searched Leah's face, as if he might find some part of Jeannie Starr that had been hiding there all along. The truth was Leah bore little resemblance to her redheaded, green-eyed mother. "Anyhow, she started dancing, and this amazing thing happened."

"Did she do a trick?"

Edward Murphy inhaled a breath Leah thought might never end. "No," he said. "She woke people up."

"They were sleeping?"

"Well, no. Not in that sense. It's just, some people . . ." Edward Murphy scratched his head. "Some people are like the elephants in your story who are afraid of being swept out to sea in their sleep. Some people just don't believe they can swim."

"Elephants are excellent swimmers."

Edward Murphy nodded. "And for some people, who don't know they know how to swim, it's like they're asleep, even when they're awake. Because they never try anything. Because they're always afraid."

"I'm not afraid," said Leah. "Her-Sweet taught me to swim."

"Yeah, you and me, we're not afraid. That's why we're not afraid to wait for someone we love to come back."

They both shot a glance toward the windows then, a habit that would last.

"Your mother, when she started dancing that night, right in the middle of that fancy ol' restaurant, she wasn't afraid either. She just started twirling while the lone piano player played, and pretty soon he started playing something more upbeat, and Jeannie took my hand and led me up, too, and then she took a woman's hand and led her up, and that woman took her man's hand, and pretty soon everyone was up and dancing and laughing, letting their filet mignons and what-have-you get cold. That's how your mother woke people up. She got them to celebrate, and it wasn't even a holiday or birthday or anything."

Leah listened intently.

"When you're celebrating," he said, looking around the room as if it were filled with dancers, "it's damn near impossible to be afraid."

THAT SEPTEMBER LEAH started first grade in a small school one town over. Because she'd never had friends her age and, with the exception of a single visit to her tent by a boy, she learned the hard way that other girls didn't relish animal bones, that a kid who spouts off random elephant facts to other kids gets cornered in the playground, where she becomes the target for the crusty remains of their lunches. She learned that kids don't like other kids to tell them stories—not even the ones Leah had heard the Puppet Beasts tell—and they especially don't like when a strange carnival kid tells them things about themselves that she shouldn't know. Pretty soon, she stopped talking to them at all.

She continued to tell stories to Edward Murphy, and she learned to tell them in such a way that sometimes when she reached the end, he had no questions, only applause. "Now *that* was enchanting," he'd say, and she'd bow. He told her stories, too, about his young life as a farmer's son, pulling fresh turnips and carrots and even the odd beet straight out of the ground and eating them with the dirt still on them. He told her about getting married before he could fully grow a beard and then losing his wife when their son was only ten. He told her that his son must have been born with "the bad blood in him, because he was mean as an angry hippo," which Leah understood was pretty mean, and that he'd grown up and moved away, not even bothering to call on Father's Day. But mostly he told her the same few stories about her mother—for, truth be told, he had only a few, which neither of them tired of—teasing them out like taffy.

Leah did the same. "One time she took me to the Hall of Windows," she told Edward Murphy. This was where she always added, "It's the best place in the House of Tricks Treats and Creatures," lest he forget. "It had this one window where there were two swings hanging over a garden of little flowers. They kind of looked like candy. And Mama picked me up and said all their names—tulip, bluebell, daisy, honeysuckle, black-eyed Susan, gardenia, lily of the valley—and the swings started moving, all by themselves. I told her she was the best magician in the world, and she said it wasn't her making the swings move."

On cue, Edward Murphy always asked the same question. "Who was it, then? Who was making the swings move?"

Leah paused at that spot in the story. "It was me."

SEVENTEEN

ARE YOU OKAY? Such a small, simple question. Leah watched the server who had asked it—Isabelle, her nametag read. An attractive woman with sensitive eyes and an explosion of dark curls springing out from her ponytail elastic, she had a smile that Leah noticed was contagious. Even from across the room, Leah could feel her warmth, and as she tried, unsuccessfully, to stop staring, she thought that restaurant servers might be the true heroes of the world. They brave the wilds of greasy kitchens, balance ungodly numbers of spillable, breakable objects on a single tray, and handle our saliva-ridden utensils and our leftovers, all while fetching countless small things—another fork, extra napkins, more butter. They use precious space in their brains to commit the day's specials to memory, and they wipe up after the messiest of children. They keenly attend to us—our hankerings and our hungers—and our desire to be served. *Are you okay?* Sometimes the smallest questions can reframe an entire life. For it was only then, as Leah wiped Essie's remains from her face, that she fully understood, all the way through her bones, how alone she had been in this world.

When Leah was finished with her grilled cheese sandwich, Isabelle returned to the table, the white frill of her dated apron brushing the Formica edge. "How about some dessert?"

"Which is your favorite?" Leah asked.

"Oh, that's a tough one. I'd have to go with the banana cream pie."

"I'll take that," said Leah, carefully wiping breadcrumbs from the table into her palm and emptying them onto her plate.

"Would you like coffee with that?"

"No thank you, but . . ." Leah paused. "I do have a question. It's kind of strange."

"Ooh, I love strange questions. Fire away."

Leah removed the will-o'-the-wisps transparency from her backpack and placed it on the white back of her placemat. "Does this look like any place around here?"

Isabelle bent over the table and examined the photograph. "Why is it see-through?"

"I don't know. It was given to me that way."

Isabelle leaned closer, and after a few seconds her eyes lit up. "I know where that is! Who gave this to you?"

"A friend."

"It's the Dog Meadow Light!"

"The Dog—?"

"Well, it's formally called the Paulding Light, but lots of people still call it the Dog Meadow Light. I personally like that better."

"I do, too," said Leah. "But what is it?"

Isabelle smiled mischievously. "A ghost."

"Of course. What else would it be?"

"Sometimes there's this strange light that shows up at night and moves around in a spooky way. On occasion, it's even been known to change color. The story is that it's the ghost of a railroad brakeman. I've seen it myself. But ghosts don't come for everyone, you know."

"True," said Leah, slipping the photograph into her backpack. "Do you think you could tell me how to get there?"

"Oh, it's very complicated." Isabelle smiled. "You just head straight up this road going north for about five miles. And then— this is the tricky part—you turn left on Old 45." She smiled. "If you need an escort, I get off in about twenty minutes."

"Well, it does sound complicated." Unable to bring herself to look at her new friend, Leah looked down at the table.

"I bet if I bring you an extra-big slice of pie, it might just last you twenty minutes."

Leah forced a glance up at this woman who, with three words, had made her feel the way she imagined her mother had made diners in a fancy restaurant feel when she invited them to dance—as if she were waking up.

THOUGH ISABELLE HAD offered to give Leah a ride, she chose to follow behind in her truck, and when they got out of their vehicles, Leah felt a sudden awkwardness in seeing Isabelle out of context of the restaurant. Isabelle had changed from her work clothes into jeans and a puffy blue jacket, and her hair, which she'd liberated from its ponytail, now cascaded down her back. "This place has gotten so famous that we now have a sign," she said, proudly extending her arm like a tour guide.

THIS IS THE LOCATION FROM WHICH THE FAMOUS PAULDING LIGHT CAN BE OBSERVED. LEGEND EXPLAINS ITS PRESENCE AS A RAILROAD BRAKEMAN'S GHOST, DESTINED TO REMAIN FOR- EVER AT THE SIGHT OF HIS UNTIMELY DEATH. HE CONTINUALLY

WAVES HIS SIGNAL LANTERN AS A WARNING TO ALL WHO COME
TO VISIT.

TO OBSERVE THE PHENOMENON, PARK ALONG THIS FOREST
ROAD FACING NORTH. THE LIGHT WILL APPEAR EACH EVENING
IN THE DISTANCE ALONG THE POWER LINE RIGHT-OF-WAY.

"It helps if you come at night," Isabelle added. "I used to come
here at night a lot when I was younger. When my parents were
sleeping, I'd pull their car keys off the hook and sneak out of the
house. Then I'd wait for the light to come." She started walking
toward the power lines, and Leah followed, quickly recognizing
the two tree lines that converged at the light in Essie's photograph.
"Once I had a car of my own though, I stopped coming here as
often."

Leah pushed her gloveless hands into her coat pockets. "Why
is that?"

"I don't know. I guess I believed in magic more when it still felt
taboo." Isabelle stopped walking and twirled in a circle, looking
up at the sky. "When I got my own car and didn't have to steal my
parents', the thrill kind of fizzled. Plus, I used to make wishes on the
light, and they never came true."

Leah stood beside her and looked out at the snow-shagged conifers and nodded. She understood about making wishes that didn't
come true. Now she was thinking about magic. She was wondering
if, like dark matter or neutrinos, it existed and people just hadn't
figured out how to measure it yet, or if it was nothing more than an
illusion, the way her mother could turn a flower into fire by blowing
on it. She was thinking about how she might say some of what she

was thinking to Isabelle, but in all the thinking, too much time had gone by, so she said nothing at all.

"Where are you from? You're not like other people around here."

"How's that?"

"There's just something different about you." She stopped walking and looked at Leah. "I can't quite put my finger on it yet."

"I thought you were going to say something about my appearance."

"Yeah, not everyone walks around wearing spikes. At least not since the '80s." Isabelle laughed. "But that's not—"

"Hey, now," said Leah, impishly cutting her eyes at her.

"I think it's cute that you're punk." She put her hand on Leah's shoulder, but Leah stepped back reflexively. She was a jumble of nerve endings, everything firing, or misfiring—she couldn't tell—at once.

"Sorry," they both said at the same time. Then Isabelle let out a sharp cackle before turning swiftly and taking off down the snowy hill. Without thinking, Leah ran after her. And by the time she caught up to her halfway down the hill, they had both fallen and were on their backs laughing. "I wore the wrong shoes," said Isabelle, holding her feet up in the air. Her canvas restaurant kicks were soaked through.

Leah's combat boots had also taken in snow, but she left them planted in it, knees bent, eyes to the sky. "I'm not punk," she said.

Isabelle turned from the sky to face Leah's profile. "What are you, then?"

A magician's daughter, Leah wanted to say. *The smallest bit of air off the smallest feather of a bird. A quark. A dream no one had.* "I don't know," she said. A strip of bulbous clouds came mushrooming over the open slice between the trees, and though she could see in her periphery that Isabelle was looking at her, she kept her gaze upward.

"Maybe that's why I can't put my finger on it."

There was nothing to say to that, so Leah gave herself over completely to the snow, letting herself sink in as she watched the next troop of clouds travel overhead, darker now. In their shared silence, which was the sweetest thing Leah had shared with anyone in a long time, she thought about Essie. Having learned about water cycles in college—transpiration, evaporation, condensation—she thought how it was possible that the clouds above could be holding water from clouds that Essie had looked up at in 1977. *When the waters meet . . .*

Isabelle cleared her throat. "You know at the restaurant, when you said you were going to ask me a strange question? I thought you were going to ask me out."

Leah turned toward Isabelle, whose brown eyes reminded her of the dun-colored bunny someone had once left at Edward Murphy's feed shop. It became the store's mascot, a treasured pet whom Leah named Velvet because of her long velvety ears. Whenever they'd let it run loose, Leah couldn't concentrate on her job because she was constantly watching to see where Velvet was going. She worried she would get smooshed by a bale of hay or that she would slip out the door and make her way into the road. At times, Velvet's vulnerability had overwhelmed Leah, causing her fingers to ache and her breathing to turn shallow, and here, in the most unlikely of places, she had that same feeling.

"I'm an empath." The words fell out like something accidentally dropped.

Isabelle looked at Leah as if she waiting for the rest of the sentence.

Leah cleared her throat. "It's why I backed away up there. When someone touches me—" she couldn't look at Isabelle for this part, so she turned back toward the clouds, "I feel too much."

Isabelle was silent then, and Leah considered the possibility that she, like the Dog Meadow Light, had just lost her appeal. She wondered if there was anything she could say. *I recently broke a date with Death. I haven't hugged anyone since I was six. I'm sorry I disappointed—*

Isabelle spoke first. "You might be the coolest person I've ever met."

Despite the compliment, Isabelle's expression had changed, quick as a door slamming shut, and Leah knew that something had ended there on the snowy hill. "Nah," said Leah, suddenly aware of being cold and wet. They walked back up the hill in a different kind of silence.

EIGHTEEN

HILDA, SOUTH CAROLINA,
THE YEAR OF BIRDS, 1989–1990

ON AN EARLY October day, as the first leaves were starting to turn, one loosened from a tree in the front yard of Edward Murphy's house. Only it wasn't a leaf. It was a scarlet tanager. Known as the flame of spring, the bright vermillion bird landed on the porch a few feet from where Leah sat on the sun-warmed floorboards. It seemed to be heralding something, opening and closing its mouth again and again while cocking its head about and flapping its black wings, except no sound came out. "What?" Leah asked. "What are you trying to tell me?" After five years of feeding birds with the best variety of birdseed in town, Leah had grown accustomed to them landing near her, but she'd never seen one like this. She watched it for many minutes—its vibrant chest, its darting eyes, its twig-like feet—as it preened and fluffed and watched her in return. "You're beautiful," she said, reaching out her hand. She thought briefly about running inside to get a handful of sunflower seeds, but when the bird inched closer, she dared not move.

Six months earlier, Leah turned eleven, and to celebrate, Edward Murphy brought home a vanilla cake layered with strawberry cream and frosted in fluffy chocolate. "Came all the way from a fancy bakery in Columbia," he informed her, lifting the cake from its pink box and turning it to face her. "See? How they wrote your name so pretty? Now let's put those candles in so you can make a wish!"

Leah, who hadn't been invited anywhere in the four years since she'd brought her fox skull to Cynthia Lewis's house, donned her cone-shaped hat alongside Edward Murphy, helped him put the eleven candles in her cake, plus one for good luck, and wished the same silent wish she wished each year: that her mother would return to her. Each year she changed the wish slightly—*I wish for Jeannie Starr to appear at our front door; I wish for my mother to come for Christmas; I wish for just one day with my mother*—hoping each time that her revision would somehow appease the wish-gods, that perhaps if she were less greedy—if she asked for only a day—she could convince them to grant her wish.

As she held her hand toward this red bird on the front porch—the very place she often imagined her mother returning—she didn't know why she had the sense that this bird was an answer to her wish. "Here," she said, urging just a bit with her fingers, "come," but the bright bird wouldn't budge. She looked up at the maple from where it had come and wondered if it had a mate and if it had enough worms and berries and seeds to eat. While she was looking away, the bird departed without a sound.

The next evening, at her bedroom window, Leah came face to face with an owl. At nearly two feet tall, it stood oddly in the grass, more like a statue than an actual owl, and it stared at her, pinning her through the glass with its yellow eyes. Thanks to her wildlife studies in the library after school, she knew this was a great horned owl and that he probably wasn't hungry because great horned owls are masterful hunters. "What?" she asked him. "What do you need?" But the owl stared back at her, as if he were the one asking the questions.

LEAH NEVER SAW the scarlet tanager again, or the owl that stood outside her bedroom window. But their presences remained. She couldn't look out her window or traipse through the yard without remembering the red flame on the porch or the owl's regal body manifest in the grass. And then more birds came.

It started ordinarily enough—phone wires and tree branches and fence railings becoming increasingly occupied by birds, until soon it was impossible to look in any direction without seeing several at once. Even looking down, Leah saw the dark shapes their shadows made as they dipped and rippled overhead. This was standard for autumn in the South, when the migrating birds passed through, hungry and garrulous. Within days, however, practically every surface was studded with birds, and the sky had become stage to a blustery epic of flight.

"Have you noticed all the birds?" Leah asked Edward Murphy, wide-eyed. They were finishing dinner. It was a year before they would take their one vacation together.

"What I've noticed is this giant basket of tomatoes we need to eat. You know Martha up the street? That woman has more tomatoes in her garden than she knows what to do with. Big ones, too—you can probably see 'em all the way from space. You can darn well bet she knows we have tomato plants of our own, but does that stop her from visiting her tomato problems on us?"

"I mean the birds, outside. All the birds out there."

"Mmmhmm," he gave a quick conciliatory nod. "I was decent, at least. I only brought her a half dozen zucchini, which I know she'll use, because she isn't even growing zucchini. Now, pole beans, that's another story. We don't have any of those. But does she bring pole beans? Nope. Just tomatoes. A big old heaping basket of tomatoes."

"Maybe we could make spaghetti sauce?"

"Make enough spaghetti sauce to feed an army is what we could make."

Leah took a bite of a sliced tomato on her plate. "It's sweet."

"Big old heaping basket of sweet tomatoes," he started, but his voice began to drift into the background as Leah's focus turned to the window, where she had spent years looking for her mother's car. Now, instead, she watched a pine limb bow and shiver under the weight of birds.

THE BIRDS CONTINUED to populate Hilda. While the sheer number of them was, in itself, unprecedented, there were other things that were different, too. For one, Leah had never before noticed so many different species of birds in one place. Since when did a bluebird perch next to a cardinal, which perched next to an oriole that was perched next to a row of starlings? And since when had parrots started coming to South Carolina? Or these white birds with green faces? Or this fuzzy-headed green-and-red fellow with sweeping tail feathers?

Perhaps most notable was the birdsong: it was largely absent. Sure, there was the occasional twitter of a catbird or chickadee, the metallic chatter of blackbirds and starlings—the usual birdsong of a usual day—but most of the birds she saw appeared to be mute.

At dinner she tried again. "Have you noticed the parrots outside recently?" They were still working on Martha-Up-the-Street's tomatoes, some of which Edward Murphy had stewed that night. Leah arranged and then rearranged them on her plate.

This time, he looked at the sea-eyed eleven-year-old who regularly said things that made sense only to her, and then peered out the window for several seconds. No birds came. "I'm pretty sure we don't have parrots here, sweetheart," he said.

The condescension in his voice vexed her. "There was a whole flock of them! Right out there! They landed on our fence and flew right down the street." She put her fork down and stared at him insistently.

"Well, who knows what this world is coming to? If you say there are parrots out there, then there are parrots out there."

"You're just saying that. You shouldn't say what you don't believe."

"Listen, young lady. Don't you go being rude now. I said I believe you, and that's enough." He glanced out the window again, but nothing stirred. "Now eat your tomatoes."

NINETEEN

LEAH'S ROAD ATLAS was beginning to look less new. She liked how some of the page corners had gotten bent from being handled, how the atlas opened a bit more softly than it had when she'd first opened it, and how Wisconsin, which Essie's spiral was circling her back to, had come to look familiar since her trip to Madeline Island. She was a traveler now. She could have told Isabelle that.

In the two hundred miles she would travel to reach the Wisconsin town called Friendship, where she would get a room at a motel called Inn of the Pines and, after days of driving on little sleep, snooze past checkout time, Leah would wonder about how the town had gotten its name. Why weren't there more evocatively named towns? For a while she drove thinking of possibilities—Happiness, Elephant, Somersault, Tulip, Candy, Love . . . —until she switched back to thinking of other things she could have said to Isabelle. *The shell of an Oriental hornet converts sunlight into electricity. The heart of a blue whale weighs over a thousand pounds. I'm carrying a dead woman in my backpack. I don't know where my mother is. I have a road atlas and am still lost.*

Essie had given Leah one item of advice—*have the courage to love*—and as Leah drove and the daylight trickled off into the deep vat of night, she wondered if love was like magic, this immeasurable thing that can be conjured by even the smallest acts. A person like Isabelle, Leah was certain, wouldn't need Essie's advice.

She wondered what would happen in Isabelle's life tomorrow, a year from now, ten. As she drove farther and farther away from her, she could feel the nascent strands between them pulling apart.

She thought about Bob O'Malley, too. He'd written his address and phone number on the note he'd left on her truck, and now that she was circling back to Wisconsin, she considered contacting him. But when she imagined actually calling or showing up at his door, she decided that she would send him a letter instead.

How strange to think that of the few people Leah would call friends in her twenty-one years of life, three of them were people she'd met only once. The third was a story she'd never told Edward Murphy, one that she'd kept for herself for all those years, until now. Reaching across the cab of her truck, she unzipped her backpack and folded down the front flap so that the top half of Essie's urn was exposed, the stones turning on each time Leah passed a highway light. "Now it's my turn to tell you a story," she said to a quick glint in the dark. "I made a friend once, in the carnival, and it wasn't Her-Sweet or the Rubberband Man."

))) ● (((

IT HAD BEEN a blistering August day when, for the first time since Leah had stepped into her role as child oracle, another child walked into her tent. Perhaps it was because children tend to live so fully in the moment that they were never interested in standing in Leah's long line only to sit down and have a conversation about something as abstract as their futures when there were rides to spin and jostle them, hot dogs and cotton candy to devour, water guns to shoot into the mouths of clowns. So when a tousle-headed, hazel-eyed boy walked into her tent, Leah assumed he was lost.

"What are you looking for?" she asked, as the boy, who she guessed was a couple of years older than she was, stood just inside the nylon flap that was the door.

The boy looked around the tent, taking his time to acknowledge each thing: the four small tables with four burning black candles, the elephant poster, the blue tops of his own sneakers, the cassette player broadcasting Romani music, a fan whirring at full speed, and then finally Leah herself. "I'm not looking for anything."

"Then why are you here?"

The boy glanced at the door behind him, then back at Leah. "To get my fortune told."

Leah scratched her forehead. "But you're a kid."

The boy shrugged his shoulders. "So are you."

Leah, who had grown accustomed to the easy power she held over the adults, suddenly found herself flustered. Though children populated the carnival like flies at the cotton candy spinner, she tended not to interact with them very often. For one, kids her age were whiny, crying all the time about every little thing—dropped ice cream cones, skinned knees, losing at the ring toss—while Leah, on the other hand, almost never cried, not even when she fell on broken glass and cut her knee to the bone. She wasn't about to be thrown now, by this curious boy still standing by the door and surveying her tent. She folded her hands on the table and asked the question she'd asked hundreds of times by then. "Would you like to have a seat?"

The boy nodded but didn't move. "Do you have any goblins?"

"Goblins?"

"Yeah, goblins. Or ghosts?"

"That's not a fortune," said Leah. "Besides, a ghost is the same thing as a goblin."

The boy sat down. "No it's not."

Nonplussed, Leah folded her arms across her chest. "What's the difference then?"

The boy fixed his eyes on Leah. "A goblin is a dwarf who plays tricks on you. And a ghost is the spirit of a dead person."

"Well," said Leah, not wanting to be outdone, "we have both. Now put your hands on the crystal ball, please."

"What do you mean you have both?" the boy asked, placing his hands on the crystal. "Where?"

"Shhhh, I can't concentrate if you talk." Leah gently put her hands on top of the boy's hands. For the first time, she neither felt nor saw anything; she smelled something: a rose—sweet, slightly astringent, unmistakable.

Leah took her hands off the boy's hands and looked at him in disbelief.

"What's my fortune?" the boy asked.

"Shhhh," Leah said again, unsure what to do next. She looked at the boy, who patiently looked back at her, his hands still on the crystal, and she tried again. But as soon as she placed her hands over his, the scent returned, so she took her hands off again and simply looked at him, as if he might transform into an actual flower. They sat like this, blinking at each other, the boy's hands in place, Leah's hands worrying a cluster of sequins on her cape, until the buzzer went off and startled them both. Already they were out of time, and Leah hadn't told the boy anything. She quickly stopped the buzzer. "You wanna see goblins?" she asked.

The boy's eyes widened. "For real?"

Leah reached her hand out to the boy, and he took it, and the two of them darted out of the tent's back door. They ran through the throngs of carnival-goers, Leah leading the boy past the Maze of Mania, where people bumped into the same walls again and again; past the Olde Tyme Photo Booth, where women slipped garters up their thighs; and past the Grave Digger, the ride that swung people inches from the ground—until they arrived at the House of Tricks Treats and Creatures.

Leah allowed herself a momentary flush of pride in being able to take the boy to the front of the line and receive instant admission, and as the door closed behind them, they stood for a moment as their eyes adjusted to the dim light. "Whoa," the boy said, gaining focus, "your head! It's so *long!*" They were facing the row of distortion mirrors that lined the House's entryway, watching their reflections bend and stretch. "Look at your stubby legs!" said Leah, and they both giggled at their hideousness.

Leah had never really been interested in the mirrors—to her they were a silly and static prelude to the real magic of the House—so she wasn't expecting the wavy reflections they both giggled at to shift. But there in the glass, she watched the boy turn old. She watched his tousled hair grow and gray, then slough off like dust, as if the entirety of his life were unfolding there in a time lapse. Her own reflection remained largely unchanged, save for the almost indiscernible specks of alarm that had suddenly appeared in her eyes, and for a moment she wasn't sure if the uneasy feeling in her body came from watching the boy go so far so fast, or from being left behind. But the boy didn't appear to notice what had just happened in the mirror, or if he did it didn't faze him, because he just kept on laughing about Leah's misshapen head.

"C'mon," she said, taking his hand again, leading him into the House's center chamber, where children and adults alike purchased magic tricks and candy and games, where the Shelves of Specimens loomed in their grotesqueness, where the music and shrieks and mechanized hauntings pressed on the ears in cacophonous delight. She led him through clusters of children, past Orelda the skittering rat, past a talking head on a silver platter. "It's a nice day for hopscotch," the head said. "It's a nice day for green beans." And as they passed, the head turned, blinking its long eyelashes, smiling.

The boy was wonderstruck. He didn't know where to look first, and twice he tripped trying to see everything all at once. "This way," Leah announced, leading him to the Hall of Figures's big black door. To prevent too many people from entering at once, a carnival employee almost always guarded the door. That day it was Perilous Paul, the carnival's premier fire swallower, glass eater, and all-around daredevil.

"Look who it is! Leah Fern and a guest! Tell me, mister," he said, lowering his voice and leaning down to face the boy, "do you have a special ticket to be here?"

"A ticket?" the boy asked. He looked down at his hands, as if half expecting a ticket to materialize, and then at Leah, who simply shrugged, and finally back at Perilous Paul. "No."

"No ticket, huh? No ticket." In a flash, Perilous Paul drew his hand forward like a sword, and the boy stepped back. "Quick—name three cartoon dogs."

Someone from inside the Hall of Figures shrieked. The boy scratched his head. "Dino," he said. "You know, from *The Flintstones*?"

Perilous Paul snapped his fingers. "Quick, quick!"

"Snoopy!" said the boy, smiling.

Perilous Paul kept snapping.

"Pluto!"

Perilous Paul leaned close to Leah but said loud enough for the boy to hear, "The kid's naming planets now."

"The *dog*!" he insisted, giggling.

"Yes, yes, of course," said Perilous Paul, addressing the boy again. "Now, do exactly as I say."

The boy locked eyes with Perilous Paul and nodded.

"Rub your belly while patting your head."

The boy clumsily obliged.

"Do five jumping jacks."

The boy jumped into the air.

"Sing 'Jingle Bells.'"

The boy tried not to laugh as he sang, "Jingle bells, jingle—"

"Okay, okay, that's enough." Perilous Paul gave a bow and opened the door to the hall. "Entrez!"

"You have to pull the curtains open to see what's inside," explained Leah as they approached the first nook. The boy hesitated. "Go ahead!" she urged.

"Alakazam!" the boy exclaimed, sweeping the first curtain open in a sudden rush.

Behind the curtain, an unrecognizable crumpled thing lay on the floor. For several seconds nothing happened, but then it began to twitch, and then to shake, and then to seize violently. "What *is* that?" the boy asked. And to answer, the thing unfurled and shot straight up, opening its single eye. "Ew!" the boy yelled out.

The cyclops jigged and jagged, wobbling on its single leg. "Did you take my other half?" it implored. "Give me back my other half!"

The boy quickly drew the curtain shut, and they moved onto the next, where Harvey Skybanger, a mail carrier whose postal bag bulged with slugs, looked up and muttered, "Everyone's looking for the sky. Can you find the sky? I can't find the sky." The boy gripped Leah's hand as they went from curtain to curtain, while Leah beamed with vicarious excitement. They watched Donny Osmond's silent white smile grow, so slowly at first that it seemed almost like nothing was happening, though one could feel something was amiss, until there was no denying the widening, the grin expanding until his head hinged open like a locket. "Eeek," said the boy, shuddering, though this time he didn't immediately close the curtain. And when Leah tried to rush him past the next curtain without opening it, he refused. "I want to see them all!"

So Leah obliged without telling the boy that this was the one curtain she would rather not open. Above it, a name glowed in red lights: Matri-Roachy. The boy pulled the thick burgundy fabric aside and sized up the woman inside: a bloodied bride clutching a roach-covered bouquet. The boy started to close the curtain, but the bride lunged forward abruptly, sending him springing back on his feet. "How *could* you!" she accused. "How could you?" Then she slumped forward, and the boy closed her curtain.

"C'mon," said Leah as they made their way past Perilous Paul and back out into the center of the House, "there's more to see."

Leah waved the boy over to the tunnel lined with red lights. "In here," she said, getting down on the floor. "You have to crawl."

The boy followed Leah into the tube, and when the lights went out, she felt the boy reach out and touch the bottom of her shoe. "Just keep going," she assured him. "The lights always come back on." They crawled in the dark, and by the time the lights came back on, they were exiting the tube back into darkness: the room that housed the Puppet Beasts.

The show had already started, and the room was jammed with kids. Leah tried to see the boy's face, but aside from a few slim spotlights on the stage, there was no other light, so she imagined him as a boy and as an old man and as a cluster of intertwined canes of roses.

A former customer had once lodged a complaint to the town, alleging that the Blazing Calyx Carnival must be in violation of several ordinances. But when a police officer came out to check that everything was to up to code, Leah told his fortune, and her mother gave him a private show, and miraculously, the carnival received a clean bill of compliance.

Now, in the packed room of the Puppet Beasts, a bat fluttered across the stage while a red-eyed mongoose told a story: "Even the faraway children, the ones in the fancy houses with the frilly bed-clothes, were lured out in their sleep by the tune of the hill and how it called to them. They sleepwalked to it through rain, across highways, past bedded-down deer in the forests, their bare feet turning dark with dirt and tar. They could not turn their heads. They could not look back. They forgot math equations. They forgot their birthdays. They forgot the names of their stuffed animals. Each step they took removed another layer from their lives, until they arrived at the hill empty and beastly with hunger. 'Feed me,' they cried. 'Feed me.' In the darkness, their veins bulged through their skin. Their teeth grew. They twitched. They were no longer their parents' children; they belonged to the hill. Always, they crested it, its deadened grass, its sharp rock, and then, like mosquitoes, they vanished, never to be seen again."

This was one of the best days of Leah's life, made even better when they crawled back into the main chamber. "It's Dylan and Dandy the Dwarves!" Leah announced. In tandem, they were juggling foil-wrapped chocolates in the shapes of insects—Dandy in an emerald cloche bedecked with bright pink flowers, Dylan in a top hat encircled by a band of shark teeth. "Get your sweet cockroaches!" they called out. "Get your chocolate beetles!"

Leah leaned into the boy's ear and whispered, "You asked for goblins?"

But the boy, whose enthrallment Leah could feel like a million tiny lights under her skin, looked at her with uncertainty. "Just because they're dwarves doesn't mean they're goblins," he said.

"Wait here," she told him, before dashing over to Dandy.

"Well, look who it is," Dandy said, catching the airborne insects. "Little Miss Leah Fern! Do you need some chocolate, sweetie?"

Leah shook her head. "Actually, I was hoping you could show my friend over there the rose."

"The rose?"

"You know," said Leah, trying unsuccessfully to wink, "the *special* rose."

Dandy's face lit up. "Ah, the *rose*! Yes." But as she started off toward the basket of tricks, she turned back to Leah and furrowed her forehead. "Shouldn't you be telling fortunes, little lady?"

Leah shook her head. "I'm taking a break!" Then she returned to the boy, whose mouth hung agape as he circled around and around, reaching for a kaleidoscope, a tarantula, a taxidermic owl.

"What's that?" he asked, pointing at a bowl filled with green slime, but before Leah could answer, a tiny voice emerged between them.

"Would you like to smell my rose?" Dandy was holding a dark red flower up to Leah, who politely bent down to sniff it. "That smells *divine*!" Leah said, imitating what her mother always said when she sprayed herself afresh with Mitsouko.

"How about you, mister?" Dandy asked, holding the flower up to the boy. "Would you like to smell my rose?"

The boy followed Leah's lead and leaned over to smell the rose. Leah clasped her fingers together and held her breath. Dandy pressed the button on the stem, which sprayed a stream of water into the boy's face. "Trick!" Dandy said. Then she handed him a chocolate grasshopper wrapped in green foil. "And treat!"

How the boy laughed then, wiping his face with one hand and clutching his candy with the other. How Leah delighted in his laughter, that warm current running through her. And how quickly the laughter shattered.

"What the hell are you doing?" Hank, the oily and baleful carnival owner and paramour to Jeannie Starr, towered over Leah. "You've got a line a hundred miles long and you just walk off and leave all those people standing in the heat?" He grabbed her arm, and a bolt of pain shot down to her fingers.

"Don't touch me!" she said, trying to wriggle from his grip.

"Go easy, now," Dandy said, reaching way up to put her hand on Hank's chest. "Have yourself a chocolate cockroach."

Hank let go of Leah and swatted the cockroach out of Dandy's hand.

"That'll be twenty-seven cents," she said.

"This isn't a joke! I'm running this show," he barked, looking down at Leah. "And Little Miss Know-It-All here isn't going to ruin things for me."

Humiliated, Leah turned to the boy, who, for the first time since she'd led him out of her tent, looked truly afraid. She wanted to do or say something to comfort him, but all she could muster were the words "I'm sorry" before she ran from the House of Tricks Treats and Creatures, without ever having asked the boy his name.

After that day, Leah never abandoned her post as The Youngest and Very Best Fortuneteller in the World. But how wonderful it was, just that once, to take a boy's hand and run.

TWENTY

IN THE PARKING lot outside the Friendship post office, in the haven of her truck, Leah clutched the latest envelope from Essie—labeled with the number three and an arc of orange paint. She wasn't used to being excited about things, and the feeling unsettled her so much that this time she saved the letter for last. Instead she pulled a wooden star from the bottom of the envelope and ran her fingers over the finely sanded wood—another of the coven's gifts, this one from Dee—engraved with a prayer: *Luna, illuminate our truths* . . . The sun cut through Leah's windshield and illuminated the wish.

Into that same shaft of light, Leah lifted the transparency, a photograph of a woman's hands. They were holding something the camera couldn't see, fingers at the verge of fanning open, suggesting that the hidden thing was about to be shown. Though the hands were disembodied from the rest of the subject, Leah recognized them instantly. They were her mother's hands.

She would know them anywhere—the long slender fingers, the little crescent moon scar over the middle knuckle of her right hand, and the way, even in a still photo, one could see how the fingers moved with the fluidity and grace of an anemone. Leah could still remember how it felt to be touched by them; it was like being touched by a zephyr you never want to end. As Leah held her mother's hands in her own, she realized she was also holding the proof, lest she had even one molecule of doubt: Essie East and Jeannie Starr had known each other.

July 21, 1998

Dear Leah,

Your mother was born a magician. She once said that her hands came into the world knowing more than she did, and sometimes it was as if they operated by their own volition. She was quite young when she discovered her gifts, and once her classmates caught on, they were always inviting her over to entertain them by making their trinkets disappear and reappear. She was grateful for that time away from her parents, who drank and fought and broke things, but even when she was home, she hid in her room and created her own secret world of magic, imagining the day she, too, would disappear.

She confided this to me one night while she was falling asleep. In the light of a single burning candle, she launched a flock of birds into shadowy flight along the wall. Her fingers moved as she spoke, but she never acknowledged what she was doing, and I was afraid to say or do anything that might stop

her, so I stayed as quiet as I could, barely
even wanting to take a breath.

You must be wondering about the circumstances
that originally led your mother to my New York
flat, or why she stayed for six months. In due
time, you'll know—but we're not at that part of
the story yet.

The five of us arrived in Watersmeet on
February 3, 1977, a day before the full moon,
a day after Imbolc—the celebration of the
beginning of spring. But that evening it
was snowing when we ventured out to see the
Dog Meadow Light, a mysterious light said to
appear like a ghost in the crux of a valley. We
drove up a narrow road and sat waiting while
snowflakes wended down. It was so cold that
we stayed in the car and kept it running, the
windscreen wipers squeaking our view clear.
Then the snow stopped and the almost-full moon
appeared as if someone had snapped it into
place. Claire was sitting beside me, her leg
against mine, and I kept stealing glances at
the side of her face. Eventually, as promised,
a glowing orb began to rise up out of the
valley like another moon. Mesmerizing as it
was, it was her face I kept turning to see.

The next night the full moon hid behind
clouds, and we never caught a glimpse of it.
"You don't have to see it to feel it," Claire
said, and that made me feel it. When we got to
Sucker Lake, the second point of our spiral

and one of three hundred and two lakes in Watersmeet, we parked on the side of the road and trudged in deep snow on a slim path through dense woods to get to the edge of it. I don't think I've ever been colder.

Athena cast our circle and tossed five handfuls of red poppies into the center. Then she lit a white candle and pushed it into the ground, and from it we each lit a red one. "Moon and sun, silver and gold, Shiva and Shakti, let us be whole in all we are and all we create!" Athena dipped her stone wand into an oil infused with myrrh and rounded the circle, anointing each of us. When she touched the wand to my third eye, it left a warmth there I can still feel.

Together we turned to salute each of the four cardinal directions. We raised our arms to the hidden moon. We knelt to touch the frozen earth. We held hands. We chanted. *"When the waters meet, they don't forget. Water bodies, we unite. We carry fire. We are one with every current, with every burning star."*

Some might say that what we were doing was ridiculous, perhaps even insane. I wouldn't have blamed them. But in that dark frozen world, I couldn't deny that I felt something I'd never felt before. And the truth is, it terrified me.

Throw my ashes to the wind at Roche-a-Cri.

Next stop: Post Office, Cosmos, Minnesota,
56228.

Yours,

Essie East

"Cosmos," said Leah. "Interesting name for a town." And as
she sat in her truck and refolded the letter and watched sunlight
waver on her steering wheel and hands, dimming and brightening
as clouds passed by, she wondered how big the spiral was and how
far it would take her, and she wondered how she hadn't wondered
those things before. It was as if she were waking from a dream, like
a sleepwalker being guided by a hypnotist, and it was all she could
do to put one foot in front of the other. It wasn't an unpleasant sensation. In fact, there was something about that feeling of surrender that reminded Leah of the few times she could remember being
held—fully carried—by her mother.

She took her mother's hands into hers again and peered into the
ghostly photo for any hint of what her mother might have been holding then—a flower? A tree frog? A feather? But then it occurred to her
that maybe it was the absence of a thing she was holding, as happened
in those moments right after she made something disappear.

Though Leah could imagine her mother projecting shadow-
birds on Essie's wall, she couldn't imagine what circumstances
would have led her mother to New York City in the first place, or
why she'd be falling asleep beside the likes of Essie East. If anything,
Essie's letters were generating more questions than answers, and
with each new bit of information, Leah felt even farther away from
her mother. It was almost as if Jeannie Starr were a myth instead of

a real person—as if she had always existed in a world of untouchable shadow-birds.

"SCREAMING ROCK," LEAH said aloud, drawing on her high school French as she entered Roche-a-Cri State Park, home to a single three-hundred-foot butte jutting up amidst miles of flat, forested land. According to the entrance sign, the sandstone butte had once been an island surrounded by a glacial lake. "I'm getting a theme here," she said to the urn that tapped against her back as she walked.

Aside from a few passersby, the park was mostly empty. The snow was melting, exposing the rich brown humus of years past and the scent of pine. Leah tread lightly in her combat boots as she followed Mound Trail to the butte. Indigenous tribes had once etched petroglyphs on its walls, and despite years of wear and graffiti, Leah could still make out the stars and moons and the tracks of thunderbirds.

Leah climbed the 303 stairs, and Essie bumped against her back the whole way. About halfway up, when she started feeling winded, she found herself wondering about Essie's last breaths. Had she died in her apartment? If so, how had Leah missed the commotion? Or had she died in the sterile light of a hospital? Had it been "quick as an explosion," the way Essie had predicted in her first letter? And if so, had it been painful? Had it been a relief? Had she been alone?

When Leah finally reached the top of the monolith, she was startled to find a family occupying the small space of the wooden deck that overlooked miles and miles of Wisconsin. Two exceptionally blond parents and two exceptionally blond children, a boy and girl, had all turned to stare at Leah. "Hello," she said, running her hand through her spiky hair. Then she stepped over to the empty side of the platform.

They greeted her, and then the parents and the boy turned back around to face the great expanse, which had turned rosy in the late afternoon sun. But the girl stayed fixed on Leah.

"Stop staring," the mother admonished. "It's not nice."

But the girl ignored her. "Who are you?" she asked Leah.

"Leah."

"Alexis, leave the young lady alone," her father said, tickling the top of her shoulder with his fingertips. "Look at the lake in the distance. Can you see the water, sweetie, way out there?"

The girl, however, would not be deterred. "Why is your hair like that?"

Leah shrugged and turned to face the girl directly. "The same reason your hair is the way your hair is, I suppose."

The girl ran her small, dimpled hands over the two pink barrettes in her hair. "Because your mother does your hair?"

"No," said Leah, wishing she'd given a better answer.

The girl looked down and pulled something invisible off the front of her shirt. "My mother does mine. I don't like it."

"Alexis! That's enough," said the mother.

"I like your hair," said Leah. "It looks like corn silk in the sun."

The girl searched Leah's face, unconvinced, and said nothing.

"And also a cloudless sulphur," Leah added.

The girl took a step in Leah's direction. "What's a cloudless supper?"

"A butterfly."

"A butterfly," the girl repeated, touching her hair again.

"Okay, time to go," the mother urged, taking the girl's hand.

"Your hair is a bat," the girl said, now craning her neck to look at Leah as her mother led her briskly down the stairs, her father and brother following.

"I like bats," Leah said.

The girl disappeared, leaving only a voice that peeped up from the stairs below. "I like bats, too!"

LEAH LET HERSELF feel tall as she trained her sight on the horizon. A gusty wind moved through an empty sky, and she thought of the people who'd carved the thunderbirds into the rock. What had they wished for then? Freedom? Love? Sustenance? Flight? Aren't we all just wishing some version of the same wish? She wondered how many people had stood where she stood and also dreamed of flight. And she wondered how many had done it—had tested gravity and winglessness, and jumped.

Though it had been many years since Leah had wished upon the silver ring she'd found in a pile of leaves as she walked home from school while being teased by a gaggle of kids who had since gone nameless in her mind, she held up her right hand, upon which the silver ring she'd once deemed magical now gleamed in the crepuscular light as if it were made of gold, and she made a wish. "Let a hawk come," she said.

She looked at the ring, its crescent moon and three stars, and then expectantly scanned the sky. Only wind came. "Let *any* bird come," she whispered urgently, still holding her right hand out. The sky remained empty.

She had never been one to beg for anything, and yet here, on the top of this screaming rock, she felt herself pleading—though for what, exactly, she didn't know. She pulled Essie out of her backpack, and this time she didn't pause to look at the stones, not even her favorite one. Everything was being washed by wind, which ruffled against her ears and swallowed the sound of the top being unscrewed and the sound of the questions and wishes in her mind and the sound of a little girl saying something somewhere about butterflies and bats. Leah carefully tilted the urn so that only a small amount of ash fell into her palm and closed her fingers tightly as she screwed the top back into place with her free hand. And then, like a sower throwing seed, she tossed the ash over the edge, and the wind took it, carried it off so fast that in a blink it was gone.

TWENTY-ONE

HILDA, SOUTH CAROLINA, 1987

ON AN ELECTRIC-GREEN spring day in Edward Murphy's backyard on Barnwell Road, Leah was learning how to make things airborne. She was nine and had been learning in school about propulsion, acceleration, and velocity. She'd also been learning about chemical reactions, an education that seemed as if it were designed to prime her for this exact undertaking. That day Leah had made off with Edward Murphy's Alka-Seltzer tablets and salad vinegar, and after several weeks of careful building and many failed attempts, Leah launched a small rocket. Made from tin scraps and electrical tape, the rocket ascended beautifully but quickly took a turn and smashed through her bedroom window.

Edward Murphy, who'd heard the window shatter and had come running outside, nodded triumphantly. "So *that's* where all my Alka-Seltzers have gone!" And instead of yelling at her or immediately sending her to clean up the glass, he joined her where she sat on the lawn, a mess of paraphernalia scattered around her. "Show me," he said, picking up an Alka-Seltzer tablet and turning it in his hand as if he'd never seen one before. "How'd you do it?"

On that April day, more than two years after her mother left, Leah Fern sat closer to Edward Murphy than she normally would, so close that their knees accidentally touched and Leah had to move away—though only an inch or two—as she showed him how she'd assembled the rocket.

"Ah, yes," he said, "I see." And then he showed her how to affix the fins so that the next rocket wouldn't break her window, and they talked about things that had nothing and everything to do with their unexpected life on that little street in that little town—how pressure builds in small chambers, how a force can act upon an inert object and set it on an endless path of motion, "like the earth," Leah said, "and the seasons." "Like the universe," said Edward Murphy, "and the stars."

TWENTY-TWO

COSMOS, MINNESOTA, 1999

LEAH SAT IN her truck in the Roche-a-Cri parking lot, atlas open. A man's voice came from her speakers, filling the small space. "I don't know what you'll be doing on this Friday night," the DJ said, talking over the beginning of an upbeat hit by Prince, "but tonight I'm gonna party like it's 1999!" She didn't usually listen to the radio, opting instead to rotate through the box of cassette tapes she kept beneath the seat, but she'd recently begun to welcome the company of the DJs' voices, even when they did annoying things like talk over the beginnings of songs.

When she finally reached her destination, she nearly blew right through the tiny town. Just over a mile in diameter, Cosmos was even smaller than Hilda, and it did not appear to have a hotel. In the last dark miles of her five-hour drive, she'd entered into a fit of yawning, her eyelids heavy, so when she saw a sign for Thompson Lake Park, she followed it, hoping to find a place to rest. In an empty parking lot, surrounded by tall trees that loomed like giant sentinels in the moonlight, she took off her spikes and lay across the seat of her truck. She unzipped her backpack enough to run her hands over the smooth wood and bumpy stones of the obelisk, which had become a familiar comfort.

She grabbed her water bottle and tapped it against the urn before taking a sip. "Cheers," she yawned. Somewhere in the umbra, an owl hooted. Another owl answered, and at some point in the conversation, Leah fell asleep.

When she awoke a few hours later, a face was hovering over her. Even in the predawn darkness she could see the pale green eyes perched over hers without apology. One inch between them, that was all. She didn't know if she was about to be bitten or loved. Her heart hammered in her chest while she held her breath. But the face was unmoving, relentless. And the eyes pierced her through. Essie's eyes.

Leah sat up, away from the dream. Soon the first traces of dawn streaked across the sky in ribs of fire-tinged lavender and pressed down in strips across the mirrored surface of Thompson Lake while the trees, still rooted in darkness, sketched smoky webs against the sky. Leah exhaled plumes of frosty white. Several times in the night she'd woken shivering and had to turn her truck on for heat.

She took the urn onto her lap and watched the stones wake in the warm light. Who had made this urn, she wondered? And why for Essie? Essie herself had referred to it, in her first letter, as "unfitting," and even Leah, who had barely known her, knew that she probably would have scoffed at such an extravagant vessel. In fact, she couldn't remember having ever seen Essie indulge in a single adornment outside of her cane, unless you count the pinstripes on her men's trousers.

Leah shook off a chill and tucked the urn away before wandering into the woods to pee behind the cover of a wide-trunked oak. From there, she meandered down to the dawn-pink lake and dipped her hands into the water. *Like in the movies*, she thought, cupping her hands to her face. The cold took her breath, but then she reached in and splashed herself again. She couldn't remember having experienced such cold in the South, such stillness. There, spring mornings brought bird chatter and peepers and whip-poor-wills, but the world here was silent, save for her stirring of the water. She took the crisp air in deeply and wondered if maybe infinity was made of soft quiet light like this.

LEAH ATE TWO packaged cupcakes with white squiggles down the center and drew three dogs in her sketchbook while she waited for the Cosmos post office to open. One dog was squat and dark with a bold expression. One was a greyhound with an extra-long snout. And one was fox-like; its fluffy tail pluming up the page, becoming feathers. She thought of Athena's hybrid dragon-leopard, and imagined what it must have been like to pull the clay for her Magical Imaginaries straight from the earth. Had it been thick? Damp? Cool? Had she dug it out with her bare hands? Leah remembered the black stone crow in her pocket. She wondered what tools Claire had used to carve it and how long it had taken her. *A long time*, she said to herself, and then she found herself thinking of the male bowerbird, who spends years decorating his bower, carefully collecting colorful items—flowers, beetles, fungi, found objects—and painstakingly arranging them. Where does the desire to create art come from, she wondered. Is it coded into our DNA? Does it arise from that mysterious thing we call a soul? That was, after all, the whole purpose of the witches' spiral, wasn't it? To make art from the soul?

Leah wondered many things that early April morning while she waited for the post office to open, not least of which was what would be in Essie's next package. She found that she was now look-ing forward to not only the letter—even the parts about Essie and the others—but also to the other objects inside. It was a feeling reminiscent of the anticipation she'd felt when she was young and Edward Murphy would sometimes bring home a Cracker Jack box and she'd immediately dig down into the box for the prize.

At precisely 7:30 a.m., Leah entered the post office and received envelope number four, which was brushed with a stroke of yellow paint, and this time she broke the wax seal before she even got back into her truck. Her hope grew a bird-sized heartbeat.

```
July 22, 1998


Dear Leah,
    It occurred to me after I finished your
letter yesterday that if I'm wrong about my
death date-that is to say, if I kick off sooner
than expected-we'll all be stuck. You'll never
know the end of the story, and in a sense,
neither will I. So I find myself rushing at
the keyboard, and then I find that this cannot
be rushed.
    I mentioned terror in my last letter.
Perhaps terror is just the flip side of
exhilaration. One spends her life wanting to
believe in magic, wanting to believe in the
countless unseen, unmeasurable things she
feels. She wants to believe in her own power,
like a sixth sense. And then one day she finds
that what she's felt-or, I dare say, known-is
```

true. She finds she *is* powerful. What then?
Perhaps there's nothing more exhilarating than
discovering that.

It happened slowly: my photography began to
change from the mosses to other things, such
as ice, leaves, water, sand, skin. I shot close
enough to uncover hidden worlds, to see the
islands within the islands, as it were. It was
a lot like the mosses, my lying on the ground
and getting intimate with things, but it was
different, too. As I explored the mysterious
shapes nature etched onto the surfaces of
those northern lakes—and by now you know
that in the north in the first months of the
year, that's a cold undertaking—I felt myself
expanding out into dimensions I hadn't been
able to see before.

I have to confess that my camera had also
begun to wander toward Claire. You should have
seen her at my little opening. Maybe it was
a coincidence, but two weeks after our first
ritual, I got my first show. It wasn't much—a
one-month gig at a small local coffee shop—
but there they were, my photographs, hanging
over people's cappuccinos and crumb cakes. And
there Claire was, beaming as if she'd taken
the photographs herself. "I'm so proud of you,"
she kept saying, reaching for my hand. And
each time she wrapped her fingers around mine
I felt a little dizzy. Maybe it was then that I
began to resent her, to resent how easily she

could unmoor the heft of me, as if I were made
of nothing but air.

Coincidence or not, I wasn't the only one
who'd begun having success. The Magical
Imaginaries kept emerging for Athena, some of
them now coiled by snakes or holding moons in
their claws, which people especially loved.
She could barely keep up and often skipped
sleep to keep sculpting. We all celebrated
when she landed an incredible exhibit at
a Chicago art gallery. Dee was writing so
many songs that she had to carry a notebook
with her everywhere she went, even into the
shower. Her music started dipping into darker
chords, her voice tending toward a growl
at times, and she was booking more gigs at
elite venues. Linda had branched out in her
painting, as well, using mixed media, building
up three-dimensional lighthouses with plaster,
trying things she'd never thought to try
before. One of her first breaks came when a
multimillionaire commissioned her to paint
four nautical murals for his mansion. Because
Claire had already been having success prior
to our spiral, it was difficult to gauge
how much our rituals were affecting her.
Everything she made, it seemed, already came
from that deepest place within her, that place
the rest of us were imbibing and incanting,
spiraling and chanting, to get to. Our
successes were welcome, but they were merely

the byproduct of our, dare I say, more noble strivings.

Back at the colony in between rituals, we didn't discuss what we were doing as a coven. There was nothing to say; there was only art to make. Then the moon would be nearing full, and it would be time again to pack up, pile into Athena's Grand Prix, and set out for as many days as it would take to get to the next turning point on our spiral.

The third point led us to Roche-a-Cri, that massive butte, which you may now know had once been an island in a lake on an island (like Bog Lake). At sunset, Athena cast our circle at its base. It was March and still quite cold, so there were only a few stragglers leaving the site as the sun went down. This time Athena cast a second circle inside the first, "*for the lake within the lake, the island within the island*." Claire told us that in alchemy, a circle inside a circle is the symbol for gold. "It's the metal of perfection," she said. "And transformation."

Athena cast a third circle inside the other two, to mark the third of our full moon ceremonies, our first trimester. That night the moon was like a silver spotlight commanding the sky. Athena anointed us with an infusion of marigold, while the orange candles we burned cast shadows onto the sandstone that made the wings of the thunderbirds

appear to move. We had each written a line of
the following incantation, which we recited
together, our voices barely above a whisper,
just to be safe:

> Think saffron, the monk's robe, the Hoodoos
>   in Utah. Think fire,
> how it becomes the witch, how she succumbs
>   to it. What is a witch?
> A shaman? A small fleck of light you never
>   saw? When they torched
> her, her skin burned like paper, her hair
>   flew up, her arms lifted:
> Hosanna! Fire animates even the dead. We
>   call on them now,
> our brilliant sisters. Let them rise from
>   the embers, and the ash.

Your mother wanted to visit all the famous
museums when she stayed with me in New York,
which regularly left us both knackered by the
end of the day. (Thankfully, by then she'd at
least stopped her late-night excursions to the
piano bar.) She and I were very different in
our approaches to museums. I could go into a
museum and spend two hours in one room, or
even one corner of a room, before leaving,
satisfied. Your mother, on the other hand,
couldn't see enough quickly enough. "Don't
you want to read any of the labels?" I once
asked her. "I don't need to be told what I'm

seeing now, do I?" she replied. Occasionally, she would swipe her hand through the air, delicate movements to and fro, as if to imagine the artist's strokes. But on one particular day, she got stuck. We were at the Museum of Modern Art, and she was standing in front of a painting by Giorgio de Chirico called *The Enigma of a Day*. I couldn't understand how, after all the spectacular art we'd seen, this unremarkable painting would stop her in her tracks, but there she stood, transfixed. "I don't like it," she said. "Well then, let's press on," I urged. But she didn't move. "I don't like this edge," she said. I wasn't sure if she meant the edge of the long row of shadowed arches, or the edge of the strange coffin-like box, or the edge of what seemed like the world. "I just want to understand what's beyond," she said, and then I understood, and went quiet at her side.

She was in better spirits that night, eating raspberries by the handful when she announced, "I want to paint!" So, the next day while she was napping, I went out and bought her an artist's kit of watercolor, acrylic, and oil paints, along with charcoals and pencils, an easel, watercolor paper, and canvases of varying sizes. When she woke up and saw the easel set up for her, she cried, "You're so good to me." And then I started to cry, because I wasn't. I wasn't good at all.

Release me at the south fork of the Crow
River in Cosmos, Minnesota.
    Your next stop: Post Office, Ear Falls,
Ontario, Canada.

                              Yours,
                              Essie

"Canada?" Leah said, with growing concern about how far this spiral would go. She pushed the letter back into the envelope and pressed her forehead to the steering wheel. She bit into it with her teeth. How wonderful for her mother, she thought, gallivanting around New York City, taking in the museums, while her daughter sat waiting, right where she had left her.

For years she'd imagined the day her mother would finally step out from the dark magic box, opening the front door of Edward Murphy's house with the gusto of a stage queen, as if she'd never been gone at all. She had meant to come back sooner, she would explain, but she had been kidnapped by a cadre of bandits and forced to entertain them with magic tricks. She would confess that she had also suffered an unfortunate fall from a mechanical bull and, in her amnesia, could only remember one thing: that she was trying to find her daughter Leah.

In the meantime, Leah had tried to find her, too. She called directory assistance on Edward's phone so many times that he locked it in a cabinet until she promised to stop, which turned out to be a relief for her. "I'm sorry," the operators had said in that impersonal, faraway tone, "but I'm not finding a Jeannie Starr." Without a direct line, Leah tried to communicate in other ways. She looked up at the moon and imagined her mother looking up at the same moon.

She sneezed and imagined her molecules traveling through the air, winding their way through valleys and over hills to wherever her mother, poor amnesic kidnapped magician, was at that moment, inhaling those same molecules. Every time she picked a dandelion, she imagined the earth beneath her mother stirring a little. She thumped sentences into the ground like an elephant: *Where are you? Come back.* And when her school got a small computer lab, she searched there, too, but always came up without a clue as to where Jeannie Starr, or the rest of the Blazing Calyx, had gone.

LEAH LEFT THE Cosmos post office and drove to the South Fork Crow River, where she pulled off the road and finished inspecting the newest envelope. She thought it odd that Essie was telling her the stories of each place belatedly, but she actually preferred having the chance to imagine what the women had done before Essie's next installment revealed the particulars. It was like predicting what's going to happen in a novel or a movie. Here at this river, for instance, had the witches waded into the moonlit water? Had they put yellow candles into small paper boats and watch the current carry them away? Had Essie whispered something in Claire's ear?

Leah took the transparency from the envelope—an abstract pattern in black and white that, with a closer look, revealed a robed figure carrying a miniature replica of itself. "The ice," Leah said, recognizing one of Essie's hidden worlds. "Ice god." And then she said it again because she liked the sound of it.

The final thing in the envelope was Linda's palm-sized painting of a moonlit sea, the last of the sigils the women had given to each other on their first ceremony together. The paint had a thick, textured feel, and the light on the water truly appeared to shimmer. Leah thought about how far these five gifts had traveled to be reunited, and how close she'd come to missing them.

Leah stashed everything inside her expanding backpack and shouldered it all down to the river. With the exception of a few small eddies, the turbid water was nearly still. She plunged her hand in, and the cold clenched back. *Let me find a tadpole*, she wished on her now-submerged magic ring as she grasped aimlessly in the brackishness, but all she brought up was algae. "Okay, Essie East," she said, drying her hand on the front of her jeans. "You want a send-off in Cosmos? You've got it." With that she drove back to the post office and got directions to a hardware store.

IN THE FAR-OFF of Minnesota, alongside a thawing field, near a slender, pokey river, in the flatbed of a black 1985 Ford pickup truck, a black-haired girl wearing black jeans with a black stone crow in the front right pocket was steady at work. The sun leaned on her shoulders and sweat trickled down her neck as she taped pieces of aluminum flashing to a four-foot-by-three-inch PVC cylinder. She took her time, making sure the clear packing tape went on smoothly and evenly before she glued an adapter onto the bottom. She flipped the pipe over and glued on a cap. It had been years since she'd followed these steps, but she remembered well those days in Edward Murphy's backyard, before the birds came, when she'd experimented with potions and with flight.

Onto the top of the cap, she glued half of a yellow plastic egg, and as she waited for the glue to dry, she used a black permanent marker to adorn the sides of the cylinder with bats and, in small print, the words PROPERTY OF EDWARD MURPHY, stopping periodically to enjoy a Peep from her newly stocked supply. Thanks to the helpful post office staff, she knew to drive south from Cosmos to a town called Bird Island, which boasted not only a hardware store but also a market that was still well supplied with leftover Easter candy and empty plastic eggs.

She sat in the flatbed and leaned up against the cab of her truck, periodically squinting up at the sky while the obelisk shone beside her. Touching each jeweled flower with her fingertip, she began to count out loud, her voice crystalline and ethereal, as if the stones themselves had birthed it. There were thirteen flowers in all. Each had a center stone and between seven and nine petals. "One hundred and eight," she announced, delighted to discover that the sum led back to the witches' moons, and also her favorite number, nine.

She had loved the number nine for as long as she could remember, even before she learned that nine always leads back to itself: multiply nine by any number, then add the digits, and you get nine: $9 \times 9 = 81$; $8 + 1 = 9$. She found the number pleasing to the eye and a joy to write, both from top to bottom and bottom to top. And she appreciated the feeling of completeness in its triplication of the triple. But now she realized something else about the number nine: it was a spiral.

She looked out at the fallow fields, a pale amber patched with snow. The day was drenched in golden light and the promise of spring, everything almost ready to erupt.

TWENTY-THREE

BLAZING CALYX CARNIVAL, 1984

LEAH'S MOTHER USED two animals in her performances. One was a floppy-eared bunny named Horatio, whom she pulled, in the standard way, out of a top hat. The other was a canary named Chipper, who flapped into being from Jeannie's wands of fire. Horatio always let Leah play with his ears, while Chipper liked to sit on her shoulder and pull invisible things from her hair. Leah was in charge of feeding them, a job for which she'd zealously volunteered. Every morning before she ate her own breakfast, she gave them theirs.

The only times Leah could remember being at odds with her mother was when they ran out of bird food or rabbit food. An all too regular occurrence, it usually went something like this:

Leah: "We're out of food again. Both this time."

Jeannie: "Just give them some carnival food like you usually do. Put a little hair on their chests."

Leah: "They don't need hair on their chests. They need food."

One night, Hank was privy to one such conversation. He and Leah's mother were slouched on the bed, passing a joint back and forth. Leah disliked it when they smoked because her mother went someplace far away from her, but what she disliked even more was when Hank spoke. "What Horatio needs is a little *hare* on his chest. Get it? A *hare!*" He and Leah's mother started guffawing like apes.

"It's not funny," said Leah, dropping a piece of stale funnel cake into Horatio's cage.

"What did you say?" asked Hank.

Leah ignored him and held a piece of funnel cake up to Chipper's beak, while Horatio chomped through his in record time.

Hank kept on her. "Go ahead. Tell me a joke, since you're a goddamned expert on what's funny."

"Tell him the one about the man who threw the clock out the window!" said Jeannie.

Leah looked not at her mother but at Hank, his greasy skin, his moustache, his slicked-back hair. "He died a painful and horrible death."

In that instant, something flared in his eyes that made her look away.

"Oh c'mon," Jeannie insisted, "that's not how it goes! He wanted to see time fly!" She started giggling and nudging Hank. "Time fly, honey!"

Hank nuzzled his face into Jeannie's neck. "I'm going to make time fly for you tonight," he said, and she broke into another laughing fit.

Meanwhile, Chipper was refusing the funnel cake. "He won't eat," Leah huffed. "He needs *real* bird food."

"Aww, don't be so serious all the time," Hank said, feigning chumminess. "I know how to help the little guy eat." He stood up and moved toward Leah as he took a long hit off the joint. Instinctively, Leah dropped the cake and closed the door to Chipper's cage, putting herself between Hank and Chipper.

But Hank crouched down beside Leah and blew a long stream of smoke at the small yellow bird. "Leave him alone!" Leah yelled. But the smoke kept coming until Chipper stuttered on his perch and fell. "Chipper!" she called. But it was too late.

TWENTY-FOUR

HILDA, SOUTH CAROLINA,

THE YEAR OF BIRDS, 1989-1990

AFTER LEAH ASKED Edward Murphy if he saw all the parrots flocking around Hilda, the birds didn't stop. Everywhere she looked there were more birds than she could count. So astonished was she by their varied beauty and their extraordinary powers of flight that she began researching them in the library after school. And Edward was the sole recipient, as he had also been of her many stories through the five years she'd been living with him, of everything she learned about birds. "That's a mighty long way," he said, when she told him that the Arctic tern flies the equivalent of more than four trips to the moon in a lifetime. "Isn't that interesting," he said, when she told him that birds get drunk on fermented berries. "Hmmm," he said, when she told him that a mother bird will spend days looking for a missing baby. "Is that so?" he asked, when she told him about the vampire finch, a small gray bird that pecks holes in the flesh of other birds and drinks their blood. She told him about the lyrebird, which can imitate any sound, even the sound of the chainsaws cutting down their habitat. She told him that some of the notes that starlings sing are too high for humans to hear, that crows are smarter than some kids, and that birds are the

only animals to have fused collarbones—wishbones. And as a seemingly endless colony of birds alighted on Hilda and into their every
conversation, he stood by patiently, half listening and half thinking
any number of unknowable thoughts. But what he heard next stopped
him in his tracks.

"I think we have a leak."

Leah had arrived in the doorway to the den without a sound,
as she often did, causing him to let out a quick startled grunt before shifting his eyes back to the local newspaper, crinkling it in his
hands as he looked down through his reading glasses. "Bathroom
faucet dripping again?"

"No, I mean, a hole."

"A hole?" He put his newspaper and glasses down on the coffee
table. "In what?"

"The house."

"Where?"

"I don't know."

"Then what makes you think there's a hole?"

"The birds."

"Oh no," he said, shaking his head adamantly. "Not the birds
again."

"They're in the house."

He scratched the whiskers on his chin. "They are, are they? Where?"

Leah gave the room a once-over and smiled, fixing her mega-
watt glacier-blue gaze on him. "Everywhere."

AT FIRST IT started with distances, with diffidence. The birds
appeared only at the far end of whatever room of the house Leah was

in, disappearing behind a doorway the second she turned her sight to them. While many people would have been disquieted by such sightings, Leah followed the birds, darting after them each time, turning all the corners they turned, only to find no trace. "Where are you hiding?" she called out, whistling to them, opening closet doors, peering behind furniture, under her bed. "It's okay. I'm your friend." But the birds didn't answer, and for days her periphery was inundated by the shy swipes of wings, brief as shooting stars.

Soon they grew bolder. On a Saturday afternoon while Edward Murphy was at the shop and Leah was sitting on the olive-green couch, forcing her way through boring homework—on this particular worksheet she had to match the shapes of the United States' original thirteen colonies to their state names—a wing flap caught her eye. She quickly turned her head, and this time the bird didn't flit behind a wall. Instead, it stayed perched in its spot on top of the ceramic rust-colored cookie jar, and, much like the scarlet tanager and the owl had, it returned her gaze. "Hi," Leah said, her voice barely more than a whisper. For fear of scaring the bird, she stayed frozen in place, her pencil stuck in the middle of Massachusetts. "Are you hungry? Do you want a cookie?"

Worried the bird would fly off like all the others and disappear through the hidden hole in the house, Leah quickly sketched it, paying close attention to its features so she could identify it when she went to the school library. Most noticeable was the brilliant red chevron adorning its chest, but she had also never seen a bird that size with such a large beak. The color of vanilla pudding, this was a beak that, in contrast to the bird's black head, was hard to miss. Turned down in the corners, it gave the bird an air of mild dissatisfaction, or possibly deep concentration, as if it were speculating about things much loftier than cookies or the shapes of states. "You probably eat walnuts," she finally blurted out. The bird fluttered off, darting through the kitchen to the back of the house, where, reliably, it vanished.

"WE'RE GOING TO need more food for these birds," Leah informed Edward Murphy when he came through the door that evening.

Normally he regarded her with a sheen in his eye, or at least a partial smile, but now the crease between his eyebrows grew even more pronounced. He pressed his palm to his forehead. "Sure, Leah," he said in a monotone as he shuffled through the kitchen and into his little den, not bothering to look back.

The television was already on when she showed up at the door and startled him anew. "Some walnuts, too, please?"

Edward Murphy nodded. "Walnuts. Check."

The television blared.

TWENTY-FIVE

AS THE SUN flooded the back of Leah's pickup truck, she noticed how the patches of snow in the field had shrunk in the hours she'd been sitting there waiting for the glue to dry. *Is there anything we don't eventually lose*, she wondered. She thought again about Essie's advice, to have the courage to love, and she realized this was one thing she hadn't lost. She still loved her mother. She still loved Edward Murphy, Her-Sweet, the Rubberband Man. She still loved Chipper. If she closed her eyes on a breeze, she could almost feel his beak rooting through her hair.

Leah packed away the urn and her array of sweets and set her backpack in the cab of her truck. Next she tested the glue on her egg-topped cylinder. It was dry. It was time.

She drove back to the part of the South Fork Crow River she'd visited earlier, and after casting a furtive glance around to make sure no one was watching, she took the obelisk back out of her backpack, decanted a small heap into the palm of her hand, screwed the top back on, and, keeping her palm flat and fingers curled around the ash, strapped the urn into the passenger-side seatbelt with her free hand. "You might want to watch this," she told Essie, stepping out of her truck. She climbed back up into the bed and deposited the ash into the plastic egg without spilling any. Then she snapped on the other half of the yellow egg.

Now she would have to move fast. She grabbed the cylinder and rested it between her legs. She pulled a yellow marshmallow Peep from her coat pocket and placed it between her teeth, then grabbed a two-liter bottle of Coke and a metal cartridge of butane. She paused to check her surroundings once more, and when she saw the street was quiet, she flipped the cylinder upside down and quickly poured in the Coke. She extracted the nozzle from her back pocket and screwed it onto the adapter she'd glued on earlier. Then it was time for the irreversible step: she injected the butane into the nozzle. She flipped the rocket back over and pulled the top off the egg one last time, and as the rocket began to tremble in her hand, she took the yellow chick from between her teeth and set it on top of Essie's ashes. That second, the rocket made a popping sound and shot straight out of her hands. How quickly it rose then, above the little river, above the little town. "To the moon!" Leah called out.

Leah kept her eye on the yellow chick until the rocket began to arc and then disappear, along with Essie's ashes, from her view. She had planned to retrieve the rocket after it landed, but a voice broke the spell. "Excuse me! Hey! Excuse me!"

A woman was speed-walking across the street toward Leah, arms swinging with purpose. "What the hell do you think you're doing?"

"I'm sorry," said Leah reflexively, and it was only then that she realized the inside of her right hand was bleeding. One of the fins must have nicked her as the rocket launched. She put her hand behind her back and rushed to the door of her truck.

"Are you fucking crazy? You could have hurt someone!"

Leah opened the door without an answer.

"Who are you?" the woman demanded.

Charon, servant to the dead.

"Answer me! Don't you know that fireworks are illegal in Minnesota? I have a good mind to call the police!"

"That was a rocket," said Leah, climbing into her truck and closing the door. And though she did regret upsetting the rigid-lipped woman who continued to yell at her from outside the closed window of her truck, there was nothing else she could do but turn the key in the ignition and push the gas pedal to the floor, sending her tires squealing down Milky Way Street.

As soon as the woman was out of view, Leah realized something: she was laughing. In that moment, the sunlight, combined with the vibrations of Leah's truck, sparked several of the gems into glittering fireballs, as though the obelisk were laughing, too.

TWENTY-SIX

BLAZING CALYX CARNIVAL, 1984

AFTER CHIPPER FELL from his perch, Jeannie hurried over. She tried to wrap her arms around Leah, but Leah wriggled away. She lifted Chipper from the floor of his cage and ran out the door. She tore through the sticky night, through the outcropping of trailers scattered at the carnival's edge, and practically threw herself into the Rubberband Man's door.

He was shirtless when he opened it, his skin pale as a mollusk. "Hey, hey, little lady. What's all the fuss?" he asked, reaching out to touch the top of her head. But Leah hadn't known how to put words to what had just happened, so she thrust her arms out and pushed Chipper into his chest. "Oh no!" he said, looking down at the limp yellow bird. "Chipper! Poor little guy." He took Chipper from her hands and kissed the top of his head and then the top of her head, and then she pressed her face into the hollow under his ribs.

"What we need is a funeral," he told her. "All beloveds need a proper send-off." He fished around his trailer until he found a blue bandana, and he wrapped Chipper inside it before handing him back to Leah, who watched as he rummaged for some kind of shovel. The best he could find was a hammer, so he put the hammer in his back pocket and took Leah's hand. He led her outside, far behind the trailers, while the carnival noise went on in the distance like an irregular heartbeat. "Here," the Rubberband Man said, coming to a standstill. He looked around. "How's this?" Leah turned her gaze to the trailer where her mother was with Hank, a few hundred feet away. Light from the windows oozed a hazy glow into the darkness. "Does your mother know what happened?"

Leah nodded.

"Do you think she'd like to be part of the funeral?"

Leah pulled Chipper more firmly into her chest. "No."

The Rubberband Man stroked the top of Leah's head. "I'm sorry, kiddo. Sometimes love gets sloppy, doesn't it?"

She shrugged and looked down at the top of the blue bandana.

"Yeah, well. I suppose it's people who get sloppy." The moonlight made his shoulders gleam like ice. "Anyhow, what do you think of this spot? That way you can always see him from your window."

She nodded, and he nodded back, and, with the claw of his hammer, he began to dig. "It's like a carving," he said, coming down hard into the earth. "We're carving the perfect place for Chipper to have his dream." He dug and dug. The moon caught the metal in flashes each time it rose from the ground, and Leah held Chipper close to her chest and wondered what his dream would be. She imagined places she had never seen—turquoise streams and trees drooping with fruit and flowers and a multicolored cotton candy sky—and she hoped that wherever Chipper went in his dream, he would always have food to eat.

The Rubberband Man stopped digging and took a moment to survey his carving. "I think that looks good and cozy. What do you think?"

Leah looked down at Chipper one last time. She adjusted the bandana so that the small dome of his head was visible and then handed him to the Rubberband Man, who carefully scooped him into his palm.

"Now, at funerals, you're supposed to give what's called a eulogy," he said, clasping both hands around Chipper. "That's where you say nice things about the person's—I mean, the *bird's* life. Do you want to say his eulogy?"

Leah shook her head and looked down at the night-black grass.

"Okay, I'll say his eulogy." He cleared his throat, once, twice, and then a third time. "We hereby lay to rest one of the finest birds ever known to earth. Chipper Fern was a canary who was as yellow as the sun, and he was also a magic bird. He was a good bird who never caused anyone any harm. Most of all, he was a loved bird. Loved by all the people who saw him and by me and by Jeannie Starr and especially by Leah Fern," the Rubberband Man's voice crackled, "who he loved back. May he rest easy. May he dream the good dream."

He held the bird up, gave him one last kiss, then held him out for Leah to do the same. "Ashes to ashes, dust to dust," he said, as he placed Chipper into the hole. And together, Leah and the Rubberband Man crouched in the moonlight and scooped their hands through the dirt until Chipper was covered and the ground was flat again.

TWENTY-SEVEN

EAR FALLS, ONTARIO, 1999

AS LEAH DROVE north through Minnesota and watched the forested landscape transition from melting snow to snow to deeper snow, which, for a Southern girl who had scarcely seen a snowflake, was a lot of snow, she wondered what Canada would be like—specifically, how cold it would be in April. In her years of studying animals, she had learned about the creatures of the cold. She knew, for example, that the Arctic woolly bear caterpillar freezes solid for the long winter and then thaws back to life in the spring. She knew that penguins huddle in a waddle for warmth and that the Canada lynx's huge fur-covered paws work like snowshoes. With only a black wool coat to protect her, she knew that, unlike these other animals, she was ill-equipped for the cold.

Though she was discovering that she possessed a natural knack for reading maps and remembering directions (she hadn't gotten lost once since she'd left Hilda), she realized, after she'd driven far enough away from Cosmos to feel she was safe from possibly being arrested, that she had also been ill-equipped for the navigation: her road atlas of the United States, Canada, and Mexico failed to include some of Ontario's more northern, less populated territories, including her next destination, Ear Falls. And when she entered the Truckers Inn to purchase a roadmap of Canada, the transaction struck her as significant, though she wasn't sure why. She had, after all, purchased a much larger road atlas in South Carolina, where she told the clerk a story about airborne harps, but carrying this slim accordioned map up into the cab of her truck felt to her like more of an emotional undertaking than a physical one (though she did feel it physically, too—the tickle in the throat, the burning behind the eyes, like crying without crying). She tried to put the feeling aside as she planned her new route and committed it to memory, but it stayed with her as she again began to travel north, into the denser forests, the lands of the sparse and of the quiet. And in those lands, the wild-eyed woman she'd encountered in Asheville pushed her way into her thoughts, as memories have a way of doing—"Cross the border when you get there," she'd directed—and it was then that Leah began to unravel the tangle of emotions the new map had brought about, or at least a thread of it, one that had something to do with thresholds, with the space of crossing over, the way a mother does when she leaves her daughter, just walks right across the threshold of the front door of a house in a tiny town, and the way a daughter does when she heads toward a border between countries to find her.

AFTER SEVERAL HOURS of driving, Leah stopped just shy of the Canadian border and found a hotel in South International Falls, where the gentleman who checked her in was kind enough to give her two Band-Aids for the slice her rocket left in her hand. "I hope you enjoyed the ride," she said to Essie as she placed her on the bedside table and flopped down onto the bed in a wave of fatigue. Like it or not, she had to admit that she felt more comfortable talking to Essie than to anyone else.

She hoisted herself off the bed and got undressed, placing her stone crow beside the urn on the nightstand. Then a strange thing happened: the hotel pen slid across the table and attached itself to the crow. Leah pulled the pen off and felt its metal clip pulling back toward the bird. "Whoa," she whispered. Awake now, she rifled through her backpack until she found the letter that described the gifts they'd given on their first ritual: *Claire carved five crows out of a black stone called magnetite—to guide us into the cosmos within* ... "*Magnetite*—of course. It's magnetic!" Leah lay back on the bed, playing with the crow and the pen, combing her memory for where she'd encountered the word before. "Magnetite," she said. "Magnetite." And as she tested the tension of the two objects, bringing them right to the point of attraction and holding them there, she repeated the word, as if it were an incantation, until she fell asleep.

THE NEXT MORNING, Leah handed the officer at the Canadian border her passport, which featured the smiling picture she'd had taken when she was planning her research trip to Cambodia. As she'd approached the border, she'd quickly thrown a sweatshirt over Essie's urn, which she'd been keeping strapped in the passenger seatbelt since her rocket escapades in Cosmos. "And what brings you to Canada this Sunday morning?" he asked. "Business or pleasure?"

A biting wind lashed through Leah's open window. "Um, pleasure," she said.

"And whereabouts are you headed?"

"Ear Falls, Ontario."

"Do you have family there? Friends?"

The question had claws that dug in deep. Leah swallowed. "A friend."

"Interesting necklace you're wearing," he said, pointing at Leah's spikes.

"You know how it is," she shrugged, beginning to feel anxious. "Artists and all."

A smile passed over his face. "My five-year-old daughter wants to be an artist."

"Ah, perhaps you've heard of my friend Linda." Leah cleared her throat. "Linda, Linda . . . *Magnetite*. She paints seascapes. She's quite famous, actually. That's who I'm going to meet. We're interested in some of Canada's smaller bodies of water—lakes and such."

"Then you've come to the right place. We have lakes galore," he said, giving her passport another look. He peered inside her truck then without returning her passport. "What do you have there?" he asked, looking past Leah to the crumpled sweatshirt covering the urn. "Buckled under the seatbelt."

Leah's stomach dropped. Suddenly nothing seemed worse than the possibility of someone taking Essie away. "Art," she said, lifting the sweatshirt to reveal the bejeweled obelisk. "I'm keeping it strapped in so that it doesn't get bumped around in my travels."

"Smart," he said, handing Leah her passport. "You wouldn't believe some of the things people try to bring in."

"I can imagine," she said, feeling her heart begin to slow.

With that, he wished Leah and her friend Linda Magnetite good luck, and Leah crossed the bridge into Canada.

As she drove north, she could see that the man was right: Ontario was rich with lakes. Ensconced by miles upon miles of dense forests—majestically towering pines, spruces, cedars, and firs shagged in snow—they, like the other lakes Leah had encountered along the way, were still frozen. "I am officially in the wilderness," she said to Essie, realizing that it had been one full week since Essie had arrived at her doorstep. "This next letter had better be worth it." She glanced down at the urn long enough to catch a celadon-colored cat's-eye stone appear to wink at her.

Leah found a rustic lodge not far from the Ear Falls post office and the next morning was already standing at the door when the clerk unlocked it for the day. But when Leah told her that she was there to pick up her general delivery mail, the young woman, who had rings on every finger and the enthusiasm of a sloth, said flatly, "We don't have that here."

Leah shifted on her feet. She was cold, glassy-eyed, stiff from days of driving. "You don't have mail here?"

"We have mail. Just not that."

Her throat tightened. "How do you know you don't have it if you don't at least look?"

Another woman emerged from the back and officiously stepped beside the young woman. "How can I help you?"

"I'm here to pick up a package for Leah Fern, general delivery," Leah nearly pleaded.

"Sure, let me go take a look. Ashley, come with me—I'll show you where we keep general delivery mail."

Leah felt herself slump forward in relief when the two women returned with Essie's unmistakable wax-sealed envelope, this one

marked with green paint and the number five. "She's new," the older
woman explained. "And general delivery mail is a rarity these days."

"So was the woman who sent it," said Leah, taking the envelope
into her hands.

July 23, 1998

Dear Leah,
When Linda's pencil marked the fourth
point on our map, I was intrigued. A place
called Cosmos? With streets called Milky
Way and Orion? When we arrived and saw the
small suburban neighborhood, I felt silly for
expecting something more. "A town can dream,"
said Claire.
That night we parked on Southern Cross
Avenue and slipped down to the Crow River.
Guided by moonlight we followed the river's
curves until we were far enough away from
civilization to feel safely out of sight. At
11:11, as we lit yellow candles, Claire's foot
touched down on something that startled her,
and she jumped and dropped her candle. "I
don't know what I thought it was," she said,
looking down at the unremarkable snow.
I didn't want to think that Claire's fallen
candle signified anything ominous. But it gave
me a bad feeling, seeing her flame go out.
"We need to reverse this," Athena said. "We
need to start over." Claire smiled in the
moonlight. "I think it's fine, really," she

said, but there was no mistaking the urgency
in Athena's voice. We blew out our candles and
walked backward, retracing our steps to the
road. Athena raised her staff as if it were
a wand. "Undo these steps from road to river.
Flame to candle, redeliver!"

Back at the water's edge, we relit our
candles. Because Claire's wick had gotten
wet, it took several tries before Athena was
able to relight hers, and once it was burning
again, we called on the spirit of the crow,
which the Romans once saw not as a symbol of
death as many others did, but one of hope, its
call (*cras*) like the Latin word for *tomorrow.*
"*Take us under your wing,*" we directed as we
clasped the crows that Claire had carved for
our initiation ceremony (we carried them with
us to every moon), "*and guide us with the
compass of your knowing.*" We circled around
her. We touched our flames to hers. We tried to
right what had fallen.

Everything we were doing was connected to
the earth, the elements, the cosmos, and with
each moon, I felt more deeply how everything
in the universe is connected. It seems that
the world isn't designed to pay attention to
such things, with its busy roads and shopping
malls, but here, in our wild, we were reminded
of our primordial selves. We were the elixirs
we drank—when we swallowed them, we swallowed
the earth; we swallowed cells from the hands

that brewed them. We were the stones we
carried—the iron in them and in our blood the
same as the iron in stars. We were the dreams
we cast up to the moon. Every flame we lit
also burned in us.

To this day, it amazes me that your mother
could swallow fire. She learned at the
carnival from a chap she called Perilous
Paul, if I'm remembering correctly. When
I asked her if she'd ever burned herself,
she confessed that in her first month of
learning, her lips were covered with blisters,
her tongue raw. "Then why'd you keep doing
it?" I asked.

She thought for a moment before she
answered. "I suppose because there was nothing
I'd ever wanted to do that I couldn't, and I
wasn't about to let fire be the first."

Your mother started painting every day after
I set up the easel. You probably won't be any
more surprised than I was to learn she was a
natural at it. She fancied the glide of the
paints, and the thickness. "Like van Gogh!" she
joked, after she finished her first canvas,
which took her weeks to create: a dark-haired
girl walking on purple flowers. "They're
kissing her feet," she explained. Then, very
quietly, she said "lily of the valley." I told
her I didn't think the flowers looked like any
lily of the valley I'd ever seen, and she said,
"I know. It's because they're not. But it's my

favourite flower to say. And saying it makes
me think of spring rain."

I didn't know it at the time, but the girl
in the painting was you. Your mother kept a
lot of secrets.

My own mother had a small apothecary in
a town called Falstone, where she offered
teas, tinctures, lozenges, salves, and odd
cigarettes. She learned herbal medicine from
her mother, who learned it from her mother in
Ireland. My father was a drunk, but at least
he was the flaccid sort.

One day a woman by the name of Beth McGovern
paid a visit to my mother. She was seeking
help for a rather delicate problem: her sex
life, or rather, her lack of it. She wanted to
know if there was anything in Mum's cabinets
that might jump-start her desire for her
husband, which had long ago waned.

Mum often chatted to me about her cases,
and eventually it became a game between us—I'd
try to guess the correct remedy based on the
person's complaint, and if I got it right, she'd
say, "You're my star!" But for Beth McGovern, I
had no answers. I was only twelve, and matters
of libido were still far from my mind.

My mother possessed considerable prowess
in the world of herbal medicine, but her
real talents lay in her intuitive abilities,
which sometimes meant knowing when people
needed active botanicals and when they simply

needed to *believe* they were taking active
botanicals. Beth McGovern, she explained,
needed a placebo. And after a week's doses of
sugar water, Beth McGovern proved her right by
finding, at long last, her libido. She found
it in bed with the men from the fire brigade,
in the back of a butcher's shop, under a church
piano with the church pianist. It seemed Beth
couldn't shag enough people—except for one,
her husband. When he found her in their own
bed with a neighbor, he strangled her. Then
he entered my mother's shop and strangled her,
too.

In court for both murders, he pleaded
temporary insanity, claiming his wife was
a tart and my mother was a witch. The court
agreed and set him free. My father couldn't
bear to attend the funeral or the trial and
instead traveled deeper into his alcoholism.

I left England eleven days later and went
to live in New York with my Aunt Sue, my
mother's only sibling. It was there that I
receded among the tides of others in a respite
of anonymity. She was a good friend to me, my
Aunt Sue—always supportive of my photography,
always steady within the quiet realm of our
shared grief. An editor for a small publishing
house, she often read passages from various
works aloud to me, and when I listened, I
liked to imagine my mother beside me, also
listening. I never saw my father again.

You can see why, at first, I wanted nothing
to do with the word *witch*. But as the five of
us entered our second trimester of moons, I
came to relish what we were doing—to *depend*
on it—and *witch* became an homage to my mother,
a deep remembrance, a thing I could inhabit,
like a home. *Let them kill me, too*, I thought,
for what could be worse than allowing my
mother's death to debilitate me with fear? Then
Beth McGovern's husband would have taken three
lives.

Of course, I didn't really want to be
killed. I wanted to shoot everything with my
camera. Suddenly the world was teeming with
images I felt compelled to capture, and, at
the age of fifty, I was alive in a way I'd
never been before, or since. I was a creatrix.
I was a witch. We all were.

And the success continued. No sooner had
I taken my photographs off the walls of the
coffee shop than I started getting gallery
shows in Baltimore and DC. *Zoom Magazine* ran
a five-page spread of my work, including a
close-up of rainbow refractions on bubbles in
a cup of coffee. Marsha Cogan, the infamous
critic who couldn't put two nice words
together on a good day, called my work "a
thought-provoking and transcendent journey
into the soul of the ordinary." Claire, on the
other hand, looked at a print of a dandelion
I'd shot and pressed it to her chest. "I love

it," she said. And there was no better success than that.

Tip my urn in Goose Bay, at the end of White Wing Road, Ear Falls, Ontario.

Your next stop: Post Office, La Sarre, Quebec, Canada.

Yours,

Essie

Leah sat in her truck in Ear Falls and stared at the road ahead, her mind a cauldron of images bubbling over each other. She saw a diorama of flowers—*tulip, bluebell, daisy, honeysuckle, black-eyed Susan, gardenia, lily of the valley—and two vacant swings, swinging.* She saw a man with his hands around a woman's throat. She saw Claire's yellow candle falling, and then she saw Chipper falling, and then she felt as if she, too, were falling, past Hank's scowling face, past a rattlesnake in the woods, past her mother, who stood sparkling on stage in her sequined bustier, head tipped back, mouth wide open to receive a wand of fire.

TWENTY-EIGHT

BLAZING CALYX CARNIVAL, 1984

ON THE NIGHT Hank killed Chipper, after the moonlit funeral with The Rubberband Man, Leah overheard Hank talking to her mother as she approached the trailer. The windows were open, as they almost always were in that Alabama field, and Leah stood in the dark and listened. "If anything, it's her fault, what happened to that damned bird," said Hank, the sound of his voice like a scrape in her ear.

"Oh, c'mon now. How do you figure?" Jeannie asked. Her voice was weary.

"The way she talked to you, damn near ordering you to get bird food? She was killing the mood. And I was just trying to lighten it up. I had no idea a little smoke would kill him."

"Yeah, well, haven't you ever heard the saying 'canary in a coal mine'?"

"That's coal, though. This was just a little reefer. Anyway, he didn't even know what hit him." He guffawed then. "*Hit* 'em, get it?"

"It's not funny, Hank. Leah was right. We should go back out and look for her."

Leah looked in the darkness toward where Chipper was still fresh in the earth.

"There's nowhere for her to go. She's probably with Her-Sweet or the Rubberband Man."

"I still want to find her."

"Listen, babe. All I'm saying is that if you don't give that girl some consequences, she'll never respect you. And you know what happens when daughters don't respect their mothers?"

Jeannie didn't answer.

"They grow up and steal their magic. And their men."

Jeannie cackled. "That's ridiculous!" But even from outside the trailer, Leah could detect the slightest catch in her voice.

"Hell, you didn't even give her any consequences when she up and left that long line at her tent to go play with some boy."

"Who can deny her that when she never plays with children?"

"Do you have any idea how much money she cost me?"

"Yeah, well how much did you pay her this week?"

"The question is how much did I pay you. Have you ever gone without since you've been with me? Anything you want, you get. Am I wrong?"

Jeannie stayed silent.

"You keep letting that kid run wild without consequences, wait and see what happens. That's all I'm saying. My daddy always gave me consequences, and look how I turned out—got a whole carnival of my own. Tonight, she finally got a consequence too. I never would have gotten up and gone over there in the first place if she hadn't been whining and being rude. But I bet she won't go ordering you to get food for that rabbit now."

"She was right to want to feed them. If anything, I'm to blame." Jeannie's voice came out as if someone had pressed it through a mill. "But I still think you owe her an apology. She loved that bird."

"What about me? Do you love me?"

There was a pause. "Of course I do."

"Well, why don't you just come show daddy some of that love right now?"

Leah thought she might throw up. Instead, she turned and ran—away from the trailers, away from the tents, away from the rides—to the far side of the carnival, where nobody ever went. Before that night, she had only spied it from a distance, a graveyard for old machinery, out-of-order games, broken pieces of rides, and in her mind, she'd taken to calling it the Isle of Forgotten Memories. As she ran toward it, the carnival dimmed and the world grew quieter, darker. She kept running, past the outer carnival lights, past the final spotlights, to where the discarded objects loomed in shadow: the sharp edge of a defunct pretzel machine, a clown face with a hole for a mouth, the rusty chains of a fallen swing. She walked deeper into the maze of abandoned parts and found a shattered mirror, an unnamable object riddled with bolts, a downed mermaid missing part of her tail. Leah spotted a cracked bumper car and climbed into it. She turned the steering wheel left and right. She stepped on the gas pedal. She didn't cry. She tilted her head back and looked up, amid all the broken things, at the stars.

A FEW DAYS later, as she walked home from her fortunetelling tent, Hank came up behind her. "Hey there."

She'd been kicking a small stone with each step and stopped at the sound of his voice.

"Aren't you going to turn around?"

Leah turned around and looked up at the rim of Hank's cowboy hat.

"Yeah, so uh, listen." Hank put his hands on his hips, down by his sides, and finally settled on crossing them over his chest. "You know, what happened with the bird. It was an accident."

"I know." She would not show him her sadness.

"Well? Aren't you gonna say you forgive me?"

"No."

Hank uncrossed his arms and stepped toward her. She did not step back. "You know what God hates? He hates someone who doesn't have forgiveness in their heart."

"I've never met God, so why should I care what he hates?"

"Because God punishes people he hates. Did you know that?"

"How?"

"How what?"

"How does he punish people he hates?"

Hank shifted on his feet, red-faced and sweaty. "He gives them plagues."

"What's a plague?"

"He'll make frogs rain down on you from the sky."

"I like frogs."

He took a strained breath and hooked his thumbs around his belt loops. "He'll put lice in your hair."

"What's lice?"

"They're disgusting little bugs that will eat your skin."

"Okay."

"What do you mean, okay?"

She shrugged. "Nothing, just okay." And she walked off, leaving Hank to stand alone.

When she got to their trailer, her mother already smelled of whiskey. Leah hated the smell but hugged her anyway. "Hank says I'm gonna get plagues."

Leah's mother rubbed her eyes and yawned. "What?"

"Frogs. And bugs in my hair."

"When did he tell you that?"

"Just now."

"Where were you?"

"On my way home."

Leah's mother turned toward the dresser and peered into the mirror, fluffing her hair, puckering her lips, examining her teeth in a smile. "What did you do to make him say you were gonna get plagues?"

"Nothing."

"Can't be nothing."

"He said I don't have forgiveness in my heart."

"Did he apologize? About Chipper?"

"I guess."

"And did you forgive him?"

"No."

"That's not very nice, now, is it?"

Leah walked over to Horatio's cage and fed him some pellets. "It wasn't very nice to let them run out of food, either, was it?" It was the first time Leah had ever spoken to her mother in that tone, and it had drawn a line between them, over which they stared at each other, silent.

WHEN THE OTHER carnival performers learned what had happened to Chipper, they wrapped Leah in their love-clutches. On a Monday night shortly after Chipper died, they gathered as they sometimes did in the back tent, where they smoked and drank and danced, and on that night, in a memorial for Chipper, they all took turns dancing with her—twirling her, dipping her, lifting her up. Someone put on Blondie's "Rapture," and the Rubberband Man began doing back flips and splits while Alexander-Alexandra was dancing the robot in a bowtie and heels and Perilous Paul was wielding a sword in the air and Dylan and Dandy the Dwarves were performing a very serious tango and Rattle the Snake Charmer was rising up from the floor not like a snake but more like a jack-in-the-box and Martulo the Legless Racer was propelling himself to the rhythm with his arms and wriggly spine and Her-Sweet was spinning under a tiny parasol and Horny the Human Reptile was standing very still except for the closing and opening of his hands and Magson the Giant was bending in angles like a series of lightning bolts and Jeannie Starr was gyrating her hips and Leah was bopping about in the center of it all, pretending her right arm was the trunk of a baby elephant. But even in the middle of the music, enfolded by the people she loved, she never lost sight of Hank, who stood in the corner of the tent, not dancing. And though she couldn't see his eyes, which were hidden in the shadow of his cowboy hat, she knew he was looking at her.

LEAH BEGAN SPENDING what little time off she had with the Rubberband Man, either in his trailer, poking through his ephemera—strange gadgets including typewriter parts, cranks, hooks, a collection of Matchbox cars with doors that opened and steering wheels that turned, and stacks of old magazines, the covers of which featured either a red-headed man with a missing tooth and big ears or naked women—or in his performance tent. The first time she saw his act, it shocked her speechless. "We are the beasts," he said, as he connected several chains to hooks pierced in his back and was lifted into the air, arms spread, eyes gleaming. "We are the dark birds of your dreams."

Later, Leah asked him if it hurt to fly like that, with all those hooks in his back.

"Sometimes," he answered. "But when it hurts, I tell myself it's just pain, and then it's okay somehow—kind of good even. Besides, there are worse things than pain."

They were eating soft pretzels on the front steps of his trailer on their shared day off. "What's worse than pain?" she asked.

"No pain."

Leah looked into his eyes and waited for more, because, as she'd learned with the Rubberband Man, there was always more.

"Pain is just the backside of pleasure." He gave her arm a little pinch. "Pain just means you're alive."

TWENTY-NINE

THUNDER BAY, ONTARIO, 1999

LEAH DROVE WITH her stereo off—an unusual silence—for the eight-minute drive from the Ear Falls post office to White Wing Road. On the seat between her and Essie was envelope number five, brushed with a single streak of green paint. She wasn't thinking of the transparency Essie had included in this envelope—a photograph of a woman from behind, walking toward the sun. And she wasn't thinking about the other two things Essie had enclosed—a crow feather and an intricate silver box with an odd elephant embossed onto the top of it. She wasn't thinking of her mother or of the painting she'd made or of Essie's mother. She wasn't thinking of anything. Instead, almost as if by necessity, she let her mind go blank as a field of snow.

She plodded out to Goose Bay, her boots once again filling with snow, the cold penetrating quickly, tapping at her bones. In the realm of remote and frozen water bodies, she had come to expect an accompanying desolation, which did not make her feel lonely—for it had been around other people that she had felt the loneliest—but rather a sense of relief, a salve of respite for her manifold empathic antennae, so she was surprised to find a man pulling a tiny lemon-colored hut across the ice on a sled. She stood at the edge, knowing there was no way to escape the coming interaction unless she turned and went back to her truck. She was curious about the tiny hut, but she was also keenly aware that not all people take kindly to a girl with spikes and a partially shaven head. There was no one else in view, no other sound but the scratching of the man's sled on the ice. He had a pleasant face with a short dark beard, and Leah detected an ease about him that put her at ease too.

"Fishing today?" he asked, stopping about twenty feet shy of where she stood. He had a burly build and didn't appear winded from pulling the weight.

She gave a small wave and smiled politely at what she thought was a joke.

"Caught three huge walleyes this morning. Nice way to close out the season."

"You caught fish? Through the ice?"

He smiled. "I take it you're not from around here?"

"You mean earth? Sometimes I wonder."

The man laughed. "Haven't you ever heard of ice fishing before?"

"Actually, now that you mention it, I think I saw it in a movie once."

"*Grumpy Old Men?*"

"Yes, that's the one."

"That's always the one."

"I hardly remember it."

It seemed they had run out of small talk—or at least, that's what Leah hoped as she started to get that anxious, claustrophobic feeling that came whenever she found herself in a small talk situation—but then he carried the conversation forward. "I'm the last one off the ice. Everyone else left yesterday morning. Had a whole little village here. Mostly not grumpy."

They both laughed a little.

"How was it?" she asked. "Having it all to yourself for a day?"

"It was nice. Peaceful. I spent the night, too. With that little sliver of moon, the stars were just too bright to leave."

"You weren't cold?"

"Not with my little ice shanty and a propane heater."

"Ah, you came prepared. It sounds . . ." Leah thought for a moment about what word to use. It bothered her sometimes to use the expected word, a generic word like *lovely*, for instance, which was the word she almost said. "Entrancing."

"Yes. Yes. Entrancing."

They stood for a moment in the bubble their words had made around them, a pause that felt natural, like at the end of an exhalation, and then the man started forward again, his rubber boots breaking the bubble, his shanty, a word Leah found charming, scratching the ice as it tagged along behind him, and she could feel that their conversation had already become a history, that they were two people now in silence, sharing a history, not needing another word. After he had pulled his shanty onto the snow and put it on a trailer hitched to the back of a truck and driven away, Leah followed his sled tracks out onto the ice. She took some of Essie into her palm, and, with a growing feeling of tenderness, she spilled her into the fishing hole.

BACK IN HER truck, Leah sat for a long time with the engine running, the heat blowing on high, her boots off, socks drying, and stared out at the frozen world, not focusing on any particular thing.

Eventually her feet began to warm, and something in her began to thaw, and she began to feel, under the layers of cold, a painful weight she recognized as sadness. This, of course, was not a new state of being for Leah, but it came on with the intensity—that acute ache—of a frostbitten appendage stuck suddenly under a faucet. The sadness, like the land around her, was vast and, in some ways, unknowable, though aspects of it were easy for her to identify, such as her sadness for Essie and for Essie's mother, whose brutal end was, if she allowed herself to dwell on it for even a short amount of time, enough to immobilize her. There was sadness for her own mother, who had lost her way. And there was sadness for Edward Murphy, who died without her ever telling him how much he had meant to her. If she could go back, she would tell him not to wait his whole life for a woman who would never return. She would tell him to let himself be loved—by anything and everything, by Martha-Up-the-Street and her tomato-heavy vines.

Leah removed the silver box from the newest envelope and examined the strange four-armed elephant. One of his tusks was broken, and a crescent moon was etched onto his third eye. He wore a crown and in his two left hands he held a lotus and a cluster of grapes. His lower right hand was turned outward, palm flat, and his upper right hand held an axe. She lifted the little latch on the side of the box and took out what she had only glanced at earlier: a silver ball attached to a silver chain. She gave it a little shake, and it chimed as it swung through the air, raining bits of lavender from small diamond cutouts. She sniffed the sweet herbaceous scent and then returned the ball to its elephant box. "What do you know about elephants?" she asked Essie's obelisk. But even the liveliest stones seemed dull that day, as if the cold had entered them, too.

By the heat of her truck vents, Leah took another look at the transparency, which to date was the only color photo Essie had given her. In it, a fair-haired woman is shown from behind, though it appears she's on the cusp of turning around. Sunlit strands of her hair ribbon out on a breeze, and her left sandal strap hangs low on her slender ankle. She's wearing a ruffled white top and a long gauzy skirt. "Claire," Leah said, remembering the long diaphanous skirt her mother had once worn.

Leah double-checked her next destination—Post Office, La Sarre, Quebec, Canada—before she tucked everything back into the envelope and consulted her new map. "Super," she said, upon realizing that La Sarre was approximately nine hundred miles away and that her journey was expanding exponentially with each new stop. "Just super." She put her socks back on. She laced up her boots. She buckled Essie back into her seat. Then she piloted her pickup truck, which was now warm and redolent of lavender, back onto the road.

WHEN THE QUESTIONS are quieted and the mulling abates, when a driver commits to the road, the driver and the road can form an easy alliance. The road calls the driver forth into a perpetual merging of tenses, future becoming present, becoming present. The road unfurls its stories in the language of landscape—stories of the earth told in water, rock, and dirt; stories of human desire told in the language of tar and bridges and streetlights; stories of loss told in the language of plastic flowers and white wooden crosses; while stories of ascension are told across the canvas of the sky. The driver, too, is a landscape. She wears her stories around her neck, in her pockets, in her cells. She carries them in vessels large and small. But sometimes, when the road and driver stretch on in easy unity, all the stories go, for a moment, quiet.

SIX HOURS, TWELVE Jordan almonds, three yellow Peeps, countless tamaracks and balsam firs and jack pines after Leah left Ear Falls, she arrived with the crescent moon on the edge of Thunder Bay, a vibrant city situated on Lake Superior, opposite Madeline Island—her resting point between White Wing Road and a nameless spot on another border between two lands.

Leah parked on the side of a street and watched the city. She hadn't seen many people since she'd stopped in Asheville, and here they seemed so full of life, wearing their scarves, walking briskly beneath the street lights, gesticulating, laughing, regarding each other and their surroundings with wide eyes and flushed cheeks. As she watched them, she felt more like a ghost than a person who could move among them, confiding in a friend in the nippy air, kissing a lover on the street corner, brushing against a stranger without recoiling. "It's just you and me," Leah said to Essie, patting the wooden top of the obelisk.

She drove through the city and found a hotel, and also a library. She had spent so many of her life's hours in libraries, where she'd discovered answers to her questions and more questions to her answers, where she'd found friends in ancient tales and dreams in secluded coves, where she'd first looked up a word Her-Sweet had given her years earlier: *empath*. All she'd found then were a few scant references to empaths as inventions of science fiction, and if empaths weren't real, she'd wondered, was she?

When she was in seventh grade, she'd found a book that had obviously been mis-shelved: *Clairsentience, Clairaudience, Clairvoyance, and the Empath: What You Know Before You Know*. She had been in the marine biology section looking for information about the proliferation of coral reefs when she saw the mermaid-green spine. "Empaths are rare," began the eponymous chapter, "but very much among us." Until that day, the library, like the House of Tricks Treats and Creatures, had been a place of wonder, a place where anything was possible. Only in the library could Leah trace the name of a bone (*pterion*) to the wing of a god (Hermes) in the seamless turn of a page, or move from the Antarctic Weddell seal to the Arctic harp seal in the reach of an arm, but on that day, the library had become something more: the one place where she could begin, at last, to understand what she was—"empaths often desire to be away from crowds, preferring instead a haven of solitude"—where she could begin to feel, if nothing else, real.

SHE ROSE EARLY the next day, grabbed a couple of pastries from the hotel's complimentary breakfast and a few brochures from the lobby before setting back out into the city. The sidewalks that Tuesday morning were still quiet, but as Leah walked, she pretended to be one of the people she'd seen the night before—just an ordinary girl leafing through some brochures, dropping blueberry muffin crumbs along the way. She learned from the brochures that the city's flag boasts the Sleeping Giant, a looming mesa formation across the water, and that the city's emblem is a thunderbird. "Of course it is," she said aloud, as if to a friend walking beside her.

When she arrived at the library, it was closed. She was hoping to learn more about witchcraft and to identify the strange elephant Essie had given her—and, if there was time, to revisit the subject of empaths—but mostly she wanted to be in a place that felt familiar, one that had always been a haven for her. The sign informed her that the doors would open at 10:00 a.m., and it was just before 8:00 a.m., so she set off walking, and as people began to appear on the sidewalks, entering and exiting shops, walking dogs, sipping coffee, Leah's thoughts turned again to Bob O'Malley. Was he there now, she wondered, sitting in his green Oldsmobile on the other side of this thawing Great Lake? Was Brenda Wright behind her red door, jingling through her funhouse? Did she sometimes look out in Bob's direction, too?

AT 10:00 A.M. exactly, Leah entered the library, and at 10:01, the rush of being in a library had its usual effect on her: she had to pee. She approached the information desk, where a lanky young man with dark uncombed hair and a quality that hovered between awkward and ethereal greeted her, his voice soft but intent. "Good morning."

"Good morning," she said. "Could you tell me where the rest-rooms are?"

He lifted one lean arm and pointed. "Just down the stairs, near Fiction and Young Adult."

"Thanks."

"I'm Brian." She'd already turned toward the stairs and had to turn back to see if he'd meant that for her. "In case you need anything."

"Oh," she said, pushing her hands into her coat pockets, "okay, thanks."

"But my friends call me Blade."

Leah didn't know why he thought she needed to know this, but it made her smile. "Good to know."

LEAH PLACED HER backpack onto a small desk facing a window that overlooked Thunder Bay and began with a single word: *witch*. Most of what she'd known of witches had come from her earliest impressions—the stories of winged witches told by the Puppet Beasts, the Wicked Witch from *The Wizard of Oz*, the craggy black cutouts of witches tacked to windows each Halloween. The *Oxford English Dictionary* offered another view: "a female magician, sorceress; a woman supposed to have dealings with the devil or evil spirits and by their operation to perform supernatural acts." She thought of her mother and wondered why a female magician was called a witch, while a male magician was simply called a magician.

According to other sources, however, the *Oxford English Dictionary* had it wrong: magic has nothing to do with the supernatural, and witches have nothing to do with the devil. *What is a witch? A shaman? A small fleck of light you never saw?* Essie's voice trailed through her mind. Depending on the book she opened, a witch might be a beautiful seductress, a wretched crone, a healer, a guardian of the earth, a polytheist, an animist, an artist, a feminist, a naturalist, an ecologist, a Jungian archetypalist, an herbalist, an aromatherapist, a mythologist, a ritualist, a necromancer, a spellcaster. Some are lone practitioners, while others participate in covens, sometimes in large organizations and sometimes in small homegrown groups with as few as three. Some covens are assembled around a high priestess and priest, while others are all female. But almost universally, covens are led by women. And almost all witches, whether practicing in covens or alone, are guided by and in relationship with the natural world. They use amulets, herbs, candles, tarot cards, brews, crystals, daggers, chalices, wands, salt, poems, and, yes, even brooms to celebrate, honor, and invoke almost everything imaginable. But whatever ways a witch identifies with her craft, she usually keeps it secret.

Leah had already learned some of this from Essie's letters, but now she saw how she could spend years studying the myriad incarnations of witchcraft all over the world, not to mention the history of witch hunts, which spanned centuries. Overwhelmed, Leah remembered something Essie had written in one of her letters: *We're a people of ritual, of symbolism . . . We make wishes upon birthday candles and stars . . .* And she wondered then if maybe, if one peeled away the many books and definitions, the many interpretations and expressions, they'd find a single tribe of people who shared a simple impulse: to believe in magic.

Leah took the strange elephant box from her backpack and placed it on the table. As she examined it, she started jotting down words—*elephant with grapes, lotus, broken tusk*—but a voice came from behind her and interrupted. "What are you researching?"

Startled, she cupped her hand over the elephant and turned around accusingly to find Blade cradling a stack of books in his left arm. "I'm sorry," she said, "but I'm kind of busy right now."

Blade shifted the stack of books to his right side but didn't move from his spot. And though she found his quiet insistence annoying, there was something about the clear-eyed eagerness with which he appraised her that softened her a little.

"Do you always interrupt people when they're studying?" she asked.

"Not usually."

"Then what's so special about now?"

"I don't exactly know."

"Great."

"My curiosity got the better of me, I suppose."

"Well, I'm sorry to disappoint you, but I actually have no idea what I'm researching."

"I see you have Ganesha there."

"Pardon?"

"Under your hand."

Leah lifted her hand from the elephant box. "What did you call it?"

"Ganesha."

"What's Ganesha?"

Blade put the books he was carrying down on her table. "A god." He leaned in for a closer look. "Wow, that's really cool."

"A god?"

"He's the Hindu god of wisdom and new beginnings. But he's probably best known for being a remover of obstacles." Blade touched the silver grapes in Ganesha's hand. "He also has a taste for sweets."

"He's not the only one," she said, suddenly craving chocolate. "How do you know all this?"

Blade shrugged nonchalantly. "I'm a librarian. What do you think I do all day?"

"Fair enough."

"Hey, would you like to have lunch with me?"

Leah scooted her chair back. "Excuse me?"

"I'm getting off soon, and I'd like to take you to lunch."

"Oh, I'm sorry," said Leah. "I—I just—"

Blade gave a knowing nod. "It's okay. Good luck with your research."

Just before he was about to turn out of her sight, Leah found that one syllable. "Yes."

Blade pivoted back toward her. "Yes?"

"Yes, I'll have lunch with you."

THE WIND CLIPPED the top of the Kaministiquia River and whisked up small white peaks. Persistent seagulls traced the sky, squawking. Leah's eyes watered in the cold. Blade walked next to her, looking younger in the sun than he had under the library lights. "How old are you, anyway?" she asked him. She was eating a vegetable panini as they walked. He had already finished his.

"Guess."

"Twelve."

"Very funny. But you're right."

"What?"

"Just reverse the numbers."

"So we're both twenty-one."

"Legal, baby."

"I thought you were a librarian. Don't you need a master's degree for that?"

"I'm a librarian in training. I finish my master's next month. Graduated from high school when I was fifteen, so, you do the math."

"Was it strange, being in college so young?"

"Strange? If you mean, was I a nervous, friendless reject who faked anaphylactic shock to get out of giving a presentation in a sociology class, then no, it wasn't strange at all."

Leah laughed. "Yeah, I hear you. It wasn't strange for me either." She took a bite of her panini. "I once thought about becoming a librarian."

"Why didn't you?"

"I went to school to become a biologist."

"Is that what you do now?"

Leah looked away and watched the river glint like metal. "No, I don't do that anymore."

"What *do* you do?"

She tried to think of a story she could tell, but all she could come up with was the truth. "At the moment, I'm driving around scattering the ashes of a woman I hardly knew."

Blade paused with his mouth open, as if he were trying to decide which of many questions he would ask. Leah took the opportunity to change the subject.

"Why do people call you Blade?"

"Why are you scattering the ashes of a woman you hardly knew?"

"Why'd you become a librarian?"

"Why'd you say yes?"

"Pardon me?"

Blade stopped walking, so Leah stopped as well. "To lunch. Why'd you say yes to lunch?"

Leah thought for a moment. "Because Ganesha removed my obstacle."

Blade smiled. "Of course," he said. "I should have known that."

"Yeah, you're slacking."

They resumed their walk along the river, the wind lapping against them, both of them still carrying the remnants of a smile. For a long time, they were quiet, and Leah was grateful to Blade for letting the small beats of the afternoon unfold without the clatter of small talk. It was she who broke the silence. "The thunderbird!" She ran ahead to a silver winged sculpture. "I saw it in a brochure this morning."

"Animikii," said Blade, as he caught up with her.

Leah peered up at its towering height. "I didn't realize it was so big."

"Yeah," said Blade proudly, as if he'd sculpted it himself. "Legend has it that thunderbirds could shapeshift and take human form. They married humans and had hybrid children."

"Could the children fly, too?"

"The children didn't know they were hybrids, so they never tried."

Leah contemplated the sculpture's skyward wing. "Sometimes I try."

"To fly?"

Leah thought about whether she should continue. Then she thought of her regret over what hadn't said to Isabelle. "I keep thinking it'll be how it is in dreams—you know, when you just lift off and then you're in the sky, gliding over everything?"

Blade looked at her, a deep look with the hooks of questions attached to it, and she could feel his yearning, like a naked thing she wanted to cover. "You have beautiful eyes," he said.

She nervously took a large bite of her sandwich and, chewing, shook her head no.

"I know. You probably hear that all the time. But it doesn't make it any less true."

She trained her sight back on the river. A seagull complained overhead. A car horn sounded in the distance. "Thank you," she finally said, turning toward him. "Thank you for everything, but I really should get back."

Now Blade stared out at the river, past her. "I knew I shouldn't have said that. It's cliché, right?"

"No, it's not—"

"Believe it or not, I don't talk to girls that much. But for some reason, you're different." He shrugged again. "I don't know why, but you made me feel brave."

Leah felt something fold shut inside her.

He took a step toward her. "May I kiss you?" He began to lean toward her, but she stopped him with a panini to the chest.

"No. I don't—"

"I understand," he said, stepping back. "I'm sorry."

In silence, they picked up their pace again, and nobody said anything until the library was in view. It was Leah who spoke then. "I can put my hands on you."

"What?" he said, visibly alarmed.

"No, not like that," she corrected. "I can *feel* people. If I touch you, I can tell you what you are." What she didn't tell him was that she didn't need to put her hands on him to know things, that she could already hear his secrets, that her offer had as much to do with her as it did with him.

"What I *am*? Don't I already know what I am?"

Flustered, Leah shook her head. "No. That's not what I meant. I mean, I can tell you things you don't know."

Blade considered this for a moment, stretching his long arms up as if he were attempting to pick an apple just out of reach. "Maybe if there are things I don't know about myself," he said, letting his arms drop, "there's a reason I don't know them."

Leah had never considered that possibility—that given the chance to know something, one would decline. "You're a librarian," she said. "The whole point is to know things."

"True. But that doesn't mean that everything can be, or should be, known."

Leah smiled. "You're right," she said. And the two of them re-entered the land of books and knowledge without so much as their coat sleeves touching.

THIRTY

HILDA, SOUTH CAROLINA, THE YEAR OF BIRDS, 1989–1990

THE BIRD THAT perched on the rust-colored ceramic cookie jar on Edward Murphy's counter while Leah was doing her homework was a rose-breasted grosbeak. Operatic singers with sturdy triangular beaks, they build their nests at the edges of woodlands, where they forage for insects, seeds, and berries. Leah learned this in the library, where she'd been pulling book after book from the shelves to find out all she could about the birds that were congregating on car roofs and mailboxes and chimneys, the ones that were dicing up the sky and getting in through the hidden hole in the house.

True to his word, Edward Murphy brought home the walnuts Leah had asked for, and she sat on the olive-green sofa with a nutcracker and opened them all. "That's quite a mess you've got there," he said, referring to the scores of shell pieces blanketing the floor and the sofa. "It's even in your hair." Leah shook her head, and a few fragments fell to the floor. It would be many months before she would chop off her hair and start shaving the side of her head. For now, her black tresses flowed halfway down her back. At eleven, her face was beginning to slim and take on a more angled, feral beauty.

"Sorry," she said. "I'll clean it up." She picked up the bowl and held it out toward Edward Murphy. "Want one?"

"Sure," he said, plunking his fingers into the bowl. "One nut deserves another."

Leah put the bowl back on the table. "I learned yesterday that rose-breasted grosbeaks only eat seeds, not nuts. So they probably won't eat these after all. But you know who does eat nuts?"

"Hmm, let me guess." He scratched his chin, pondering. "Little Leah Ferns?"

"Nuthatches! And also woodpeckers and wrens and chickadees. And magpies. We've been getting a lot of magpies in the house lately."

Edward Murphy's smile wilted. He sat down beside Leah, sending a few more shell fragments to the floor, and pressed his fingertips to his temples as he let out a long sigh. "Do you remember that time when you said I shouldn't say I believe you—you know, about the birds—if I don't?"

"Yes."

"Well, you were right. It's just—Leah, I don't see these birds. No magpies in the house, no parrots on the wires, no owls standing in the grass. I just see regular birds, the birds that are always here."

"Oh, Eddie Murphy," said Leah. "It's okay. They're just shy." She patted the sofa next to his leg as if to comfort him. "But don't worry—soon you'll see them, too."

A magpie ducked close to Edward Murphy's head, and Leah couldn't help but giggle.

AT NIGHT THEY came to her. Only then did they let her touch them. They found her in sleep and flooded her bed. They filled her hands, which she wrapped softly around them as they fluttered over her, one after another after another. They always came in a rush, the way flocks descend upon trees before they lift off again, a single susurrating body. They drew their wings against her forehead and feet. They nestled into her neck—silk in motion, tiny heartbeats. They peered into her with keen eyes while she purred and closed her own. Even with her eyes closed, their vivid colors penetrated. She was not a girl. She was crimson and emerald. She was cerulean. She was yellow as the sun. They smoothed against her, giving her everything, silent save for the flickering feathers.

"LEAH, THIS IS Dr. Stern." Edward Murphy and Leah had entered a beige building, where a tall thin-haired man held out his hand.

Leah didn't shake it. Instead, she silently assessed the man they'd driven all the way to Columbia, South Carolina, to see. "Hello," she said flatly.

"She doesn't shake hands," Edward Murphy explained.

Dr. Stern pulled his hand back and knelt down to face Leah. "Your father thinks it would be a good idea if we had a little conversation. Is that okay, Leah, if we have a little conversation?"

"He's not my father."

Dr. Stern was visibly taken aback but quickly regained his composure. "I'm sorry. Mr. *Murphy* thinks it's a good idea for us to talk."

Leah snapped and unsnapped the button on her little daisied purse, which she'd recently begun filling with birdseed and carrying around with her wherever she went. "I know. He already told me."

"Wonderful, then," Dr. Stern said. "Right this way."

Leah followed him into an office of dark wood and leather. Edward Murphy stood in the doorway. "Did you want me to come too, or wait out here?"

"Why don't you come in to start? That might make her feel more comfortable."

"I'm not afraid of you," said Leah.

"Leah, you be polite now," said Edward Murphy, taking a seat beside her on the leather couch.

"How come whenever someone tells the truth, they're being impolite?" she asked.

"That's enough," said Edward Murphy.

"Tell me, Leah," said Dr. Stern, "do you always tell the truth?"

"I was telling the truth when I said I'm not afraid of you." She snapped and unsnapped her purse.

Leah and Dr. Stern stared at each other without speaking for several seconds.

Dr. Stern cleared his throat. "I'm here to help you," he finally said. "I want to be your friend."

"You do? Do *you* always tell the truth?"

"How old are you, Leah?"

"How old are you?"

Dr. Stern laughed. It was more of a cough, really, to which he appended a forced smile.

"Leah, please," said Edward Murphy, and she could see in his eyes how important this was to him for her to talk to this man, how pained he was with worry.

"I'm eleven," she said, leaving the snap on her purse closed.

"That a girl," said Dr. Stern. "See, we can be friends after all."

Leah discreetly pinched the inside of her arm to distract herself from telling the man what she knew about him: that he was dishonest, and only modestly intelligent.

"Now, your fa—I mean, Mr. Murphy, says you like to tell stories."

"Yes, I do."

"He says that lately you've been telling stories about birds."

"Those aren't stories."

"Okay. What are they?"

"They're birds."

"Yes. Birds. And is it true that you're seeing these birds in your house? In your kitchen and bedroom, for example?"

Leah watched two finches dancing outside his office window. "Yes."

"And what happens when you see them?"

Leah couldn't help herself. "What happens when *you* see a bird?"

"It depends. Once I spotted a bald eagle, and I was pretty excited. He was just sitting there all proud, way up in his nest." Dr. Stern looked up at the ceiling as if that was where the nest was. "What about you, Leah? How do you feel when you see birds? Do you feel excited? Happy? Afraid?"

"Did you know that humans' eyes have three cones for seeing colors but an eagle has five?"

"Well, you know the term *eagle-eyed*."

"Did you know that owls can't move their eyes?"

"No, I—"

"Did you know that a mother bird will look for a missing baby bird for days?"

"Do you want to talk about *your* mother, Leah?"

"I want to talk about birds. You asked me to talk about birds, and I'm talking about them."

"Have you ever thought that maybe the birds in your house aren't real? That maybe they're like the stories you tell?"

"Stories *are* real," said Leah. "So are the birds."

"Then why do you think Mr. Murphy can't see them?"

"Maybe because he doesn't want to see them. Besides, if they aren't real, then how am I able to draw them and look them up in the library? Birds I've never even seen before?"

"Well, Leah, the mind is a fascinating thing." He folded his hands on his desk in a practiced manner. "Every day it gets bombarded by stimuli—by things you see and hear and smell—but it remembers only a small percentage of that. It could simply be that you once saw a particular bird—in a book or on TV perhaps—but have since forgotten that you saw it, though somewhere in your mind it was recorded. And that recording is springing up now, in your imagination."

Dr. Stern continued to speak, but Leah had stopped listening. The finches had returned, carrying twigs and string for the nest they were making in the shrub outside the window. She thought of how the hummingbird decorates the outside of its nest with lichen, how the edible-nest swiftlet constructs its nest entirely with its own saliva, how the golden-headed cisticola sews its nest with its needlelike beak, how the mythological cinnamon bird builds its cliffside nest with cinnamon sticks—

"Leah? *Leah*?" the voice broke through. There was the snapping of fingers, two quick strikes. "Do you see them?" The voice was louder now. "Do you see the birds now?"

Leah closed her eyes until the voice faded again, until it was on the other side of a wall of clouds that turned everything to rain.

THIRTY-ONE

IT WAS NEARING 3:00 p.m., and the library would be closing in two hours. As Leah stacked up the books on witchcraft, magic, and mythical gods, a calm came over her, a gift from an unexpected date with a lanky librarian. Not everything can or should be known, he'd said, and it was as if his words themselves were a kind of magic that had freed Leah from her compulsion to know everything now. Sure, she had waited years to know even one single thing about what had happened to her mother—a little impatience there was understandable. But the boy had, in his earnest wisdom, opened a door for her. *The present is the present*, she thought, certain she'd heard that someplace before.

She had one more thing to do in the library: visit the computer room. As she passed by the front desk, she looked for Blade, but he was nowhere in sight and an older woman was now busy behind the counter. Feeling a pang at his absence, she took a seat at a computer, where she typed *Essie East* into the internet search bar. What she found came by way of old headlines, mostly from 1978— "Essie East Walks Out on Opening, Is Ousted from Gallery"; "Photographer or Sorceress? Essie East's Photographic Powers"; "Essie (Witch of the) East Slips into Obscurity." It came by way of a few of the photographs themselves, the ones that had won her accolades and accusations, the ones that had hung in some of the most prestigious galleries: photographs of spider webs, puddles, ice. It came by way of photo credits attached to random wedding pictures on a few mostly defunct websites—overly saturated, uninspired shots of conventional love. It came by way of a single photograph of Essie herself. In it she stands in front of an exhibit of her photographs. She's looking beyond the camera, as if something far away has caught her attention. She isn't smiling. One could say she doesn't even look happy. She's dressed unglamorously in plain slacks and a wide-collared button-down shirt, and her unkempt hair falls unevenly to her shoulders. "And you had the nerve to pick on *my* hair," Leah whispered. But there was no mistaking it: the woman in the photograph was beautiful. Fierce and unusual, it was a distant sort of beauty, like a jaguarundi right before it sprints into the brush.

Leah entered four more names into the search engine. She had searched for them many times before, but this time, she promised herself, would be the last.

As she typed *Rubberband Man* into the search engine, her heart pounded so hard that she was sure the person next to her could hear it. Her search turned up little else besides references to the song by the Spinners. Her-Sweet was next, and again, the internet turned up nothing. She even tried *bearded lady*, but none of the hirsute faces belonged to the woman who had first given her the word *infinity*. Next, she tried *Blazing Calyx Carnival* and then stared blankly at pictures of flowers.

Finally, she clenched her toes and held her breath and typed in *Jeannie Starr*. Each time she'd done this in the past, her greatest fear had been discovering that her mother had died, and this time was no different. But her search only brought up more of the same: people and places that had nothing to do with her mother. *Jeannie Star, Jeannie Starr Magician Extraordinaire, Jeannie Starr carnival, Jeannie Starr Leah Fern*—it didn't matter what permutation or spelling she tried. As far as the internet was concerned, the first people Leah loved didn't exist.

Leah opened her sketchbook and made a quick drawing of a bird. And as she tore the page from her book, the paper making an exclamatory ripping sound, she felt something release from within, too.

On her way out of the library, she handed the page from her sketchbook to the lady behind the counter. "May I leave this for Blade?" she asked. The woman took the drawing, wondering aloud what kind of bird it was. Leah didn't say, *It is no bird and all birds.* She didn't say she hadn't drawn a bird for nine years. She didn't point out the word written along the soft slope of the bird's head, printed in tiny letters: HOPE.

THIRTY-TWO

HILDA, SOUTH CAROLINA,
THE YEAR OF BIRDS, 1989-1990

ON THE WAY home from Dr. Stern's office, Leah nervously poked her fingers through her purse of birdseed and barraged Edward Murphy with questions. "Do you know which bird lays the largest egg in the world?" Leah's words sped out faster than usual.

Edward Murphy, on the other hand, was slow in responding, somber. "I don't know, Le—"

"C'mon, guess."

"A flamingo, I reckon?"

"An ostrich! But good guess. Okay, what about the biggest bird that ever existed on earth?"

Edward Murphy rubbed his eyes and pulled his visor down. "A pterodactyl?"

"An elephant bird! I told you that already. Its egg was seven times bigger than an ostrich egg, remember? Don't you remember anything?"

"Hey, there. Easy now."

"I'm sorry."

"Listen, I want to talk to you about what the doctor—"

"Did you know a cassowary bird can kill a person by kicking them?"

"Leah, I—"

"Did you know the Australian magpie will peck a person's eyes out to defend its young?"

"Leah, I'm trying to defend *you*."

Leah tilted the purse so that some of the birdseed slid out into her lap. If Edward Murphy noticed, he didn't mention it. She poured out a little more, and this time it made a whooshing sound.

"I'm trying to help you."

Leah felt suddenly guilty for the mess she'd just made. "The birds are my friends. A lot of them have traveled a long way to see me."

"It's not them I'm trying to protect you from. It's you. I'm trying to protect you from yourself. The doctor said—"

"The doctor's stupid."

"Leah Fern, enough! It's not healthy to keep—" He gripped the steering wheel and shook his head as if to loosen the words that had gotten stuck in his mouth. "To keep seeing things that aren't real. You're going to need medication. And that's that."

Without saying a word, Leah tipped her purse. The seed rushed out in a thick steady spout, darkening her lap and spilling onto the seat until the purse was empty.

IN THE MONTHS that followed, the birds came with a vengeance. Aggressively friendly but never hostile, they surrounded Leah, shooting up from the ground like rockets, looping through the air like acrobats, perching and preening in the most unusual places: on a piece of toast just popped up in the toaster, along the rim of the toilet seat, beside the chalk and erasers in the blackboards at school, on the handle of a running lawn mower, on the roof of a moving car, on the back of a lazing cat. Sometimes when she walked outside, they'd be standing by, balanced like thousands of small statues all turned in her direction. Sometimes whole flocks of them would follow her. Other times they'd be soaring high, layers of them orbiting like planets.

None of the birds' odd behaviors or unprecedented migration patterns—not even their silence—caused Leah to question their realness. After all, why would she question a gift that brought her so much joy, one that to her eyes was unquestionably real? From the moment the scarlet tanager arrived on the front porch of their house on that crisp October day, she believed that at last her wish had been answered—not the exact wish she'd wished that year or on each of the four birthdays prior, but a version of it. Instead of her mother, it was the scarlet tanager who'd arrived on their front porch six months after she'd blown out her eleven birthday candles.

It turned out that the scarlet tanager was also the problem: it shouldn't have been red. When Leah finally identified its breath-takingly bright plumage in the school library, she learned that by October it should have already molted to an olive yellow. Why this stood out to her as more troublesome than a cardinal choosing a cat as a roost, when it wouldn't have been such a stretch to allow for a slightly later molting season that year, was as baffling an occurrence as everything else that was happening. Or maybe it wasn't, for some-times it's the smallest things that rouse us. Nevertheless, it was that single bird that was red when it should have been yellow that made her decide, after months of spitting out the pills Edward Murphy handed her each night at dinner, to swallow them. Maybe he was right; maybe he was protecting her from herself.

After a month of taking the pills, an amazing thing happened. The birds kept coming.

"They're real, they're real!" Leah came running into the den just as Edward Murphy was solving a puzzle on *Wheel of Fortune*.

"Sing a song of six pence!"

"The birds, they're really real!"

If Edward Murphy's face had been glass, it would have shattered. "Oh, Leah. No."

"No really, it's true! I know you haven't seen them yet and you're probably sad about that. They fly off sometimes. They hide. And they do the strangest things—sometimes they even pretend to be flowers! But they're real, and any minute now I bet you'll see them, too!" In her unprecedented ebullience, she reached to touch Edward Murphy's actual hand. "Maybe you'll even see them tonight."

"Leah, I need you to tell me the truth—"

"I am, I am telling the truth!"

"Please, let me finish. I need you to tell me if you've stopped swallowing your pills."

"That's just it. I finally started!"

"Okay, explain that."

"I admit, at first I was spitting them out. I just didn't feel sick and didn't want to take medicine for not being sick. Then I thought maybe you were right and something was wrong with me and the birds weren't real, so I started taking the pills. I've been taking them for four weeks straight. And guess what!"

"You still see the birds?"

"Isn't it spectacular!" Leah pressed her hands together in front of her chest. "On my birthday I wished they would stay, and they stayed! They're still here! They're everywhere!"

BY THEN IT was April—six months after the scarlet tanager first arrived and days after Leah had turned twelve—and the growing bird population in Hilda couldn't be denied. Maybe this was why Edward Murphy didn't act on Leah's tales of blue heron theater and egret skywriting right away, lest the birds she was reporting be the same birds he, too, was observing. Besides, he had never seen her so animated, so—dare he think it—*happy,* and he certainly didn't want to interfere.

"Do you see the little finch?" she'd ask, pointing. "Over there?" And Edward Murphy would look over there and solemnly shake his head no. "What about the macaw on the coat rack?" Again, the most he could do was shake his head. Leah felt so sorry for him that she tried talking to the birds. She asked the ones on her bedroom windowsill to roost on Edward Murphy's instead. She walked beneath the phone lines and asked a long row of painted buntings to swoop over his head when he went to Martha-Up-the-Street's to trade the season's first harvest. Even at night, during that most cherished time when they visited her bed, she whispered, "Go to *his* bed tonight."

But the birds didn't listen. They were Leah's birds, her gift from the wish gods, and all their feathered turns were for her.

THIRTY-THREE

ONTARIO–QUEBEC, 1999

WHITE LINES. YELLOW lines. Green signs. Conifers. Random deciduous branches sketched against a nacreous sky. Clearings: fields, water bodies and water bodies, frozen. Black tar. Packed gravel. Snow. Everywhere, snow. Blue light. Rose light. Amber. Blue again, and bluer. Darkness. A crystalline voice inside an old Ford pickup: "I thought I was awake, but now I'm really awake." Leah was speaking to her trusty copilot, the obelisk. She was so engrossed in the conversation that she had gone record time without plucking something sweet from her backpack. In fact, this ten-hour trek from Thunder Bay to La Sarre, Quebec, marked the chattiest she'd been in a very long time. Since ripping that page out of her notebook for Blade, she'd been feeling lighter, as if parts of herself were sloughing off, too, the way a snake sheds not only its skin but also its eye caps, its sight wiped clean. She remembered what her mother had said about shedding snakes. *It's still the same snake after, but it's also new* . . . "Or it's like a door," she explained to Essie, "and you open it, and you think you see so much, but then there's another door, and you realize how little you'd seen before, and then another door . . ."

Luna, illuminate our truths.

"Yes. It's like you think one thing is true, but then you find the truth isn't exactly what you thought it was. Or it's more than what you thought. Or something like that."

And then one day she finds that what she's felt—or, I dare say, known—is true.

That was the other thing that had changed since Leah left Thunder Bay that morning: Essie had become chattier, too. Whether in the wind batting Leah's old Ford or the thuds of bumps and pits in the road or the hissing of a passing car or the whine of an eighteen-wheeler's brakes, Leah had begun to hear Essie's voice. Sometimes it came in lines from her letters, and sometimes it seemed to come from the ether, but more and more, it was there. As the miles ticked by and the sun went down, they carried on a long conversation, the longest of Leah's life.

You don't know what you are, said Essie in the swish of a passing car.

"You don't know what I know."

Leah's truck veered a bit too far to the right and evoked the growl of the rumble strip. *The question is, will you rise again?*

"The question is, will I eat some jelly beans," Leah said, finally relenting and reaching into the bag. Deep into the darkness, deep into her thoughts, she crossed the border into Quebec.

That night she checked into Motel le Bivouac in La Sarre, where a cheery redhead beamed at her from behind the front desk. "Bonsoir! Welcome to Motel le Bivouac."

Leah cleared her throat and did her best to call upon her high school French. *"Bonjour. Merci. S'il vous plaît, je voudrais avoir une chambre pour la nuit."*

"Are you from the United States?"

"Why, did I just say something terrible?"

The woman laughed. "Not at all! What you said was perfect."

"Merci," said Leah, smiling, giving a little bend at the knees.

"Bienvenue," said the woman, curtseying in return.

MAYBE, THOUGHT LEAH, as she laid out her bedside accoutrements, lingering to admire the obelisk, and then the magnetic crow as it reliably caught the hotel pen, *I've already risen.* She opened her sketchbook and took out the letter from Bob O'Malley she'd been stowing there. She carefully tore out a blank page and began writing him the letter she'd been composing in her mind for days. When she finished, she read it several times, imagining how he would feel when he read it. The thought made her happy.

THE MORNING LIGHT revealed a charming town in La Satre, home to a covered bridge, a motto that means *I won't forget you* (*Oblivisci Nescius*), the best chocolate croissant Leah had ever tasted, and the post office that housed letter six, blue:

July 27, 1998

Dear Leah,

I haven't wanted to write this letter. I still don't.

I don't want to tell you about the scarab ring Claire gave to me. She'd carved the scarab out of turquoise and set it in silver. "A symbol of eternity, and the fire of creation," she said, slipping it onto my finger. For a

moment, I thought my heart might actually
burst through the wall of my chest. And I
thought, *Why, why must you toy with me?*

I don't want to tell you about my shame. But
it's only in telling you my story that I can
fully tell you yours.

After my mother was murdered, I felt
besieged not only by grief but by shame.
Perhaps I believed that despite everything
I knew about her—that she was kind, loving,
generous to a fault, genuinely driven to help
people heal—perhaps the people who had set her
murderer free had known something about her
that I hadn't. Had she carried some mark? Was
that mark also on me?

I hid behind my camera, where I could be
the seer, the world my object. It worked fine
for a time, and then I met Claire, who swiftly
became the dividing line of my life, though in
the end, what she divides is merely one kind
of despair from another.

Don't even think of pitying me. There she
was, sitting beside me on the hotel bed,
giving a gift she'd forged and fired expressly
for me. She beamed when she saw that it fit
my right ring finger perfectly. "I just knew
your size! I've looked at your hands a lot,"
she confessed. I didn't know what to say. No
one had ever made something so splendid for me
before, and it wasn't my birthday or anything.

It was late. We had just finished our fifth

moon ceremony at the edge of Goose Bay. Claire
and I were sharing a room at a little resort
that faced the water. This was the midway
point of our spiral, the point, as Athena put
it, between Earth and Heaven, and our art
continued to skyrocket. There was no question.
The magic of our spiral was working.

When the five of us checked into the resort,
Claire announced that she wanted to "bunk"
with me. She declared it with an unmitigated
ebullience that turned my breath shallow
and fluttery. By now it was clear that the
others suspected there was something between
us, though what that something was I didn't
exactly know myself. As she sat beside me on
the bed, her eyes shining with the gift she'd
given me, for which I choked back tears to
eventually say four words—"Thank you, it's
perfect"—it was she who said the words I was
too much of a coward to say, though I'd felt
them from the day we met. "I love you," she
said, open as the sea. "It's true," she added,
"that you're sometimes distant. And grumpy.
And afraid. But I see the you beneath all
that, and I love you." She leaned close to me
then, and I don't think I was breathing. "You
inspire me," she said, and then she kissed me.

Now, I'd been kissed before. Or really, I'd
done the kissing. I suppose you could say that
I treated women like I treated the rest of
the world, as objects. As I said, I don't want

to tell you about my shame. But if I'm being
honest at this late date, I should probably
mention that I wasn't comfortable yet with
my sexuality. In 1977, even in New York City,
being a lesbian still felt like another thing
to hide. So I took women to bed and then
disappeared, never brave enough to take them
by the hand in the light of day, let alone
love any of them.

With Claire, I had no choice. Never had a
kiss so unmoored me, so swiftly gouged out the
ground beneath my feet and sent me falling,
in every direction at once it seemed. I wanted
her so much that it physically hurt. And I
pulled back, away from her.

"You fancy men," I reminded her.

"I fancy *you*," she said, with that smile.

"You're half my age."

"I'm an old soul."

"Is this because I read you those poems?"
(About a month earlier, I'd read several poems
aloud to her from a book called *I Hear My
Sisters Saying*. She hadn't read much poetry
before, so when she heard Sylvia Plath,
Gwendolyn Brooks, Adrienne Rich, Marge Piercy,
she reared up out of her chair like a wild
horse. *More*, she kept saying. *More*.)

"Well, that's part of it," she said.
"Everything that's part of you is part of why
I love you."

There it was, the moment that I would come

to regret more than anything else in my life.
There would be plenty more regrets to follow,
believe me, but this was the one that would set
the rest into motion. Our beautiful Claire had
told me she loved me three times. She had given
me the most exquisite gift. She had kissed me
into a land of possibility I'd never stepped
foot on before. And I looked into her radiant
eyes and willed myself to go cold. "I think
it's best if I go stay in Linda's room," I told
her. And I watched the pain seep into her face.
I watched her eyes fill with disbelief, then
tears. I started to take the ring off to give
back to her, but she stopped me by putting her
hand out and simply saying, "No." Her tears fell
generously into her lap while I grabbed my bag
and left her there, sitting on the bed alone.

What can I tell you? She terrified me.

Your mother once told me she didn't feel
fear, ever. I didn't believe her at first, for
how could a person not feel this most natural,
hard-wired, self-protective impulse? Easy, she
told me. "Everything is going to happen to
us. We're going to experience great pleasure,
and we're going to suffer. We're going to run
the gamut in between. We're going to die. And
safety is an illusion. You can go to sleep
at night in your safe bed, and a tree could
fall on you. Anything can happen, good or bad,
anytime. Why not take every risk you can? Why
not say yes to everything?" If I had tape-

recorded her, I don't think I would be far off from her exact words as I recall them for you now, because what she said made more sense to me than anything I'd ever heard. I just wish I had learned that lesson sooner.

To this day, it wrenches me to imagine your mother saying yes to Hank—about anything. I never met the man, but she told me enough to make me loathe him for lifetimes. The first yes between them, however, was his, on the day she showed up at his carnival and applied for a job. When she told him she was a magician, he laughed at her. "A girl can't be a magician," he told her. Her response was to pull his wallet from a pink chiffon scarf tucked into the depths of her cleavage and return it to him. He was outraged that she'd pick-pocketed him, and completely smitten at the same time. Needless to say, she got the job.

She was pretty broken down by then, and he was like no one else she'd ever known. "Arrogant, aggressive, but a puppy underneath," as she put it. He took her in at a time when she felt she had nowhere else to go. You weren't born yet, but you would be soon. She never said who your father was, if that's what you're wondering. Even when I found out about you, at the very end of her six months with me, I didn't ask. Your mother told only what she wanted to tell.

My urn must feel lighter now, yes? When

you're finished, only the stones will be left,
and the wood carved by a woman some might call
a fairy. Let it be lighter still by releasing
me on a small island bisected by the border
of Quebec and Ontario. Here are the directions
as Claire wrote them in our Book of Shadows:
*From La Sarre we drove south on 393. Fleetwood
Mac's "Dreams" came on, and the five of us sang
along with Stevie. "Women, they will come and
they will go . . ." We turned right on Chemin
de Gallichan, right on Route Centrale, left on
4e-et-5e Rang O, right on Chemin de la Plage
Fortin, and left to stay on Chemin de la Plage
Fortin. From there we drove to the end of the
gravel road, past the campground, and parked.
At the turnaround we went through the woods to
get to the shore of Lake Abitibi. Then we swam
to the small island, the in-between land, and
the water flashed all its colors at me.*

Your next stop: Post Office, Plains, Georgia,
31780.

Yours,

Essie

Leah's jaw clenched, and she felt her two chocolate croissants
rise up. It was too much. Too much story. Too much pain. Too much
wisdom. Too many directions to a nameless island. And exactly zero
directions to her mother. "This is a wild goose chase," she said to the
urn. "That's what this is."

Our lives, for a time, coincided in ways you might be interested in knowing about.

It was then that she had to admit what she hadn't wanted to admit to herself: Essie had never promised anything more than a story. And that's what she was getting.

There was nothing she'd ever wanted to do that she couldn't, Essie's voice sounded again in her mind.

"I guess she didn't want to be a mother then." Leah felt the claw of her own words, along with a deeper ache she couldn't bring herself to address. She looked out at the empty road and up at the canopies of trees. "You're cruel," she added, throwing her coat at the urn. "You're a cruel person."

"What am I even doing here," she whispered, this time to no one in particular, "alone in the middle of nowhere?"

You're not alone.

"What do you call this?" she argued. "I'm having conversations with an urn."

The voice insisted, *You've never been alone.*

Leah let her gaze travel as far as it could down the QC-393, the road she'd come in on. The sun showered through the trees, dropping webbed shadows onto the lanes. A sudden remembrance of pedaling Brenda Wright's bike on the empty roads of Madeline Island rushed over her—she could feel that wind, that light.

You've always had yourself.

She took a deep breath and pulled her coat off of Essie, and the obelisk shone back at her like an old friend. "Georgia, huh? At least we'll be heading someplace warm."

First there was another icy lake to find, another place to let more of Essie go. Before that, there were two more things waiting to be discovered inside Essie's envelope. The photograph was first: a shot of an open suitcase filled with neatly packed clothes and a book—an odd shot for what Leah had become accustomed to from Essie. Like the last photograph, this transparency was also in color, but unlike all the others, it seemed more like a document than art. Leah took a closer look at the book in the suitcase. BOOK OF SHADOWS was written in thick silver calligraphic letters on a black cover. Vines wound up both sides, sprouting leaves and flowers not dissimilar to the ones on Essie's urn. "Claire," said Leah, realizing she was looking at Claire's suitcase—her camisoles and blue jeans, her writing on their sacred book. And suddenly she was certain that it was Claire who had made Essie's urn. "But why?"

This time, she heard no answer from Essie.

As she lingered over each visible item in Claire's suitcase, wanting to touch the lace and the silk, the silver calligraphy, wanting to see what was beneath and beneath, she began to feel as if she, too, had known Claire, as if she, too, had loved her.

Leah removed the last thing from the envelope, a small green velvet box. She played with the tension of the hinge's spring, holding the top and the bottom just a little bit apart, like when she'd held the crow and the pen apart, in that sweet spot of pull and resistance. The box was open just enough to want to snap back shut but not enough for her to see what was inside. She already knew what was inside. But she wasn't ready to see it, to have it so close and exposed and present, so she continued exerting a sequence of micro-movements upon the box, keeping it held in a state of inbetweenness, not letting it clamp down, not letting it fully open, as if her fingers were gods controlling a universe of velvet. But eventually the top, in a millimeter's moment of momentum, sprung up and revealed the turquoise scarab, symbol of infinity, another winged being Claire had carved.

Leah slipped the ring on the middle finger of her left hand, and it fit. She held it up then, ready to make a wish as she had so many times before upon the ring on her right. "Wishing ring," she said, and she noticed how the words sounded like another language. As she said the words again, she found that, for the first time in a life brimming with wishes, she didn't know what to wish for. "Wishing ring," she said as she studied the intricate details of the scarab—the triangle at the center of its back, the delicate lines on its head— "wishing ring." And then the wish came out, as if from a back door in her mind while she wasn't paying attention, in a whisper almost too soft to hear. "Let the birds come back."

THIRTY-FOUR

HILDA, SOUTH CAROLINA, THE YEAR OF BIRDS, 1989–1990

IT STARTED WITH a simple blood test, "just to make sure everything's in working order," Edward Murphy reassured Leah. Leah almost never got sick, and in the four years she'd lived with him, she'd been to the doctor only twice, for standard immunizations. Now, as they sat in the waiting room, her breakfast sloshed around in her stomach.

"I'm really okay. I don't feel sick at all, I promise," she said. She even touched his arm with the tip of the *Highlights* magazine she was reading. "Can't we just go home?"

"It'll just be a little prick, and then it'll be over."

It wasn't the prick she was worried about. It was the contact. Would the doctor have to examine her? How long would his hands be on her?

Leah redirected her thoughts to a fact of nature that had been a thorn in her awareness for days: the problem of cuckoos kicking fairy wrens' eggs out of their nests and replacing them with their own. Because the cuckoo egg hatches more quickly than the fairy wren, the hatchling ousts the remaining eggs from the nest and is raised by the fairy wren, while the cuckoo mother is free to fly unfettered by the responsibilities of child-rearing. As she waited for the doctor, she imagined that maybe she could build a fairy wren birdhouse with holes too small for cuckoos, or maybe she could apply some sort of cuckoo repellent to the fairy wren's nest, or—

"Leah Fern?"

Leah looked up at a woman holding a chart in her hand. "Go on, now," urged Edward Murphy. "I'll be right here."

Leah followed the woman into a room. She was wearing a navy shirt adorned with cartoonish lions, elephants, and giraffes. "Did you know that a giraffe's tongue is black so it won't get sunburned?" asked Leah.

The woman apparently didn't care much about giraffe tongues because she ignored Leah's tidbit and handed her a folded paper robe. "Take off all your clothes and put on this gown, okay? And leave the tie in the front."

"I'm just getting a blood test," Leah informed her.

"You're getting a physical," the woman corrected, holding out the robe.

Leah obediently took it, but when the woman left the room, Leah hopped up onto the table without putting it on.

When the doctor walked in, he hadn't finished closing the door behind him when she blurted out, "I'm just getting a blood test."

He chuckled, but not in the fake way Dr. Stern had. "Easy there, partner," he said. "At least allow me to introduce myself."

Leah folded her arms over her chest.

"I'm a man of wealth and taste. Just kidding—that's a song. I couldn't resist."

"The Rolling Stones," said Leah, recognizing it from the radio station Edward played in the car.

"You're one cool cat," he said, still smiling. "I'm Dr. Charles. And you are?"

"Leah Fern."

"That's a beautiful name."

"I'm just getting a blood test."

Dr. Charles' eyes softened. "Well, I have to examine you, too. But it won't hurt."

"I don't want to be touched."

"Okay. May I ask why? Has someone touched you in an inappropriate way?"

Leah shook her head. "No one touches me."

The doctor nodded as if somehow, he understood. "I see. How about I examine you without touching you? Would you be okay with that?"

She thought for a moment and then nodded.

"Thank you. It'll be easy, you'll see." Dr. Charles stepped closer to Leah. Even without his hands on her, she could feel him, mostly in the way of warmth. He smelled like licorice. "Now I want you, without moving your head, to follow my two fingers with your eyes, okay?"

Leah nodded, and the doctor waved his fingers back and forth and up and down in front of her face, while she followed.

"Okay, great. Now smile for me."

Leah smiled.

"Excellent. Now close your eyes and touch your right fingertip to your nose, and then your left."

Leah did everything he asked. She stuck out her tongue; she put her hands on her thighs, then turned her palms up and down rapidly for ten seconds; she listened to a tuning fork and nodded to indicate she could hear it; she walked back and forth across the room; she stood with her eyes closed; she answered his questions: she was born on April 4, 1978, George H. W. Bush was president, her favorite color was black.

"Perfect," said Dr. Charles. "Now let's get you that blood test." He called for the woman with the animals on her shirt, and when she came in, he explained that she would have to be extra gentle, which she was as she tied the rubber strip around Leah's arm and asked her to make a fist—so gentle, in fact, that she'd hardly made any contact with Leah at all, save for the quick brush of a gloved finger. Dr. Charles stayed in the room, asking Leah questions about what her hobbies were and why her favorite color was black, and before she knew it, the needle was out and the test was over.

"WE'RE GOING TO have to do one more test," Edward Murphy informed her, after Dr. Charles found nothing amiss on the neurological exam, after her blood test came back normal. He was standing in the doorway to her bedroom, and she was sitting on her bed, paging through *World of Birds*. "Dr. Stern says we'll probably know everything we need to know once we do something called an EEG. It doesn't hurt. Don't worry—I asked. It just measures brain waves." He scratched his head. "I think that's what he said. Brain waves."

Leah looked up from her book. She had just been reading about a type of hummingbird called an amethyst woodstar, but she didn't bother to tell him about it, and he didn't ask. Something had changed between them. They had become more formal in their interactions, regarding each other with a tentativeness that harkened back to their earliest days together—as if one wrong move from either of them could shatter them both.

SURELY EDWARD MURPHY hadn't meant to lie when he told Leah there would be only one more test, but after she lay on her back in a dimly lit room and allowed twenty-one electrodes to be pasted to her head, after she closed her eyes and tried to think good thoughts but instead kept remembering falling—a yellow bird falling, her own falling as she chased a car going too far too fast—the EEG showed no abnormalities, and Dr. Charles recommended a CT scan.

It was hard to tell for sure, after the EEG, whether or not the bird population was dwindling. Leah had the sense that there were fewer birds around, and certainly fewer in their house, but the weather was so lovely that spring that she figured maybe they had fewer reasons to want to come in. After the CT scan, however, she was certain: the birds were starting to disappear. They were also losing their sense of humor: no longer did they perch on the backs of neighborhood pets or the brim of the mailman's cap. Each time she stepped outside there were fewer of them, until the thousands had thinned to only a hundred or so, only one or two of which still looked in her direction. It was okay, though. She still had her night birds. A flurry of fluttering wings, they descended upon her faithfully each night in full force, draping over her, a shroud of rapturous whispers, until all that could be seen of her were feathers.

When the CT scan was normal, an MRI followed: the shot of gadolinium, the insertion of her small body into a dark tunnel, the loud strange knocking and clanging. *I'm not afraid*, she thought, imagining people with Hula-Hoops bopping around to the irregular rhythms. *It's just dancing.* This, Edward Murphy had assured her, would be the last of the tests. *Last one*, she sang in her mind in time to the drumbeats. *Last one*.

She still had some birds left. The test was normal. And it wasn't the last one.

For the next test, Leah was asked to remove her clothes and put on a gown. This time she was told to leave the tie in the back. This time there would be no negotiating.

Leah rolled onto her side and brought her knees up to her chest as instructed, while Edward Murphy waited somewhere out of sight. She winced at the gloved fingers against her spine, the cold antiseptic they rubbed onto her skin. "Now you're going to feel a couple little pricks and then some pressure, and it's really important you don't move. Can you promise us you won't move?"

Leah knew she should agree, but the most she could do was faintly nod her head. She was lost. Someone had lost her. "This is important, now, Leah. Don't even move your head, okay? Don't move anything."

She squeezed her eyes shut and didn't move anything. She felt the two pricks meant to numb her, but they weren't as uncomfortable as the fingers still pressing on her spine. "Okay, now you're going to feel some pressure." Leah didn't move then, either, as the main needle entered her low back and she felt it happen: a sky-full of birds rose up—a galaxy of them, the last of them—and flew away.

FOR TWO DAYS after her lumbar puncture, which had also been normal, she lay flat in bed, avoiding the headaches that came with sitting up. There were no birds on her windowsill, none on her stack of books, not even the quickest flash of one from the corner of her eye. Edward Murphy brought milkshakes to her bedside, which at first she refused. "Just a little?" he pleaded. "Just a sip? It's chocolate, your favorite." She wouldn't even look at him, but when she heard his voice crack and finally let her eyes wander to where he knelt beside her, she saw how he'd aged in the last months, how tired he looked, how papery his skin had become, and she took a sip of the milkshake.

If she would have known, on the night before her lumbar puncture, that it would be the last time her night birds would visit her, she might have begged them to stay, or at least thanked them for all the nights they'd come to her, but instead she let them lavish her as if they would always return. Those next nights, as she lay flat in the darkness of her room, she felt the emptiness all around her, not only in her bed and in their house but also outside, on the surfaces of things and deep in the crevices of things, and she felt that emptiness move over her, too, until all that was left of the birds was their silence. It entered her, that silence.

Edward Murphy didn't realize at first that Leah had gone mute. "You've got to stop being mad at me sometime," he said. "I did what was best for you, and you need to stop being so gosh-darned defiant all the time."

Leah sat beside him at the table, poking her spoon into her cereal without taking a bite.

"At least be polite enough to say good morning."

But it wasn't a matter of politeness anymore. Leah had been emptied out like a nest. She had no words left.

In the following days, Edward tried a variety of things to get her to speak. He begged. He asked her questions about elephants and Arctic animals and giraffes (he did not ask about birds). He pretended to sneeze. He threatened her with another visit to Dr. Stern. He brought her gifts: a new sketchpad, a set of colored pencils, a book of rare animals, a stuffed bear. But she offered nary a thank you for his gifts, nor a bless you for his sneezes, nor an answer to a single question. She simply stared off like a blind girl.

Two weeks went by, and Edward's face was awash in a perpetual look of anguish. He became so desperate, in fact, that as he drove her home from school, he even resorted to talking about birds. "Look!" he said of a conflagration of starlings lifting off from a stand of trees. "Look at how they pepper the sky!"

She knew what he was doing, but it barely registered. Who cared if he was on her side now? Who cared what birds he saw or what enthusiasm he dredged up in seeing them? She didn't even bother to look up.

SOMETIMES, IN HER first years with Edward Murphy, Leah would entreat him to tell her a bedtime story—not one of the true stories about her mother or his childhood or the time Martha-Up-the-Street's hat blew off and skidded all the way down Barnwell Road before he managed to catch it for her, but a made-up one. He wasn't the most original storyteller, but just as he'd made Leah a better storyteller, he'd also learned a thing or two from her along the way. "One sunny afternoon, a polar bear emerged from his ice cave," he once began.

"He wasn't a *regular* polar bear, was he?"

"No," he said, taking the hint, "definitely not. This polar bear had the rare ability to laugh like a human. But his voice was so deep that when he laughed, huge pieces of ice would crack, dumping anyone near him into the sea. So all the other animals—"

"Like the Arctic foxes and the oxen and the reindeer?"

"Yes, the Arctic foxes and the oxen and the reindeer—they did everything they could to be serious, you know, to avoid making him laugh. But they were so nervous about it that it made them clumsy. They would trip and slip and spill their tea, and then the boom of laughter would come."

"So what did they do?" Leah wanted to know. "Did they move away from the polar bear? Did they teach him to laugh more quietly? Did they make a sound-capturing helmet for him? Wait. Don't tell me! I don't want to know the end!" Those were the times she loved Edward Murphy the most, as she lay under her blanket and stared at his furrowed skin in the warm light of her bedside lamp while he sat on the edge of her bed and did the best he could to make something for her, something that existed only there, in the air between them and in their shared imagination.

"TELL ME A story," he finally said, a month after Leah had stopped speaking. Her teachers were irate. The bullies at school were relentless. Edward Murphy was looking more gaunt by the day. It wasn't until he asked her for a story and broke their unspoken rule by putting his hand on her hand that she fully felt the enormity of his despair, which, in the end, eclipsed her own.

Finally, her voice broke through the silence, mellifluous as a nightingale's. "Once, in the faraway of time, a girl lived in the green hills of the earth. People would have called her Cliff Child, because she liked to stand at the edges of the bluffs. But no one else was alive then, so there was no one to call her anything. In fact, the hills had made the girl from silence. And as she roamed and looked out at the hills, there were no words to get in the way of her senses. She wasn't lonely. She could hear the music of the taproots sipping water and the air rolling over the hills. She could smell the first summer strawberry turn red and a storm coming when there wasn't even a cloud in the sky. And that was all she wanted: what she already had. Not a thing more. Not even you."

A YEAR AFTER the scarlet tanager appeared, one last bird arrived: a crow. It appeared on the same fence post in their front yard every day, cawing at her whenever she left or returned. It was huge, glossy black, raucous. But she wouldn't acknowledge it. She wouldn't believe it was real.

As crows go, it was the most insistent crow she'd ever encountered. When she ignored its vociferous complaining, it flapped its wings as if it were in a battle to the death. When she ignored those displays, it began bringing her gifts—a red button, a safety pin, a shiny penny, a blue piece of plastic, a white pebble—leaving them on the fence post and ascending dramatically whenever she was near, as if to point them out. But she left them there, untouched. The crow added a few more offerings to the collection—a silver charm, a book of matches, a mollusk shell—and for a moment, she was tempted to gather them and take a closer look. But she let the moment pass, and soon the crow and its gifts, which got rained on and scattered by the wind, disappeared.

After the crow left, Leah, who had sprouted up in recent months and had lost the last traces of roundness in her face, entered the bathroom with a new razor and a pair of scissors. Cut by cut, stroke by stroke, she watched her hair fall into the sink, watched the new skin of her scalp emerge. Black and blacker, her hair collected in the white basin—like feathers, the last of them.

THIRTY-FIVE

WITH THOUGHTS OF Georgia sunshine on her mind, Leah followed Claire's directions to a vacant campground, *Camping Municipal de Roquemaure*, and found herself facing a looming wall of snow partway down the road. The story was in the tracks: the snowplow operator who had cleared the rest of the road had decided that this was far enough, and that was fair, for who in their right mind would have cause to travel here, in waist-deep snow, now? Leah appraised the giant snow mound, which was bolstered by hunks of ice churned out by the plow. "We're just going to have to climb it," she finally decided. Why she chose to climb the snow mound, which towered twice as high as her truck, when she could have gone around it, is anyone's guess—though it should be said that sometimes making an entrance has nothing to do with logic. Sometimes a body just wants what it wants.

She turned her truck around so that it was facing the plowed part of the road, unbuckled Essie and wedged her into the backpack, and finished the Cadbury egg she'd been nursing, letting it melt in her mouth while she pulled up the hood of the black sweatshirt she was wearing and buttoned her coat.

As Leah got a foothold on the snow mountain, which was densely packed and therefore surprisingly easy to scale, she smiled. "Nothing stops me!" she rejoiced, ascending. Just then, her foot shot down through the snow and she fell forward onto her chin. She checked to see if she was bleeding, and when she saw she wasn't, she extracted her leg from the hole she'd made and said again, though with a bit more reserve, "Nothing stops me."

Unfortunately, the mountain was just the beginning. She still had more than a mile to walk, and the snow was more than three feet deep in places. She pushed her slight body into each step, and the snow pushed back. Soon she was sweating and breathing heavily. "Nothing stops me," she gasped, flipping off her hood and opening her jacket. And she kept going.

In the months after her mother left, she kept dreaming the memory of chasing her car, and sometimes she would actually get out of bed mid-sprint—a swift movement, a combination of a fall and a leap that would awaken her. Then a strange thing would happen: something invisible would stop her from moving. She thought of it as a hand, this force that pressed into her chest and prevented her from taking even a step, though she never saw anything. There was just air around her, and all the usual things in the usual places. It didn't matter how hard she pushed against the invisible hand—all her strength meant nothing. Only after the passing of some amount of time, which she guessed to be only seconds (though it felt much longer), would the force relent and give way. It happened enough times that she understood it was a waiting game, that the hand would always give way, but nevertheless, she still fought it every time. Once she broke free, she'd stumble forward into a run only to find herself outside Edward Murphy's door, where she took comfort in the resonant snores of a man who would have gladly woken and put his arms around her, if only she would have let him.

Now no force would stop her. She parted the snow as if by the sheer force of her will alone, throwing herself into each step, lugging her weighty pack, sweating and breathing victoriously, slinging off her coat altogether and tying it around her waist. She did this for an hour until the road forked and she entered the forest, where the pine boughs had shielded the ground from much of the snow and made her footsteps easier.

Soon she could see it, the clearing beyond the trees, the frozen lake. She rushed forward and emerged from the woods, and the view took what was left of her breath: miles and miles of glittering white in every direction. Was she on the edge of the world? Was there anyone else, anywhere? Was she alive? *As for you, you're already dead.* But no, she *was* alive. She had never been more alive. And, lightheaded from a mixture of elation and hypoxia, she took her first step onto the ice. It held her firm as marble. A door opened.

NOW SHE WAS untethered. *There is more than one way to be born.* (Had the ash-woman said that? No, the ferrywoman had.)

Now she was born. Born of ice. Born of the world below it, glowing blue. Born of the hidden fish and the flashy schools of silver. Born of the scutes of ancient sturgeon. Born of the algae wavering upward toward the bright ice ceiling. Born of the flecks of fossils gleaming red and green. Born of the glycoproteins released by the sleeping creatures wedged into the sand. Born of the slick eel. Born of the slime, the pearly spheres, the translucent skin. Born of the sediment. Born of the cold. Born of the quiet. Born of the luster and the sinew. Born of the leg muscles—gastrocnemius, quadriceps, hamstrings—that were leading her forward.

THOUGH LEAH WASN'T generally prone to such gestures, she opened her arms wide and spun around. If someone had said to her two weeks earlier, "Hey, wanna go stand on a frozen lake in Quebec all by yourself?" she would have laughed. But nobody would have been able to give her the answer that now pulsed through her as she spun alone on the ice, where the milky sky began drawing down and a fine mist began rising up to meet it. Dizzied, Leah stopped spinning and breathed in the mist, which was almost sweet, while the sugary world kept turning around her. She spotted a small island about two hundred feet from the shore and knew it was the one. She watched the lake right itself as her equilibrium recovered, and then she headed forward, toward the border.

When she stepped onto the little island, she noted how, unlike the frozen lake, which was swept free of most of the snow, the island's vegetation held onto it. Leah set her backpack down and imagined what it had been like in June 1977, when Essie and four other women must have swum through these waters to get to where she was standing now. She narrowed her eyes and could almost see through time to the smooth strokes of five women moving through the coruscated blue of the water.

Leah took a deep breath as the fluid world of her imagination turned solid again. She watched the mist continue to gather and spread across the ice. She removed the obelisk from her backpack and poured some ash into her hand, closing her fingers around it. "This is for blue," she said, as blue after blue flickered through her mind—the Little Prince by the well in his blue suit, the enchanting sky in Rousseau's *Sleeping Gypsy*, the cobalt swirls of van Gogh's nights, the endless motion of Kandinsky's *Blue Rider*, the iridescent wings of the blue morpho butterfly, the bright feet of the blue-footed booby, the "blue trains" and "blue of sand" in Diane Wakoski's "Blue Monday." A blue silk scarf specked with silver. A blue silk scarf coming undone. A blue silk scarf swathing the empty eye socket, the jaw. Blue of the vein, of the stone. Blue of the rare poppy, blue of the hippo tang. The blue sheen of a first bicycle, hitting the ground. The black blue of the blink of time. The sea-blue bits of sky between birds. The cellophane blue of the immortal jellyfish. Royal blue, lapis, azure, cyan, cerulean, periwinkle, indigo, teal: paint on the fingers, on the brush, on the white. Blue beyond a girl's night ceiling, her blue eyes beaming through the endless hall of mirrors of the self.

She tossed the ash. Some fell onto the snow; some fell onto bits of protruding sedge; she imagined some fell into Ontario, and some fell into Quebec. As she capped the obelisk and tucked it away, she heard again the voice of the woman who'd approached her in Asheville on the first day of her trip. *Cross the border when you get there.* Leah could picture the white-haired woman in her tattered layers of faded black, could still feel the shock of how abruptly she'd appeared, barking her directive with the certainty of a soothsayer, or a madwoman—Leah wasn't sure which—before veering off into the crowd. Could this be what the woman meant? Could she have known? How much did anyone know? How true was the book about clairvoyance that Leah had found in the library so long ago, or John Muir's idea that everything was hitched to everything else in the universe? What would happen if she listened?

She remembered sitting on the front fender of her truck on the shoulder of the highway, preparing to cross that first border, between South Carolina and North Carolina. How easy it had been, after all those years of fearing it, to traverse that line. How easy it would be now, to do the same.

A warm thrill vibrated through Leah's hands and feet, and, with the swiftness of a jackrabbit, she leapt forward, wondering where, precisely, the border was, and whether she was truly in Ontario. *Maybe just a little farther*, she thought, taking a few more steps. *Just a little farther.* Soon she was back on the ice, on the other side of the island. She moved a little farther still. The fog was thickening, and she kept moving into it, as she had that night when she walked barefoot through a field outside the carnival. How familiar this fog was, its dreamlike hovering, its slow sprawl.

There was no one to tell her not to wander. As the lake went on and on and the fog went on and on, Leah, in her wandering, had the sense that if she wandered far enough, she would emerge, as if through a wormhole, into that field of her former life. Through the smoky gray she could almost see the warm lights of the carnival as they had always been, unstopped, unchanged, whirling and flashing, glowing with such quenching beauty. She could almost hear the electric din; she could almost smell the sticky sweetness.

When she arrived, she would wake up from a long dream, one in which she'd come to love a man named Edward Murphy and a woman made of ash, and she would find the moon-headed, mollusk-skinned man who'd once dug into the earth with a hammer, and she would find the voluptuous bearded lady who'd taken her to her first lake, surrounded by green and fecund with summer. Just there, a few steps farther, she could almost see them, smiling, waiting for her, ready for another adventure. Who she couldn't see, peer as she might into the vapor, was her mother.

A chill seized Leah. Wet from sweat and fog, she untied her coat from her waist and put it back on. *Just a little farther*, she kept thinking, treading carefully. *Just a little more.* She kept going, kept peering into the fog in search of the dazzling birthplace of her imagination. But then an unsettling awareness shot through her—she had gone too far.

The reverie fell away. She was not in Alabama. She was in Canada, with no trace of her carnival life, and no trace of the small island where she had just released Essie's ashes. Regret surged through her then and would not relent. She pirouetted on her feet as she looked for a clearing in the fog that enveloped her. There was none. "Hello?" Leah called out. "Anyone?"

"HELLO?" Leah waited. "HELP!" The fog billowed around her. She tried again, hitting a volume she didn't know she had. "HELP! HELP! HEEEEEEELP!   Help?"

It was no use. There was no one to help her. There was nothing left to do but keep walking in the direction she thought was right. She walked and walked, this way and that. Several times she tried what she thought was a new direction, but how could she be sure she wasn't walking in circles or, worse, farther away from the shore? How big was this lake anyway? How could she have been so stupid?

Finally, she stopped. She dropped her backpack onto the ice and sat on it. She put her hands in her pockets, while the chill worked its way through her wet wool coat and the fog grew so thick that she couldn't see her boots.

She lay down on the ice, not bothering to put her hood up. It didn't feel as cold as she expected it would. *Stupid, stupid*, she thought, seeing nothing but soupy gray vapor in every direction. Had she ever made a good decision?

She closed her eyes. Her mind plunged deeper and deeper back, to the hirsute goddess of her early life, to one of the most glorious summer days she could remember. *Let me go there now*, she thought. Even her thought was another kind of fog. Still, she reached through it, for the warmth of Her-Sweet's hand.

In another corner of her mind, she knew that soon the temperatures would drop. Maybe she would take her coat off then. Maybe she would freeze solid, like the woolly bear caterpillar. Maybe in weeks, when the ice would eventually break, she and Essie would drift down, together, to the bottom.

THIRTY-SIX

ONE AFTERNOON, HER-SWEET surprised Leah by taking her tiny hand and leading her to the outskirts of the carnival and into her rusty Ford. "It's time you learn how to swim," she said, putting the car in gear. Leah, who rarely got the chance to leave the carnival grounds, gazed out the window like a puppy as they turned down one street and then another, while the world she knew disappeared behind them. Leah pressed her nose to the window and peered with wonder at every tree, every field, every lamppost they passed.

When they arrived at the lake, it was shining like blue glass. An orchestra of birdsong, insect chatter, and frog grunts rose up, then quieted, then rose up again, as if it were being directed by a conductor. "The thing about swimming," said Her-Sweet, stripping out of her red dress, "is that you have to relax. Panic is a drowning woman's game."

Leah dropped her own clothes into a small heap at her feet, and the two of them stood naked side by side, holding hands and facing the water. Whenever Leah touched Her-Sweet, she could feel the emptiness she carried, but it was a quiet emptiness, one that asked nothing of her.

"We're born from water, after all," Her-Sweet continued, as they made their way through the marshy ground to the water's cusp. "It's natural, just like being naked is natural."

"It's cold," said Leah, meeting the edge with her toes.

"Aw, that's nothing! Try swimming in the ocean. You're just used to shower water is all." Her-Sweet took a couple of steps into the water, leaving Leah at the edge. "Feels delicious if you ask me."

Leah followed her into the water and took her hand again, and the two of them descended until the water was up to Leah's armpits and Her-Sweet's thighs. "Now, think of yourself as a bird, and pretend the water is the sky, and move your arms like wings."

Her-Sweet placed the flat of her palm under Leah's belly, and Leah followed her instructions, sending up huge splashes of water into their faces. The sun raked over their bodies, making the water droplets on their skin shimmer.

"Okay," said Her-Sweet, laughing. "I didn't so much mean *flapping* as I meant *gliding*. Like this." She demonstrated by sweeping her hands over the water's surface. "Smooth. You see?"

Leah tried again, and this time she felt how the water both carried and resisted her arms. "Now kick your legs!" Her-Sweet said, and when Leah started kicking, she swam right off Her-Sweet's hand.

"That's it! That a girl!" Her-Sweet called, making Leah feel like she could swim all the way to the other side.

ONCE THEY'D DRIED off and were sitting with their peanut butter and marshmallow sandwiches, Leah watched bugs skim the surface of the shining lake and a groundhog galumph into a tall patch of grass. There was something exotic about the slowness of the day, the quiet, that made her feel dreamy, peaceful.

"So," Her-Sweet asked her, "how do you do it?"

"How do I do what?"

"How are you so good at telling people's fortunes?"

Leah shrugged. "I don't know. I just feel what's inside of them. I feel what they feel."

Her-Sweet slapped the top of her thigh so hard it made a loud cracking sound. "Oh my god, Leah Fern, you sweet little honeybee. You're an empath!"

"An imp path?"

"An empath!" She put an arm around Leah's delicate frame. "That's a rare gift, my dear."

"Elephants feel other elephants' feelings," Leah said matter-of-factly.

"Well then you must be part elephant!"

Leah smiled, while the sun beat hot on her shoulders.

"Her-Sweet?"

"Yes?"

"How come other women don't have beards?"

Her-Sweet smiled a generous smile, her teeth as white as clouds. "Because they can't. Couldn't grow one even if they wanted to. Well, most of them anyway."

"So you're rare, too."

Her-Sweet nodded and ran her hand over her beard, this time slowly and with great deliberation. "People are always trying to erase what makes them special, just so they can be like everyone else. But do you want to be just another kernel of corn in the can, or do you want to be a whole mutant stalk still standing in the field, the ugly one getting all the sun?"

"I want to be the ugly one!" said Leah. "I want all the sun!"

THIRTY-SEVEN

BORDER, ONTARIO AND QUEBEC, 1999—LEXINGTON, KENTUCKY, 1999

KATERVIC EEL.

Leah's cheek twitched.

The harrow wheel.

Leah swatted an invisible bug from her ear, strange little voice. She was lying flat-backed on the ice. She was in the process of freezing.

The crow was real.

Leah opened her eyes to fog. She was a cloud now. She would drift, drift. She closed her eyes. The cold was a distant stone.

And did you get up?

Leah's voice was a wisp. "Hmmm?"

When you fell? Did you get up?

"Mmmhmm."

Then get up now.

"I'm busy."

You're a fool.

"Good night."

Get up.

Leah opened her eyes again. "There's nowhere to go." She began to shiver.

Ask the crow.

"Why do you always interrupt me when I'm trying to die?"

Such histrionics.

Leah sat up. "I'm lost, in case you haven't noticed."

Ask the crow.

"Of course. Why didn't I think of that? I'm already arguing with a dead witch, so why not have a conversation with a crow?" Leah reached into her pocket for the stone crow and looked into its carved eyes. "Oh, Great Magnetite Crow, can you tell me where to go?"

Without even a moment to relish her sarcasm she realized something crucial: Essie might be right.

Leah examined the crow's meticulously sculpted wings, the wide fan of its tail feathers, the sharp point of its beak. She thought of the hotel pen sliding across to reach it—how had she not realized it sooner? This wasn't only a magnetic stone; it was a lodestone, a compass! She remembered now. Magnetite, which she'd learned about when she was researching birds in the library, exists not only in rocks but also in the beaks of birds. The tiny crystals work like a compass, telling the birds which way is north and in which direction to fly.

She turned the crow upside down and ran her finger over its smooth underside. "The beak must be north, right?" Then she noticed something she hadn't noticed before, a small etched word under the right wing: EAST.

Leah pulled the last of a chocolate rabbit and a bottle of water from her pack. She consumed what was left of the rabbit's head and filled the plastic mold with water. Then she floated the cap in the water and placed the crow on top of it. At first, it bobbed up and down, riding the wave of her unsteady hand, so she put the container onto the ice and waited. And when the water eventually stilled, the crow turned.

"How about that!" she exclaimed. "It actually works!"

She picked everything up and began walking in the direction of the crow's right wing. Several times she stopped and leveled the compass on the ice to be sure she was still on course, making small adjustments and continuing on as if she'd been orienteering her whole life. Meanwhile, the fog began to loosen and drift apart in patches. Through it she could see trees. "Good crow!" she said. But the crow couldn't tell her how far north or south she was in relation to where she'd begun, so she dumped out the water, pushed the crow back into her front pocket, and stepped off the ice into the woods, wishing with every snowy step for a house, a person, a sign, a road, anything. And after all the un-granted wishes, all the lost things, all the trudging through the frozen wild, she got her wish. She knew, from the snow-covered picnic tables and barbecue pits, that she had, miraculously, stumbled onto the empty campground she'd driven past on her way in.

From there it didn't take her long to make her way back onto the plowed road, where she ran, breathless, through the remnant wisps of fog to a beautiful sight: an old black pickup truck. Then how easily the ordinary began again: the turn of the ignition as it would turn on any other day, the music coming through her speakers, the familiar rush of the vents. And as the truck began to warm, she took off her boots and changed into dry clothes, making sure to transfer her trusty crow to her new front pocket. She took Essie from her backpack and strapped her into her copilot seat. "Time to go to Georgia," she said.

THE NEXT DAY, after she crossed the border back into the United States, she stopped at a post office in Niagara Falls, this time not to pick up a letter but to mail one. She asked the person behind the counter, whose nametag read Terry, if she could buy an envelope and also a stamp.

"You can *have* an envelope," Terry said, handing her a business envelope. "But are you sure you only need one stamp?"

"Actually, I'll take a sheet of those," Leah said, pointing to a collection of Arctic animals.

In the corner of the post office, she reread the letter she'd written to Bob O'Malley before folding it and putting it in the envelope. And when she finished writing the return address, she couldn't help but smile as she imagined him opening it. It was a tough call, stamp-wise, between the Arctic fox, the Arctic hare, the snowy owl, or the polar bear, but in the end, she settled on the owl.

LEAH FACED THE thunderous rush of the falls. She gripped the railing, upon which countless other hands were gripped, but something about the power and the volume of the falls erased the hands and the people they were connected to, or rather, they erased any connection she felt to them, so that for the first time in her life, she could stand in a crowd without feeling any particularities belonging to someone else. What she felt instead was the absence of feeling, *like being washed clean,* she thought, but then the falls washed the thought away before it finished forming.

Leah wanted to stay longer, where rainbows formed in the mist, where she felt delightfully small, invisible practically, but she wanted the letter waiting for her in Georgia even more, so she got back on the road and continued south, pulling off at rest stops, loading tapes into her stereo and sweets into her mouth, until she arrived late that night in Lexington, Kentucky.

It's true that she was tired. It's true that, in addition to the Cowboy Junkies and Luscious Jackson, she was also replaying Essie's letters in her mind. It's true that she exited the highway onto a dark road, looking for a place to pull off and sleep for a few hours, and that her mind wasn't fully on the dark road. It's true that the moon was new that night, which made the dark road especially dark. But it's also true that at the second of impact, she was fully focused on the road. She saw the deer bound out in front her. She saw its eyes. She felt the sharpness of her own reflexes move through nanoseconds. She turned the wheel and hit the brakes, but after days of driving in snow—deep snow, icy snow, wet snow, fluffy snow, packed snow—her truck spun out on the dewy asphalt and she hit the deer.

She left her truck on the wrong side of the road and ran to the deer, who was lying on her side. Her head was up, and she was looking around. She didn't appear to be bleeding. "Hey there, little girl," said Leah, hoping with all the hope of her life that the deer was merely stunned, that in a moment she would leap to her feet and bound off, just as she had sprung out into the road. As Leah got closer, the deer got antsy and tried to get up, but she could only hoist herself halfway before her legs wobbled and she fell back down. "Whoa there, sweetie. Just wait. We'll figure this out. Just wait, just wait, just wait." Leah didn't know what she was saying. She didn't think it was a kind of prayer. "Please," she kept saying. "Please." Slowly, she inched her way closer to the deer, who was still holding her head up, looking at Leah with her enormous eyes. Leah hadn't thought to put her hazard lights on, so the next car that came along screeched to a halt only feet away from them. The deer flinched, but Leah didn't. "Please, get up," she urged. "Go on now."

"Oh my god, are you okay?" A voice came from behind.

Leah didn't turn away from the deer. "No. Yes. I'm okay. But I hit her."

"I'm calling 911!"

Soon traffic was backed up on both sides, and the deer, who had finally laid her head down, was roused back up by the people who had gotten out of their cars and begun to amass around them. For some reason there were small flashes of light. Someone was taking pictures. There were voices, like at a party. Leah slid even closer to the deer in an attempt to shield her, but she moved too quickly and spooked her, and the deer tried to get up again, this time managing a few steps before she thumped back down. Was that laughter Leah heard? Surely not. She turned to see a crowd. A siren sounded in the distance. Someone was definitely laughing. "Be quiet!" Leah barked. But the crowd didn't seem to hear her. The siren drew closer. The lights swirled over everyone.

Shiny shoes, legs—that's all Leah saw.

"Excuse me, miss. I'm going to have to ask you to step out of the road."

"I have to help the deer."

"We'll take it from here, miss."

"I can't—"

"We'll take it from here." The shoes were insistent.

"I'm sorry," said Leah to the ethereal face, the eyes still gleaming with life. "I'm so sorry." She stood then, and she faced the people, and a camera flashed, and she opened her mouth to say something, but it came out as a scream, as the loudest sound she'd ever made, as if she herself were Niagara Falls, and the sound hit them all, and it kept going. It traveled over a school and its dark playground. It swept over a row of ancient elms. It broke into pieces, and they broke, too, though they kept shooting through the air, over the tops of things, breaking and breaking until they were tiny shards of glass, and then bits of glitter that rained down, twinkling onto roofs, over gardens, into the open mouth of a baby bird, whose eyes grew big with the taste of it.

THIRTY-EIGHT

AFTER THE BIRDS left, Leah became fixated on death. She didn't stare into womanhood with the yearning and wonder that other twelve- and thirteen-year-olds did, the ones she heard in school talking about boys and wedding dresses and diets. For Leah, that yearning, that wonder, belonged to death. Maybe the Blue Öyster Cult song "(Don't Fear) the Reaper" was partially to blame, but what made her swoon inside wasn't a boy or thoughts of a first kiss or a pretty dress; it was a black-cloaked death angel who would come to her and carry her off in his clutches, his cape blooming out into infinity, where, at last, she would be fully loved.

Not that Edward Murphy hadn't tried his best. Few men would have loved her as he had, and she knew this. But there remained between them the simple problem of loss. Through no fault of his own, he would always be linked to the day her mother disappeared. In Leah's mind, he was also the reason the birds had disappeared. He'd meant well, but she couldn't reconcile his intentions with the fact that in the end, she was left barren.

A gulf spread between Edward and Leah, though in that same year, during their late-autumn vacation at Folly Beach, he'd requested that she start calling him Dad. Though she hadn't wanted to, she agreed, because she loved him, too. If anything, this new name had only drawn attention to their distance, their increasing awkwardness and unfamiliarity with each other. To avoid this, Leah began spending even more time in the library and in the woods and fields, where she examined death close-up in the clouded eyes of a frog, the open mouth of a vole, the maggots boring into the chest of a dove, while Edward Murphy spent more time in the den, reading the paper and watching game shows. But they still sat down for dinner most nights, even if it was only for a few minutes before Leah ran off or Edward Murphy took his plate to the television. And it was in those few minutes, as they touched on the small points of any given day, tidbits about the seed shop or school subjects or Martha-Up-the-Street's garden, that their love was also in attendance—intact, indestructible—as all true love is.

THEN LEAH GREW up. From their distant posts, they forged a new relationship, not so much as father and daughter as much as two friends. By the time she'd turned twenty, they'd established new rituals together, like Saturday Pasta Night—the two of them always making it together, Edward slicing the garlic razor thin, Leah preparing the salad, the two of them reminiscing, as if the whole of her childhood and his parenthood had been one long grueling trip that they could only now, from the safety of their new relationship, laugh about. They reminisced about the rocket they'd built together, about all the lobster and crab they'd eaten on their vacation together, and even about the birds. "That time you spilled all that birdseed in the car, I thought I was going to career right off the road! You sure were a feisty thing!"

"I was under the influence of tomatoes," Leah protested. "Do you remember how you made us eat them for like two weeks straight?"

They both laughed.

It was a rainy night when Leah came home from the feed shop at her usual time for Saturday Pasta Night and Edward Murphy didn't rush to greet her. Normally, he would already have the cutting board on the counter and a pot on the stove and a record playing, but now the kitchen and living room were empty and dark. Raindrops tapped at the windows, and from the back room, the television murmured softly. "Hello?" Leah called. "Dad?" She walked slowly to his little den, stopping just shy of the door. "C'mon, now, you've already solved every *Wheel of Fortune* puzzle there is." And when he didn't answer, she felt the impulse to turn and run as fast as she could back out the door. Maybe if she left now and came back later, he'd be stationed at the kitchen counter as he always was. "Dad?" She inched a little closer, listening, wanting fiercely to un-know what she already knew, and when she finally braved the doorway and found him sitting in his chair, his eyes cloudy, she felt the breath rush out of her, as if her own life had come lurching to a halt.

FIVE DAYS LATER, the few people who'd read the town obituary and had known Edward Murphy showed up for his memorial, along with a few other people who just wanted to gawk at Leah. She was wearing her one dress, dark-purple velvet, and her one pair of shoes, her combat boots. "Sorry there aren't more chairs," she said to the elderly folks standing awkwardly with their paper plates of cheddar and celery and a smattering of mayonnaise-y salads. On the counter, among the food and flowers, stood a framed picture of Edward Murphy. He was standing in his garden, smiling, squinting into the sun.

"Such a lovely picture of him," Martha-Up-the-Street mused. She was holding onto her patent leather purse with both hands. She must have been Edward Murphy's age, but she reminded Leah of a little girl.

"He always loved your tomatoes," said Leah.

Martha brightened. "Really?"

Leah smiled. "He talked about them all the time."

"Oh, how lovely. That's just . . . that's good to know." She grabbed a tissue from her shiny purse and dabbed at her eyes. "I'll keep those tomatoes coming. And now you'll have to be the one to tend his garden."

Leah didn't tell Martha what the lawyer had told her—that she had only three months to stay in the house, even though Edward Murphy had paid off the mortgage years ago. She also didn't say that house now belonged to her mother, who was nowhere to be found.

At first Leah had been hurt by the news. How could he have neglected to change his will, which left everything to her mother, after all those years? But her hurt was short-lived, for she understood why he hadn't. It was the same reason she had wished some version of the same wish on all of those stars and all those birthday candles through all those years, the same reason she hadn't gone to Cambodia: faith. And never were two people more faithful than they were to the three words Jeannie Starr had left them with: *I'll visit soon.*

"Aren't you going to say a eulogy?" one of the women more demanded than asked.

He was a loved bird. Leah could still hear the exact timbre of the Rubberband Man's voice. *May he rest easy. May he dream the good dream.*

She cleared her throat, and the guests fell to a hush. "He was my father," she began, "and I loved him. He was the best person I've ever known. And he never let an animal go hungry." Several people laughed fondly then, knowing personally the generosity of the man who had fed their animals for decades.

THIRTY-NINE

PLAINS, GEORGIA, 1999

SHE WAS LOOKING for a majestic lone pine in the middle of
a field. She wasn't finding one.

That morning Leah had driven into Georgia from Kentucky
in a blur of sadness. The accident the night before had left a broad
dent in the side of her truck and an ache in the center of her throat,
though as the miles ticked past, the ache began to turn to anger
and, eventually, to lightning flashes of rage—at the people who'd
laughed at the injured deer, and at herself for having driven for too
long. As she passed exits for towns in South Carolina, she even felt
angry at South Carolina. Though she'd paid for her apartment for
another month, she had no desire to go back.

Even when she'd finally arrived at the Plains post office and
stepped out of her truck into the blessed Southern warmth, even as the
sun shone on her face, even as she got back into her truck with letter
number seven in hand—indigo—she was awhirl in a storm of anger.

August 20, 1998
Dear Leah,
The magic continued. Dee got a record deal
and no longer had to play other people's

radio hits in smoky bars. Word got out
about Linda as far as my homeland, where
a member of the Royal Family commissioned
one of her watercolor seascapes. Elena's
Magical Imaginaries had become popular
enough for her to start casting them in
numbered collections and selling them in
boutiques all over the country. I suspect
that people could feel the magic in the
things we made and wanted some of that magic
for themselves. As for me, there were days
I couldn't shoot fast enough—everything was
vibrating, chattering like a million voices
just under the radar, commanding me to take
a closer look. Patterns were everywhere, in
all their endless striations and undulations.
I received a Guggenheim Fellowship for my
photographs, which was terrific but also a
trifle anticlimactic. You see, the only thing
I wanted, besides my camera, was the woman I'd
turned away.

What about her, you might ask—what magic had
our moon rituals been manifesting in Claire's
art? None, it seemed. Though she continued
to sell every piece of jewelry she made as
quickly as she made it, there appeared to be
no difference from before. I couldn't help but
wonder if things might have been different if
she hadn't dropped that yellow candle.

Back at the colony in between moons, we
still met for lunch each day at our picnic
table overlooking those green hills. We still

joked, I still sat beside Claire, and she was radiant as ever. What was different was me. I was twisted in a knot of regret so tight and so massive that at times I found it hard to breathe, and I was convinced that only Claire, in her dexterous ways, could untie it. Just one more try from her was all it would have taken. I would have rushed to her, coward that I was, if only she had given me any indication she was still interested.

Instead, there she was, wrecking me every single day I laid eyes on her, fluttering about as if what happened between us hadn't happened, as if pain were a language she didn't know how to speak. It was that very insouciance, which I'd come to adore in her, that turned its thorny side to me, making me even more aware of my own pain. I felt like a toy she'd grown tired of before she'd even taken it off the shelf.

Still, I tried to recapture her interest. I wore her scarab ring every day, waiting for her to notice. I read poems to her about longing and love. I let my gaze, and on braver days my touch, linger on her. She continued to regard me with a newfound blitheness that gnawed at me mercilessly. The truth is that I began to quietly, just a little, hate her for it.

When we arrived in La Sarre on May 31, it was a blessed eighty degrees, but on June 1, our sixth full moon, the temperature didn't get far above fifty, as I recall. As we stood

on the shore, the sun was setting and the
moon was rising, so there was still plenty of
light. "Let's go in," Claire said, stripping
off her clothes. "Let's swim to the little
island!" As her layers fell to the ground, I
couldn't take my eyes off her.

The rest of us undressed, and soon there was
a riot of splashing. I teetered on the edge.
I wasn't much of a swimmer to begin with, and
the moment I stepped in, I thought I might
drown from the shock of it. Then I saw Claire
swimming toward that tiny island with such
buoyancy and determination that I felt I had
no choice but to follow her, my arms slapping
the surface in desperation. Eventually my
strokes found a rhythm, and the water stopped
being a thing to fight against but instead a
thing that carried me. I could feel the water
holding our bare bodies under the rising moon
as if we were one body.

Soon Athena, Dee, and Linda were standing
on the island, while Claire was still in the
water. She appeared to be flailing. A bolt of
fear stabbed through me, launching me forward
to swim in a gear I didn't know I had. As
I neared her, I realized she was leaping to
and fro in the shallows, pulling up rainbow-
colored shells. "They're everywhere!" she
called out, though it seemed only she could
see them. And as we gathered on the small
island, Claire turned toward me. "Here," she
said, reaching out her hand. My heart and hand

reached back, and she pressed an iridescent
spiral into my palm. "Ammonite." It was an
opalized fossil, she explained, showing me how
the colors changed when she moved it in her
hand, and it had once grown according the same
path we'd mapped for ourselves: a Fibonacci
spiral.

On our way back to Tennessee from Canada, we
decided to go dancing. We stopped in New York
and piled into a single Midtown hotel room,
where Athena, Dee, and Linda glommed together
like teenagers at the bathroom sink, applying
various paints and potions to themselves.
I had no interest in such pageantry, and
historically, neither had Claire, but after
a few minutes of being alone together in
the room, she excused herself and joined the
others in the bathroom. Dee dolled her up with
black eyeliner and lip gloss, and I couldn't
help feeling betrayed as I watched her natural
beauty turn into a banner.

Claire told us she'd never been in a
nightclub before, and I could see her taking
it all in—the dance floor that lit up in
multicolored squares, the DJ high up in his
booth, the suspended cages where women posed
in time to the beat. We got a table and sipped
ornate drinks until the DJ played Donna
Summer's new hit, "I Feel Love." I remember the
song because as soon as I heard it I decided
that would be the night I would tell Claire I
loved her. I took her hand and led her to the

dance floor, and as we danced, she shone as if she were the source of every light in the room.

Let me pause here now. Let me stop the music, just for a moment, and behold her there, shining. Let me tell you how, in this suspended moment, Claire Silver, who has her head tossed back, whose skin is flushed with the rush of the young, is happy.

Because the music must continue. And soon Claire was being swallowed by men on every side of her until I was edged out. I danced alone on the periphery, occasionally catching a glimpse of her between all those bodies. She didn't seem to even notice I was gone. As the men crowded in, she smiled and flung her hair about and let herself, in the spirit of the song, be loved.

I chose the first gal who was willing, a slinky brunette, and brought her back to our table. Dee, Athena, and Linda were shimmying in their seats, drinks in hand, and eventually Claire returned, too. I willed myself not to look at her, but from the corner of my eye I could see she was trying to say something to me. "Aren't you going to introduce me to your friend?" Claire yelled over the music. I remember how the strobe lights caught the sheen of her silver halter, and how badly I wanted her. I hadn't bothered to ask the brunette her name, and wouldn't. Instead, I put my hand behind her neck, locked my fingers into her hair, and kissed her. Anger, desire, passion—I let it all flow into the mouth of a stranger, and when I snuck a quick peek at Claire, I saw her crumple a little in her seat.

I reached for the silver pillbox in my pocket. Like *Charlie's Angels*, Jell-O molds, and gold lamé, Quaaludes were everywhere in 1977. I placed one on the brunette's tongue and then on my own. After I put the box back in my pocket, I noticed Claire looking at me indignantly. I had never seen that expression on her face before, as she thrust her hand forward, palm open. She had always stayed away from drugs and barely even sipped off the top inch of a drink, but I obliged and pressed a pill into her hand.

So let us turn again to Claire's own words, in our Book of Shadows, which she so dutifully kept. *In Buena Vista, Georgia, we went south on GA Hwy 41 until we came to a fork in the middle of nowhere. We were eating ice cream cones from the Banana Split, a local shop run by woman of our tribe. Chocolate marshmallow for me.*

It felt like years since we crawled around on the big map and watched Linda mark the turns of our spiral, yet it had been only months. Maybe there is no such thing as time. We turned left at the fork on GA Hwy 30, then right on GA Hwy 45, just past a church. And after we turned right on Hagerson Road we saw the grand old pine wearing a gown of moonlight

in the middle of the field. "Primordial,"
Athena called it. We made its trunk the center
of our altar, where we burned mugwort and,
in the rainbow of our candles, we lit indigo.
Clouds streamed over the moon in shifts as we
passed around the obsidian scrying mirror I'd
made for the occasion. Athena looked into it
first and saw a plateau of dinosaurs. Linda
saw herself turn into a child. Dee saw a
garden of flower vines and ripe melons. Essie
saw herself as a man in Victorian England. I
saw nothing.

I told you in the beginning of these letters
that I never cared what others thought of me.
That had been true until Claire, and now you.
I hope you won't think ill of me for the way
I'm telling your mother's story, or mine. I
don't know any other way to tell it.

After your mother made the purple-flowered
painting of you, she never painted another
picture on the easel I gave her. "Don't you
want to paint anymore?" I eventually asked
her. "I've already painted all I need to
paint," she said, looking over contentedly
at the easel that held what I now know was a
striking likeness of you.

Scatter my ashes below the lone pine. You
can't miss it.

Your next stop, Post Office, Holbrook,
Arizona, 86025.

Yours,
Essie

Leah couldn't remember the last time she had cried, but she could feel the dam beginning to push toward breaking. "Just tell me where my mother is," she said, taking the obelisk into her hands. "Just tell me . . ." she let the question trail off. She still wasn't ready for the answer.

Let me pause here now. Let me stop the music . . .

As the weight of tears receded back into the unknown place they came from, Leah put the obelisk down and reached back into envelope number seven for an object wrapped so thickly that it barely fit inside. As she unwound it from its cocoon, she came to see her own reflection in the scrying mirror, the one that had shown Claire nothing. The forged silver handle was cold in Leah's palm. Coiled vines wound up the mirror to cradle the black glassy stone, into which she peered. At first, she, too, saw nothing but herself, but then, in the dark of her hair, in the dark of the mirror, she saw the faintest form: a wing in a flash of flight.

When Leah reached back into the envelope, she found her face again, this time in Essie's transparency. It was a photograph of Jeannie, taken from behind. She was painting Leah. In another circumstance, Leah might not have recognized the woman in the photo as her mother, for her frame was much thinner than she'd remembered. She studied the photograph in the light and in the shadow, holding it high and low and in between. She traced the outline of her mother and felt her feet tingle. So many people—the hopeful, the dreamy, the lost, the heartbroken—had once come into her tent, all asking some version of the same question: Am I loved? And now Leah knew that, whether she ever found her mother or not, what she held in her hands was proof. Her mother hadn't forgotten her. Her mother had loved her.

THAT MORNING LEAH followed Claire's directions to the field where the lone pine stood. Only, there was no pine. Leah drove up and down the road and checked her directions and atlas several times, but there was no primordial tree in sight. The pine that had stood in 1977 had since been replaced by a farm.

She pulled over on the side of the road and looked out at the fresh dirt and neat rows that had recently been tilled and planted, a fact the pungent scent of manure confirmed. A silver irrigation arm roughly two football fields long spanned over the land and ended at what appeared to be a cesspool. "Maybe it has an island in it," Leah remarked as she headed out into the field, smiling at her joke, carefully stepping between the seedlings. "If somebody shoots me for trespassing, I swear—"

On the heels of her tribulations at the border between Ontario and Quebec, she kept looking back over her shoulder to check that her truck was still in view. Once she was far enough away from it to feel a twinge of discomfort, she stopped. She was tempted to pull out the scrying mirror and ask it if this was the right place to let Essie go, but she had the feeling that she should probably move quickly, so she unzipped her backpack right there between what she presumed to be two different crops—one planted east-west, the other north-south—and, as if her hand were full of seed, Leah scattered Essie's ashes to the east.

"Now you can become a zucchini, maybe," she said, zipping the obelisk away again. And just in time, because at that moment, the sound of a motor starting up behind her announced that it was time to get out of the field. As she hustled back toward her truck, she couldn't tell where the sound was coming from, until a loud hissing sound ripped through the air and she realized that the enormous

irrigation system was turning on. She started to run, but she wasn't
fast enough, and a soaking mist came straight down on her. She
tried darting sideways away from it, but that's when the power jets
turned on, shooting water in both directions with surprising force
and soaking her in the process. "Arrrrrgh!" she screamed, running
erratically through the field. By the time she got to her truck, she
was panting and coughing, her eyes burning, her clothes dripping
irrigation water onto the road.

IF SHE HAD to find something to be grateful for that day, it
was that she'd zipped her backpack tightly, so no water had gotten
in—and that she'd made it out of the field without getting shot by
anything other than an industrial irrigation pipe.

There in her truck on the side of the road, she changed into
the last clean clothes she had and drove into the center of town in
search of a laundromat. She found many things—the Jimmy Carter
historic site, a peanut shop, a souvenir shop, a dollar store—but she
did not find a laundromat. Meanwhile, the wet clothes that she'd
draped over the seat to dry had filled her truck with a smell so fetid
that she had to pull over and throw them into the back. And it was
there, at a gas station featuring a disturbingly tall peanut statue with
only one facial feature—an enormous toothy grin—that Leah had
a craving for ice cream. She wanted chocolate marshmallow, like
Claire had gotten.

At first when she asked someone at the gas station if they knew
where the Banana Split was, he just shook his head and said, "No,
I can't say that I do." The next person she asked offered a similar
response, so she went into the Mini Mart to try once more, and

though the woman behind the counter hadn't heard of the place either, she called to the back of the store and asked another woman if she had heard of it. The woman in back thought maybe it sounded familiar, but if she called her friend Jenny, Jenny would definitely know, so she dialed the phone, and Jenny didn't know but was sure her mother would know, so Jenny was going to call her mother and call the store back. Leah, in the meantime, took the opportunity to replenish her candy supply, and when Jenny called the woman in the store back, Leah had almost given up on the idea of ice cream. "Her mother says it used to be up the 280 a ways. A bunch of women owned it, must have been twenty or so years ago, but then they stopped selling ice cream, and now it's just a house. Can't miss it though—it's painted bright purple. I must have driven past it a thousand times and never realized what it used to be." Leah thanked the Mini Mart women and returned to her truck, carefully avoiding making eye contact with the peanut's teeth. No laundromat, no ice cream, nothing to do but hit the road and start the long haul west to her next post office, in Holbrook, Arizona.

Before she'd even begun to settle in to her driving rhythm, she came upon the purple house and felt compelled to stop. It was just suddenly so *there*, so purple. Twenty minutes passed before she gathered the gumption to get out of her truck, and another several minutes passed during which she ascended and descended the porch steps three times. If she didn't knock soon, someone would probably call the police. She thought of Brenda Wright's shiny red door and how gracious she'd been, inviting her into her whimsical home, arm extended, bracelets clinking, and that gave Leah the nerve to finally knock.

After a moment, a voice came from inside. "How do you do?"

Granted, Leah hadn't knocked on many doors, but she'd never heard a door answered that way before. She leaned forward, her mouth close to the purple paint. "Fine, thank you. How do you do?"

"South of bad, north of good."

"Sorry, I think I have the wrong address."

Leah had already descended the stairs when she heard the door open behind her. She turned to find a plump elderly woman in a flowery dress standing at the top of the steps, smiling at her. "What address are you looking for?"

"I'm so sorry to bother you." Leah patted the sides of her legs. "I just made a mistake. I was told this used to be an ice cream shop, but I shouldn't have disturbed you."

"Well, it was! Who told you that?"

"A lady . . . at the Mini Mart. A lady's mother actually. I don't know her name."

"Sue Williams?"

"The daughter's name was Jenny. But I don't—"

"Blaze Pedersen?"

Another woman appeared at the door then. Dressed in brown pants and a stiff navy shirt, she offered Leah more of a scowl than a nod. "Blanche," said the flowery woman, elbowing her friend, "this young lady knows about the Banana Split! Says someone at the Mini Mart sent her here."

"Actually," Leah started to correct, "they didn't send me here per se."

"Per se?" asked the flowery woman.

"Per se?" accused the scowling one.

"You see, there was this woman named Essie East, and I have these letters—"

"Essie East? You know Essie East? *The* Essie East?"

"Yes. I knew her recently. In South Carolina."

"Is that where she ended up?" She nudged the woman beside her again. "Did you hear that, Blanche? She knows Essie."

"Yes, I heard it. I'm standing right next to you."

But the flowery woman appeared unaffected by the sourness of the scowling one. She smiled, and the lines around her eyes lit up like sunrays. "Tell us, how is she doing?"

"Oh," said Leah, suddenly not knowing what to do with her hands. She looked at the ground, repositioned her backpack, and finally settled on folding her hands behind her and bowing a bit forward. "I'm sorry to tell you this, but she passed away."

"Why don't you come in, dear?"

ENTERING THE PURPLE house was like being propelled through a time portal to the 1970s, replete with green shag carpet and a lava lamp in full jig. The flowery woman, Laurie, sat beside Blanche on a pink velvet couch, and Leah sat across from them in a tall-backed rust-colored chair.

"You're sitting on strawberry," said Laurie.

"I beg your pardon."

"Right there, where you're sitting. That's where strawberry used to be. We had three soft serves, chocolate, vanilla, and strawberry. Then we had the churned ice cream we made ourselves, all those wonderful flavors. People came for miles just for our peanut brittle ice cream. Best around, anywhere!"

"I don't know about *anywhere*," said Blanche.

"Anywhere," said Laurie, with convincing flourish. The two of them, side by side, reminded Leah of the famous theater masks, Sock and Buskin—one face perpetually laughing, the other forever turned down in torment.

"How long did you have the ice cream shop?"

"We had it for fifteen years. Closed up at the end of 1977. But oh, what a year that was! With Jimmy Carter getting inaugurated and all, everyone wanted to come see what little old Plains, Georgia, was all about. At just about any time of day that month we had a line at least fifty people long." She looked over at Blanche. "Wouldn't you say?"

Blanche nodded. "It was a long line. That's true."

"We were like a bunch of cats living here—must have been eleven of us then—all piled up in this little house, which was even smaller then on account of the ice cream shop taking up all that space in front. We were a fun group of women, weren't we, Blanche?"

"It was a commune," she said, examining Leah as if she were looking for some specific reaction.

"It sounds wonderful," said Leah, offering a polite smile. "I bet that peanut brittle *was* the best."

"Best anywhere!"

"Probably not anywhere."

"Anywhere."

Leah cleared her throat. "What made you decide to close the shop?"

"We don't need to talk about that," said Blanche.

"C'mon, quit it now," said Laurie, shooing at Blanche with her hand. "She's a friend." Laurie leaned conspiratorially toward Leah and lowered her voice. "You get a bunch of women living up in a house like this, all beautiful and free, selling more ice cream than a lady's got a right to, and, you know—people get the wrong idea."

"That's enough," said Blanche. "Why doesn't the young lady tell us how she knew Essie?"

"Yes, dear. Why don't you tell us? Or wait, how rude of me! Let me bring you something to drink first. How about some sweet tea?"

"Sure," said Leah. "Thank you."

Laurie scurried off into the kitchen, leaving Leah and Blanche to sit across from each other in awkward silence.

"Your home is lovely," Leah finally said.

"You smell like a swamp."

Leah self-consciously touched her matted hair. "I accidentally got sprayed by an irrigation pipe. Something must have been in the water."

"Swampy," said Blanche.

"I'm sorry. I looked for a laundromat but couldn't find one."

"Okay, okay, let's hear it!" said Laurie, returning with a tray of three tall glasses. "How did you know Essie?"

Leah exhaled the breath she didn't realize she was holding. "We lived in the same house."

"You lived with her!" She leaned into Blanche then. "She lived with her."

"I know. I heard her. I'm sitting right here."

"Are you in the Arts, too?"

Leah felt herself blush. "I guess so. I paint sometimes."

Laurie chuckled, and even Blanche joined in. "Not *that* kind of art," said Laurie. "You know, the *Craft*. Magic."

"No," said Leah, shaking her head. "No. Not me. I didn't live *with* Essie. We each rented an apartment in the same house."

"Oh," said Laurie and Blanche simultaneously. The two women shot each other a glance, and Leah got the sense she'd disappointed them.

"But we're, um, *close*," she added quickly.

Laurie leaned forward. "Tell us, dear, how did you and Essie become friends?"

Leah felt suddenly exposed. "Actually, she and my mother were friends."

"How did she come to know your mother?" Blanche asked.

Laurie grabbed Blanche's forearm with both hands. "Come, now, Blanche, let's give the poor girl a rest." Laurie turned back to Leah. "Unless of course you *want* to tell us," she added, her voice rising expectantly.

Leah cleared her throat and reached for her tea.

"Ooh, what a lovely ring!" exclaimed Laurie, noticing the turquoise scarab.

"Essie's friend Claire made it," Leah said, grateful for the distraction.

"Oh goddess! Did you say *Claire*?"

"Claire," said Leah, "yes."

"Claire," said Blanche with a plaintive drawl.

"Claire," repeated Laurie, as if she might never say any other word again. "Everyone loved her."

Blanche nodded. "Everyone."

"It was a coincidence how we met them," Laurie explained. "They came into town on a road trip, and we became fast friends. In fact, we're still in touch with Linda to this day—we exchange holiday cards and such. Anyway, as I recall, they were doing some kind of extended ritual, a nine-month thing." She elbowed Blanche. "What did they call themselves? I believe it was the Bog Witches?"

"No," Blanche said in an authoritative voice. "They were the Mud Witches."

"Don't be ridiculous. Who would call themselves the Mud Witches?"

"How is a bog any better than mud?"

"I think it was the Moss Witches," Leah interjected.

"No," they said simultaneously.

"In any event," Laurie continued, "as I recall, they weren't following any of the traditional, you know, *approaches*. But I believe what they were doing had something to do with math. Gosh, it's been so long. Do you remember, Blanche?"

"I think they were making a shape. A pentacle, probably."

"No, everyone does pentacles. It was something else, something numeric—I remember that."

"A pentacle is numeric."

"It wasn't a pentacle," said Laurie, stopping to sip her tea. "The point is they were doing some big ritual that same year they came here to the Banana Split."

Laurie dabbed at her mouth with a napkin, and Leah was about to clarify that it was a golden spiral, but Laurie chattered on before Leah could say it.

"I remember Claire showing us a collection of rare stones." Laurie nudged Blanche's arm again. "Show her the one we have, Blanche!"

Blanche got up and left the room, then returned with a rock the size of a hummingbird.

"Sugilite, they call it," said Laurie.

Leah peered into Blanche's hand at a purple stone with pink striations. "It's beautiful."

"Just like she was," said Laurie. "Everyone loved Claire."

"Everyone," said Blanche.

"But Essie, she was a different story."

"You can say that again."

"Kind of the opposite of Claire." Laurie sighed. "Such a shame what happened to her."

"What? What happened to Claire?" Leah asked.

"I'm surprised you don't know," said Blanche, "being so close with Essie."

Leah swallowed past a sudden lump in her throat. There was no question now, as she sat on these women's tall-backed rust-colored chair where strawberry used to be, that even from her distance of time and space, she, too, had come to love Claire. She unzipped her backpack and pulled out a letter, holding it out in front of her like a shield, like the one document in the world verifying her existence.

"I don't know the whole story yet, because Essie hasn't told me. She's asked me to scatter her ashes along the same journey they made in 1977—it was a golden spiral they charted using the Fibonacci sequence—in exchange for installments of the story, part of which has to do with my mother, who disappeared. Now I'm trying to find her, and I've been picking up these letters at post offices all over. I'm heading to Arizona next. I hit a deer last night. I got lost in Canada. And this morning I got sprayed with an irrigation pipe." Leah noticed that her hands were trembling, and in a quick jittery move to return the letter to the safety of her backpack, she accidentally kicked it, and it fell over, launching Essie out onto the floor.

Both women gasped. Leah reached for the obelisk and quickly tried to stuff it back in.

"What on earth?" exclaimed Laurie, rising from her chair. "What is that stunning vessel?"

Leah pulled her backpack close to her chest. "It's Essie."

Laurie reached out her hand. "May I?"

For a moment, Leah didn't move. She considered leaping up from the rust-colored chair and sprinting out of their house. Instead, she handed the urn to Laurie.

"Would you look at that? This thing must be worth a fortune!" Laurie stood up and carried Essie across the room, with Blanche following behind. "Look at all these stones!" They carried Essie off into the next room, and Leah followed behind with a growing sense of dread. "Stunning, just stunning!"

"Yes," said Leah, reaching for it. The women ignored her gesture and held the obelisk between them, turning and tilting it as Leah had done so many times. It was only then, in watching them, that she realized how deeply attached to it she'd become.

"Truly no end to Claire's talent," mused Laurie.

"How do you know Claire made it?" asked Leah, reaching for it again.

Laurie handed the obelisk to Blanche. "Just *look* at it!"

"I see, I see," said Blanche, who carried the urn to a window and held it up to the light. After what felt like eons, Blanche left the window and handed the urn back to Leah.

"Thank you," she said, clutching the urn tightly. "Will you tell me what happened to Claire?"

"It's very sad—"

"Tragic," interrupted Blanche.

Laurie picked up the purple stone. "Yes, tragic. Claire passed away some time ago. She was still a baby."

The blow made Leah physically double over. "What happened to her?"

"We don't know," said Laurie. "One day we received a letter from Linda that told us she had passed, but she didn't give any more details than that."

"It's not the kind of thing you go asking questions about," said Blanche.

Leah sat back down and zipped the urn away. "I appreciate your hospitality," said Leah, "but I should get going." She needed Essie's next letter, and even if she left now, it would still take her days to drive to Arizona.

"Nonsense," said Laurie. "You'll spend the night here, with us. It sounds as if you've been through the wars and could use a bit of a rest, not to mention a shower."

The women spent the day telling Leah stories, most of which had nothing to do with Essie, Claire, Athena, Dee, or Linda. They talked about the town of Plains, about the places they had traveled, about the commune, about the garden where they'd once grown the berries for their ice cream. Leah listened as attentively as she could, though her mind was wed to Claire.

Eventually Laurie and Blanche ran out of energy like two coin-operated rides that slow to a halt, and Leah took that opportunity to excuse herself and launder her clothes and backpack. After a shower, she found the women in the kitchen, garrulous again. "We're having ham hocks and greens with boiled potatoes," Laurie informed her. "Used to be we were all vegetarians, but these old bones need some meat nowadays. Plus, I think it's a law in the South—can't cook greens without pork. Isn't that right, Blanche?" Something warm passed between the two women, and Leah saw Blanche smile for the first time.

That night, as she lay in their guest bedroom, she thought about how she was sleeping in the same house Essie and Claire had once slept in, how she was walking in their footsteps, just as she'd once followed her mother across an Alabama field ablaze with summer. Claire's voice came to her then—*Maybe there is no such thing as time*—and she fell asleep not knowing where she was.

At some point later, she woke to a strange sound, a kind of moaning. She sat up in her bed and listened. Was someone crying? Howling? She couldn't tell. All she knew was that it was time to leave.

Quietly, slowly, in the dark, Leah moved like a cat as she gathered up her things, except for a stash of candy that she left on the bed, another gift of gratitude. The moaning continued as she slipped through the house, and far as she could tell when she looked back at the dark house from outside, no one heard her close the door.

FORTY

THAT BIKE THAT she'd used to chase her mother with? The one that dumped her to the ground? The one Edward Murphy locked in the shed after promising to get training wheels, the slick click of the dead bolt conferring a finality that, like the training wheels, neither of them mentioned again? Leah wasn't finished with it.

A few weeks after her mother left, once she saw that she could pad around the house without disturbing the snoring Edward Murphy, once she saw that she could even make noise—clinking cups down on the counter, dropping magazines on the floor, opening and closing the front door—without waking him, she slipped out. She could hear her mother's voice telling her not to wander, and she could hear the din of the carnival still spinning in her mind, even though Hilda was as dark and quiet as an unborn soul.

On that first night, she took the key that Edward Murphy kept with the other "hidden" keys in a ceramic jar labeled NUTS, and ventured out into the yard in her pajamas. She stood for a moment, letting her eyes adjust to the darkness, and then she opened the door to the shed. She pulled the bike out carefully, hoping that maybe it would be careful with her in return, but by the time she got down the driveway, she'd already fallen twice. And that's how it would be for days, her stealing out in the middle of the night, smacking the ground repeatedly with various parts of her body, breaking open scabs, getting the wind knocked out of her, ripping a gash that would leave a scar on her knee for life. When Edward Murphy asked about the bruises and cuts, she told him she'd fallen out of a tree, tripped while running, slipped getting out of bed. "You sure are a clumsy kid," he told her.

But then came the triumphs—the night she made it down the driveway without falling, the night she made it to the intersection of Barnwell and Broughton, and the night she kept going, past it.

For years she swept through the sleeping town of Hilda and beyond, gliding along the dark roads, the dark trees towering up around her, the dark wind in her hair.

FORTY-ONE

IN THE DAYS after Leah left the purple house in Plains, she felt locked into a new sullenness. The news of Claire's death worked in her like a virus, while Essie's scant revelations about her mother played themselves again and again on the screen of her mind as she drove through farmland and forest, rolling hills and red earth; as she spent the night in Little Rock, Arkansas; as she drove through the Great Plains and ranch lands and bedded down in Amarillo, Texas; and as she steered through the Rockies and into the high desert of Arizona. With each mile, Leah became less enchanted with Essie.

"Maybe you need to learn a better way to tell a story," she said as she arrived at the eighth post office of her journey, only minutes before closing time. It was the first thing she'd said to Essie since she'd left the ice cream witches in Georgia. She looked over at the passenger seat, but it was empty—for the three days it had taken her to arrive in Holbrook, Arizona, she hadn't bothered to strap Essie into her seatbelt. In fact, she had hardly looked at the urn at all.

Some stories take time.

"Whatever."

Then, despite herself, Leah felt a trickle of hope when the man behind the counter handed her the envelope with the violet paint and the number eight. She thanked him, climbed back into her truck, and broke the red wax seal.

March 8, 1999

Dear Leah,

I almost didn't finish these letters. After the last one I wanted the curtains to close. I lost track of the days, forgot to eat, didn't care about bathing. I became quite ill and wondered if death would come for me sooner than I'd thought. Let it come, I willed, but then I caught a glimpse of you walking toward your truck one afternoon, and even without seeing your face, I knew you needed to read these letters more than I needed to write them. *She's not long for this world,* I heard a voice say as I watched you drive away. And now that I feel my own death nearing, I know that I must move quickly.

Your mother, Jeannie Starr, was Claire Silver. Yes, the metalsmith, the magician, the woman who drew the world toward her as if by the power of her very inhalation, the woman who brought shadow-birds to life on the walls, the woman I loved and pushed away, the woman I loved and took in, were one and the same. And on October 30, 1989, she left us all. You've been carrying us both in the beautiful urn she made.

You might think me unkind or deceitful or
worse for not telling you this sooner, for
not telling you outright that Claire's story
and Jeannie's story were different parts of
the same story. But I wanted you to know your
mother as she was before drugs pulled a veil
over her, before she dyed her hair and changed
her name, before she took on a Southern drawl
and returned to the magic she'd abandoned as
a child. You see, when she finally fled her
parents, she hadn't needed that kind of magic
anymore. Instead of tricking people or hiding
things, she now felt free to bring things
to fruition instead, to let her art become
her magic. I remember how sometimes when I'd
visit her in her studio, her hands would be
going, working a piece of silver or gold wire,
and she would hardly look down at what she
was doing while we talked. Then she would
casually put the piece on the table as if
nothing had happened. But each time, the wire
would have transformed in her hands, into a
flower, a bird, a spiral. For a time, she was
a different sort of magician. And in writing
you these letters, I wanted to give you your
mother as she was then, when she was free.

When your mother ran away from home at the
age of twelve, she led a hardscrabble life, as
most runaways do. Because she was a natural
beauty there was no shortage of men wanting
to give her shelter in exchange for what she

could give them. She lived this life until she was fourteen, and then she went into the woods outside Philadelphia and built a tiny hut for herself with sticks and vines and mud. For sustenance, she ventured out to the closest grocery store and stole ready-made sandwiches and candy bars, until one day a woman caught her slipping a sandwich up her sleeve. "What do you think you're doing, young lady?" the woman asked, but your mother didn't register the question at first because no one had ever been keen enough to catch her sleight of hand. The woman stepped directly in front of her and told her she had seen her stealing, and though your mother didn't mean to, she started to cry, for she could see behind the woman a terrible future: police, prison, or worse, a return to her awful parents. But the woman had other plans. She took the sandwich from inside Claire's sleeve and added it to her cart. Then she took her home.

Maternal to the core, Glinda was a kind and humble woman who made your mother's bed with crisp cotton sheets edged with dainty eyelets and ran bubble baths for her and took her to art classes and brought her stacks of books from the library and baked muffins and cookies and cakes for her. When Claire showed an interest in geology, Glinda took her mining for tourmaline in Maine. When she showed an interest in shaping stones, Glinda bought her

a lapidary wheel. Wherever Claire turned her
sights, Glinda, who had never married or had
children of her own, arrived on the scene to
swing the door open for her. It was in those
same years that Claire discovered her love for
metalwork, which married well to her love of
stones.

When I asked your mother whether she had ever
gone back to school or what Glinda's last name
was or what Glinda did for a living, she just
rolled right over my questions as if I'd never
asked them. Then one evening, toward the end,
your mother asked to watch *The Wizard of Oz*. At
that point, whenever she wanted something, she
wanted it *now*, so I ran out into the October
cool without finishing my supper and went
to three different libraries before I got my
hands on it. That night, with a fire going and
hot apple cider in our hands, with the wicked
witch cackling and Toto barking, I realized
that the kind woman who took Claire in as a
teenager and the good witch in the movie shared
the same name. I wondered then if what she'd
told me about her own Glinda, and about her
hut in the woods, had all been a story, and I
had harrowing thoughts about what might have
actually happened to her in the true story of
her runaway life. But then I stopped myself.
Who was I to doubt her?

Your mother was sick when she came to me,
though she was sparse with even those details.

"With what?" I'd asked her. "Sickness," she
answered. It was one of the first things she
told me when she showed up at my building
unannounced. When the doorman rang to tell
me there was a Jeannie Starr to see me, I
told him they had the wrong apartment. Then I
heard her voice in the background, urging him,
"Tell her it's *Claire*." And though I recognized
her voice instantly, there was something off
about it, which I realized later was her
acquired Southern accent. When I opened the
door, I had to bite my lip to stop myself from
crying. I hadn't seen her in twelve years,
and what I saw standing before me was a
shell—still beautiful, yes, but hollowed out.
Even in an oversized sweatshirt she appeared
dangerously thin, and despite a heavy-handed
makeup application, her skin was as pale as a
reflection in a window. The canvas bag slung
over her shoulder looked as if it might knock
her over, though it wasn't a large bag by any
means. She had dyed her blond hair a shocking
red that seemed stronger than the rest of her.
She arrived, perhaps not by coincidence, on
your birthday. But on that day, I had no idea
you'd even been born.

Rewind twelve years, and things were
changing in our coven. Your mother had
begun to keep her distance from me, as if
I were contagious, though she was still her
gregarious self with the others. And though

I knew I didn't have a right to be hurt after
the way I'd treated her, I was crushed.

She was already on to another love, drugs,
though I didn't yet know how far she had sunk.
Sometimes I would catch her nodding off or
staring out at nothing, but I told myself she
was just tired like the rest of us. Between
our art, our travels, and our magic, we hadn't
stopped for seventh months. Maybe I just
couldn't bear the thought that I had done this
to her. I had given her that first pill. I was
the one who'd caused her to want it.

Imagine, if I had not been a petulant
coward, filled with jealousy and insecurity,
and had told her I loved her that night—if I
had reached to kiss her instead of a stranger—
how things might have been different.

For our seventh ceremony, we lit indigo
candles under that old lone pine. We touched
our foreheads to the earth and bowed to its
grandness. We danced around that wondrous
tree. I'd never felt comfortable dancing until
we formed our coven, and even then, it was
Claire who anchored me to the joy of it. But
in Georgia, for the first time, Claire didn't
hold my hand.

On our way out of town, we stopped at the
Banana Split, a popular ice cream shop run by
a coven of eleven. Witchcraft was extremely
secretive then, but we recognized each other,
and they invited us to spend the night before

heading back to Tennessee. We all piled up
in the living room that night, Athena on the
couch, Dee on a loveseat, and Linda, Claire,
and me on the floor. Claire made sure Linda
was between us. It was very late when we
finally turned out the lights after a night
of laughing and imbibing, and once everyone
was asleep, I sat up in the dark and watched
your mother sleep. I never would have guessed
then that twelve years later I would spend six
months doing that very same thing.

By the time we arrived in Yosemite for our
eighth moon on July 30, 1977—our second moon
that month and therefore a blue moon—Claire
was no longer Claire. The drugs had burrowed
in deep, and after we'd returned to the colony
from Georgia, we all watched helplessly as she
disappeared. She started showing up less and
less at our daily picnic-table lunches until
eventually she didn't come at all. We took
turns knocking on her door, but she didn't
answer. Part of me didn't think she'd show up
for Yosemite, but then on the morning we were
due to fly out, she appeared. She'd been busy,
she explained nonchalantly. But at 7:00 that
morning, she already reeked of liquor.

In Yosemite we drove to Glacier Point and
hiked part of the way down Four Mile Trail.
We lit our violet candles on a rock that rose
into a natural altar, and we made offerings
to infinity, the horizontal 8, with apple

blossoms and ammonite spirals Claire had found in the lake. Dee and Athena had written our invocation: *We arrive at violet, the end of the spectrum, the edge of what is seen. With crowns of violet light, let us gaze into the wet mirrors of the earth, into the mirrors of infinity. Let the spirits of duende rise as we carry the colors toward darkness.*

At some point Claire must have taken something because as we started to hike back up, she began to stagger. Dusk dropped a haze over everything, making it hard to see. Athena tried to steady her, but she insisted she was fine, then tripped and started stumbling forward. Instinctively, I grabbed her arm to catch her, but she tried to yank away from me. "Don't touch me!" she warned, but I didn't let go. She pulled away more violently then, jerking us both out of step, but I still didn't let go, not even as we fell off the side of the trail. We tumbled over each other until my hip hit a stone plateau and she landed on top of me. Pain drilled down my leg. I immediately asked if she was okay, and miraculously, she was.

Of course, I blamed myself, so I was grateful to at least have been the one to cushion her fall. You take grace where you can get it, I suppose. And as we lay there in near darkness, waiting for help, I finally said the words I should have said months before. "I

love you," I told her. "You don't know how to
love," she replied.

X-rays showed a small hairline fracture
in my hip, for which there was nothing to do
but rest. In a pall of silence, we flew back
to Tennessee, where I spent a month in bed.
During that month, Claire disappeared. Linda
came into my studio to tell me the news, and I
think it was worse hearing it from her than it
would have been from anyone else, because she
was so terribly calm when she said the words,
"Claire left." I hoisted myself up from my bed
and hobbled over to Claire's studio. Though I
knew it was true, I had to see for myself. But
even before I entered her studio, I could feel
her absence. I don't know how to describe it
except to say it was like a thinness to the
air. All of her belongings were gone, though
no one had seen her go. She left one thing
behind: our Book of Shadows, closed on her
workbench.

Several months later I received a package
in the mail, forwarded to me by the colony.
Inside it was the urn you've been carrying,
our urn. There was no return address, but I
knew Claire had sent it because I recognized
the handwriting on the package. For days I
stared at the outlandishly ornate vessel, and
then it occurred to me to open it. Inside
was a small folded piece of paper penned by
Claire. "This is to mark the death that you

caused." I doubled over at the thought that
she might have taken her life, but almost
as quickly as I thought it, I knew she was
still alive. It may sound strange, but I could
feel her. And what she sent me was the most
beautiful slap in the face I'd ever received.
She must have used all her best stones to
make it.

When Claire materialized as Jeannie Starr
that early April afternoon and she saw her
last bejeweled creation on my mantle, she
pointed at it and laughed. "I suppose that
was a bit dramatic, huh?" "Maybe just a bit,"
I agreed, smiling. That's when she told me she
was sick with sickness. "How sick?" I wanted to
know, but I knew better than to ask.

Eventually I found the nerve to ask her
where she picked up her accent. "It picked *me*
up," she said.

In the years since we'd seen each other, the
arthritis in my hip had become debilitating,
though I was still too stubborn to use a
cane. "It gives you swagger," she said of my
ghastly strides, on a day when I was having
a particularly hard time. "It's kind of *sexy*."
But for me, my wretched hip was nothing but a
lifelong reminder of my biggest mistake.

And even with this uncanny—and, in some
ways, unkind—second chance with the only
woman I've ever loved, I was still guarded,
stifled, petulant in moments. Some people just

come into the world with thorns. Your mother, on the other hand, came in without any, and perhaps that was to her detriment.

Your mother made the necklace inside this envelope from a blue morpho butterfly she found near the picnic table where we spent so many afternoons together. She picked it up and spoke to it as if she could conjure it back to life. "C'mon," she told it. "Fly, fly." And when it didn't, she carried it back to her studio and spoke to it for several more days before she decided to preserve it in crystal. Of all the jewelry she made, that was the only thing she kept for herself, this glowing blue symbol of transformation. And she wanted you to have it.

We fell in Yosemite on Four Mile Trail. This time, let us fly.

Your next stop: Post Office, Santa Cruz, 95060.

Yours,

Essie

Leah calmly read the letter until the end. She sat, blinking.

And then she crumpled the letter into her fist and squeezed it hard. A small cry escaped her throat as she felt the blood drain out of her face. Was she about to faint? Dissolve? Explode? Her body hadn't caught up yet. Her heart didn't know how to take in the information any more than a house knows how to take in a tornado. She simply sat, ravaged.

"How could I not have known?" she finally whispered.

With the suddenness of a match strike, she felt her body go hot, as if small flames were spreading under her skin. And deeper, she felt what had always been inside her, a herd of elephants, now unleashed. It was as if she were made of nothing but trampling feet and thunder. She hurled the letter at her backpack. "Fuck you, Essie East," she said, putting her truck in reverse. She squealed out of the parking lot, all force and storm and fire, and gunned her truck down the road. "You deserve each other."

With her pedal to the floor, she peeled onto the highway heading back the way she'd come. "We're done," she said calmly, too calmly. "Do you hear me, Essie East?" Her truck was barreling ahead, into an uncertain rattling, pushing eighty miles per hour, then ninety.

Safety is an illusion.

"Shut up! I don't want to hear your voice in my head anymore!" The old truck was up to ninety-five miles per hour now, the motor roaring.

I put my death in your hands.

"And now," Leah started rolling down her window, "I put your death on the highway." Her truck was shaking and her hands were shaking as she steered with her knees and unzipped her backpack. She yanked out the urn and lifted it toward her open window. In that same second the sound of a gunshot sent her Ford swerving off the road.

She dropped the urn and gripped the steering wheel, and her truck careened into the desert. As she swiftly cut the wheel back and forth to avoid the cactuses, she realized that her tire had blown out. "Oh yeah?" she said, flooring it again, kicking up thick clouds of sand. "Is that all you've got?" And so she went, on three tires and one rim, ripping through the desert, farther and farther from the road, until the road was out of sight and all she could see behind her was dust.

When she finally came to a stop, the sun was an orange disk descending toward the horizon, turning the desert gold. Her radio, which must have gotten knocked in the chaos, crackled bits of static through the speakers. Her hands were still trembling and her mouth was dry. The elephants were gone.

She picked the urn up off the floor and placed it on the seat. Then she stepped out of her truck, the dust still settling, and assessed the damage to her right front wheel. Her rim was scratched and bent, but it was still on. "Good truck," she said, patting the hood.

Why she felt so calm then, as she climbed back into her truck, which was now some indeterminate number of miles from civilization, she didn't know. It felt good though, this feeling like a settling in her bones, a lightness about her, an ease to her breathing.

For most of her life, Leah had been stuck in a purgatory between grief and hope. But now the question had been answered. Now she could finally let that hope, and all that was attached to it, go.

Leah reached down to pick up the letter she'd balled up and thrown. She flattened it out as best she could and slipped it back into the envelope. For the second time in her spiral of letters, Leah knew, when she pulled out a small wrapped box, what was inside: the blue morpho necklace her mother had made. The pendant hung from a strand of hand-knotted silver beads stamped with small leaves, which Leah immediately fastened around her neck. The butterfly wing landed where she thought it might—at the center of her chest, over her heart.

True to form, there was another transparency waiting for her in this envelope, and as she took it out and held it up in the last of the coppery light, her mother's face appeared in color. Her mother is laughing, her chin tilted toward the sun as the light lands unabashedly on her face. She's holding a half-eaten ice-cream cone. She's wearing the necklace her daughter would one day wear. There's a sign behind her featuring a black-and-yellow drawing of a banana in a top hat, its legs in motion, kicking up dust. THE BANANA SPLIT, it reads.

Leah thought of the gold dolphin necklace Edward Murphy had given her for her thirteenth birthday. Though she had never worn it, she regretted not bringing it with her when she'd left Hilda, as it was only now that she realized she had not a single physical reminder of Edward with her. If he ever noticed that she wore the silver moon and star ring she'd found in a pile of leaves but not the dolphin, he didn't say. And she didn't say that several of the girls who picked on her wore dolphin necklaces—they were apparently very fashionable animals then—and that the necklace symbolized all that she wasn't, all she would never be. But now she wished for that dolphin, wished that she would have worn it for him, even if only once, when he was alive.

Leah gazed at her mother, so young and fresh-faced with happiness. From the photograph you would never know that the drugs were already taking hold. But you would know, from the way her eyes fell on the photographer in the midst of laughter, that she loved her.

Beyond the photograph, against the sky, something was moving. Leah put the transparency down and watched a flock of doves in flight, the white crescent moons of their wings sailing across the sky. *Let the birds come back,* she'd barely dared to whisper in Canada, and now she couldn't help wondering if these birds were the answer to her wish.

As she watched them disappear into the expanse, she realized something that flooded her with waves of chills. The birds that had come to her in October 1989, six months after her eleventh birthday, had arrived around the same time her mother had died. She held the photograph back up in the last of the light and asked her mother, "Did you send them? Was that your final trick?"

She tucked the photograph back into the envelope. Then she left everything inside the cab and climbed into her truck bed, where she leaned back and watched the night come on. She watched the cactuses slowly disappear as the scuttling sounds of lizards and the excitable calls of coyotes scratched at the new darkness. She watched the setting crescent moon take on a brighter shine. She watched the first constellations poke through the fabric of the sky—Sirius, Orion, Taurus, Gemini, Virgo, the Big Dipper. She watched Mars appear, a steady red jewel. She saw the Pleiades—the Seven Sisters upon whom she'd made seven wishes sixteen days earlier, another lifetime ago—appear low in the west. Soon they would disappear until October. She thought about wishing on them again but then decided to let the wishes she'd already made stand. *I wish my mother a happy life*—that had been her sixth wish. And now she heard her mother's words as Essie had remembered them: *Anything can happen, good or bad, anytime. Why not take every risk you can? Why not say yes to everything?*

Yes, her mother had been happy. Her mother had been everything.

Leah felt the temperature drop as a light wind rolled over her skin. She heard a jet rumble past in the distance. She watched the sky deepen into blackness, and when she thought it was as black as it could get, it grew blacker still. Now the heavens were strewn with stars, like snowflakes against a dark road. She thought of her mother's scarf packed away in her suitcase, and how she'd always thought of the silver specks as stars. But here were the real stars, glimmering above them both.

As more and more stars came into view, Leah lay flat on her back and let herself remember. All those years, she and Edward Murphy had built an entire woman based on a few select memories, the sparkly ones, the ones that, over time, received more and more embellishments, making them sparklier still. But they had cheated themselves in the process. They'd created a woman that no real person could ever live up to, a wall of loneliness no one could ever scale. They'd created a myth. And in doing so, they'd ignored their own real wounds, and therefore the ability for them to heal. But Essie had changed all that. She had, in the only way she could, given Leah her mother as a real person, both flawed and filled with light.

As Leah gazed into the vast and mysterious universe, she let the memory of her last morning with her mother arrive with the stars, this time without resisting anything.

))) ● (((

NOT LONG AFTER Chipper died, her mother woke her early one Sunday. "Mornin', pumpkin. Guess what!"

"What?" asked Leah, slowly blinking awake.

"We're going on a little trip today, just the two of us."

"A trip?"

"We're going to have a little adventure, just you and me. Now I want you to get dressed and pick out a few outfits and a toy and put them on the bed here. I'll pack a bag, and we'll hit the road."

"But what about the people?" Leah asked. "The fortunes?"

"Oh, don't you go worrying about the people. The world can go a day without gettin' its fortune told. Now go on, get your stuff together. And go say bye to the Rubberband Man and Her-Sweet."

Leah scrambled out of bed and picked out her clothes. Then she stood before her many elephants. She immediately chose her favorite, the bronze one whose trunk pointed up at the sky, a gift from her very first customer. But just as quickly, she changed her mind and put her back on top of the small dresser. "You have to stay here and watch over everyone while I'm gone," she instructed her. Next, she chose a ceramic elephant standing in a patch of daisies, but she worried it might break, so she put it back and selected a stuffed yellow elephant with pink ears, only to put that one back, too. And each time she chose another, she felt bad for all the ones left behind, until she finally announced that she didn't need to bring an elephant after all.

Leah knocked on the Rubberband Man's door first. "We're going on an adventure!" she said.

"Oh goodie!" he said mid-yawn. "Where are we going?"

"No, silly. Not *us*. Mama and I." She stepped inside his trailer of wonders.

"Oh yeah? Where to?"

"I don't know. It's an adventure!"

"Well, come here, then, Leah Elephant Fern, and give me a hug."

He knelt down, and she palmed his bald head and breathed in his neck, and he made her feel like streamers in the wind. "I have to go say bye to Her-Sweet," she said, heading back to the door.

"Don't forget to pay the toll," he urged, arching himself into a backbend. She crawled under the bridge of him and put imaginary money on his belly before heading back out into the dazzling morning.

She found Her-Sweet in her trailer next. She was still in her nightgown. "I'm going on an adventure today," Leah announced, heading straight for the marshmallows, "with Mama."

"Isn't it a bit early for marshmallows?"

Leah held the bag thoughtfully for a moment. "No," she said, reaching in.

"Thought not," said Her-Sweet with a ravishing smile. "So where are you two headed?"

"I don't know. It's a surprise."

"A surprise, huh? That sounds exciting." Her-Sweet put her coffee down and swooped Leah up. "You be sure and remember everything you see, okay?" she whispered into Leah's ear. "Then you can tell me all about it when you get back."

"I will," said Leah. "I'll remember everything!" And she ran back to their trailer, where her mother was waiting with Leah's small, packed bag.

Leah didn't know yet that only her clothes were in that bag, and not her mother's. She didn't know to turn back and look at the carnival one last time.

AS SOON AS the first light began to rake across the desert, Leah followed her tire tracks toward the road, carrying her backpack over her shoulder and a silver-specked blue silk scarf in her hand. When she came upon a perky cactus standing taller than the others, she stopped and gave the scarf one final sniff before loosely tying it around one of the cactus's arms. *Let the birds unravel it and use it in their nests*, she thought. *Let it be a better thing than it was before.* She unsnapped the spiked collar she wore around her neck and shimmied it down next to the scarf. Then she continued toward the road without looking back at the things she'd been carrying too long.

FORTY-TWO

AFTER LEAH HAD walked nearly three miles from her truck to the road, a cheerful woman driving a Volvo with two small children in the back saw Leah and pulled over. She called a tow truck for her on a phone that was mounted in her car, then kindly insisted on waiting with Leah while her kids provided musical entertainment in the form of an endless round of "Row, Row, Row Your Boat" until a hulking man with a bedraggled beard showed up. Leah climbed up into his tow truck, and they followed her tire tracks out. When they finally found her truck, he gave her a sidelong glance. "Had a joyride there, did you?"

"You could say that."

"Coming from South Carolina?" he noted her license plate.

"Yes. In a roundabout way."

"You drove all this way in that old thing, and all you got was a flat tire? Somebody must really be looking out for you."

"Two," corrected Leah. "Two flat tires." She didn't mention the dent in the side.

As they drove out of the desert and cut through a section of the Petrified Forest, past all those hunks of wood turned to stone, past the striated hills of the Painted Desert, Leah wondered if Bob

O'Malley had received her letter. And she wondered if the tow truck driver was right—that someone had been looking out for her all along.

Neither of them spoke until they approached a sign pointing to a town called Snowflake. It was the rickety wooden sign below it, featuring a crudely etched turtle, an arrow pointing south, and the words PETRICHOR ANIMAL SANCTUARY, that made her pop up in her seat. "What kind of animal sanctuary is that?" asked Leah.

"Oh, that place? It ain't worth your time."

While Leah appreciated the man's willingness to haul her truck through the desert, she didn't appreciate being told what her time was worth. "Why not?" she asked.

"Just not much to see."

Leah kept her eyes on the sign as they passed.

Later at the repair shop, a mechanic informed Leah that her truck needed not only a new tire but also a new rim and a long over-due oil change. While he was at it, he would give her an old spare at no extra charge. She found a playground nearby and waited on a swing, and in a moment when no one else was around, she unzipped her backpack just a little and peeked in at the urn. All this time, her mother had been with her. All this time it had been not only Essie's bones in her hands but also her mother's. "I'm sorry I almost threw you out the window," she whispered into the small opening. But there was no reply. Since she'd careened into the desert, she'd stopped hearing Essie's voice. She whispered a bit louder. "I said I'm *sorry*. I understand now why you told the story that way." A child scuttled down a slide on the other side of the playground, squealing the whole way. "I understand why you did everything you did." But Essie stayed silent.

LEAH MADE HER way back to the mechanic's garage in time to find her truck restored. "Next time, try to stay out of the cactuses," he advised, handing Leah her keys. Leah thanked him and offered him a Cadbury egg, one of her precious last pieces of Easter candy. "Thanks," he said, "but I'm layin' off the hard stuff."

Leah left the garage, but she did not drive west toward Santa Cruz, where her last letter from Essie was waiting for her. Instead, she drove back to the sign with the turtle on it—PETRICHOR ANIMAL SANCTUARY—and followed the arrow.

The first thing she noticed when she arrived forty minutes later was the zebra. He was standing at the corner of a pasture fence, while behind him a disinterested pony munched on grass and two alpacas stood by stoically. In the next paddock, three deer frolicked about, as if they were excited by the sound of Leah's tires crunching over the gravel path. When she reached a small hut with a wooden welcome sign, she parked and got out of her truck.

She stood for a moment, taking in the shrub-studded desertscape and the warm dusty air. There were several small buildings scattered about, including a ranch house even smaller than the one she grew up in. She walked up to the hut and looked in through the screen door. "Hello?" she called. When no one answered, she pushed the door open and poked her head inside. She spotted a wooden desk, a set of bookshelves packed with books, several beanbag chairs, and a dog crate. A sign hung from what she presumed to be a bathroom door, featuring a questionable drawing of a rooster and a hen. She noted several photographs of various animals on the wall, a box of ginger snaps on the desk, and a small succulent near a window. But there was something else in that hut that she didn't see.

"Hello?" she called again. Something came scampering over her boots, startling her as it scurried into the hut.

"Oh, that's just Army," a voice called from behind. "He won't hurt you."

Leah turned around. A young man was walking toward her, smiling. He wore a tan-colored cowboy hat and a blue gingham button-down with the sleeves rolled up. He appeared to be made of the desert itself, his skin fashioned from sand, his eyes from the burnt umber of far-off rock formations and the green flecks of desert broom and sage.

"Army?"

"The armadillo. He tends to go inside in the morning and nap all day."

Leah nodded as if that were the most natural thing she'd ever heard.

"Did you know that a three-banded armadillo is the only armadillo that can roll into a perfect ball? Seals itself right up, so not even a wolf can break it open."

"I, uh—" Leah looked down at his cowboy boots.

"Of course, Army's not a three-banded armadillo."

"Of course," said Leah.

"He's a nine-banded. Did you know armadillos are really excellent swimmers?"

"No," said Leah, smiling. "Did you know that *elephants* are really excellent swimmers?"

"Hmmm," he said, tapping his chin. "I can't say I've ever seen an elephant swim. But I would imagine they're pretty floaty."

"Floaty, yes."

"I've never had an elephant here. But boy would I love one! I get animals from all over the world. People like to have exotic things, but taking care of them is another story. I guess you noticed the zebra?"

"He was the first to greet me."

"That Albert's a friendly one. I've got a ring-tailed lemur, too— Jack. He's shy, though. Still figuring out where he is. But most of the animals here are local. A lot of the time, people find them as babies and think, 'oh, how cute, a baby,' and they try to keep them as pets. But then this weird thing happens."

"What's that?"

"They grow up. Suddenly they're not so cute anymore, and they're not like dogs or cats, and they bite and smell and destroy things, and then they end up here at Petrichor."

"I see," said Leah, feeling mildly dumb. "Is Petrichor the name of one of your animals?"

The young man's eyes brightened. "You know, that's a good idea. I should really do that."

"Do what?"

"Name an animal after the sanctuary. It would have to be a really special one, though." Just then he pulled a monocular out of his pocket and scanned the horizon. "Anyway," he said, taking the lens away from his eye, "nobody ever knows what petrichor means. I'm not sure if that's good or bad."

"I think it's good," said Leah. "What does it mean?"

"You know that smell that happens when the earth is dry and it starts to rain?"

Leah closed her eyes and conjured it. "I do."

"That's petrichor."

"That's beautiful."

"That's a scent I rarely get out here, as you can imagine. Anyway," he said, glancing toward the gravel road, "would you like a tour?"

"I'd love one."

"Right this way," he said, extending his arm out to the side with a bow, and they set off walking. "What's your name?"

Leah shoved her hands into her front pockets, where the magnetite crow greeted her right fingertips. "Leah."

"Nice to meet you, Leah." He looked into her eyes as if he were trying to see who she was beyond her name. "I'm Cal."

"That's quite a condo," she blurted out. They were approaching a large, multilevel enclosure that housed a pig, a jackrabbit, and three goats.

"Yeah, they're good buddies. The goats like to climb, so I keep telling them I'm going to build another addition. I built two already, and it'll keep going up, like Manhattan. But it's mostly just me running the place, so I also keep reminding them to be patient."

"How'd you end up running an animal sanctuary?"

He stepped into the enclosure, pulled a burr off the chest of one of the goats, and came back out. "I inherited the land from my grandfather. Never even met the man, but then I ended up here. And I've always loved animals, so it just made sense, you know, to share the land with them."

"I've always loved animals, too."

"So what brings you out here?"

"I'm kind of on a road trip."

"Ah, a road trip. I lived on the road as a kid, so it's relaxing to be in one place for a while." He gave another look through the monocular. "There he is!" he announced.

"Who?"

"Ernie. I'll be right back!"

Cal ran off to one of the shed-like structures and returned with a bowl full of pellets.

"Alfalfa," Leah identified.

"Impressive."

"My father owned a feed and seed shop. I nearly bankrupted him feeding all the animals in our neighborhood."

They both stopped then and looked at each other for a few seconds longer than strangers tend to, and Leah felt an odd sense that she had seen him someplace before. Cal cupped his hand around his mouth and called out, "Eeeerniiiiee!" He shot another quick glance through the monocular. "Yup, he's coming. Likes to go down to Silver Creek and drink."

At first Leah saw nothing. She wasn't even sure what she should be looking for. But pretty soon a large tortoise came moving toward them at a surprising pace.

"You have a tortoise that comes when you call it?" she asked, incredulous.

"The power of alfalfa," he said, putting the bowl on the ground just in time for his arrival. "Leah, meet Ernie. Ernie, Leah."

"Nice to meet you, Ernie," she said, bending down to get a closer look. Ernie stretched his neck out and got busy chomping.

"He's our mascot. We used to have Burt, too, but sadly, he passed away. Anyway, Ernie was my first rescue. I found him on the road after he'd been partially run over. That's him on the main sign, which I'm guessing you saw."

"Yes," she said, recalling the sign's rudimentary design. "Did you make it?"

"Sure did! I'm no artist, but I think it came out looking kind of like Ernie."

"I can definitely see the resemblance," she said, following Cal to the next pen, where a barn owl perched in the center.

"Do you want to pet her?" he asked as he unlatched the gate.

Leah nodded and swallowed back the feeling that a bunch of balloons might come floating out of her mouth if she opened it.

"She imprinted on me when she was only a few days old. Someone found her fallen from the nest and called me to come get her, and we bonded immediately. Right, Mushroom?" he asked, rubbing her between the eyes. She pressed her face into his hand. "C'mon over," he said to Leah. "I think she'll like you."

Leah approached the moon-faced bird tentatively. "Is she real?"

Cal chuckled. "She's as real as you are."

She stroked the owl's soft white chest and wondered if she was in a dream.

"Did you know owls can't move—"

"Their eyes," Leah finished the sentence.

"Yes, exactly."

"Did you know reindeers' eyes change color with the seasons?"

"No," he exclaimed. "I didn't know that! How do you know so much about animals?"

"I've studied them all my life. Someday I'd like to work with elephants." She hadn't meant to say the second part out loud.

"Wow," he said, "tell me more!"

Leah shrugged. "I don't . . . I'm . . . still figuring things out."

Perhaps he sensed her reluctance to talk about it, because he let it drop, and the two of them fell into an easy silence as their hands moved together in a kind of dance against the owl's small body—gentle circles, long strokes, light scratches behind the neck. She could feel the owl's wariness but also her trust in Cal. And she could feel in Cal an openness as expansive as the desert. She was curious about this openness, which she herself had lost so young.

Maybe she'd already sensed that something fundamental had shifted within her in the desert the night before. Maybe that was why, when her hand accidentally touched his, she didn't pull away. This time, she felt no pain. She felt, instead, a rolling sensation, like driving on a hilly road, like laughter. At the same time, she thought she detected the scent of roses.

"What colors?" Cal asked.

"Pardon me?"

"The reindeers' eyes."

"Oh yes," said Leah, "the reindeer. Their eyes are blue in the winter and gold in the summer. The blue allows them to capture more light during the winter darkness. That's the theory anyway, according to a professor I once had."

After several long blinks, the owl closed her eyes. "I think she's asleep," he said.

"Yes," Leah agreed, remembering what she'd learned about owls having three lids, "it looks like her lower lids are up."

"I don't know where you came from," said Cal, "but do you want a job?"

"Sure," said Leah. "Full-time feeder of creatures—that can be my title."

"Perfect!" he said as he led her out of Mushroom's pen.

Once the many animals of Petrichor were fed and Leah and Cal had exchanged a litany of animal facts, she thanked him for the tour and asked if she could use the restroom before she left. He led her back to the welcome center and pointed her toward the door adorned with the rooster and hen.

"You grow roses in the desert?" Leah asked, wondering how she hadn't noticed the fragrant bush of deep-purple blooms when she'd arrived. "I've never seen that color rose before."

"Ebb Tide roses. They grow surprisingly well here."

"They're wonderful," she said, stepping inside. "Hi, Army," she said, waving at the small armadillo who looked at her sleepily from inside his crate.

Leah put her backpack on the bathroom floor and unzipped the top. "I just fed a lemur," she whispered, peering in, "and petted an owl." The bathroom light flattered the urn, making the few visible stones sparkle like mad. "Did you hear me? Anybody home?" The obelisk stayed silent.

When she came out, she found Cal sitting at the desk. "Before you go, will you sign my visitors' book?"

"Sure," she said, taking the pen from his hand and sitting down across from him. "What's today's date, anyway?"

"Wait, no. That's wrong."

"I'm sorry?"

"That's not the question I meant to ask you," he said. "I meant to ask you if you'd like to stay and have dinner with me."

"Oh . . . I . . . uh . . ."

"If it's any consolation, I've never invited a guest to stay for dinner. Granted, I don't get that many guests, but still."

Leah fidgeted in her seat across from one of the most charming humans she'd ever met, and though the word *yes* rolled forward like a marble that wanted to spill out of her mouth, she felt a deeper pulling, perhaps not unlike what the crow in her pocket felt toward north, and she once again recalled Essie's one bit of advice—to have the courage to love—and she realized then that the one person whom she'd never thought to love was waiting for her to get back into her truck and continue west, on a spiral that was charted before she was even born. It was her. She'd been waiting for herself all along. And it was only here, facing someone who she sensed was more like her than anyone she'd ever met, that she realized it. "That's a very tempting offer," she finally said. "Do you offer rain checks?"

"Of course," said Cal, "a rain check it is. Oh, and today is the twenty-first of April."

She wrote her name and the date in his book, but when she got to the address column, she didn't know what to write. Hilda didn't feel like home, but no place else did either. Finally, she decided on a single word: *Spiral.*

"As in a galaxy?" he asked.

"Exactly," she said, looking up with a grin. And then something caught her eye. "What's that?" she asked, pointing.

He turned to the shelf at which she pointed. "You mean the elephant? I thought you were an expert," he teased.

"Where did you get it?" Leah bit her lip.

"It's my good luck charm. She watches over the sanctuary, and over sleepy Army."

"That's really sweet. But where did you get it?"

"You really are a curious one." He picked up the elephant—bronze, with a long trunk pointing skyward—and looked at it fondly. Was that nostalgia she saw flash across his face? "It was a gift someone gave me a long time ago. It's a long story. Why do you ask?"

Leah's heart kicked up. "It looks like . . . it looks familiar."

"I know the feeling."

"Will you tell me the story?" she asked. "About the elephant?"

"I'll tell you when you cash in your rain check."

"Fair enough," said Leah, taking a moment before handing him back his book and pen. "I'll look forward to it." She wanted to say so many things then, but something told her there was time. "Thank you."

"Travel safely," he said, holding out his hand, which she took.

AS SHE DROVE out on the gravel road and passed the last paddock, she stopped her truck. Albert the zebra came up to the corner of the fence where he'd first greeted her, while she got out and reached for the painting that she'd slipped behind her seat in Kentucky. She carried it over to the paddock, stopping to give Albert's face a stroke, and against a small boulder in front of the fence, she leaned the elephant she'd painted on her twenty-first birthday, its trunk lifting toward the sky.

FORTY-THREE

YOSEMITE NATIONAL PARK,

CALIFORNIA, 1999

IT WAS A crystalline day in Yosemite: sunny, still, just shy of warm. Leah was sitting on a large rock off the path on Four Mile Trail, looking out at Sentinel Rock. Who knew the earth could look like this, so magnificent and jagged, so alien compared to the flat, balmy South? Sure, Leah had seen pictures in the library—she had traveled the world, page by page—but it was different being in it, looking out from a great height and feeling gravity in a new way. She'd been sitting cross-legged on that rock for a long time, backpack cradled in her legs, though for how long, she didn't know; she hadn't much considered time since she'd reached into her grandfather clock and stopped the pendulum.

She listened to the hikers come past in waves and to the silences in between. She'd never realized before how many kinds of silence there are: desert silence, mountain silence, frozen lake in the middle of nowhere silence, the silence that follows a long conversation.

She still hadn't heard a word from Essie, and she couldn't help but wonder if she'd scared her off or broken some spell, which now she wasn't sure she'd wanted to break. There she was, at the end of the spectrum, the violet point on the spiral, the eighth, with only black to go. Essie and Claire were almost home.

Leah slid the obelisk out into the sunshine and, in a breezier moment, threw a handful of ash off the mountain. How quickly it dispersed, out of sight. She thought of the ash she scattered from the top of Roche-a-Cri and of the ash that went up in the rocket. Where had it settled? Where would this ash settle? Would some fine particles be carried along in the air? Would they land and get blown up again by a breeze? Would they become the heart of a snowflake that might one day land on her cheek? How far could they travel? Leah had once imagined that the molecules of her sneezes might travel through the air and find her mother, who, in turn, would breathe them in. But now she imagined her mother's ashes mingling with Essie's, traveling the routes of birds and beetles, gathering more stories to tell.

THAT DAY LEAH drove across the San Joaquin Valley and up into the hills, over the San Andreas Fault, and back down into the plateau over the Pacific, past fields of flowers and strawberries, artichokes and asparagus, until she arrived that evening at the coast. For most of her journey, she'd been playing old memories on the turntable of her mind, the way she'd once played Edward Murphy's records, investigating again and again each dark chord. But in these most recent miles, most of the memories were recent ones: two women sitting side by side on a velvet couch, a girl talking about bats on the top of a butte, a deer lying in the middle of a dark road, a brown-eyed woman named Isabelle, a magnetite crow turning north, a woman with jingling bracelets and the man who loves her across the water, a tortoise named Ernie and the man who saved him, a bronze elephant so similar to an elephant a woman had given to her long ago, when she was The Youngest and Very Best Fortuneteller in the World.

When the Santa Cruz post office opened the next morning, Leah was there to collect letter number nine, the final letter, black. She took the envelope, which was heftier than all the others, to a quiet place on the beach and sat holding it for at least a hundred wave breaks on the shore before she was ready to open it. She wanted to open it fast and slow at once. In a way, she never wanted to open it.

Leah took a deep breath and broke the seal. Yes, she, too, was loved.

March 9, 1999

Dear Leah,

It's fitting that I should finish my story to you on the ninth of March. I wasn't sure we'd make it to the ninth moon, both now and then. Though the five of us had already purchased our plane tickets for the complicated journey into the Arctic Circle, part of me didn't expect to see your mother again after she left the colony. She showed up as we were packing Athena's car for our trip, and even then, I couldn't quite believe my eyes. A man much older than she was had brought her, and though she didn't introduce him when he got out of the car to hug her goodbye, I now know he was Edward Murphy, the man who raised you.

But I didn't need to be introduced. I didn't need to know anything about him. I could see everything in his eyes when he looked at her. I recognized that love.

Athena, Dee, and Linda rushed over to flood her with hugs and questions. *Where have you been? Are you okay? Who's that man? Does this mean you're coming back?* I stood a few paces back, afraid of somehow saying or doing the wrong thing and making her disappear again.

It wasn't until we were en route to the airport that I spoke to her. "I'm glad you made it," I said. We were both sitting in the back, with Dee between us and Linda up front with Athena. "Of course I made it," she said. I think we all needed to see the spiral through.

Though no one ever said the words out loud, it was clear that our coven wasn't going to survive the changes yet to come, namely our branching out into our different regions of the country. After Claire left, the rest of us agreed that it was time for us all to leave the colony and fully inhabit our lives as artists. I would go back to New York, where my gallery openings would spill out into the streets, where I would be the guest of honor at parties, where beautiful women would, for a time, distract me enough to soften the edges of my pain. Athena would move to Chicago to teach sculpture at the School of the Art Institute of Chicago. Dee would settle in San

Francisco, though she would spend most of
her time traveling the globe with her band,
The Ninth Moon. And Linda, not surprisingly,
would end up on Peaks Island, Maine, where
she continued painting seascapes. I stayed
in touch with her the longest, but eventually
even that communication receded into the sea
of memory, where we all shared a secret about
the moon.

When Linda plotted the final point of our
golden spiral on the large map on the floor,
we were gobsmacked to see that it ended as
it had begun, at a lake on an island. But
there was more we couldn't see on a map. The
journey was arduous, as you will soon see for
yourself. I shall leave it to you to find your
way, as we found ours, using the coordinates
as Linda mapped them: 69°47'32.6'N 108°14'25.8'W.
It is best to go between June and August, when
the tundra softens in the brief warmth.

A young man had taken us in his fishing
boat on the six-hour journey from Cambridge
Bay to the lake. To avoid suspicion, we'd told
him that we were marine biologists who wanted
to examine the waters of the region, hence the
little inflatable dinghy that Linda had packed
in her suitcase in lieu of clothing. Our plan
was to paddle out on the lake by ourselves and
then return to our guide, but suddenly our
plans changed. Our spiral lit up. Even now I
can feel it glowing gold. From the boat, we

spotted an island inside the lake; by the laws of math and the mystery of magic, our spiral's end now fully mirrored its beginning. My skin tingled at the sight of it. Dee wiped a tear from her cheek. "Actually," said Linda to our captain, pointing, "we'd like to dock there." "We end as we begin, and we begin again," Athena whispered.

On that inner island, we climbed (I hobbled) up a small hill. My hip hadn't fully healed, and the pain at times was blinding, but when we got to the top, all the pain of my life was at once diminished by what I saw: there before us shone another lake, and nested inside it were four more islands. I had the sense then that, like the spiral, we could go on forever.

Linda wasted no time inflating her tiny boat and ferrying us to the largest innermost island. When we stepped onto it, I reached for your mother's hand, and for a moment she wrapped her fingers around mine before letting go. Please release what's left of us there, as we complete the spiral for the second time, this time truly together.

When you go, it will be your second trip there as well. Though none of us knew it back in 1977, your mother was already pregnant with you that August. I'd chalked her nausea and pallor up to what I'd presumed was her continued drug use, but in her last days on earth, she swore to me that she never touched

a drug or had a drop to drink once she knew
she was pregnant with you. She said it was the
only thing she'd ever done right as a mother.

By the time she finally told me about you,
I could already feel her dipping her toes into
the waters on the other side of the veil. She
was gravely weak by then and spent most of
her hours relegated to the hospital bed I'd
had brought in. I'd hired her a nurse, but she
was always sending her away. Her voice was
frail and thin like the rest of her, but when
she spoke your name, it came out as solid
as a flagpole in a field of wavering grass.
"I'll find her for you!" I pleaded, feeling
the urgency of time tugging at my heart. "No,"
she said, forcing herself to sit up. I could
see she was in pain, though, like so many
things, she did her best to hide it. "No," she
repeated. "You have to promise me right now
that you won't contact her while I'm alive." I
tried to interject, but she wouldn't have it.
"I already left her once; I won't do it again."
She reached for my hand. "Promise me." What
else could I do but take her hand and promise?

"Do you remember," she asked, lying back
down, "when I told you I was never afraid?"
Certain that if I opened my mouth I would
cry, I simply nodded. "I lied. The truth is I
was afraid of being a mother. I was afraid of
being a bad mother." I squeezed her hand. Even
in the depths of her sickness, her eyes were

luminous. "But there's one thing I might be able to still do for Leah," she added. Then she told me a story.

When you were a fortuneteller at the carnival, a boy came into your tent. Perhaps you remember him? You ran off with him and found yourself in some trouble with–oh, how I still loathe saying his name–Hank, as a result.

Well, the boy certainly remembered you, so much that he came back again, looking for you. I remember how animated your mother became as she told this story, almost as if it were playing out again word for word in an unlatched safe in her mind. Afraid I would forget, I took notes in a small blue notebook.

When the boy came back for you, you were already with Edward Murphy, and your mother had taken over your role as fortuneteller. By her own admission, she wasn't very good at it, but someone had to at least try to fill your shoes. "When I sat in that tent, *her* tent, it was as if she were right there with me," she recalled. But when the boy came in, he appeared dismayed. "Where is the youngest and very best fortuneteller in the world?" he asked. Your mother told him you were on vacation and suggested he check back in a month. At the time, she didn't know that what she was saying was untrue, because she had still meant to come back for you. "I just felt at that time that I needed to get her out of there," she told me. "Call it intuition."

Yes, the boy agreed, he'd come back in a month. But he was just a small boy, not much older than you were, and your mother hadn't actually expected him to reappear. One month later, however, he returned. And when your mother saw him enter the tent, she didn't know what to say. The boy, who looked like he might cry, folded his arms across his chest and confronted her. "You said a month. How can you be a fortuneteller if you don't know a month?"

"I'm afraid I'm not a very good fortuneteller," your mother admitted. But the boy didn't budge.

By then the once-sprawling line outside the tent had dwindled to an occasional passerby, so your mother followed in your footsteps and led the boy out of the tent without anyone noticing. She asked him if he liked elephants, to which he answered an emphatic yes. But when she took him into her trailer and showed him your collection, she disappointed him yet again. "I thought you meant real elephants," he said. "Oh, but these *are* real elephants," she corrected. "They're even more real because they're magical." She invited him to pick one, and after some deliberation he carefully tucked one into his pocket.

Your mother spent the rest of the afternoon with him, taking him on rides, letting him

play as many games as he wanted, getting him
any treat he craved, until the big watch on
his small wrist showed 4:00 and it was time
for him to meet his aunt in the same spot
where she had dropped him off. He thanked your
mother for the day, and as he exited through
the turnstiles, she realized she'd never asked
his name.

She also never returned to your tent again,
opting instead to stick with what she knew
best, magic. But now she had to perform her
magic while carrying a heavy weight in her
heart. "I could still do the tricks," she said,
"but magic doesn't mean much when there's no
love behind it."

Eventually the carnival unhitched itself
from that Alabama field and took to the road
again, only to disband some time later. This
is where your mother was sparser with the
details. How long she stayed with the carnival
and what she did after, I will never know in
this life.

In the end, she became happy again. Even
sick, she was happy. And when she became too
sick to go out anymore, I brought the world to
her.

My apartment filled with pots and vases of
flowers and books that grew in stacks from
the floor up. You had to brave an obstacle
course to travel ten feet across the room,
but there was something I think we both found

comforting in the disarray. Questions came
off her like pollen—she wanted to know how
it is that fireflies make light, whether the
universe has an end, whether there is a fixed
amount of energy in the universe, who exactly
the Great Masters were, how to tell the
difference between a rabbit and a hare, what
the first words ever spoken were—and I pored
through those books, doing the best I could to
answer her.

Of all those books, what your mother liked
most was a book she'd been carrying with
her for years, *Twelve Moons* by Mary Oliver.
"Because of you," she'd told me, and for a
moment I'd felt like maybe I'd done something
right. In the last few weeks, she wanted me
to read the same poem to her each night:
"Entering the Kingdom."

One night after I thought she was asleep,
her voice startled me. "Once we cross over,"
she said, "we'll know all the answers."

I sat up in the half-light. "How do you know
that?"

"The obelisk told me."

We shared a laugh, but then I saw her
wince in pain. I reached quickly for the
bottle of morphine on the table, but as I
started to open it, she said "No." She held
out her hand, so I reached to hold it. "No,"
she said again, pulling it back. "What do
you need?" I asked, but as I asked it, I

realized it was the whole bottle of pills
she was asking for, not just one. I wanted
to say no in return, but I wanted to give
her anything she wanted even more than that,
so I put the bottle in her hand. Her eyes
lit up then. And I don't mean figuratively.
I mean, there was light in those eyes. And
in a single magician's swipe from her other
hand, she made the bottle vanish. She smiled
then and closed her eyes and made even death
beautiful.

It would take me days to find the pill
bottle, still full. I will never know how she
managed to get it into a vase full of tulips
that was clear across the room, but part of me
likes to think she wasn't like the rest of us,
that she was born with a kind of magic that
wasn't entirely human, and that's why there was
always a part of her that was unreachable to
the rest of us, and maybe why she couldn't stay
too long.

Your mother was the greatest gift of my
life, and these letters, as much as they have
fallen short, were my best attempt to share
that gift with you. To do it, I had to honor
the story as it was, not as I wanted it to be.

What I remember most about the inner island
in the Arctic was the quiet. Though we were
far from our guide, we moved in silence.
Athena's bag had gotten lost on the flight
from Yellowknife to Cambridge Bay, so we were

without our ceremonial herbs, our flowers, our black candles to light and wish upon. Claire brought no stones. Leave it to her, though, to bring a small jar of honey, which we used to draw spirals on each other's tongues. That was it, and maybe that was best. Maybe the ninth moon has always been yours, starseed in the belly of a magician. All you have to do is claim it.

For a decade, I wondered what would have become of Claire and me if I'd reciprocated her love when she offered it; I castigated myself relentlessly for robbing us both of the chance to find out. But change any one thing, and you change everything.

Don't you see? Perhaps had I not failed so epically, you would not have been born. Therefore, your life, Leah Fern, is one of my life's greatest blessings.

Now our Book of Shadows, with its many still-blank pages, has found its rightful heiress. Let these blank pages be a reminder that there are always new paths to blaze. But perhaps you might consider treading a trifle more softly in future, for the love of anyone who might find herself living beneath you for a spell.

With gratitude,

Essie

Leah sat with the letter well into the afternoon, reading it again and again, as she would all the letters, before she finally reached into the envelope and took out the Book of Shadows. She ran her fingers over the silver vines her mother had drawn onto the book's black cover. She brought the book to her nose and inhaled the faint scent of herbs and smoke that still clung to it. She flipped through the pages, letting them flutter against her skin. But she wasn't ready to read it yet. What she had now was time.

She took out the final transparency and held it up, but this one was blank. She smiled as she looked through it: there was the world, her world, unfolding in the now. There were the countless small gifts being washed up onto the shore—shells and stones, sea glass and driftwood. There was the ocean glinting under the sun like the many jeweled facets on the urn her mother had made.

She flashed back to the BEGIN envelope, which she'd opened on the floor of her apartment. Essie's prediction had been right: she'd died nine months after writing that first letter, which spilled out pieces of a ripped-up picture of Leah that Essie had taken without her ever knowing. How intently she had sat on the floor arranging the pieces, not even recognizing herself at first.

Now this Southern girl who had driven over 7,500 miles, who had taken on snow, ice, grumpy men, ghosts, and an industrial irrigation pipe, all in the combat boots that could no more protect her from the elements than they could from the battle she'd been engaged in for most of her life, was beginning to realize that she was not the sole scatterer in this arrangement. Essie had also cast Leah out—onto the infinite spiral, into the blank slate of her future, where the fractal repeated, the one where a girl, piece by piece, makes herself whole again.

))) ● (((

LEAH HAD ALWAYS wondered about the desert. She'd seen on TV how people see mirages of shimmering oases in the distances of the sands, and she'd wondered, during her night in the desert, if she would see one, too. But now, having walked for miles along the Pacific coast, having watched the sun splash itself onto the water in strips of lilac and tangerine before slipping under the horizon, as she lay back on the sand and looked up at the stars, she saw the opposite of a mirage. She saw, for the first time, as clearly as she saw the moon, her mother. She saw the facets of her mother the way she had meditated upon the facets of the stones in the urn that now held her. And a grief unlike any Leah had ever known branched out inside her and made her feel as if she might shatter. Her mother had, in many ways, been an extraordinary person, and an extraordinarily *good* person. But she had not been a good mother.

Sometimes, when a person saves up a lifetime of crying, it seems as if it will drown her when it comes. It seems as if it will never stop. So unfamiliar was the feeling to Leah that, at first, she thought maybe she was dying. In moments she thought her chest might explode or that she might cough up an octopus or that her eyeballs might fall out and wash away into the ocean. But she let the deluge carry her out anyway, and she wept for all the years she hadn't cried a single tear. She wept for her mother's pain, for Essie's. She wept for Edward Murphy. She wept for the birds and for the deer and for her own loneliness. She wept for the girl who, nineteen days earlier, had almost ended her life. And she wept with gratitude for the man who knocked on her door on Easter, and for every gift that had followed.

She wondered if her mother had spent much time at the ocean. She wondered if she'd ever made jewelry from seashells. She wondered so many things, and for a time, it seemed the questions would never stop arriving. "You're named after magic," her mother had told her, and Leah realized then that her mother had named herself for magic, too—not only the magic she performed on stage, for those were merely tricks—but for the magic of transformation, an art she'd been practicing all her life.

Eventually the tears began to abate. Eventually Leah was able to take a breath again without it getting caught. Eventually what she was left with was the sky.

The stars seemed even closer now, in these dark hours before dawn—the Milky Way stretched across the sky like a riverbed of rock-sugar—and she felt their light pour over her, felt herself slipping into something, an unfamiliar feeling that at first made her uncomfortable, until she realized what it was—peace.

She let the peace come, as she had let the tears come, and she took a deep breath, and her eyes grew heavy, and as she fell into a new kind of sleep, she imagined the stars in her mouth, sweet and dissolving.

LEAH WROTE ONE letter while she was in Santa Cruz. For the stamp, she chose an Arctic fox.

Dear Cal,

Did you know that dolphins give themselves names? What name would you give yourself?

Sincerely,

Leah Fern, Feeder of Creatures

One day, perhaps, she would ask him about the bronze elephant. She would ask him if he'd ever been to a carnival in Alabama.

In the meantime, she would rent a room in Santa Cruz, where she would work nights as a ghoul for a haunted house attraction on the boardwalk. She would fill her sketchbook with new trees—redwoods and sycamores and blue oaks on hillsides—along with surfside studies of starfish and sand dollars and seabirds. She would enter another library, where she would turn her attention north.

FORTY-FOUR

VICTORIA ISLAND, ARCTIC CIRCLE, 1999

IT WAS TIME. After planning the route she would need to take to get to the nested island on Victoria Island—San Francisco International Airport to Calgary to Yellowknife to Cambridge Bay to a floatplane to the specific coordinates of an island within an island within an island—Leah purchased her ticket and hired the only floatplane pilot she could find. Then she drove to San Francisco and boarded a plane.

Two days later, she arrived in Cambridge Bay. At her hotel on Victoria Island, a message was waiting for her from the pilot: *Bad weather tomorrow. Will have to reschedule. Call when you get this.*

Leah had been planning to deliver Essie and her mother to their final point on the spiral on Monday, June 28, the night of the full moon—also known as the strawberry moon, the rose moon, the honey moon—and that was tomorrow. Leah's hands were trembling as she picked up the hotel phone and dialed his number.

"Listen, you got my message? We've got a serious weather system coming in tomorrow, but I can fly you to where you need to go on Saturday."

Leah tried not to sound desperate. "Saturday will be too late. I have a ticket that I can't change." Whether or not she could change her ticket wasn't the point, but she didn't know how to explain how important it was for her to go there on the full moon.

"I wish I could change the weather."

"Can we go by boat, then?"

"I'm afraid not."

"You're saying that there will be no chance to go tomorrow, no break in the storm, nothing?"

"That's what I'm saying. Sorry."

Out of habit, Leah turned the obelisk in her hands, stopping at her favorite stone. "What about tonight?"

"Tonight?"

"Tonight. At midnight. Then it would technically be tomorrow. This is the land of the midnight sun, isn't it?"

"Well—"

"Please," she said. "I've traveled a very long way to be here."

Another long pause stretched between them, peppered with bits of static.

"Okay," he finally said. "I'll do it."

"You'll do it? You'll do it! Thank you!"

"Can't say I haven't been asked to do stranger things," said the man who would soon pick her up at her hotel and drive her to a dock where a small yellow aircraft with two white pontoons mounted beneath it waited in the water.

"Does it have a name?" Leah asked as they walked along the pier.

"A name?"

"Like boats have?"

"Nah, I suppose I never thought to name it," Bill said, reaching from the pier to open the door for her.

Leah stepped across to the passenger seat and felt the plane bob like a boat. "Did you know that the sooty shearwater bird migrates forty thousand miles a year?" she asked nervously as he untied the ropes holding the plane to the dock.

"That's a long way," he said, climbing into his seat. He handed her a pair of headphones, which she put on, and he started the plane.

Over the vibrating buzz of the engine and the loud whir of the propeller, his voice crackled through the headphones. "Ready?"

Leah felt for the crow in her pocket. "Ready," she said.

Bill nodded, and then, faster than she'd expected, they were gliding across the water's surface and lifting off like the lightest bird. How quickly they were airborne. How quickly they rose over the pristine waters, over the scattered tawny landmasses, and through the clouds. And when the nameless craft emerged above the clouds, Leah gasped.

"Beautiful, isn't it?" said Bill.

Leah could only stare, mute with wonder, at the moon and the sun, silver and gold, perched on opposites sides of the sky, so huge they seemed unreal.

The plane bounced five times during its water landing, and Leah remembered why she'd never liked the carnival rides. But the moment passed, and Bill led the plane uneventfully to the shore. "You know," he said, "I've never been here before. In fact, I wouldn't be surprised if no one has."

Leah smiled and kept her secret to herself, while a circle of five women—wild and brave and draped in layers that billowed when they danced—burned their candles in the depths of her mind.

"I won't be long," she said, removing her headphones and opening the door. She secured her backpack over both of her shoulders and stepped out onto the pontoon.

As she was about to close the door, he leaned over her seat and asked, "Do you have any ideas?"

"Pardon?"

"The plane. Any ideas what I should name her?"

Leah didn't have to think. "*How* about *Essie*?"

"Essie?"

"*Essie East*. She was a great explorer."

"Essie. I like that."

Leah smiled and closed the door and stepped onto the island.

She looked down at the sand and inhaled deeply. At last, she had made it.

She walked along the edge of the island until the plane was out of sight, and then she stopped. She wanted to remember everything about this moment, exactly as it was—the muted hues of the sand and sparse grasses, the water rippling beneath the undulating clouds, the low ridges in the distance. In the weeks leading up to this night, she'd imagined the full moon boldly presiding over her final scattering, but the clouds were thickening, the moon and sun on their opposite sides tucked away beyond them. Still, even if she couldn't see the moon, she could feel it there, just as her mother had. And that was enough.

Leah took the obelisk from her backpack and set it on the silty ground. She pulled out all the gifts the women had once given each other, including the crow that had taken up residence in her pocket, and placed them around the obelisk, along with the vial of water collected from Watersmeet and Ganesha, god of beginnings, remover of obstacles. Then she took a talisman of her own from her backpack—a fox skull in two pieces—and pressed it into the sand, arranging it so that it looked whole again, its jaw pointing upward, ready to drink the rain.

She pulled two final items from the backpack she'd been carrying every step of the way. The first was a candle, a tall black pillar, which she lit with a match and set in the sand. The second was their Book of Shadows. She opened it to a page dated April 4, 1977—the day of the Moss Witches' fourth full moon, exactly one year before she was born—and she read her mother's words:

I've always known some things about magic, but nothing like the magic of our coven. There's a special power in what we're creating together, a synergy that feels like a mystical entity of its own. Our rituals are beautiful. They make me believe in my own soul. What I love most, though, are the simpler moments, just being in each other's company, like when we're all laughing about something silly, or when Dee plays her guitar and we start singing. We're a family now, and that, to me, is the most magical thing of all.

Leah tucked the Book of Shadows safely away again and watched the flame of her black candle dance under the slate-colored sky, while all around her the quiet earth sprawled as naturally as if it had never been named. She had wanted to say something about black absorbing all the colors, but though she'd imagined this ritual many times, she knew well that rituals don't always go as planned: suddenly, she couldn't continue.

She cleared her throat and knelt down to face the obelisk. "Hello? Essie? Claire?" Her voice was a small wavering leaf. She waited for a minute, and then another, but she heard nothing. "I'm wearing the ring," she tried again. "And the blue morpho necklace." The flame flickered, then grew tall, while tears escaped her eyes and fell onto the island, where it would soon rain, and onto the obelisk, which would soon be empty. "Just say something," she pleaded. "Just one more thing."

And then she heard it, Essie's voice: *Now,* it said, and that was all.

Leah smiled. "Now," she repeated.

She took the obelisk into her hands and unscrewed the top as she had done at each point of the spiral, but this time, with both hands, she gave it one fervent shake and released all that was left inside. "May you dream the good dream," she wished.

Now her mother and Essie were clouds in the air, moving away from her. She watched them drift like mist and disappear.

Suddenly, there was a trembling. Whether of the earth or of her body, Leah didn't know. But it came on like a shadow, like the first thought the earth ever had. It was the sky. It was the sky darkening. It was the sky being painted and erased in swift grand swoops. It was a murmuration of starlings. They moved as if directed by a God that loved them, shapeshifting into a single wing sweeping through the air, then an enormous wave stretching beneath the clouds, bits of sky between them like white water, before they collapsed back into a tight bud and were born again, this time rushing out into a sail, an hourglass, an arrow going up—the birds that had finally come home.

MEANWHILE . . .

ON A SUNNY day in April, as winter relinquished the last of its grip and Superior churned a deep blue, an old man with watery eyes and a tweed jacket boarded a ferry. As he walked in the bold sun, he felt the days of his past moving alongside him. He felt his stomach overworking the toast and egg he had for breakfast. He felt the hitch in his one tricky knee. He was nervous, yes, but another part of him was calm as winter quiet. How is it possible to have nothing and everything to lose at once?

When the letter arrived, Bob O'Malley hadn't noticed the postmark: Niagara Falls, New York. What he'd noticed was Brenda Wright's name and address in the top left corner. He'd ripped the envelope open as quickly as his fingers would let him.

> *Dear Bob,*
>
> *The first signs of spring have arrived on the island, and I find myself thinking of spring across the lake, where you are. Surely there must be subtle differences. Maybe we can talk about them over tea sometime? I found a yellow kettle that feels just right for the season.*
>
> *If you come, please don't call first. And don't mention this letter. Just knock on the door like an old friend and tell me you came to*

see my unfinished sculpture. Then I'll know you were meaning to
come all along.

Affectionately,
Brenda

As he walked past the fairy statues and copper wire dragonflies and ceramic birdbaths and multicolored ribbons streaming from branches and shiny glass orbs in purple and blue and stepped up to the red door, he was launched back to his high school self, full of apprehension and inchoate yearning. Maybe the years had been a dream. Maybe he had been standing here his whole life.

He knocked.

Brenda Wright's wrist jingled when she opened the door, and her pretty face became even prettier as she smiled. "It's you," she said, breaking into the softest laughter.

"I came to see your unfinished sculpture," he said. And soon the two of them were standing there, on opposite sides of the threshold, laughing and laughing as if there were nothing in the world but joy.

What happened after he crossed the threshold and she closed the door? Did they have tea first, out of the yellow kettle Leah remembered, or did they go straight to the sculpture? Did they undress unabashedly in the full light of the afternoon, or did they spend those hours tinkering with the many wonders inside her home, gongs and flutes and strange dolls? We may never know the exact order of how things unfolded. What we know is that a man crossed a threshold he thought he couldn't. What we know is that even the most lost people can find their way.

ACKNOWLEDGMENTS

I AM DEEPLY grateful for and humbled by those who have contributed to this book's existence. My eternal gratitude goes Maggie Cooper, who is a dream come true and whose faith in this book kept me afloat; to Janet Silver, who believed in this book when it was still mostly an idea and who saw it through with so much care; to Alyea Canada, who opened the door for Leah and helped bring her to life; to Kirsten Reach, whose genius and huge-hearted insights made these pages better; and to Carl Bromley, whose tireless enthusiasm, guidance, and good cheer have been a lifeline.

Thank you to the endlessly talented, creative, and devoted team at Melville House for ushering this book into the world, especially Mike Lindgren, Sammi Sontag, Amelia Stymacks, Beste M. Doğan, Emily Considine, Peter Kranitz, Janet Joy Wilson, Tim McCall, Valerie Merians, and Dennis Johnson. You are the coolest people.

To Kathy Daneman, illustrious boss-goddess, thank you for your meteoric energy, incredible inventiveness, and unshakable commitment to this book.

I am enormously grateful to my magical friends who read early drafts and whose valuable input and encouragement have sustained me: Mira Bartók, who drew pictures in the margins; Cathy Chung, my unicorn co-conspirator who always knows; and Dawn Eareckson, who gave me that first book of poems, and so much more.

Huge thanks to my beloved family and friends for their belief in me: Norm Ephraim, Billy Leonard, Joanne Zaks, Kiana Logan, Lesley Shore, Joel & Susan Bloom, and Michele Pedersen.

To Larry Chin, thank you for getting in the boat with me. There is no earthly measure for how much good you bring to my life.

To C. E. Courtney, dream keeper, map maker, first reader of every page, thank you for the countless ways you've supported this book and, most of all, for your love. I couldn't have done this without you.